THE NIGHTGHOSTS' CHILD

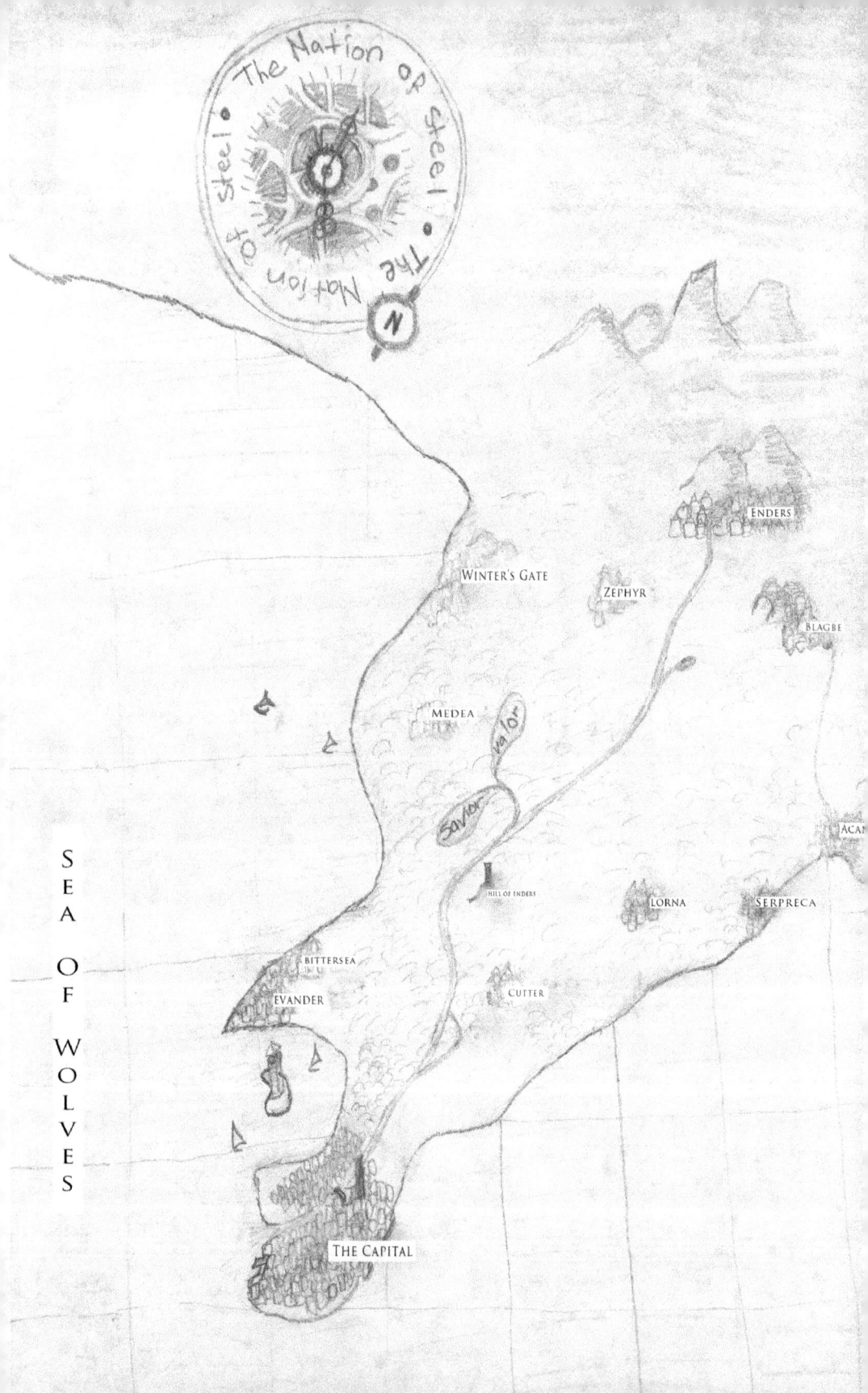

THE NIGHT GHOSTS' CHILD

S. K. GABRIEL

Futurological Press

Washington • Massachusetts

ISBN-13: 978-0615675275
ISBN-10: 0615675271
Copyright © 2012 by S.K.Gabriel
map illustration © 2012 S.K.Gabriel
cover design © 2012 S.K.Gabriel
All rights reserved. Published by Futurological Press, an imprint of Westry Wingate Group, Inc.

Printed in the U.S.A.

Body text type set in Adobe Goudy Old Style
The decorative clockwork text type set in *Time to Get a Watch* font designed by Melissa Choyce

To my mother, who made this story possible
And to my sister Meera, who saved two fictional lives and made
it better

The Man From Space

Above
October 31st, Year 119 A.C. (After Colonization)

T he epiphany came to Markus Walker in the brightest flash of light. It blinded him at first before his vision quickly returned. Markus rose to his feet, his chair spinning away from him across the metal floor. A cacophony of voices surrounded him. Videos played on the screen behind him, messages from friends and family that would have been opened one by one during his journey, if it had gone right. They felt like ghosts now. He looked down at the lines of control buttons on the console in front of him. All useless now. Glancing upwards through an expansive curved wall of glass, Markus saw the world he was headed for, a swirling blue and green orb. He knew to everyone on the ground he had been lost for so long he was now little more than a ghost haunting them. People would say he must be dead, but he knew the ones who mattered would never have given up on him. Markus knew something else as well, something he realized he should have known from the beginning. This spaceship was his coffin, and today he would die.

"But I'm not going the way you want me to," he whispered through gritted teeth. "I'm not going to be your explosion. I'm not landing."

Markus turned away from the window and ran. He heard the clanging of the ship and the sound of metal doors and barriers being thrown in his way as some hidden program tried to stop him. A pain inside of him began to overwhelm him, driving him to his knees as he heard the ticking of a clock somewhere far inside the ship. Markus dragged himself across the floor and quickly slammed his hand between the airlock doors, preventing them from closing and crawled inside. He saw the door in front of him, beyond which lay the vast emptiness of space. Markus readied himself, shut his eyes, and then placed his palm to the hand-print lock to open the outer airlock doors. He waited but nothing happened. He grasped the bar handle running across it, but it didn't budge. It was stuck fast in place. He forced himself to walk, leaving the airlock behind. He tried the other exits but knew before he reached each one they would not work.

"No!" Markus screamed in frustration as he sank against the last closed door.

He swallowed hard and looked at the control panel in front of him. There was only one option left. It couldn't have been corrupted; they couldn't have found this, the last solution. No one outside Samson Magler's space program knew it was going into the vessel, and it was separate from every other program. He remembered the instructions Magler had given him before takeoff, "just in case." His hands flew across the controls.

"Password?" the computer asked.

He sighed trying to remember. It seemed harder, knowing what he needed it for, but he couldn't let the computer land the ship, not with him on-board.

"Um..." Markus said. "Okay, 9,0." Birthday.

What else would he have used for a password?

"Edwin." His best friend.

"And..." He felt as if he'd been rent in half. "Lavender."

"90EdwinandLavender," blended together in the computer's electronic voice.

The words sounded bizarre. Markus let out a choking laugh that turned into a hysterical fit with him screaming out at the top of his lungs. A rattling noise from deep within the ship stopped his screaming and he was thrown off his feet. He lay sprawled on the cold metal floor. *It is going to end now*, he thought.

"You promised me it wouldn't come to this," he whispered under his breath. "That Defense would never get me. Not after I left. You promised me I would be safe, Magler. You liar!"

The rattling inside the ship grew louder, and he shut his eyes. *A bad dream about to end*, Markus thought. It had all been one hellish nightmare. But the ship didn't explode, it plummeted.

****

"I am Lavender Kawaguchi," she spoke into the tiny window, hearing her voice echo on the other side of the metal tunnel that carried sounds into the locked room.

"I am Lavender Kawaguchi," a garbled voice answered, sounding vaguely like a male child.

"No!" she stifled a laugh. "I'm talking *to* you, understand? You're supposed to answer. What do you answer when people say their names?"

"Encantado," the voice answered, sounding slightly unsure.

"In English," she said.

The voice replied, "Nice to meet you."

"You're getting much better, but we'll still have lots to work on tomorrow." Lavender stepped back and reached for the panel that covered the window, emblazoned with a yellow zero.

"It is...dark in here."

Lavender jumped and turned back to the window. "What did you say?"

"It is...empty...in here."

"Stay there!" Lavender grabbed the panel with shaking hands, put it back in place, ran through the dimly lit corridors of the building, and burst out the front door onto the pavement outside. She quickly shut and locked the door. She ran down the street, unaware of the frozen traffic and the crowds of people lingering on their phones. She entered a grand, but somewhat unkempt looking mansion and ran through the rooms, but all of them were empty until she came to Edwin Ambrose's bedroom on the second floor. The door was ajar; her roommate was sitting on a chesterfield couch covered in dirty laundry, newspaper cutouts and a pile of books on child psychology, an old television playing in the background.

"Edwin, he's finally doing it, he's finally independently...." She stopped, as he looked up at her. There was something wrong about his expression. "Edwin, what's going on?"

"Look," he pointed at the television and she followed his gaze.

A reporter stood on the crest of a hill, pointing down towards a stretch of highway that had been sectioned off. Something odd was sitting in the middle of it, but Lavender couldn't tell immediately what it was.

"That is the spot where it fell earlier this morning," the reporter said. "It crashed straight through the protective dome around the Nation. We're not sure what went wrong, contact was lost some time ago and it was assumed that the vessel had been lost, but it's returned. For our viewers tuning in now, this is the ship of astronaut Markus "Mark" Walker, who left six months ago on the first manned expedition into space, only to vanish a day later."

Lavender turned to Edwin, pale-faced. "He's dead?"

Edwin looked back at her, shaking his head. She stared at him, confused.

"I'm going in for a closer look...oh, it looks like they've managed to get him out." The camera zoomed in on a figure being carried away from the wreckage by stretcher, badly bloodied, but apparently alive. He clutched a piece of twisted metal in his hands. As a team of medics struggled to carry the stretcher away, he suddenly jumped up and brandished the piece of metal wildly with a crazed expression on his face, crying out, "No! No!"

The medics surrounding the stretcher tried to calm him down, but he continued screaming, "No, I told it to self-destruct! I told it to self-destruct! You'll die! All of you will die!"

"What's wrong with him?" Lavender asked, looking in horror at her screaming fiancé.

He gave one last cry, "No! Not you, Lavender!" and collapsed back onto the stretcher, perfectly still.

PART ONE

Curiosity killed the man from space
Curiosity stopped the clock by the staircase
Hear their steps as they walk with grace
Little loves run to your hiding place
Pull the sheets over your face
Shut your eyes, leave not a trace
For the Nightghosts have come to chase
And rock you to sleep in their embrace

-from *The Parable of the Nightghosts,*
circa. January of 120

![1]

Earth
The Nation of Steel: Capital City
Late Fall, Year 141 A.C.

Alaska Donnel didn't remember being twelve. That year was like a black empty canvas in her mind. All she remembered of that year was waking up in bed in her room all of a sudden and feeling like something was wrong, as if something massive had happened, and she had missed it. And then there was the dream, a dream which came again and again, even after four years had passed. A dream with an imaginary friend named Winter, who always slipped away from Alaska, no matter how hard Alaska tried to catch her.

"I'm going to find you!"

A dark-haired, impish little girl splashed through deep puddles, before running across a muddy field, whipping past bracken and heather. Rain fell heavily, and the world was shaded a dim gray as things passed by in a flash. The sound of birdcalls filled her ears. She stopped short by a thick trunked, strange, bark-less tree on the edge of a steep slope.

"You didn't go down there, did you?" she asked, looking down below, but she couldn't see anything. "That's cheating, I told you before!"

She sighed, shook her head, sucked in her breath and then

spread out her arms. She jumped, the earth surged away from beneath her feet, and then she was flying, not falling, flying gently above the ground.

"Alaska!"

Startled, she crashed to the ground and looked up as darkness closed in around the world.

"No, stop it," she said, as it spread like a black cloud and then everything crumbled and vanished.

"Alaska!"

Alaska Donnel opened her eyes. She was in the Capital again, lying in a sunlit bedroom. Sketches covered nearly every inch of the walls, sketches of cloaked figures, some in red and some in black. Alaska saw her mother hovering over her, an impatient expression on her stern face.

"Wake up!" her mother said hurriedly. "You got it! You got it!"

"What?" Alaska asked sleepily, sitting up.

She saw the housemaid Tarana enter, and then her eyes fell to the slip of red paper in her mother's hand.

A panicked expression crossed her face at the sight of it. "No, they can't have. I'm rude. I'm brash. I'm the worst student in the class. I would never be chosen."

"You have to go to school! Just a few more months!" Her mother seemed not to hear her, her voice overjoyed as she crossed to the door. "My daughter, a Defense officer at seventeen!"

Alaska kept going over the slip in her head. Few people got early graduation, but she would be graduated in December, on her seventeenth birthday. What had she possibly done to deserve that? And what would she do now? She had always planned to enter the reserves like her brother Malcolm, but early graduates weren't allowed to opt out.

****

"Mudflat Scum!"

Alaska stopped on the street and turned her head in the direction of the yell.

She saw a frightened, emaciated young woman with wild honey-brown hair, dressed in raggedy washed-out clothing, running away from a group of children throwing stones at her. The woman tripped and fell on the cracked pavement, trying desperately to shield her head with her hands.

"Get away from her!" Alaska screamed at them, plunging forward as she recognized Tarana, her family's maid.

The children looked at Alaska and ran away. Tarana looked at her, her thin, bony fingers shaking.

"Thank you," she whispered in a cracked voice, wide-eyed.

"It's okay, let me —," Alaska started, when she heard her name being called.

"Alaska, hurry up!" Alaska's best friend Hugh stood on the steps of a nearby museum. "The whole class is here already."

She ran towards Hugh, crossing under a sign that read Glory Of Defense Museum and followed him inside.

"You know we're not supposed to talk to people from the Mudflats!" Hugh whispered in her ear as she slipped past him, sounding scandalized, but Alaska ignored him and stood on tiptoe to see over the heads of the students in front of her.

The students had formed a chain down the long gallery of the museum as their tour guide, a teacher clad in white robes, led them past various exhibits.

"A skeleton of a Provincial, see the severe damage, from their... barbaric practices. Magler's pocket-watch, in which he always kept a bit of poison in a hidden compartment to kill his enemies, and, some say, to quench his insatiable thirst for human blood. Ah, and quite a fascinating and rare curiosity, a glass model of the Nation, found at Magler's estate shortly after his assassination, and the saving of the Nation from his tyrannical wrath."

Alaska turned and saw the model, a giant glass dome with tiny figurines and houses inside of it. The figurines were made of brass clockwork and moved on a rotating circular base.

"But this, this is the pièce de résistance, class. It is a great honor for you to be able to see this. This is a replica of Markus Walker's vessel," the teacher said, as he stopped in front of a giant case, beneath which was a twisted mass of metal.

Alaska squinted, making out the inscription on a plaque:

This is the embodiment of Contagion.

"Contagion," said the teacher sternly as he walked back and forth in front of the crowd while a tall harsh-looking man in red stood behind him, surveying the crowd with a severe expression. "A disease that spreads among society. A harmful influence that poisons civilization. Defense is the only reason you stand here today, in the wake of the actions of Magler and Markus Walker. If it were not for Defense, you would all be dead now — Alaska Nasrin Donnel!"

She jumped, tearing her eyes away from a window. "Sir," Alaska said, straightening herself as the teacher approached.

"Are you looking for something?"

"No, Mr. Gizel."

He reached his hand out. "Give it to me, Alaska."

His usually soft voice was biting and angry, but his face was sympathetic. Behind him, however, she could see the man in red, a Speaker, glaring down at her. She looked down at the piece of paper crumpled in her grasp, before the teacher forced it from her hand, stared at the crude scribbling, and asked, "What is this, Alaska?"

It was a drawing of a marbled brown winged creature curled up in a ball, caught in a cage carried by figures in black cloaks. Black cloaks. How could she have been so stupid, she thought, before staring up into the teacher's face with the most innocent look she could muster.

"A dream I had last night, Mr. Gizel. About a...bird."

"You know birds are only mythical creatures, long extinct if they ever did exist. Clearly this is just another example of your fanciful imagination, Alaska, and I think it would be better for both of us if you did more listening and less dreaming."

She watched him shred the scribble in front of her eyes. The pieces floated onto the floor as the Speaker fast-approached, forcing his way through the crowd.

"I do listen, Mr. Gizel."

Alaska winced the moment she said the words, wishing she had stopped as hushed remarks spread throughout the crowd.

"Good then, maybe you can tell us what happened in 119."

Alaska stared back at him blankly. Some of the students started teetering. The teacher's eyes narrowed.

"Alright then, I'll have to —"

"Everybody knows about the plague," said Alaska.

The room fell silent, except for the soft voice of Hugh behind her whispering, "Just be quiet. Just be quiet."

She ignored him, "But we never ask why. Why did Markus Walker disappear? Why did he crash? How did he contract the plague? Why did it spread everywhere? Why was Defense the only one to find the cure? Why...exactly?"

Gasps filled the air. This was not the thing to say. Alaska looked down, her face burning.

"Hugh," the teacher said turning to him. "Will you escort Alaska out of the building? She will be returning home."

Hugh reached for Alaska's hand to drag her out, but the Speaker barged his way to the front, and held up his hands for Hugh to stop.

"The thing about contagions," said the man in a low voice. "Is they must be bled out."

Alaska looked to Hugh pleadingly, but nobody spoke a word as the Speaker drew out a thin metal device and hit the back of her hand with it. It whipped across her skin, and she saw blood drip onto the floor. He grabbed her hand, squeezing it tightly in his grasp, and Alaska grit her teeth to keep from screaming as he held it up in front of her eyes. She saw the letter "U" staring back at her, carved in flesh and blood.

"For the rest of the day, this girl is a provincial. She is to be treated accordingly."

She turned to leave, but the Speaker stopped her. She looked up into his cool gray-green eyes with hatred.

"I look forward to continuing this lesson when you join Defense, Alaska Donnel," he said in a menacingly soft voice.

She pulled her hand free and ran, hearing the silence behind her, then the sound of footsteps as she burst through the doors of the museum. She hurtled down the steps two at a time, running towards home. Alaska heard footsteps behind her and turned to see Hugh following, gasping for breath as he caught up to her.

"I'm sorry, Alaska!" said Hugh. "It wasn't fair, he shouldn't have done that to you."

She didn't answer and barged on past him. He caught her hand and slowed her down.

"You're not supposed to do that," said Alaska, flashing her wounded hand in front of his face. "'U', remember? I'm a bloody provincial for the day. Untouchable."

"Well, you shouldn't have spoken out," Hugh couldn't contain his impatience as he began to lecture her. "If you want to finish school, you'll have to stop doing that. They'll kick you out if you keep this up."

Hugh, the model student, could be absolutely maddening at times, she thought as he looked down at her with a very patronizing glare from behind his thick-rimmed spectacles and very yellow blond bangs. She wondered why they hadn't chosen him for early graduation. He seemed their ideal. He wanted to be a Defense officer.

"Maybe I don't want to finish," Alaska spat, speeding up so Hugh fell behind her. "Maybe I don't want to be like them. Did you see the Speaker? He enjoys it!"

"You don't have to be like that," Hugh said quickly. "You could be like your father. He's a Defense officer. He doesn't have to carry out executions, or —"

"Do you think they'll let me choose?" Alaska asked angrily. "They're forcing me to graduate early, Hugh. They're going to make me become whatever they want."

A look of astonishment passed across Hugh's face, and then, just for a moment, jealousy. Why couldn't they have chosen him?

"Why does it all have to be such a bad thing, Alaska?" asked Hugh. "I've dreamt about being an officer."

So have I, Alaska thought, *in my nightmares.* "I'll just drop out and become a pilot."

"Don't be stupid," Hugh sighed heavily. "You're scared of riding in cars. How do you expect to fly a ship?"

"I don't mind air-ships or trains, just cars," Alaska said indignantly, staring intently at an empty patch of land in the distance. "I don't know why."

Hugh craned his neck, following her gaze. "Is something wrong, do you see something?"

"No," said Alaska quickly, turning to look at him.

"Something is wrong! You've got a funny look on your face, like you're worried about something. Are you worried about your brother and his fiancée?"

"No, I don't know why they're sneaking out to the shop every night, but I'm going to find out," she assured him. He stared at her for a moment, then nodded his head, accepting her answer.

She kept an eye out for anything strange as Hugh went on and on, going over their lessons for the day, about burial practices during the plague, word etymology and other boring things she wasn't going to bother herself with. No, the thing that preoccupied her most was the feeling of being followed, of someone watching her. When Mr. Gizel caught her staring out of the window, she had thought she saw something, just briefly, just for a second. But outside in the smoggy air, with officers carrying briefcases running past in the opposite direction, people out walking agitated dogs and cars flying past at dangerous speeds on wide roads, it was like looking for a needle in a haystack. The city was a tangled jungle of concrete and glass, the only trees odd metal replicas that rose thirty feet above street level, covered in gray-blue lights. Red flying objects like oversized fireflies, called messengers, whizzed past in thick flocks, carrying electronic memos. Overhead was the constant soft drone of passing Defense air-ships as they darted across the sky. Everything was fast-moving, flashing before Alaska's eyes. She felt there was something wrong in all the hustle and bustle, that it was right there in front of her eyes, but she couldn't single it out.

"And then at the end of the plague the Act of Defense was written and signed by every loyal resident of the Capital today, to protect them and their descendents from the rabid provincials who had supported the dictator Magler's ridiculous space plan and helped cause the spread of the plague...," Hugh continued babbling on.

She halted in her tracks. On the steps of a circular, fort-like prison building, a cloaked figure stood and stared back at her. It was a tall, imposing figure. She couldn't tell if it was female or male. She felt her heart stop. They were still watching, whoever they were. What did they want?

"Alaska?"

Alaska turned her head towards Hugh for a second. He'd stopped several feet ahead of her, realizing she was no longer moving. She looked back towards the prison steps, but the figure had vanished. The only one on the steps was a red-haired, pale young man in a Defense uniform running down them at breakneck speed.

"Never mind," Alaska said.

"If something's bothering you..."

"I said never mind!" She turned sharply, rejoined him, and they both walked onward in silence until they reached an intersection where they were swamped by a horde of people, all running away, all looking terrified.

"What's going on?" Alaska cried, trying to keep from being crushed by the crowd.

Hugh tried to get a look over the heads of the crowd, but he couldn't, and was knocked to the ground. Quickly he managed to pick himself up and grabbed Alaska's hand.

"We have to get out of here!"

"What...?"

Suddenly the air was filled with loud popping noises and flames. Alaska saw a wave of black flags and gasped. They were protestor flags, anti-Defense flags. Screams, panic and the sound of smashing glass came from every direction. Hugh pulled her away, and they both ran with the crowd. Somebody trying to push their way through slammed into Alaska and for a moment all the breath was knocked out of her as she tumbled to the ground. She struggled to get back up, but couldn't with people running everywhere, knocking into her, trampling over her fingers, not seeming to realize there was somebody on the ground in front of them. She screamed out Hugh's name but he was lost in the maze of legs frantically propelling their owners in every direction. A ghostly white car appeared in the middle of the chaos, speeding out from a side street, and people panicked even more. Several people fled sideways, jumping over barricades lining the road. Alaska stepped back, unsure whether to run or stay, but then the car door flew open.

"Alaska, is that you? Alaska!"

She ran to the familiar voice, and saw her father staring back at her from inside the car, wordlessly helping her inside. She looked around wildly for Hugh, and caught sight of somebody who might have been him struggling through the crowd, but then the car door was shut, and they were hurtling down the road as she clipped on her seat-belt and shoved the hand emblazoned with the "U" in her pocket.

They turned onto a narrow side street surrounded by high stone walls. Alaska heard the chaos of explosions, shattering glass and screams of pain just on the other side, and then the noise died down, leaving them in silence. Alaska braced herself as the shock started to subside, and the fear that set in every time she was in a car came washing over her. She felt suddenly panicked and gritted her teeth.

"Are you okay?" her father asked, and Alaska nodded her head.

"What happened?" she asked, still shaking slightly.

"Several criminals showed up at a clinic and were denied. They caused a commotion, and," her father sighed. "A whole lot of damage was done. I think they may have been trying to steal medicine."

"That's horrible! Why would anybody do that?" she asked.

Her father sighed again, "I really don't know, Alaska."

Benjamin Donnel's detour took awhile, but Alaska was just glad to be home when they stopped outside the house that had been in the Donnel family for three generations. The house, a crumbling, quirky canary yellow colonial set on a tiny, narrow lot looked odd next to its blocky, concrete neighbors. Its three stories looked as if they had been haphazardly stacked on top of each other, and it had a front porch with open latticework topped by a sleeping porch with heavy steel shutters drawn down over the windows. Alaska ran up the stepping stone front walk past empty fish ponds, their inhabitants long ago eaten by sneaky alley cats. She rushed inside of the house. Her nineteen-year-old brother Malcolm and little sister Leila were already there, both safe, seated around the television. They jumped up the moment Alaska and Mr. Donnel arrived.

"Where's Amina?" Mr. Donnel asked, looking around fearfully.

"Mother's upstairs," Malcolm answered quickly. "What about Marianne? She was working nearby, is she okay? Is she safe?"

"She's fine, I checked with her grandmother. She made it home safely, she's coming over here for dinner by a different route."

The door opened behind them and Malcolm's fiancée, Marianne Poesy, entered looking disheveled, but fierce, her short black hair in her face. She briskly swept it out of her face and dropped down immediately on the sofa.

"It's brutal out there," Marianne said, staring intently at the television. "Things are escalating."

"It's just a one-off," Mr. Donnel said quickly.

"There's been fifty one-offs this year around the country," Marianne pointed out.

A funny look crossed Malcolm's face, and Alaska stared at him. All those times she had walked in on him and Marianne in the kitchen, talking in low voices. They always stopped when she entered, looking uncomfortable, but not before she caught whispered snatches, caught the name, Pomander's Lid.

"I know," Mr. Donnel settled down into an armchair. "The protests are getting more frequent, but the best we can do is crack down on the possible perpetrators before these things happen."

"As a Defense officer don't you ever wish," said Marianne

carefully, glancing at Mr. Donnel. "That you could find out what's going on inside these people's heads? Know what's changed so suddenly that so many people are attacking clinics?"

Benjamin Donnel's eyes narrowed as he stared from her to Malcolm. "No."

Alaska quietly slipped away to the kitchen. She passed by a six-layer cake set aside for her brother's wedding that was taking place the next day. She stole a raspberry off it, before rummaging through a drawer where Tarana, the housemaid, kept medical supplies. Alaska managed to find a large bandage. She pasted it over her hand. If her parents asked, she'd say it was only a cut she got during the riot, she decided. She started to close the drawer when she heard the snapping of a branch outside. She went over to the back door window but couldn't see anything except the overgrown, untamed rose bushes climbing up everything, and rusty train tracks. Then, as she opened the door and stepped out further into the yard itself, she saw it standing among the roses, over six feet tall, cloaked in black, a faceless form.

"What do you want?" she asked in a shaky voice, as it moved towards her.

Alaska ran for the house, hearing the sound of movement behind her, close by, closing in. She threw open the back door and hurtled inside, locking it behind her. Alaska turned away, cowering with fear.

"1,2,3," she whispered, repeatedly. "1,2,3. 1,2,3...."

Alaska looked over her shoulder. The backyard was empty.

leven thirty-four p.m. Alaska could see the monolithic Capital clock from her window, rising out of the nearby Sea of Wolves and towering over the city. The massive brass clock with spindly hands jutted out from the structure's pale gray stone, and was held up by two enormous human statues standing on ledges made from elaborate ironwork. The clock chimed twice a day, once for the beginning of the 1 a.m. Capital curfew, and once for the end of it, at 6 a.m. Alaska looked away from the clock, clutching her hand. The "U" cut into her hand was burning with pain and swollen, even though she'd cleaned and bandaged the wound before bedtime. She went to the bathroom, hoping to find something to relieve the pain, and ran into Tarana, wiping the floor.

"Sorry," said Alaska hurriedly, searching for an excuse to get Tarana to leave without raising suspicion. "It's kind of late, isn't it?"

Tarana only nodded and quietly left the room. She wasn't supposed to talk to Alaska, and Alaska hadn't expected her to, but it was odd and awkward. When Alaska was a little girl and her parents were out of the house they had often read stories and played silly games together like hide and seek. Tarana had been like a close friend then but somehow in the years that had passed she had become a shadow in the house, moving silently from one room to the next. Alaska rummaged through the bathroom drawers, but didn't see anything and was about to leave when she caught a glimpse of her reflection. She saw a bird-like girl barely over five feet tall with a dark olive complexion, long, straight nose and oval face. Thick black ringlet curls encircled her head and dropped down over her forehead, shadowing her chocolate brown eyes. There was something strange in them, something people always said looked haunted, or wild. Her reflection always unnerved her, but she didn't know why, and drew away quickly, not wanting to see anymore. Alaska returned to her room, gritting her teeth as she tried to bear the pain. She pulled up a few floorboards near her bed, revealing a hidden cubby. Wedged into it was a pile of storybooks with bright covers. She pushed *101 Fairytales* and *Through the Looking Glass* out of the way, unearthing a wad of maps. She replaced the floorboards and spread the maps on the floor, quickly becoming lost in a world of far-away places she'd always wanted to go to, but knew were impossibly distant. The Nation of Steel took up a large chunk of an island once called Australia. The country was surrounded by sea on three sides and mountainous, impassable desert on the fourth. An invisible dome shielded it, cutting them off from the outside world, listed on all the maps as simply "Otherland." According to Defense textbooks the dome had been built by the first colonists to defend the Nation from barbarian invaders and their cruel endless wars. At its edge by the Sea of Wolves was the Capital City, which had once had another name under Magler. Only fools, traitors and Defense officers left the Capital, her mother always said. The city was cut off from the provinces by a red barbed wire fence. The provinces were a swath of brown on the maps and Alaska had marked locations, such as Enders, Cutter and Winter's Gate on them with small black dots. Alaska turned her head, and saw the time on the clock again. 11:45 p.m. Marianne had gone home six hours ago. Alaska was waiting for something, but it was not quite time yet.

"Miss Donnel?"

Alaska heard footsteps and quickly shoved the maps under

the bed. She stood in front of it with the most innocent smile she could muster on her face. Tarana appeared, stopping in the doorway.

"I was leaving for home, but I remembered I'd brought you these." She smiled at Alaska, unearthing a set of yellowed maps from her bag.

Alaska took them, staring at the maid in surprise.

"I...I just noticed," Tarana stammered, nodding her head towards the edge of a map, poking out from under the bed. She pulled a small, pink bottle from her pocket. "Take this for your hand. They never cut shallowly."

Tarana held out the bottle, and Alaska stared at her in shock. "Cut?"

"The Defense officer who cut your hand," said Tarana. "I'm sorry, but I have the same injury. I knew it didn't happen in the riots. But don't worry, I won't breathe a word of this to your parents."

Alaska accepted the pink bottle, staring at Tarana in utter surprise. "Thank you."

Tarana nodded and quietly slipped out of sight. She heard Tarana leave to walk alone in the night towards the decrepit, dark part of the Capital called the Mudflats. The clock read 11:50 p.m. There was a banging sound as a door downstairs shut. Alaska quietly slipped out of her room onto the landing beyond, climbed down the ladder to the second floor before she descended narrow steps, skipping the rotten one, and entered the living room. Her mother had hung red and white silk rose garlands in the afternoon around the room for the wedding, and they were collecting dust and cobwebs. In the dim light Alaska made out the cracked clock embedded in the old marble mantel of the fireplace that had never been fixed and collections of dusty photographs. She walked past all of them, unable to see the details in the low light, but she could remember all of them in her head — a 6th birthday party, a family outing, her brother's graduation in a freshly pressed Defense uniform, the only time she'd ever seen him wear one. None of them included her at twelve. Her parents said they had lost all the pictures from that year. A light flooded the dark room and she turned to see the headlights of a car pulling silently into the drive. Alaska heard the soft noise of the bathroom door being opened and closed again. A moment later the stairs creaked as someone descended. She was ready for them.

"Alaska!" Malcolm said, sounding surprised and uncomfortable as she sprang out from behind the stairs. "What are you doing down here?"

"What are you doing?" she countered.

He said quickly, "I was going to get water."

There was a click and the front door opened. Marianne stood in the doorway. She looked from Malcolm to Alaska.

"Why is she here?"

"I was just about to ask you that," Alaska turned to her brother.

"We're just going out," Malcolm said quickly. "Aren't you supposed to be in bed?"

"You sneak out of here every night."

"How do you know that?" Malcolm stared down at her, looking shocked.

"My best friend told me. You go to his father's shop and talk to him every night. What are you doing?"

Malcolm shook his head, throwing on his coat. "It's none of your business."

"Fine, then," Alaska said as she started to climb up the stairs again. "You won't mind me telling Mom and Dad?"

He and Marianne exchanged a glance at her threat.

"Wait! You'll have to go in a car," Malcolm said resignedly.

Alaska glared at him. "I know that."

"Okay. As long as you promise not to tell them."

Gleefully Alaska threw on her bright yellow coat and followed them into the autumn chill that clung to every surface like an icy blanket. Alaska sat in the back seat, clenching the armrests to steel herself for the drive ahead, watching as her brother locked up the house and then drove down the dark road, illuminated only by tiny streetlights. She pressed her face to the window, staring through the darkness and knew somewhere out there were the security cameras, just out of view, their watchful eyes following everybody who passed by. Marianne stared out of her own window as they passed by each streetlight, anxious, alert, watchful, but for what reason Alaska didn't know. She hadn't expected them to take her with them; they had to be terrified of her and Malcolm's parents knowing. Something big was going on.

The car stopped in front of a battered looking antiques shop. It was built from limestone and looked like it had once had three stories, but the third story had crumbled away, leaving only two. Bars covered the windows, many of which were missing glass and boarded up. They got out of the car into a light drizzle and stood at the deep front doorway as Malcolm rang the bell. A small window opened in the door, and Alaska saw a gray eye. A moment later the door opened and Hugh's father, Maisel, the shop's owner, ushered them inside. He nodded to Malcolm and Marianne, but gave Alaska an odd look.

"Stay down here," Malcolm said, and before Alaska could protest, he and Marianne disappeared with Maisel upstairs to the flat where Maisel and Hugh lived.

"Alaska?"

She turned to see Hugh in pajamas and slippers, peering out from an open door.

"What are you doing here?" he whispered.

"I'm so glad you made it back home. But I told you, I'm going to figure them out," Alaska whispered back.

"Alaska, I'm..." Hugh looked unsure whether or not to say something, and finally said, "My father's up to something."

"What sort of something?"

"He...he had this guy come earlier, after school. Somebody I've never met before. My father talked to me afterward, and he said a lot of things." Hugh bit his lip. "He doesn't want me to go down into the basement. He hid the key, but I found it."

"Well, we should go then," said Alaska excitedly. "Maybe that's why my brother keeps coming."

Hugh left, then returned and led her to a door with flecks of paint peeling off of it. He pulled out a key from his pajama pocket and unlocked the door. As he forced it open, Alaska tried to see through the darkness beyond, just managing to make out a set of stairs, old, narrow and crumbling. A horrible rank smell drifted up from the bottom of them. They descended carefully, Alaska feeling with her foot for each step.

"I don't know what Marianne and Malcolm are doing, but it's important," Alaska said as she followed behind Hugh, using the walls as a guide. "Your father and Marianne both like to keep secrets, but not Malcolm."

"Weird things keep happening and I keep an eye out for them," Hugh said as they reached the bottom of the stairs. "My father can't screw in a light bulb. If somebody's using him for something I..." Hugh trailed off, mumbling to himself.

The basement was a cavernous, earth-smelling space, full of old antiques lifted off the wet floor. Alaska wondered how Hugh's father had possibly gotten some of them—gold chalices, a dusty chest carved in the shape of a wolf and pendants with gems that glinted in the moonlight pouring in from narrow, broken windows. As they passed a cracked black marble statue of a tall, slim man holding a torch, Hugh asked, "Anything weird at your place, Alaska?"

Alaska opened her mouth to speak but thought better of it, thinking of the cloaked figure and that strange name — Pomander's Lid. She shook her head, trying to force the memories away.

"Nah, everything's fine," Alaska told him.

They came to the back of the basement, and Hugh picked up an old LED lantern off a nearby table, switched it on and illuminated the space. Alaska stepped back at the sight in front of them. At the back of the basement sat a battered air-ship, dark like Defense's air-ships, but crude and blockish unlike the new ships Alaska usually saw through the chain link fences surrounding their launchpads at the Defense airfields. This air-ship's metallic body was covered in dents and flaws where it had been clumsily repaired and patched back together. All the former Defense markings and insignias had been badly covered up with fresh paint.

"It must be a fake," Alaska said, open-mouthed.

Hugh walked around it, shocked. He tried prying open one of the doors, but to no avail and finally stepped back. "It doesn't seem to be. I've seen Defense ships in books. I've gone over the specs numerous times. It's real." Hugh looked like he wished it wasn't.

"How...how did your father get it?" Alaska asked.

He stared back at her.

"No,...he didn't steal it, did he?" Alaska asked, horrified. "If Defense finds out he'll be executed!"

"Don't tell anyone," Hugh said quickly. "We can't let anyone know."

There was a rustling noise from somewhere else in the basement. Alaska took one look at Hugh and then ran for the stairs, Hugh racing after her as they ascended two steps at a time despite the darkness.

"We'll forget we saw anything," Hugh gasped, breathing heavily. "There is no ship in the basement."

"But there is," Alaska started. "What if it is connected to Malcolm and Marianne?"

"No ship," Hugh said forcefully. "Your brother's wedding is tomorrow, isn't it? Maybe they want my father to come up with something for it. That's all."

"This isn't about any stupid wedding!" Alaska countered fearfully.

Despite Defense having saved the country from the plague, very few held the illusion that it was a benevolent government catering to the every need or whim of the citizens. Nobody in his or her right mind crossed Defense. Marianne had always told her they were truly loved by few, but truly feared by most. Over time, she had become aware that there was more to it than what her father did. Things people were hesitant to speak about. Strange sudden deaths, nighttime disappearances, mysterious mutilations. Alaska had seen public executions and people dragged down alleyways by white uniformed officers, though she tried to walk past like everyone else, pretending not to care or hear the screams, when inside she felt like screaming herself. She knew Hugh had every right to be scared. She was, but she didn't want to show it and she wasn't going to. The sound of voices came from above. Hugh relocked the basement door, sinking against it and letting out a sigh of relief.

"I almost forgot to give you something," Hugh said, reaching into his pocket and pulling out a notebook, with a tiny screen and keyboard. He handed it to her and Alaska flipped it over, trying to seem happy about it. It was a nice one, after all. It had probably cost a lot of money, and Hugh wasn't living in the Goldcage.

"Thanks," said Alaska, trying to sound slightly grateful.

"You don't have to pretend you like it," Hugh said quickly. "It was an antique my father got. He refurbished it, but there wasn't much demand. It'll work fine, the only thing he couldn't fix was the typo, see?" He pointed at a date on the bottom of it, by an inscription that read: *For Winter. 2100.* "They accidentally put a "2" in, so it's at least forty one years old..."

"Hugh, I hate writing, I—" Alaska started.

"Just try," Hugh interjected. "I just wanted to thank you for being a friend to me when nobody else wanted anything to do with me. You helped me start talking, so now I'm going to help you start writing."

"Thanks," Alaska said, a little puzzled, but trying to sound enthusiastic as she stuffed it in her coat.

"Tell your brother and Marianne congratulations for me at the wedding," Hugh added.

Alaska stared at him, nonplussed. "You can tell them yourself."

He shook his head darkly, "I can't. Don't come over to the shop tomorrow."

"Why?"

"My Dad's planned a trip," he said and slipped away to his bedroom.

Alaska stood alone in the hallway. Suddenly, she heard a strange scraping noise and looked back at the basement door. Something was definitely moving on the other side.

"Maisel?" a muffled shout came through the door. "Maisel, help me!"

She backed away and heard a sharp yell from behind her, "Alaska, move out of the way, you're blocking the stairs!"

She stepped back as Malcolm, Marianne and Maisel descended the stairs and she heard nothing more from the other side of the basement door.

"One a.m. curfew," her brother said as he rushed to the front door. "We have to go."

"I heard somebody," Alaska said. "I think it was a man. He said your name," she nodded at Maisel.

"There's only us here," Marianne said, trying to steer Alaska towards the door.

"I heard somebody," Alaska repeated more certainly, shrugging her off.

"Someone outside?" Marianne glanced at Malcolm.

"Inside the shop. At the basement door."

"Hurry up!" Malcolm interrupted, holding the door open for Alaska. "We can't be caught on the road after one."

"But somebody's in here! What if it's a break-in?"

"It's late for all of us," interjected Maisel in a tired voice. Hugh had ambled in, pretending to be groggy with sleep and Maisel put a hand on his shoulder. "You three should be leaving."

Malcolm glared at Alaska pointedly, and she followed him reluctantly out of the shop in silence, but the moment they'd gotten into the car and started off again she exclaimed, "I heard somebody, I'm not imagining it! They were moving on the other side of the basement door!"

"You didn't hear anything, Alaska."

"Yes, I did."

"Listen to me," Malcolm snapped, whirling around to face her. "You didn't hear or see anything, understood?"

"Mal!" Marianne grabbed the steering wheel before he drove the car into a lamppost by the side of the road. Alaska screamed, feeling an oddly familiar fear. Malcolm turned back quickly and brought the car under control.

"I'm sorry, Alaska, but there wasn't anything there. You must be tired, like the rest of us. We're tired and worried, that's all there is to it," he said, his voice even again. "You shouldn't even be up at this hour."

"I'm not twelve years old anymore, Malcolm, though I don't think you've noticed. I did hear someone," Alaska snapped with stubborn indignation, though her certainty was wearing.

She knew she had heard something. But as they got further away from the shop, closer to home, Alaska couldn't help but doubt it. And that ship? Thinking about that just made things worse, more jumbled up in her head, along with ghostly figures that watched her and the mysterious excursions of her brother and sister-in-law-to-be. By the time they pulled into the drive and the Capital clock began to chime, the voice was not so clear, but fuzzy, more of a whisper. Perhaps just a thought.

Two Years Ago

A thirteen year old boy ran past a cracked stone bench through thick gray snow, sopping wet, his long auburn hair plastered to his head. He skirted around rows of uniform, crumbling tombstones, with a swift, but slightly awkward gait. Everything was laced in a morning fog, though the fog hardly made a difference from the heavy gray curtain that always hung over the city. He came to a grinding halt, hearing the cacophony of people's voices, a public television somewhere blaring out a funeral march, the sound of breaking glass and screeching cars. Several Defense vehicles sped past the derelict graveyard. He hid in the shadow of a small, shed-like stone structure until they passed, then slipped out cautiously and found the rotted, old wooden door. Someone had graffitied 'Liars, Thieves, Murderers' on the door in now faded red paint. He found the rusted handle and pushed the door inwards. It groaned, and finally gave way, a plume of dust hitting him in the face as he carefully descended a short set of steps. Inside was musty and dark. He pulled a flashlight out of his pocket and switched it on. Black mold climbed up the walls and badly cracked ceiling. Several inches of snow had collected on the floor. Lying in the snow was a young captive around the same age as the boy. He was dressed in a ripped, dirty school uniform and huddled in a corner of the room. One of his arms had been chained to a hook in the wall.

"Help me," the young captive whimpered, his fingers trembling and frostbitten. "Thomas and Yuri grabbed me. I've been here for hours. I can't get free."

The boy had no idea who Thomas or Yuri were, but he got down on the floor by the captive and wrenched at the chains. After several tries he managed to break them, and the captive's eyes widened as he scrambled unsteadily to his feet, freed from the wall.

"Wow, how did you do that?"

"It's not hard," the boy said. "I'm Gareth."

"I'm Jamie. Jamie Campbell-Boyd."

Now

The boy who called himself Gareth splashed through the crypt. In the years passed it had become even more decrepit, and the water in it pooled around his ankles. Across the room was a marble plaque projecting out from the wall:

In Loving Memory of
Nimue Ambrose
Edwin Ambrose
Lavender Ambrose
Ianto Ambrose

Go tell the wolves from whose den I have escaped, I will slay Goliaths, I will find the Cure, and at the dying of my day's light, I will be perfected.

"Odd sort of thing to be put on a grave."

He spun around to see his best-friend Jamie Campbell-Boyd standing on the crumbled steps inside of the door, weighed down by schoolbags with a red apple in his hand.

"Come on, Gareth, this place gives me the creeps."

He followed Jamie outside where it had stopped raining. They passed under a rusted, half-fallen sign that read: 'Protestor Grave-site 99, Visitor Be Warned.'

"Why do you keep going there anyway?" asked Jamie chattily, taking a thoughtful bite of his apple.

"I'm looking for ghosts."

Jamie's mouth fell open slightly, an expression that made him look even more like a mix between a beaver and a pet mouse, perhaps dim-witted, but harmless.

"Anyway, what are you doing here? Aren't you suppose to be home studying?" asked the boy called Gareth, though that was not his real name.

"Um...with some other friends," Jamie mumbled, and the boy felt a pang of jealousy, before he realized Jamie's long, drawn-out pause meant he was lying.

"Really?"

Jamie sighed, though his tone was nonetheless decidedly cheery. "I was in detention. My parents are going to kill me!"

"Third time this month!" Gareth mimicked in perfect imitation of Jamie's mother's voice which made Jamie jump, a look of bewilderment crossing his face, before he laughed nervously.

"Don't do that, Gareth."

"Scared?"

"No! Just...don't do that, right?"

They passed by the Disc theatre, modeled after an ancient amphitheatre called the Colosseum. Like so many of the Capital's buildings it had been built by Samson Magler, and reclaimed by Defense, painted in the official colors of red and white. A man in shabby, gray clothes stood outside the entrance, calling out with a loudspeaker, "Come and see a real battle! Which beast will win, the wolf or the rebel? David or Goliath?"

A group of young men and women clustered around the man, handing over money for tickets. Gareth snorted, watching them.

"They could save their money. It's always the wolf, not the human that wins. Their 'Goliath' has been beaten, tortured, starved and dehydrated. Doesn't stand a chance."

Nearby was the Glory of Defense Museum, then further down were rows of small, shabby faded houses. Jamie talked chattily, not noticing that his friend pulled the hood of his jacket over his head, and walked more in the shadows.

"I wish at least my parents would recognize I'm not doing anything wrong. I just found a non-Defense book. I hardly read it."

Gareth stopped immediately, staring at Jamie. "You found a non-Defense book?"

"Yeh, 1948 or something," said Jamie, frowning slightly. "I just read a page and they threw me in detention!"

"Where did you find it?" Gareth asked sharply.

"By that h—" Jamie pointed and stopped, his eyes widening.

Gareth followed Jamie's gaze and saw a house down the street smoldering, bits of it falling from the upper stories down onto the ground. Gareth and Jamie watched from the curb as emergency teams arrived, but there was nothing left to save. All they could do was protect the houses next door.

"What about the people in the house?" Jamie asked one of them as he and Gareth passed by.

The emergency worker looked at Jamie sadly, "All dead."

"But...."

Gareth glared at Jamie, grabbing his arm. Jamie wrestled his arm free and the emergency crew looked at the two of them suspiciously, before the last standing portion of the house collapsed and diverted their attention.

"What do I always tell you?" Gareth admonished Jamie as they started down the sidewalk.

"Shut up?"

"Besides that."

"See, I'm telling you, these are the types of things that don't make any sense!" said Jamie. "They're everywhere but they're so mundane and commonplace, nobody seems to notice it. Who thinks twice about a house fire they're told is normal?"

"Shut up."

Jamie turned to Gareth, and his expression changed to one of sympathy.

"I'm sorry, I know..." He bit his lip, before saying in a rushed voice, "But don't you understand? You, of all people, should understand, after what happened to you."

"Stop trying to find a hidden meaning in everything," said Gareth.

"But what if those people—"

"They deserved it then," Gareth said coldly as he walked down the sidewalk.

Jamie stopped walking.

"You don't actually believe that, do you Gareth?" Jamie asked quietly. "You don't actually believe they deserved it?"

Gareth stopped and turning back to look at Jamie who had an expectant look on his face. He opened his mouth as if to say something and then turned around and kept walking. Jamie caught up with him. They walked the rest of the way to Gareth's house in silence. Several houses down from his own, Gareth stopped and turned to Jamie.

"You better go back now, I'll meet you later."

Jamie didn't protest; he had met Gareth's grandfather only once before, but had no wish to repeat the experience.

"I'm going to look into signs of arson," Jamie said before leaving.

The boy who answered to the name of Gareth but was not, watched his best-friend run off down the street in the direction of the Defense library.

He walked up the steps to his house, an old Victorian with peeling paint, its gray brick chimney crumbling to the ground. Badly rusted bars covered the doors and windows. He passed the porch's heavy, block-like columns and stepped inside into the vestibule, skirting the drop floor trap his grandfather had installed recently, in a fit of paranoia. Arthur Ambrose was waiting in a rocking chair in the middle of the hallway, facing the door as he ruffled through a dog-eared newspaper, antiquated like most of the items in the house. He'd moved the television into the hallway as well where it blared at full volume at the foot of the stairs behind him.

"What were you doing outdoors, Ianto?" Arthur Ambrose asked the question without looking up, in his gruff, hardened voice.

"I was walking, like a normal person."

"But you are not a normal person," Ambrose snapped. "I told you to stay upstairs, boy. What if somebody recognized you? What if they are tipping off Defense right now?"

"Nobody's going to recognize me. They all think I'm dead."

"Do you want to end up like me, boy? Is that when you will learn?" He pulled up the sleeve of his left arm, twisted and burnt. The claw-like, gnarled fingers of his uninjured hand closed around Ianto's arm. "Defense will not think you are dead until you are dead. Understood?"

"Let go of me," Ianto said coolly.

"Understood?"

Ianto ignored his grandfather and glanced at the television.

"You're watching the funeral?"

Ambrose let go of Ianto, crossing his arms. "You can't change the subject with me, boy."

Ianto ignored this. "Since when do you watch public funerals?"

Ambrose hesitated. "Do you know who he is?"

"Yes. He's my grandfather. My maternal grandfather."

"Then you understand why I am watching."

"No, I don't. Why are you celebrating a thief? He stole vaccine from clinics. He condemned a lot of people in the future to die."

"Maybe he did, maybe he didn't. We will see, won't we?"

Ianto slipped past his grandfather into the kitchen. It was a sterile room every inch of which Ianto had scrubbed over the years until the smell of cleaner permanently lingered on everything. He shut the door, grabbed the key chain he had stolen that morning out of his pocket, and quickly locked it. Then he rushed over to the back door.

"Don't try it!" Arthur Ambrose's voice boomed behind him.

"How did you get in?" said Ianto as he glanced over his shoulder to see his grandfather standing in the doorway.

"Did you really think I keep only one set of keys?" his grandfather shook a laden key-chain in his face. "Upstairs."

Ianto stared him in the face for a long moment, then said coldly, "Didn't you have your sixty-fifth birthday? When is Defense coming for you, instead of going after a kid who didn't do anything except have a pair of murderers for parents?"

Before his grandfather could answer Ianto pushed past, heading up the backstairs to the second floor, hearing his grandfather's impatient response right before he slammed the kitchen door shut.

"How would that help you, boy, with me dead? Do not forget I saved your life!"

The door to the second floor stairs locked behind Ianto as he ascended. His room was at the end of the upstairs hall, and the moment he was inside he heard a soft click. His grandfather had installed an automatic locking system while he was gone, but if he thought that would thwart his grandson, he'd never been more wrong. The room was small and mostly empty, except for a mirror, bed and television. The latter had been left on purposefully. The funeral was playing here as well, the glass coffin making the final stretch of its journey around the memorial to all those who had died in the plague, before the end of the dictator Magler and the rise of Defense out of the chaos.

"Turn of–," Ianto started to say, before he noticed something staring back at him out of the mirror on the wall.

Two figures stood on either side of his reflection, waving back at him.

"No," he whispered. "Why do you have to do this?"

It had to be his grandfather, punishing him for running off. To one side of him stood a relaxed-looking woman with warm eyes and bushy hair. To the other side was a man who looked like he could be an older Ianto, same reddish-brown hair, same inquisitive gray-blue eyes. Ianto hurled the remote at the mirror, and it smashed into shards across the bedroom floor, but they still stared back at him from the pieces. He kicked it all under his bed. He would not look. He would not look at the reason he was locked away in this life forever, without ever being able to be a normal person. Not at the people who had betrayed him.

4

Everyone in the Capital went to a clinic promptly at six a.m. to receive the cure pills, the blood red tablets that tamed the plague, turning it into a sleeping tiger, instead of a raging menace. The virus was still there, coursing through every human and animal body, spreading like wildfire through the population, but there was no pain, or fevered madness, or agonizing, prolonged death. Defense had controlled it two years after the beginning of the plague, two years after Markus Walker's crash, and no one had found a better cure since. Alaska swallowed a red pill as she stood on a short bridge. It crossed a stream which snaked out from the river, following its parent to the Capital's marina and the open sea. She could see glass bottles filled with messages folded into paper ships, bobbing in the placid water, cast by children in the morning after visits to the clinics. She remembered casting her own as a young child, planning one day to follow one all the way to the end of the river, even though she knew it was not likely she was ever going to the end of that seemingly ceaseless band of water. A vague shadowy awareness of having been on the bridge with someone, someone important, very long ago came to the forefront of her mind, but she couldn't remember anything. The memory was like a story with a thinly fleshed out setting, but no characters or plot. Memories of when she was twelve were always like that.

She put an old spyglass to her eye, but couldn't see anything around Maisel's antique shop. It was empty and locked down, none of the lights on inside. Perhaps they would be back from their trip later. The shop was close to the church, so Alaska decided to go back home and slip away again during the wedding. A small crowd was assembled at the house, ready to go to the wedding, though there was an odd tension in the air that Alaska knew had nothing to do with the wedding. There had been another "incident" early that morning. Leila, her younger sister, stood near the television playing a Defense news update. She had dressed herself in a white jumpsuit stuffed with pillows and put a cardboard box with eye cutouts over her head.

"Look, I'm a spaceman!" Leila shouted as she turned to Alaska and contorted her face into a crazy, zombie-like expression as she stretched out her hands like claws towards Alaska.

"Alaska!" Mrs. Donnel's sharp voice rang out through the entire house.

Alaska ran towards the front door again, but she was caught and dragged by one arm upstairs into an empty bedroom by her disheveled-looking mother.

"Why are you fussing with me when Leila's walking around as a zombie space-man downstairs? I don't think that's usual wedding—."

"I'll deal with Leila later. You're older and should know better," said her mother, throwing a horrid, lacy peach pink gown on the bed.

Alaska stared down at it in utter hatred. "On second thought, can I be a zombie space-man?"

"No," said her mother simply, crossing her arms and Alaska sighed, picked up the dress, and grudgingly took it with her to change in the closet.

"My friend said something odd," Alaska said through a small crack that ran straight through the door.

Her mother's eyes narrowed. "What friend? And where did you run off to earlier? You could have been late."

"Hugh. He said something odd. Last...yesterday."

"You risked missing your brother's wedding for that?"

"What if something's happened to him? Like..."

Alaska remembered the family who went missing at the beginning of the year. They had lived just a couple of blocks over. Alaska remembered them as being nice, all pink-cheeked and cherubic and ginger-haired, though the girl in her year had been a bit dim. She finished putting the dress on and slipped out of the closet.

"The Robinsons!" Alaska said, remembering their name suddenly.

"I don't remember them," Mrs. Donnel said tight-lipped, fussing with Alaska's hair.

"Yes, you do! And Davies, and the Alexanders...and Carters! They went on vacation and never came back."

"You have an overactive imagination. Go to the church!" Mrs. Donnel said roughly, pushing her out the bedroom door.

Alaska went downstairs where everyone had gathered as a light rain began to fall. Chatter filled the space, and she knew someone would beckon her over and want to talk to her if she didn't get out of the way. She headed for the door, picked up an umbrella, and stepped outside, staring up and down the street. There was perfect silence, curtains drawn over every window, not a single air-ship in the overcast, gray sky, and it was beginning to rain harder. As she opened the umbrella, something flew in front of her face, coming to a stop on the bridge of her nose. A red messenger. Alaska picked the metal insect off her nose. She flipped it over several times, but there were no outside markings. Alaska started to pry it open to see the message locked inside, when she heard footsteps and looked up. A man stood in the middle of the road. He looked gaunt, old and withered, sprouts of ginger hair beginning to grow unevenly out of his shaved head. The face was familiar, yet so changed it took Alaska a moment to recognize him.

"Mr. Robinson?" Alaska said, startled.

The man collapsed on the street and Alaska ran towards him, noticing something fall from his hand. A crude child's drawing. She turned away from it, dropping down beside him, trying furiously to remember first aid.

"There's someone hurt!" she yelled over her shoulder at the house. "I think he's unconscious!"

"Step away!"

Alaska looked up and recognized the Defense officer approaching. She'd seen him before, running down the steps of the prison, a young, red-haired officer. Up close, Alaska saw he had a rather odd, skeletal face. He looked grim as he reached her and Mr. Robinson and began to drag the collapsed man away.

"Oh, thank you," Alaska said, scrambling to her feet and following him. "He just dropped in the middle of the street, I don't know what's wrong with him. He went missing some time ago." She realized the officer wasn't listening to her as he pulled Mr. Robinson towards the backseat of a white car parked nearby. "Wait, sir! You're going to take him to the hospital, right?" she asked, unsure.

The officer reached the car and pulled open the doors. Mr. Robinson's eyes suddenly opened and he stared about wildly through cloudy, green irises.

"Wait. He's awake!" Alaska exclaimed in relief while the officer dumped him in the backseat of the car. "He's awake!"

Hands reached out from the car, thin, bony, spiny hands. They closed around the young Defense officer's throat, and in one quick movement the officer removed a laser gun from the belt of his uniform and fired into the car. Alaska saw the blindingly white light, heard a thump as the man fell onto the car seat. Blood dripped from the car, staining the rainwater running away from it scarlet. The officer shut the door and turned to face her, a small, lonely figure with nothing but an umbrella.

"No, you didn't have to kill him!" Alaska screamed angrily. "He was just scared."

There was a booming crash, a flash of lightning in the sky. Alaska realized the laser gun was now pointed at her. She stared back at him, frozen.

"Alaska!" her father's voice rang out, as he appeared in the doorway of the house. "Coming, Alaska?"

The officer slipped his laser gun back into its casing, and without another glance in her direction, he got into the car and drove away.

****

"What's the matter with you, Alaska?" she heard her mother snapping at the corner of her ear. "You look frightful! This is your brother's wedding. Don't mess it up. Try to pretend to be happy, at least."

Alaska ignored her, one hand firmly stuck in her dress pocket, clenched around the child's drawing she had retrieved off the street. The memory of what she had just seen was fixed in her mind. She wanted to tell someone, but she knew what they would all say. Forget about it, forget about the man, the officer. Pretend it never happened. Be quiet and look pretty. They filed into the massive, modern glass church, a warm escape from the icy, wet fogginess outside. Images of people moved in the window, leaves blowing gently as if touched by wind. Newly inset gold sparkled in the ceiling around skylights. Commandments of the council of Defense, the unseen rulers, saviors and benefactors of the Nation and sponsors of the science team that had discovered the cure to the plague towered in alcoves set into the church's thick walls. Alaska slid into one of the metal pews.

"Look, an old woman!" said Leila suddenly, her eyes wide as

if that was something novel. It was Marianne's grandmother, Antoinette Poesy, approaching. Alaska immediately felt the urge to get up and walk away, remembering past meetings with Antoinette, but her mother put a hand on her shoulder before she could move, and turned to quiet Leila.

"She's nearly sixty-five, the Cleaners will be coming for her soon. Be nice to her." Despite her words, Alaska's mother looked like she wanted to get up and leave, too.

Alaska looked more closely at Antoinette, a thin, gray hawkish woman with an enormous pink hat. It was hard to like her, but it was undeniable that she'd been through a great deal of horrors during the Plague, losing nearly everyone she'd known. Defense didn't care; in six months they would have her rounded up and executed, an old woman without the life right privileges of a Goldcage resident or senior Defense officer. It was all humane, merciful and honorable, they promised, but Alaska had seen the tears and fear on people's faces as they were hauled away in the Cleaners' sterile white vans.

"No more comfortable after all these years," grumbled Antoinette, sliding into one of the pews near them. She stared into Alaska's face, "What's wrong with you?"

"Alaska is graduating early from the Academy," Alaska's mother bragged to the old woman. "She was labeled as one of Defense's best future prospects, our wild rose." She looked at Alaska fondly.

"Defense's best prospect, my foot. She's too small and see her eyes. Feral, like a dog's. Looks like a wild puppy to me," said Antoinette. "I'd keep my eye on her, you know what they grow into."

The old woman began to cackle and Mrs. Donnel glanced at Antoinette distastefully, whispering something under her breath that sounded a lot like "old dingbat."

Mr. Donnel looked out of the double doors at the church

entrance as guests streamed in, an anxious look on his face, as if waiting for something. Amina Donnel seemed nervous too, looking about herself and constantly fussing with her hair, then wringing her hands. Alaska's father didn't have hair, so he scratched his bald head and shook the guests' hands a little too vigorously. Malcolm entered and Antoinette started crying, then wailing, looking miserable while Leila screamed as Mrs. Donnel attempted to stop her from removing her green hairpins for a third time. Alaska silently slipped away from the madness of the church through a back door. Mr. Robinson was dead. Fog hung eerily over the gravestones surrounding the church, invisible from inside, but everywhere here. Hugh's house was very close. Alaska ran through the rows, leaving behind the main graveyard and entering a separate, far more decrepit section. From there she looked up and saw where the shop should have been. Except that now there was only a hole, surrounded by burnt grass. She felt herself swaying and a hand landed gently on her shoulder, steadying her. Alaska jumped, but it was only her father.

"Come on," he said softly.

"But..."

"Please, it's your brother's wedding," he pleaded.

They walked back and Alaska said, trying to keep her voice even, though she could hear it shake, "His house is just gone."

"Something wrong?" one of the guests, a dark-haired young man who looked close to nineteen poked his head out the back door, looking concerned.

Alaska didn't recognize him, but his voice was familiar.

"No, everything's fine, Alaska was just feeling a bit crowded, needed a moment to take everything in," Mr. Donnel said. "Just go back inside and enjoy yourself."

The guest disappeared and her father led her back inside. He guided Alaska towards a pew then sat down beside her. Alaska could see him wringing his hands.

"I didn't know you were friends with the family until your mother mentioned him earlier. Hugh Maisel was his name, wasn't it?"

Alaska nodded her head.

"I'm sorry, Alaska, but his father was doing things he shouldn't have. He couldn't be allowed to escape. I believe they were taken by Defense."

"What sort of things was he doing?"

"Weapons supplying to rogues, protestors."

Alaska remembered the air-ship in the basement, and felt a sinking feeling in her stomach.

"Why would he do that?"

"I don't know. For the money, perhaps," he told her. "Times are hard for all of us. Been so for twenty-two years, ever since Mark Walker's spacecraft crashed. Some people can't deal with the fact we can't go back to before, that Defense is doing the best they can to find a cure and keep people alive, but there is no magic panacea."

"What happened to them, Dad? Where did the house go?"

"I don't want you to get caught up in all of that, Alaska," he said firmly. "Promise me you won't, okay?"

"Okay, but what about—"

"What happened to you?" Alaska turned as her mother appeared, a look of horror on her face. "Benjamin, what did you let her do?"

Alaska realized for the first time she was drenched and splashed with mud from running through the churchyard. She opened her mouth to respond, but she was already being pulled away. As she was pushed back into place on the pew with her mother and sister, Alaska felt sick. Hugh's house being gone couldn't mean anything good, but he'd warned her the previous night not to go. Had he known something was going to happen?

"Marianne Poesy," a voice boomed over hidden speakers.

Marianne entered and there were hushed exclamations.

"The wedding dress is black!" Alaska heard Antoinette exclaim in a horrified voice, but screeching organ music in the background drowned out her ensuing tirade. The old woman lumbered down the pews as fast she could, brandishing her cane at anyone in the way. Marianne took her arm and started forward. She reached the front where Malcolm stood. Alaska saw Marianne and Malcolm beam at each other, but at the same time they seemed to be whispering softly. She tried to make out what they were whispering to each other.

"Place your hands on the stone." A computerized voice boomed over a speaker, as a metal pedestal rose from the floor, topped by a flat tablet on which was an indented space for two hands to fit.

"What are they doing?" Alaska heard Leila asking their mother, who leaned over and told her, "It's part of the ceremony, to make sure they are an acceptable match, to the code of the Defense council Commandments. For instance, if one was from the Capital, and the other was actually a—"

"There's really no point. Malcolm might be a failure, but he's not a dirt-licking provincial and neither is my granddaughter," snapped Antoinette who had returned to sit beside them on the pew. Marianne glared at her, and she grudgingly fell silent.

Marianne stretched out one of her hands as Malcolm did, and they placed them on the stone. The stone glowed a soft blue for a moment, and then they lifted their hands away, and all seemed to be fine as the organ blasted a particularly high note when a siren blared. Defense officers streamed in from every door, surrounding the room, weapons at the ready. Everyone stopped and stared about in shock.

"Which one of you is Hugh Maisel?"

Nobody responded until Mr. Donnel stepped forward, looking tired.

"Clement, what's going on?"

"He wasn't there," Clement said in a low voice. "At the house. His father, but not him."

"But why here?"

"We have evidence he was invited," Clement said, stepping forward away from the other guards.

Alaska stared at the officers in shock, and then looked away as Clement's gaze briefly settled on her.

"This is ridiculous!" Mrs. Donnel snapped, jumping to her feet, "Why would—?"

"Look, I'm sorry, Amina, but we have to do this." Clement flashed her an apologetic look.

Everyone watched in silence as the Defense officers proceeded to scan the room, going from person to person.

"That's it, I've gotten everyone in the room," Clement said.

The guards pulled away, but then one of them asked, "Isn't this a wedding? Where are the bride and groom?"

Alaska turned around startled, realizing Marianne and Malcolm had disappeared.

"Who do you think?" Clement said impatiently, pointing at two random strangers Alaska had never seen before, a woman in a evening dress and a man who was probably older than her father in a plaid suit, both standing a couple of rows down. The plaid-suited man opened his mouth for a moment, then quickly shut it.

"No sign of Hugh Maisel," Clement glared at Mr. Donnel, as if it was his fault. "I suggest you all clear out now."

The crowd immediately got to their feet and hurried out but Alaska didn't move, watching as her father started to leave, and Clement laid a hand on his arm.

"You better be careful, Ben. It won't be enough for Johnson.

Nobody believes it wasn't your son and most departments aren't going to be as lenient as mine. If I were you, I'd be planning a vacation."

"I don't know what you're talking about," Mr. Donnel said, though he gave Clement a grateful look before wrestling his arm free and leaving the church.

Alaska quickly turned around and started to leave with her mother and sister, pretending she hadn't heard any of the exchange. Everyone got into the car, and Mr. Donnel drove them home. Nobody mentioned Marianne and Malcolm's disappearance until they reached the house. The television was blaring and Marianne was sitting in the living room watching it, her arms folded. She had changed into a plaid flannel shirt and jeans. Alaska looked for her brother, but didn't see him.

"Is...?"

Before she could finish, her brother came out of the kitchen, still wearing his suit.

"Turn off that bloody noise," Mrs. Donnel snapped at Marianne before turning on Malcolm. "What were you two thinking? You could have gotten us all killed. They suspect us because you two vanished off in the middle of a raid. Alaska, get upstairs, pack bags for yourself and Leila now!"

Alaska started up the stairs, but stopped on the landing as Marianne replied defiantly, "If they didn't suspect us they wouldn't have carried out the raid in the first place. Don't pretend that was all about Alaska's friend." She didn't turn off the television.

Alaska remembered the red messenger from earlier, reached into her pocket, and pulled it out. She had stuffed it unconsciously into her dress pocket when she ran to help Mr. Robinson.

"Turn it off!"

Upon hearing her mother's infuriated scream, Alaska looked up and saw what Marianne was watching on the television.

The screen zoomed in on a glass coffin. The man contained inside looked brutally beaten, bruises covered all his face. His hair was mostly long, but the hair around his face had been cut back so none of it was covered. Alaska knew she had seen that face before.

"They're replaying Apollo Kawaguchi's funeral," Marianne said. "They want to show us what happens if you join the protestors."

"Shut it off!" Mrs. Donnel ran towards the screen as the coffin was paraded along a long, winding path in the cemetery, the national anthem blasting in the background as red and white flags flew high, and a moment later the screen went dark.

"Don't turn that on again," Mrs. Donnel said in an uneven voice and then she headed for the stairs.

Marianne rose to her feet and heatedly stormed off.

Alaska flattened herself against the wall as her mother ran past, Leila and her father trailing behind.

"You okay?"

She saw Malcolm staring at her from the bottom of the stairs, an awkward expression on his face. She resisted the urge to snap at him over his stupid question. "What's that messenger for?"

Alaska stared down at it in her hands, half opened.

"Nothing. I'm fine," Alaska said quickly. "Just—"

"Just what?" Malcolm climbed up to stand beside her on the landing.

"I...I saw something earlier, before the wedding," Alaska said. "You know Mr. Robinson, right? He was walking down the street. I don't know where he came from. He looked horrible, though not as bad as that Apollo guy on TV...and then a Defense officer came out of nowhere and he...he killed him."

Malcolm's eyes widened. "In front of you?"

"I saw a flash of light from inside the car where he dragged Mr. Robinson, and blood...and it doesn't matter whether it was in front of me, or in the car, does it? He wasn't doing anything wrong. For a moment it looked as if he was going to try to strangle the officer, but he was weak and dazed, the officer didn't have to kill him."

"That's Defense for you."

"Dad works for Defense," Alaska pointed out. She could still feel the pain in her hand, from the "U" engraved beneath the bandages. "Malcolm, what's Pomander's Lid?"

Malcolm stared at Alaska in shock, then grabbed her hands, messenger and all. "Where did you hear that?"

Alaska wrestled free of his grip, glaring at him. "I won't tell you if you act like that."

"Fine then," he said, breathing heavily. "I don't want to know. Just don't mention it again."

This was not what Alaska wanted. "In school," she lied.

"In school?" Malcolm looked doubtful, and he stared into her face.

She looked down, playing with the messenger, slowly pulling it apart into two pieces, revealing the metal rod inside that had a screen and a button to make the message play.

"Alaska, how much do you know about the plague?"

"Everything. Mr. Gizel tells us about it in school everyday. It's all he ever talks about."

"And about the protestors?"

"Nothing," Alaska said, pushing the button.

"Good," Malcolm replied, not noticing her preoccupation. "Keep it that way. Don't ever mention Pomander's Lid again. Do not tell anyone about it, understood?"

"Why? It's just a name isn't it?"

She stared in confusion at the words in front of her, scrolling across the messenger's screen in glowing red: GET OUT. There was an earsplitting wail from outside. Alaska looked up from the messenger and with a huge bang the world was rent apart.

Flames raced up the stairs. Alaska jumped off of them before the flames reached her. She stared around wildly for her brother, but he had vanished, lost in a dense curtain of smoke. An unnatural white light permeated the wall of red-orange fire, blinding her.

"Alaska!"

Leila. Alaska forced herself to move and reached through the smoke while covering her eyes. Alaska felt a small hand clutch her own. Quickly she crawled forward, leading Leila with her. Alaska coughed as she burst out of the back door and rolled onto the grass of the backyard. Flames exploded out the windows and doorways. In a daze Alaska watched the flames feed on the house. She was laying on the ground, gasping for breath, and heard Leila's own labored breathing beside her. Alaska finally managed to get to her feet and looked around the side of the house. Three figures were being dragged out the front door. One of them twitched as they were shoved onto the backseat of a white car which took off down the road. Malcolm.

"Come on!"

Alaska turned around to see Marianne running towards her and Leila, covered in soot, with bruises on the side of her face.

"Follow me. Do not say a word unless I tell you to," Marianne said.

"But what about—"

"Just go."

Leila and Alaska ran after her as she crossed the train tracks into an empty field. Alaska cowered down and hoped the tall grass of the untamed land would hide her.

"What's going on? Why are they taking them? Are they going to be alright?" Alaska burst out finally, breaking the silence. "What happened? Where's—?"

Marianne plunged forward wordlessly, forcing Alaska and Leila to follow her into a narrow alleyway, where everything was covered in a thick slick of mud. The building adjacent to the alley seemed to be crumbling into it, bricks missing off of its facade, shingles peeling off the roof, forming piles on the ground they had to jump over, though Marianne did it expertly, as if she'd been there many times before.

"This is where we're going?" Alaska asked, nearly tripping over a pile, but Marianne didn't reply.

She knocked on the side door of the crumbling building once, then five more times. It slid open and a woman with a pinched, narrow face, and graying hair peered out.

"Who is it, Marianne?"

"Family," Marianne said and the woman's eyes widened.

"Come inside, then," the woman said and Marianne hurried inside.

Alaska followed cautiously with Leila. She could see several others in the living room and they all nodded to Marianne respectfully, before scrunching up their faces in pain.

"I thought Malcolm got medicine from the clinics for them," Marianne said sharply, turning to the woman who shook her head, eyes narrowed.

"He did, but it's not enough. I've had to ration it. The Pain will start in four days. Thankfully though, there's a transport for tomorrow and maybe the facilities will have a store."

Alaska was too dazed to ask why they couldn't just go to a clinic. She slumped down on a torn sofa, putting a hand over her face as she felt the urge to gag at the house's stench. Leila settled beside Alaska, her nose scrunched up, and asked, "What happened?"

Alaska turned to ask Marianne the same question, but she was staring into the room full of coughing people.

"Hello everyone," Marianne said in a forcefully cheery tone, but she frowned as she gazed around the room. "There's people missing."

"They moved to a different safe house," the woman said. "I managed to arrange a safe transport that comes every Monday and Wednesday. I guess you three are the luggage for this Monday."

"What happened?" Alaska asked Marianne, who dropped down on the sofa across from her.

Marianne stared at her silently, and at first Alaska thought she wasn't going to respond again. Then she said, "This is home now."

Ianto crept out of bed and walked across the cold floor in his
bare feet. He went over to the security system's microphone
and cleared his throat.

"CoalSmotheredCrimson9919929965," Ianto said, copying his
grandfather's voice.

The door unlocked, and he crept down the hallway, carefully
avoiding tripwires and security cameras till he made it to the back
stairs, where he checked for his grandfather. He slipped into a pair
of the old man's golf shoes, lacing them tightly, before prying open
a window. A huge whirring noise filled the whole house as the
system went off, but he'd already jumped out, hitting the ground
hard, and took off. As promised, Jamie had left a bicycle for him
by his grandfather's old shed, once a mechanics shop. The bicycle
was a little dented and old, but it still worked. He headed for his
friend's house, and on the way passed by yet another smoldering
wreck, not far from the one he and Jamie had happened upon
earlier in the day. The entire street had gone deathly silent, windows
of the houses next door shuttered. Everyone knew something was
wrong. He hesitated for a moment, then shook himself, and went
uphill, stopping on the edge of the Goldcage. He remembered
the first time he came to the Goldcage a few years ago, stumbling
about in the snow, drinking in a world that was all new to him.
That had also been the first time he escaped from his grandfather's
house.

Two guards stood by the gate and he flashed a pass Jamie had
lent him, then slipped through the Goldcage's invisible barrier.

The night changed the moment he entered, from cold drizzle to a breezy warmth. The houses stood as garish monstrosities, each trying to outdo the other in extravagance and color. They looked like clown palaces, Ianto thought, hiding people little different than the ones downhill, though perhaps a bit fatter. He stopped in front of Jamie's house, parked the bicycle and went up the walk to the gold-plated door. His knock was immediately answered by Jamie's mother.

"Oh, it's you," she smiled at him, though he saw her eyes looked beyond him, going up and down the street, a wary expression in them. "Come inside."

He stepped through and heard the loud, high-pitched barking of Jamie's dog.

"Jamie's in his room," she said and Ianto started for the staircase, but she caught his arm. "Can I ask you something, about Jamie?"

Ianto nodded his head, looking startled. "Yeh, uh, sure."

"Is...Is Jamie doing anything he shouldn't be?"

Ianto hesitated, "Does he seem to be?"

The woman dropped onto a chair, looking extremely drained. "I don't know. No, of course he isn't," she said firmly to herself. She turned back to Ianto, "Just tell him to be careful, won't you? He's so impressionable, I worry about him. There's things going on that can seem very attractive, but he needs to know they're not."

Ianto nodded to her quickly, "I'll tell him that."

"Oh, thank you, Gareth."

Ianto cringed inside at the name, before ascending the stairs. Jamie's room was at the very top of the house, a circular, concrete structure with 360-degree windows, though few of them had glass, allowing in an unnaturally warm, balmy breeze from outside. Jamie was manning a telescope protruding out of one of the glassless openings. He didn't turn around as Ianto approached him and Ianto looked down at the photos scattered across every surface. Several of them were of the same person, a man with a narrow, slightly harsh face, piercing gray-blue eyes and thinning dark auburn hair.

"Who is that?" he asked.

Jamie turned around, his arms crossed. "You tell me."

"What do you mean?"

"Your parents didn't just die in any fire, did they? And your Granddad's not just being a grump wanting you to stay in the house. Your name is Ianto Ambrose."

The color drained from Ianto's face. One of the photos, which he had picked up, slipped from his fingers onto the floor.

"Hey, it's okay," said Jamie quickly, scurrying across the room towards him, as Ianto began to collapse to his knees.

"How—?"

"I was looking for the people who lived in that house," Jamie said. "And I ended up finding a whole bunch of outdated Defense wanted lists. I found your parents on one of them by accident."

"How do you know they're my parents?"

"No offense, but you weren't exactly careful, Ianto," said Jamie. "I asked you once who your parents were, and you said Lavender and Edwin. I looked at the inscription in the crypt and I found a Lavender and an Edwin Ambrose listed there, so I looked them both up. Your Dad looked a lot like you."

Ianto sighed, looking down at the photographs. "Then you know everything?"

Jamie nodded, "Is that why you didn't want me to investigate? You didn't want me to know what your parents—"

"I'm not like them!" said Ianto immediately. "I hate them like Defense does. I hate what my parents did!"

"I'm not telling anyone," said Jamie quickly, putting up his hands. "I just wanted to know, that's all. I'm really not going to tell anyone about you. Your secret's safe with me. Here." He gathered together all the photos, and tossed them in the fire. "No more, I promise. I'll leave you alone. I won't bother you about anything I do. Just...I think your grandfather is right. I don't think you should go out anymore. It's too dangerous."

Ianto stared at him, speechless, then left the room. He heard Jamie calling after him, and ignored him. He'd been completely exposed, and now he was supposed to spend the rest of his life locked up in Arthur Ambrose's giant cage? He ignored Jamie's mother as she said something to him, slamming the front door in her face. In his anger he saw nothing, not even the white car parked just outside the house, not even the metal eyes suspended from streetlights that followed him home, adjusting themselves to his every step and turn.

****

Arthur Ambrose rose from bed. He had definitely heard something. After years of hiding, he knew better than to sleep too deeply. He peered out the window, but didn't see anything in the darkness. Tiptoeing down the hallway he passed Ianto's room. The door was slightly ajar and Ianto lay in bed, his eyes shut. Arthur closed and relocked the door, grumbling to himself under his breath as he walked down the cold stairs. He stopped halfway down, unlocking a hidden cabinet in the wall with his fingerprint, revealing a locker containing stun guns, a wicked looking rapier, and an antique laser. He went over them, and finally chose the laser. *Better not to leave anything to chance*, he decided. Locking the cabinet again, he alighted on the first floor and opened the front door, staring out into the dark night. It was silent, no sound, not even air-ships. The windows of the annoying neighbor across the street were shuttered, and for once, their dog wasn't barking. He started to close the door again, deciding he was finally going senile, when he noticed something on the front step. He leaned over, picking it up.

"What the—?" Arthur Ambrose whispered, his face pale.

It was a blood red messenger.

It was not until the next morning that the deadweight set in. Alaska awoke to the six a.m. chime of the Capital clock on a tattered sofa. Everything had seemed to pass in a crazy, movie-like whirlwind the previous day, and now it all registered in the dim morning light, hitting her like a ton of bricks. She took a deep breath, staring out of a window at the gray skies and heavy rain, feeling sick, wondering if perhaps the Pain, that excruciating stage of the Plague before death, felt a bit like this. She vaguely remembered the last things Marianne had told her the previous night, but it was as if she had dreamed it. They were runners now, escapees. Marianne and Malcolm were criminals, rebels, protestors who had been stealing from clinics. *No, not criminals,* Marianne had said, but Marianne had been the one doing it. They had not stolen medicine, like Apollo Kawaguchi, she had said. They had taken equipment to find a real cure, not the bandage that Defense offered, stopping the Plague as long as it was taken. But Defense could not find a cure, Alaska had countered, and they had all the scientists, proper, registered scientists, not criminals conducting experiments without permission.

"Won't they release the others?" Alaska had asked. "Maybe you and Malcolm were involved...and I don't want either of you to be locked up," she had added quickly at the murderous look Marianne gave her. "But Leila didn't have anything to do with it and our father, he's a Defense officer. He'll explain all of this away. They'll understand it was just a big mistake."

"Do you really think Defense would be that compassionate?"

Marianne had said.

"Clement was ready to forget it."

"Was he? And then we all got captured. Defense is not to be trusted."

"Don't forget my father is a Defense officer!" Alaska responded defiantly.

"I'm not saying he's a bad man, but he was a fool. Don't challenge me, Alaska. How could anyone whose not one or the other follow Defense? Ultimately run by people you never see, men behind curtains. All that is visible is the outer tendrils, and I think that gives you enough of an idea what you're signing up for."

Alaska had risen to her feet then and crossed to a heavily curtained window. She had peeked through the gap in the curtains, seen the grim street beyond. "Maybe he was afraid," Alaska had said, adding under her breath so Marianne couldn't hear. "Like I am."

In the end, Alaska did not know what to think anymore. She did not want to believe any of it, most of it seemed too incredibly ridiculous to be real. She could not imagine her brother doing something so horrible, though she was not sure about Marianne anymore. Perhaps she was crazy, delusional. A small trickle of light started to poke through the curtains. The city was slowly dragging itself out of its curfew slumber as people made their way to the clinics. But not Alaska, Leila, Marianne, or anybody in this house. Marianne had made that very clear, though she had no answer when Alaska asked how they were supposed to protect themselves from the plague without pills. Already Alaska craved them, feeling a growing hollow, dull aching inside of her, and it had only been a few minutes after she would have normally taken it. She went to the kitchen unable to bear the gnawing feeling. The woman with the pinched face was there. According to Marianne the woman's name was Sarah Graye. She was dressed from head to toe in white, and had a distant, dreamy, almost crazed look in her eyes, though she calmly offered Alaska food. Alaska looked down at the barely edible offering and rejected it. She didn't feel hungry; she wanted to get moving, to get out of there, to go home. She wanted to find out where Malcolm and her parents were, and bring them back from there. Her father was a Defense officer, he could explain all this away, she was sure. But then if Defense was responsible for the fire...

"Here," Sarah Graye's voice attracted her attention, and Alaska saw her open a kitchen cabinet, pulling out a small bottle of pills.

Red. Very, very red. Tiny, and easy to swallow. She handed Alaska one, and she immediately gulped it down.

"Feel better?" Sarah Graye asked with a twisted smile, and Alaska nodded her head.

"What about Leila and Marianne?"

"Marianne has had hers. I'll give one to the little girl when she comes down," said Sarah Graye, as somebody coughed nearby.

There was medicine in the safe house, but Alaska could tell all of the people were severely under dosed. She had heard people could make it for fourteen days without a single dose, though how she could not imagine. It only took twelve days for the worst part of the Plague, the Pain, to completely set in. Nobody her age had ever seen it, but Alaska had heard the stories of writhing, crazy mobs going into terrible rages, burning and sacking, killing anything and everyone in sight. Eating all that they left dead in their wake. A lot of people died just trying to defend themselves long before the final stage of the plague, coma and death, set in. A sudden, quick death, followed by immediate burial.

"Go wake Leila. And get changed, there's a wardrobe upstairs."

Alaska jumped at Marianne's voice. The young woman walked into the kitchen, red-eyed and weary. Alaska slipped past Sarah Graye and went up a set of rickety stairs to the second floor. People floated in and out of rooms like ghosts. They appeared quickly, walking almost soundlessly with bare feet, then just vanished around doorways. Their strange and piercingly cold eyes darted from corner to corner, taking in every detail, every noise around them. She did not know what they had gone through, but she could see some of it etched in their faces, engraved there forever. Was that her fate? Leila lay in the last room on the floor with a bunch of other small children. They were all clustered on cots. Leila's bushy hair encircled her face in a halo, the edge of the blanket tightly clenched in her hand. Alaska knelt beside the small figure, brushing her hair, whispering in her ear so as not to startle her, "Time to wake up."

One of Leila's eyes opened and she looked up terrified, then relaxed as she saw Alaska's face.

"Alaska, I had a bad dream."

"It's okay, we're in a safe house," Alaska reassured her. "Go downstairs and Ms. Graye will give you a pill. Okay?"

Leila nodded her head absently, and Alaska got back onto her feet and found the wardrobe. Inside was a baggy pair of linen trousers and a moth-eaten wool sweater. She changed out of her tattered peach dress.

In one of the rooms on the floor a group of ghostly figures were crouched around a mattress together. She caught the words "Lossit" and "Mariner" before one of them noticed her listening and got up. The emaciated woman glided soundlessly across the room and pushed a button beside the door. It snapped shut, but Alaska could still hear voices through the thin walls like wispy murmurs. Alaska turned away and went back downstairs. She wanted madly to do something, but she did not know what to do.

"Alaska?"

She turned around and saw a thin, tall young man with a mop of blue-black curls. He was not a ghost, but a living person, with a voice that seemed oddly warm and inviting. Familiar, she realized, as was his face.

"How do you know my name?" she asked, annoyed.

Hypocrite Marianne. She must have been giving out their identities when she kept telling Alaska she was not careful enough, that they could not trust anyone anymore. She stopped, finally reconizing him. He had been one of the guests at the wedding, that's how she knew him. But there was something else, something from before that...

"Here," he threw her a coat. "You'll need that."

"Thank you," she said, catching it. "Who—who are you?"

"Get out now," he whispered hurriedly, not answering her question. "Just get out."

"That's what we're doing. We're going on a transport today," Alaska told him, startled by the urgency in his voice.

"No, that's what I mean. Get away from the safe house. Don't go on the transport."

"Why?"

Before he could answer Sarah and Marianne appeared, and he vanished.

"Where's Leila?" Marianne asked Alaska.

"She's still upstairs. Marianne, this person—"

Marianne was already gone. Alaska knew the stranger had been scared of something. He had meant it when he told her to get out, but why remained a mystery. She turned her head and saw Sarah staring at her curiously.

"What were you about to tell Marianne?"

Alaska started to tell her when there was a loud rumbling from outside, and Sarah left her and hurried to the door. Alaska craned her neck to see a truck out the window, painted white, not terribly distinctive. She would have thought nothing of it if she didn't know it was their escape route, and somehow that knowledge now made her feel very uncomfortable. Some men in shabby, dusty uniforms alighted from it, shaking Sarah's hand. They spoke with her for a moment, and Alaska could see the impatience in their faces. Then Sarah Graye reentered the house as Marianne ran down the stairs as fast as she could, leading Leila behind her.

"Ready," said Marianne.

Sarah gave a pill to Leila, then gestured toward the door. "Hurry, they won't be able to wait long."

As Alaska followed after Marianne she saw the young man again, his face just visible in one of the doorways, mouthing something to her. She didn't know what he was saying, but she could understand his expression and the side to side shaking of his head.

"Marianne, maybe we—"

"Be quiet," Marianne snapped.

"Marianne, I don't know about the people on the truck."

"Just listen to me, and we'll get out of here safely. I trust Sarah Graye. I've worked with her for years. Everything is fine."

"Sorry," Alaska whispered back to the stranger.

The moment she stepped into the drizzle outside she was herded towards the vehicle. The transport was larger on the inside than it first appeared, and several of the others from the safe house were pushed in ahead of her. She had a moment to look back, and saw Sarah Graye and the stranger standing side-by-side, waving them off, grim-faced. *There's still a chance*, Alaska thought. She could jump out with Leila. Then she was pushed inside and encased within the truck's metal walls. The doors closed with a resounding thud, enveloping them in total darkness. The truck pulled away.

Ianto opened his eyes. He blinked, but the Defense officers standing around his bed did not vanish. A round-faced woman stepped forward, smiling kindly at him, though the smile did not extend to her almond-shaped eyes, which were hard, cold and unblinking. Unlike the other people, she was not wearing a Defense uniform, but a red dress and matching six-inch heels. She had the type of face that was difficult to place an age on, but he did not think she was older than forty.

"Gareth?" said the woman in red, stepping forward.

Ianto could tell from the woman's clipped, sharp accent she was from the Goldcage. He sat up, speechless.

"Maybe you'll answer to Ianto," she said in an even harsher voice, and she moved out of his view, revealing his grandfather behind her, looking down pointedly at the floor instead of his grandson.

Ianto's expression hardened.

"No," said the woman, as if reading Ianto's thoughts. "No, Ianto, it wasn't your grandfather, though I have to say I expected better precautions from a sympathizer harboring a protestor. And did he really think he could stop us single-handed with a laser?"

Ianto found his voice.

"I'm not a protestor," he said, and she laughed, a cloying sound that made Ianto cringe.

"What's the point of hiding it now?" she said and then nodded to one of the guards standing nearby. "Get him and the traitor into a car. No, on second thought, make sure they're separated, I don't want them passing any ideas."

She tapped the side of her head, then turned away and left. Ianto was forced out of bed by guards and marched down the stairs in his pajamas. He looked past them, trying to see what his grandfather was doing, but in the hallway the group split up. Ianto was taken down the main stairs while his grandfather descended the back. When they reached the kitchen, Ianto suddenly attacked the guards and they lost their hold on him. The guards scrabbled after Ianto as he swiftly grabbed a knife off the counter and hurtled towards the door to escape.

"I wouldn't do that if I were you," the woman in red said, stepping forward.

She was holding a laser gun. Ianto dropped the knife.

"Good boy," she mockingly praised him as the guards grabbed him again, more firmly than before.

They exited the house. Ianto gritted his teeth. He knew there was no way of escape as he was pushed head first into a ghostly vehicle. It was completely whited out on the outside, but transparent on the inside, its mechanisms churning silently beneath Ianto's feet. They seemed to match his heartbeat as the car started. The guard next to Ianto looked down at him suspiciously, noticing the change in him as he resigned himself to being taken away. Ianto ignored this as he stared at the people watching along the street. They were all silent and unmoving as statues, as if expecting the officers to turn on them if they dared move a muscle, dared blink an eye. The silent observers of his final moments alive. *Someday you'll all die the same way,* he wanted to yell at them. The guards pushed buttons on the car doors as they shut them, activating a myriad of seat-belts that strapped him down to the seat. He watched in confusion as he was bound in place, then sensed someone watching him and looked up. The woman in red stared at him through the safety glass that separated the front and back compartments of the vehicle.

"Take him to Lossit," she demanded suddenly. The guards stared at her in surprise as the direction of the car changed and they drove to Defense headquarters.

Alaska listened to the sound of Leila's snoring in the dark. Alaska was squashed between two other people and tried to avoid unwanted thoughts as the transport rattled along on a road somewhere. The people on either side of her whispered assurances to one another, but Marianne said nothing. Marianne was composed. *She seemed to have almost expected the attack on the Donnel house,* Alaska thought. *She had known they were all in danger. Why had she not warned them?*

"Was it at a clinic?" Alaska asked Marianne.

"What?"

"Did they find out about you and my brother at a clinic?"

"Oh, no, it was probably a rally," Marianne said quietly.

"What about?"

"Everyone had a different cause," Marianne said in a low voice. "It all leads to the same end, the same basic need: for Defense to be gone. Malcolm and I were there about the treatment of people Defense labels 'Stills.' You know what they are, don't you? People affected by the plague in a different way than most. They don't die but they become severely impaired, and even the cure can't fix it. But there's always certain things that they become unusually good at."

"I know," Alaska snapped. "I'm not stupid."

"Then you know some of them can make educated guesses about the future, predictions that can be incredibly accurate."

"But they're completely useless otherwise, they're not really part of anything, just...there."

Even in the dark Alaska knew Marianne was glaring at her.

"They are not useless. Defense uses that word, but you shouldn't. If they're useless, one day you'll be too. The Cleaners will come and snuff you out, and some other girl will be saying 'she was just useless.' Nobody is 'useless.' Don't ever say that. You're just repeating Defense's propaganda."

"Okay, okay," Alaska said quickly, hearing the rage in Marianne's voice.

"Defense grants asylum to those who'll work for it, and executes those who don't, seeing them as an unnecessary strain on society. Just like they'll do to you and me when we become too rebellious or old."

Alaska opened her mouth to reply when the truck stopped suddenly, and she was thrown roughly against the back wall.

"Why are we stopping?" Alaska asked. "We can't be—"

She stopped speaking as the sound of weapons fire came from outside the vehicle. Suddenly the doors were blasted open and a rush of blinding sunlight flooded inside. Alaska blinked, trying to see what was going on. The drivers of the truck seemed to be fighting people firing stun guns from out of sight. Defense officers, she thought in a panic and then she realized something. The drivers were holding lasers of the type she had only ever seen Defense officers with. Something was very wrong. Instinctively Alaska jumped down out of the truck. She heard Marianne and Leila running behind her, and the others struggling as the drivers realized the truck had been hit, and they were getting away. The sound of pounding feet surrounded Alaska. A hand snaked out to grab her, revealing the edge of a Defense uniform under a dark sleeve.

"Stop it, let go of me! I'm not a runner! I haven't done anything wrong!" Alaska pleaded, but the driver Defense officer was already dragging her back towards the firefight and the truck. "Stop!"

Alaska screamed. A shot from a stun gun missed Alaska by inches and hit her captor in the shoulder. The driver staggered back, howling in pain, and she ran before he could recover. She found herself in a dark, murky alleyway. Alaska sank against the side of a building to catch her breath and listened for the sound of pursuers. It was then she realized she had no idea where Marianne and Leila were anymore. Had they escaped and gone a different way?

Alaska heard the sound of someone approaching and froze. She looked around for a hiding place and saw a set of discarded, old metal trashcans lined up by a high, crumbling brick wall. Alaska quickly slipped behind them and peeked out through a gap between them. A man in a Defense uniform appeared, his eyes flitting around the alleyway in his search for escapees. She recognized him immediately, the same red hair, and hard, cold face. It was the officer who had killed Mr. Robinson. He turned and faced the trashcans. Alaska felt as if his gaze was looking straight through them, seeing her. She felt sure she was going to get caught. *Maybe Defense will be lenient*, Alaska thought, though she knew immediately it was a hopeless wish. She was a runner and would be locked away in the Crypts, a place where few came back from. She waited, but the officer turned around and walked away. Alaska stared in open-mouthed shock as he disappeared out of sight. She thought for sure he had seen her. She breathed a sigh of relief, but then jumped as something landed beside her. She leaned over and cautiously picked it up. Another red messenger. Alaska looked up, but couldn't see where it had come from; it seemed to have just fallen out of the sky. She slowly pushed a button and a message appeared on the screen:

It's all right. Your escape was all part of the plan. I'm coming for you. Just stay where you are. Oh, and I told you not to get into that truck!

"**D**o you know who I am?" The woman in red asked and Ianto nodded his head.

"You're Melissa Johnson, one of Defense's scientific founders. Now you're a Speaker."

A smile spread across Johnson's face. "I am *the* Speaker for Defense's council. But, yes, that's mostly right."

"You have reached your final destination," the car blurted out in a slightly overjoyed voice.

"Thank you," said Johnson, alighting from the vehicle.

Lossit loomed in front of them, its dark glass glinting in the direct sunlight. Huge marble steps climbed upward to its entry, a tall set of swinging glass doors framed by flagpoles bearing oversized versions of Defense's signature banners, each larger than Ianto himself. A slab of white marble was set above the doors, bearing the ouroboros icon of a dragon eating its own tail, symbolizing the immortality of Defense, the soul of the world, the giver of life and death. Below it had been added a second, metal plaque, with 'Gild, Patria, Pleb, Untouchable' written on it, marking the four classes of citizens. Ianto was dragged from the parking lot into the monolith. He noticed some of Johnson's confidence ebb away as they went through the swinging automatic doors into a packed lobby. She became tense, an apprehensive look crossing her face. Johnson pointed down a dark hallway to their left.

"This way. Quickly," she said and the guards followed with Ianto between them.

They reached a large atrium that stretched far out of sight, light spilling in from every direction. The only way across was a glass train floating across a track in midair, all of its inner workings visible like gold clockwork.

"Get on," Melissa Johnson said to Ianto, pushing him as guards surrounded them.

The train took off. Between the gaps in the guards shielding them from view, Ianto could make out bits and snatches of the inside of Lossit: blurry faces, signs marking different departments, and above, an elaborate stained glass ceiling, in the center of which was a marble dome engraved with the council of Defense's ten Commandments. Young officers in white marched mechanically on a floor far below, blasting entrancing, anthemic music that made Ianto freeze and shut his eyes. The train twisted and turned, and then came to a stop. They got off in a concrete cavern with a wall standing directly in front of them, seemingly floating in the middle of the space. Melissa put her hand to the wall. It glowed a cool blue, and then slid out of the way into the floor, revealing a concrete tunnel, and beyond a glass bridge. They entered, spilling out onto the bridge. Light poured through it, and Ianto could see some of the outside world beyond Lossit's confines before he was surrounded by walls again. People walked by casually, chatting away with an air of joviality. Yet this was to be the place of his execution, no doubt, the last people he would ever see, his first and last walk across that bridge. They marshaled him through another set of swinging doors into a windowless rotunda with a high, domed glass ceiling and rows of wall lights. The center of the room was crowded with desks. Johnson relaxed and returned to her former state. A few people said, "Hello, ma'am," or nodded politely as she passed, and she ignored them, not stopping until they had reached a large, sterile white office with only one window that looked out onto the rotunda.

"Wait here," she told one of the guards. "Keep the boy with you, run tests for me. You...," she turned to the other guard, "with me."

She left and Ianto stood awkwardly. He looked around the room. There was a long desk that stretched nearly from one end of the office to the other. There was nothing on it except a few stray papers and a computer console. The room oddly had two doorways, but the second one seemed to be locked, and a chair piled high with equipment was positioned in front of it, indicating its infrequent use. Ianto sat down on the floor. He turned to the guard, looking for some sort of objection, but the guard ignored him, and turned to an instrument on a nearby rolling cart. Ianto looked through the window to the main rotunda where a woman had just entered, trailed by a boyish young man. Despite the woman's suit, she had a decidedly shabby look, out of place in the grandiose, marble-floored rotunda. Her face was harsh and wasted, eyes strangely dead-looking as they hawkishly scanned the room. She swept strands of thin, graying brown hair out of her face and slammed a folder down on one of the desks with shaking hands.

Faintly, Ianto could hear the desk's owner say, "How was vacation, Ira?"

He noticed the young man standing next to the woman. He was nothing like her, dark haired, quite tall, thin, but not hollowed and skeletal like his guardian, extremely good-looking, with an air of being very well cared for. He responded, then as the folder distracted the people around him, he turned his head, discreetly making a strange symbol. Ianto followed the young man's gaze and saw a pink-haired girl watching. Ianto strained to see better, then jumped back as a metal shutter soared downward like a guillotine blade, obstructing his view.

"No seeing out of this room," the guard said sharply.

"Why do you care?" Ianto snapped. "I'm dead already, aren't I?"

He ignored Ianto, turning back to the machine, and as he reached for a syringe from one of the drawers Ianto saw an opportunity and bolted for it. He threw himself at the door which slid open, but he was grabbed by the guard around the waist and pulled to the floor. He heard the door slide shut again and fought furiously, kicking and biting as the guard attempted to keep him under control. The guard drew out a long knife and pointed it at Ianto.

"I don't care if that woman wants you," the guard hissed. "You keep this up, I'll rip you in half right here and now."

Ianto took a deep breath and held still, allowing the guard to move away and wipe off his bloodied face on his uniform shirtsleeve.

"What do you mean the woman wants me?" Ianto asked.

The door of the office slid open once again, but this time it was Johnson, followed by the young man Ianto had seen earlier in the rotunda. She stared in disinterest from Ianto, unblemished, to the bleeding guard.

"I told you to take a blood sample of him, not yourself. Get out of this room, before I fire you."

The guard obeyed immediately, flashing Ianto a dirty look before the door slid shut behind him.

"Now, meet Ianto Ambrose, Ira Graye," Johnson said.

They nodded to each other.

"Ianto and Ira, lovely," Johnson mused. "Ira, let's see if you're as useful as you've been the past thirteen years."

"What about me? What do you want with me?" Ianto asked.

"You're the son of the late Edwin and Lavender Ambrose. We can use you."

Ira's gaze immediately snapped to Ianto's face, his mouth falling open.

"Your parents..." she continued, "were traitors, but at the same time they were geniuses, the pair of them." Her voice grew slightly bitter.

"What about my grandfather?" Ianto asked.

"Oh, he's alive, Ianto. He is a Gild, he has life rights. He's exempt from the touch of the Cleaners."

Ianto's eyes widened. He had never known of his grandfather's status and wondered why he had lived in an old wreck instead of a mansion in the Goldcage.

"But," Johnson continued, "that doesn't mean he's exempt from death. We moved your grandfather to a secure compound on Defense grounds for officers' families. He can stay there, safe. As long as I see some purpose in you."

"Their son?" the statement seemed to escape Ira's lips involuntarily. Johnson's eyes narrowed as she glanced at Ira, but when she spoke there was no hint of suspicion in her voice.

"You'll be Ianto's mentor," she said, before looking back at Ianto. "Usually I give the rules for outside contact, cover stories to tell friends and family because what we do here is often very sensitive, but I don't think that'll be necessary for you. Here is your identifier." She went over to a desk drawer and punched in a lock code. The drawer unlocked and slid open. She reached in and removed a thin piece of metal from it. She walked back over to Ianto and clipped it around his wrist.

"Any Defense computer can tell who you are by it, whether you're living or dead. It's most useful in the field. Eventually it will fuse to the skin of your arm."

Johnson held out her hand, "Welcome to Defense, Ianto Ambrose."

"I"m a Defense officer now?" said Ianto, incredulous.

"What your parents did isn't your fault," said Johnson sweetly, taking his hand and shaking it. "We all have something in our pasts we're ashamed of. I think you'll fit into Defense very well."

She started to leave, then added, "By the way, Ianto, a few people including Ira and myself will know about your past, but I suggest if you want to stay alive you tell no one else, even the others working in this department. Is that understood?"

Ianto nodded, "Okay."

"Dismissed."

11

laska stayed hidden. She saw other people run into the alley, terrified looks on their faces. They hid and then left throughout the day. She wondered if she should just run, too. But this person, if it really was the same man as the one who had warned her at the house, had offered her good advice before. If she had listened to him, she wouldn't be hiding in the alley and Marianne and Leila wouldn't be lost somewhere. Alaska shivered in the cold despite her coat as the sky darkened overhead until it was night. Curfew approached, everything began to fall silent. Except....Alaska froze as she heard voices. They came from somewhere above her. She thought of curfewmen, thieves who defied the curfew to rob whoever they could on the Capital's dark streets. Only really desperate people would do that, or lunatics. She remembered some of the ones who got caught and went to their executions laughing like hyenas, trying to pick the pockets of their guards, just for the sake of one last crime. Alaska doubted they would have any scruples about killing a runner hiding in a lonely alleyway. She forced herself to remain calm and looked upwards, blinking as a harsh light shone in her eyes. As her eyes adjusted, she saw two figures lean over the wall and stare down at her. A pink-haired girl and a large young man with strikingly pale green eyes.

"This is her?" the girl said, though she did not seem to be speaking to her companion, and a moment later another face appeared.

Alaska recognized this one.

"Yes," said the young man from Sarah Graye's house. 'Yes'—simply, a single word, yet an undeniably familiar voice and she finally realized where she'd heard it before. The wedding...and his was the voice she had heard at the basement door in Maisel's shop. So it had been real.

"What's next, Ira?"

He opened his mouth to speak, but the green-eyed young man, who sounded annoyed, cut him short.

"We could try getting down there," he said, before climbing over the side of the wall and landing heavily on the ground near Alaska.

The girl followed, and then Ira.

"You were the voice in the shop," said Alaska to Ira vaguely, and a small smile spread across his face.

"Yes, that was me. And the 'Get Out' messenger note. And the wedding. The safe house, too. I'm Ira Graye, Sarah Graye's my mother. Oh, and those two," he pointed at his companions, "are Guinevere Graves and Owen Jarrah."

"Did your mother know the drivers were Defense officers?"

"Yes, that's what she does and I try to stop it," Ira said seriously. "Come on, we haven't got much time. Curfew's soon."

Alaska followed the three of them and then saw a truck waiting at the end of the alleyway.

"No!" she immediately cried, recoiling at the sight of it. Ira took her by the hand and led her aside.

"It's not like the other one, Alaska, I promise. I'm trying to save you, not capture you. Ginny and Owen too, they're safe. The drivers will take you to a real safe house."

"What about my family?" Alaska asked. "Did you see what happened to Marianne and Leila?"

"They were caught," Ira said sadly. Alaska looked stricken. "But we'll get them out. We're getting you to safety first, and then I promise we'll do the same for them. Johnson likes to keep people a little while, so there's time."

"Johnson?"

"They're imprisoned by Speaker Melissa Johnson," said Ira. "But that's not important."

"I've seen Speakers before," said Alaska quickly. "They're cruel. What if she—?"

"I'm getting them out, Alaska, with Owen and Ginny. Trust me," he turned briefly to look back at Owen speaking with the drivers of the truck, "You have to go now."

Alaska nodded her head, as Ginny waved at them.

"Ready!" she called, and Alaska hurried over. The back of the truck was opened; she could see a white space with a compartment in the floor.

"If the drivers tell you to hide, you go in there," Ginny said, pointing and Alaska nodded before clambering inside.

Ginny took hold of the doors to shut them, and Alaska said a quick, "Thank you," wishing she knew something more to say.

Ira nodded his head. Ginny closed the doors and Alaska felt the sway of the vehicle as it started off again. Alaska took a deep breath, steeling herself for whatever happened next.

12

"Ianto!"

The scream, a woman's scream, reverberated in Ianto's mind as he opened his eyes, sat up and looked around the gray, metal-clad room that was now his home. He was just remembering, he told himself, going over memories of that horrible day when he had nearly died four years ago. Then he realized there was still a scream, far off and muffled, but there. It went on for several minutes before silence fell. Ianto got out of bed, and eyed his new red and white Defense uniform folded on top of a metal dresser by the door. There was a light blue access card in the pocket. Ianto quickly changed into the uniform and grabbed the access card before leaving the room. The chime of the Capital clock went off, signaling the end of curfew. Ianto ran faster, crossed the rotunda, and continued onto the glass bridge. There was a door at the end which would let him out of that section of the building. He slid the card against the door's scanner, but the door refused to move.

"It won't open."

Ianto turned away from the door at the end of the glass bridge and found himself face-to-face with Ira Graye. Ira nodded at the blue access card in Ianto's hand.

"It won't open for you. You need a red card to leave."

"I'm the only one locked in, aren't I? How many have higher cards?" Ianto demanded.

"Almost everyone," Ira admitted. "You're supposed to be dead."

"I'm not," said Ianto flatly.

"Are your parents—?"

"They died," Ianto interrupted. A funny look flashed across Ira's face, but only for a second.

"How much do you know about the history of the Nation, Ianto?"

Ianto thought for a moment, before saying, "I know that the Nation was built by some colonists. They found this place and created the dome. Samson Magler was the first child born in the colony and grew up to be a great leader who brought the citizens together and created a society where everyone would be provided for. I know that he was supposedly a genius innovator and that the manned space flight was his idea of getting more knowledge about the outside world. But something went wrong and the crash unleashed the plague, though no one knows how that happened. Then Defense killed him and took over."

Ira stared at him. "You've never been to school, have you?"

****

Ira and Ianto entered a gray metal room with a placard on the door that read 'The Box'. It was dimly lit by harsh blue lights in the ceiling. Rambunctious ten-year-olds were sitting on rows of seats going all the way down to a large stage platform below. A young woman with an odd heart-shaped face and piercing brown eyes was standing on the stage, reading something on a notebook. She was in Defense uniform and had an electronic name-tag hanging around her neck that read Evita. The children quieted as Ira and Ianto entered, looking at them in wonder, and Evita looked up.

"Ira," she said simply, and Ira pushed Ianto down into a chair.

"I've brought a new student," Ira said.

"He looks a little old," said Evita, and the children snickered.

Ianto looked at the young students coolly, and they quickly turned back to Evita, whispering amongst themselves.

"We have lots of room," said Evita quickly, and when she spoke next, it was to everyone. "This is the simulator. One of the many things it can do is show us the past."

She snapped her fingers, and the air around them pixilated. Images appeared out of thin air all around. Ianto watched in amazement as pyramids popped up on the stage around Evita. They were circled by bright red, two-story buses while knights and samurai on horseback ascended up the aisles, the roaring whinnies of the horses ringing around the metal walls of the room. The children gasped and awed in excitement. A white horse neared Ianto, and he reached out his hand. His hand passed through the animal, the image distorting and bending around his fingers, and he realized it was only a projection. Evita clicked her fingers again, and it all ended, fading away into nothing.

"This is all part of the history of the outside world," said Evita. "All of what you've seen is gone. The people of the Nation, the first colonists, fled from the wars and destruction encompassing the world. They came to this place, and they created the dome to protect it. In the beginning, the Nation of Steel was one shining paradise and nothing seemed like it could ever go wrong. But then Samson Magler was born to two colonists."

An image appeared on the stage, of a baby in a black cradle, watched over by two twisted figures in dark cloaks.

"They say he never seemed quite right. He always seemed as if there was something wicked about him," Evita said in a soft voice that somehow seemed to fill the room with an ominous feeling. "But he was the first child of the colony and loved. He grew up and took control of the Nation. He was clever and he knew what he had to do to get control of it. He poisoned people's minds with lies that made them turn against their better nature, against what they knew was right. He spoke of curiosity and created horrific experiments to terrorize his people. Then he did the worst thing of all, he broke the rules that had kept the colony safe for over a hundred years. He decided to let a spaceship leave it, to break the dome."

There Samson Magler stood, young and brash and completely, undeniably evil, with a long, sharp dagger in his hand. The children shrunk back from him with looks of terror. Behind him, a spaceship took off, hurtling upwards to the ceiling of the room, which hovered with puffy white clouds and twinkling stars.

Evita's voice boomed as she cried, "He created the space program, saying that we must not be ignorant, but curious, that ignorance was death and curiosity was freedom!"

The spaceship hurtled back down out of the sky, smashing into the stage at Evita's feet. A black cloud spread across the stage, engulfing her and then everyone, and some of the children screamed and cried in the darkness.

Then there was a whisper in Ianto's ear, "Curiosity brought the plague. Curiosity is evil. Curiosity is death. Ignorance is life."

The cloud evaporated, and Evita stood alone on the stage, beaming at the class of sniveling, teary-eyed ten-year-olds.

"Don't be afraid. A group of good people, sponsored and protected by the benevolent Defense council, realized how evil Magler was and found a cure for the plague. The Defense council restored the rule of law and created the Speakers to protect order in their name so that no one like Samson Magler would rise again to dominate over the citizens of the Nation of Steel. You'll find lists of the Defense Commandments in your pockets," said Evita brightly. "Never forget to follow the rules."

The children were quick to leave, and Evita walked up the rows to where Ianto was sitting, Ira standing behind him.

"This is Ianto, the..." Ira started, but Evita cut him off.

"The new officer!" said Evita, reaching over and shaking Ianto's hand warmly. "I have something for you to do."

Ianto looked at her apprehensively, but before he could speak

Ira asked for him, "What is this 'something'?"

"The simulator isn't just for scaring little children," said Evita, still ignoring Ira and speaking to Ianto. "We've been making changes to it, and it has a new function now. It can connect to your brain, decode what you're thinking and display it for you, as if it's real. Though it has a preference for less savory memories."

Ira's eyes widened. "Where did this come from?"

"It was a summer project," Evita said without looking at him.

Ira said sharply, "Whose summer project? Johnson just okayed the return to production of MRI machines. She never allows..."

"You want us to test it, don't you?" said Ianto, interrupting Ira. Evita smiled like a Cheshire cat.

"Thanks for volunteering," she said.

Ianto hesitated, "I thought you said it triggers 'less savory memories.' What does that mean for me?"

"It'll do its best to take you back to your worst memory. Here," Evita handed him a headset. "Ira and I will leave, but we'll be waiting right outside."

Ira flashed Ianto an apologetic look and then stepped out of the room with Evita. The door slid shut behind them. Ianto put the headset on, as the room went pitch black. He settled down in a seat to wait for whatever would come. It didn't take long before the air around him pixilated, forming a narrow street lined with streetlights. The pixilations were fuzzy, or seemed displaced, as many different references in memory merged together like screens over screens. They straightened out until the first layer shone through, almost crystal clear. He could hear the far off wailing of an ambulance, the sound of people walking a street over, somewhere above the whizzing propellers of a helicopter. Clinic doors were being unlocked as six a.m. drew closer. Suddenly a car whizzed by, and he stared after it, trying to suppress the memory, but unable to as it surged forward. August 13th, 137. He was now watching through a barred window as a green car parked on the road outside the house. Turning his head, he could see through the door to the next room, where there was a woman painting, humming some children's rhyme under her breath. A door slammed below. Ianto rose to his feet and ran out of the room into a hallway. He stood at the top of the stairs and stared down at the man, so much like himself in appearance.

"Go to your room, Ianto," the woman slipped past him, going down the stairs. "Edwin? Edwin, what is it?"

Edwin Ambrose dropped his bags on the floor and went into the living room, followed by Lavender. Ianto heard urgent whispers, then the scene was splintered, and flames shot from all directions mixed with the sound of shots.

"Ianto!" the woman screamed from somewhere beyond the flames encircling him.

"Ianto!"

"Leave him." Edwin's voice.

"Ianto! Ianto!"

"Don't leave me!" Ianto screamed, but their voices were disappearing and he flew down the stairs to escape the flames, falling off a misjudged step and landing in a heap at the bottom.

"Leave him!"

The voices stopped, and he screamed after them, screamed for them to come back for him, crawled towards where they'd been, but they didn't come back.

"Stop it!" he yelled at the computer, but it was an inanimate, unthinking machine. How could it understand him? He shut his eyes, hearing the commotion, the crackling of the fire, seeing the flash of the Defense officers' shots. He could see the Box's computer as clearly as if it was in front of him.

"Shut down," he instructed it. "Turn off now."

For a moment nothing happened. Then he heard real yells,

not the hard electronic noises, faded from being locked away in memory. These were real and clear.

"Ianto? Are you alright?"

His eyes flickered open and he saw Ira's face looking down at him in concern. He lay spread-eagled on the stage. Nearby Evita looked in astonishment at a control panel on the wall.

"What happened?" Ianto asked, groaning as he lifted himself into a sitting position.

"The Box just shut down," said Ira. "I'm not sure why, but when it shut down you passed out. Something must have gone faulty with the headset."

"With the whole thing," interjected Evita, joining them, a frown on her face.

"I made it shut down," he said suddenly, looking from Ira to Evita. "I'm sorry, I couldn't take it any longer, so I told it to stop."

"You can't just tell it to shut off," Evita said, sounding irritated. "You don't have voice command to shut off the system."

"But I did," said Ianto. "I did, Evita."

13

Alaska wasn't sure when she fell asleep. It was her first deep sleep in a long time, and she felt anxious when she awoke, but relaxed as she saw she was still in the back of the truck.

"Hey," one of the drivers, a young woman, pulled aside the window separating the back of the truck from the front seats. "Time to get out."

"Tarana!" said Alaska, recognizing her in surprise. "What are you doing here?"

"Ira said you might be more comfortable if I was one of the drivers," Tarana smiled at her, before quickly saying, "I meant the bit about getting out NOW."

They ditched the truck at the shore of the river, and Alaska watched as it slid into the dirt black water, pushing through clumps of junk until it disappeared out of sight, swallowed up by the muck to join the rest of the river's unnatural contents.

"We'll walk the rest of the way," the other driver said.

Alaska had forgotten how cold it was outside after traveling in the warm truck, but now she found herself rubbing her hands together and hugging the thin coat Ira had given her at the safe house.

"Here, love," Tarana offered Alaska her own thicker coat, which Alaska accepted gratefully, throwing it on over the first.

They walked along a twisting path that bordered the lake, then veered off of it and climbed uphill towards the highway. Alaska hung back. She didn't see any Defense officers, but she feared there could be some hiding, or security cameras.

"Here!" said Tarana quickly and suddenly she plunged out of sight.

Alaska looked around, bewildered, unsure where she'd gone, then the other driver grabbed her hand, and she was pulled through a trapdoor in the ground that had been hidden by a covering of grass. They tumbled underground, landing hard on the rocky floor. Alaska groaned and scrambled onto her feet, watching as the drivers quickly put the trapdoor back into place.

"Somebody there?" She whipped around and saw a figure approaching.

"Jakob!" said the male driver, relieved. "It's us."

"Plus one," said the figure, closer now.

Alaska could see his face, illuminated by the flashlight he was carrying. He wasn't much older than her, and there was something very familiar about him. At first she thought he looked exactly like Ira Graye, but as he drew closer, she could see he had a slightly harsher face and feathery, lighter brown hair that was already starting to gray a little. His hands were covered by worn, fingerless leather gloves. He glared at Alaska. She glared back at him.

"Just escaped Lossit," Tarana said.

"Oh, that hellhole. But I can tell she wasn't actually incarcerated," Jakob stared at Alaska curiously. "Bit young, isn't she? Who will you bring next, a five year old?"

"I'm sixteen," Alaska pointed out irritably, and one of his eyebrows rose.

"Could have fooled me," he said, turning to the drivers. "So did Mummy's Boy and the Teen Brigade make it out of this one, or will I start having to dust off the epitaphs I filed for them?"

"They saved your life. You should be more respectful," Tarana snapped and he narrowed his eyes.

"For what exactly?" he said. "Ira did that because he owed me.

Now he can see me suffer worse than I did before...and glory in it."

"What are you talking about?" Alaska asked, staring between the two drivers, who looked disgustedly at Jakob.

"What revolutionary nonsense have you been pounding into this girl's head on the drive, aye? Same lovely little speeches you gave me? Well, ha, they don't work in the long run, do they? The truth wins out in the end," he snapped.

"They saved me, and they're going to save my whole family!" Alaska said defensively and he turned around, sneering at her.

"You've still got one then. How lucky for you," Jakob said, and he walked off down the tunnel without another word.

"Don't mind Jakob," Tarana said, guiding her down the tunnel after him. "His family was killed four years ago, and well...that's hard enough for anyone, never mind the fact he witnessed it all as a twelve-year-old. We saved his life, but I wish we could have saved the rest of them." She looked after him sadly.

"I am right, aren't I?" Alaska said to her. "You really will get my family out?"

"Don't worry," Tarana said comfortingly. "We'll get them all out."

"Promise me then," Alaska said, and when there was no answer, she repeated herself in a shaky, uncertain voice.

Tarana just looked down at Alaska. "Let's get you cleaned up."

****

The room she was given was small, serving as both a bedroom and a bath with a stone tub in the center of the room. Alaska noticed a bucket in the corner that she guessed the purpose of, but didn't want to think about. She changed into the uniform khaki clothes that had been left for her, and Tarana entered the room carrying a pile of blankets.

"It gets very cold at night," Tarana said, setting them down. She noticed Alaska's slight shaking and dazed look.

"It's okay to be scared," Tarana said gently. "I was scared when I first came to this place, I wasn't brave at all. But then I learned it was going to be okay." Tarana gave Alaska a faint smile, then gestured for Alaska to follow her.

"Ask any question you want," she said to her, as they entered a small library with a few lingering people. They weren't quite like the ghosts of Sarah Graye's safe house, but there was still something thin and unreal about them. Alaska and Tarana sat down at a table.

"What day is it?" Alaska asked.

"Tuesday," Tarana said and Alaska nearly jumped out of her chair.

Not that much time had passed, yet she'd gladly have given up a year of life for those days to have never happened.

"Any questions?" Tarana asked her patiently, and Alaska asked as many as she could think of: why Tarana was here, how this all got started, what they were doing, what was her future; and Tarana answered them as best she could.

"There are plenty of people who want more control over their own lives, instead of where they'll go in life and how long they'll be allowed to live decided by some nameless, faceless council in the shadows. People who want the end of Defense. Some pretend to lead normal lives, as I did, while working underground," Tarana said. "They usually operate in small groups though and get picked off quickly. If they're too public, Defense cracks down, no matter how big or small. We believe we should be able to build our own nation. A place where we needn't cower from Defense, or watch the disadvantaged brutalized."

"I know they've done awful things. I've lived through it. But I can't help thinking about the plague," Alaska said. "If there's no Defense, how will we keep from dying? Everyone is infected. If it wasn't for Defense's discovery of the Cure we'd all be dead."

"That's it," said Tarana, smiling slightly. "We need to get beyond Defense's patch, which makes us so reliant on them. We need to make our own, and not just a patch, a real cure that'll destroy the sickness."

"But Defense tried to and they haven't—"

"Did they try?" Tarana asked. Alaska stared at her in bewilderment.

"Are you saying maybe they didn't?"

Tarana didn't reply.

Alaska asked, "What do you do here?"

"Different facilities have different functions. At ours, we save people from Defense like yourself, and do a bit of the cleanup work," Tarana said. "We're only a way station, though. You'll be moved in a day or two."

"Where will I go?" Alaska asked and Tarana went quiet, something Alaska hated.

"Tell me," Alaska said desperately. "Last time I was just shipped off somewhere it didn't turn out well."

Tarana just shook her head, "I'm sorry, but I don't know myself. One of the more permanent stations."

"Have you seen these stations? Are you sure they exist?"

"They do, I can promise you that," Tarana said. "I'll get you there myself, if you want."

"Thank you," Alaska said, a little more relieved, then she added, "Will my family be there?"

"They may or may not be," Tarana said. "There's no news from Ira, but when there is I promise you the first thing I'll want to know from him is about the Donnels, and then we'll send them straight to wherever you are."

Alaska flashed her a weak smile, trying to feel reassured at her words. She looked past Tarana at the bookcases and recognized a word on the cover of a spine. She stood up and crossed over to it as Tarana watched her in surprise. It was a heavy black volume next to a book called *The Lives and Deaths of Scissor Children*.

"*In The Name of Pomander's Lid*," Alaska said, opening it to see the author's name on the first page. Edwin Ambrose. "'Pomander's Lid'. I heard my brother and Marianne talking about it once but it's so strange....I'd never heard of a name like that before. Is it a protestor term?"

"Aye," said Tarana, her voice low. "It's best not to talk of it."

"Why keep it hidden?" both Tarana and Alaska turned around to see Jakob striding forward.

"In the end isn't that where she'll end up? Where we all hope to go? Glorious Pomander's Lid, the shining city, the grand metropolis, the great land, heaven on earth, Eden, paradise, utopia?"

"Don't say another word," Tarana said, an edge to her voice.

"No," Alaska said as she put the book on the table and folded her arms. "Tell me. It's got to do with my brother, it's got to do with me. I want to know."

Jakob smirked. "She's more curious than the others, I'll give her that."

Tarana's head dropped into her hands, but she didn't stop him from continuing.

"Pomander's Lid," he said, very slowly, seeming to enjoy the torment he was putting Tarana through as well as Alaska's impatience as she mentally screamed at him to hurry up and tell her. "Is our Nation."

14

Hallucinations, Evita told Ianto. The scream, his control over the Box. It was all in his head. He felt as if he'd heard that a thousand times before from his grandfather, when he looked in the mirror and felt something wasn't right, or suggested he wasn't quite the same as Jamie, as if there was something broken, or wrong inside of him. Now he was hearing the same thing in Lossit, and locked away just the same way as he had been all his life. But in Arthur Ambrose's prison he'd known how to escape. Here he had no idea as he lay on the floor of his steel-walled quarters listening to the heavy thump of guards' boots as they patrolled hallways. Ideas flashed through his mind, then very suddenly all of his thoughts were wrenched away by a horrible, sickening scream. He jumped to his feet and followed the direction of the noise, eventually coming to a partially open door marked "Ira Graye." The sound was so loud he felt as if his head was on the verge of exploding. He slipped inside and looked around the room, which felt like a tomb. It smelled of dust, everything was antiquated and the windows were covered in metal shutters that looked as if they had not been raised in a hundred years. Ianto glanced up and saw the panels of security cameras watching on the ceiling. Moving photographs played in frames on the wall, all sepia toned portraits of the same three people: Ira, an unsmiling man Ianto guessed was Ira's father, and a woman Ianto could barely see as Ira's mother, but supposed must be, with a forcibly large smile. He turned away from the pictures, taking in the rest of the room. There was a shelf with pieces of taxidermy, tiny rodent organs swimming in formaldehyde, and medical volumes, a long, winding line of stacked up dominoes standing in front of them on the edge. A few tubes of paint sat on Ira's desk beside sheets of red stationary, a plaque that read 'Award of Excellence In Flight To Ira Graye, Pilot, 14' and a dusty mother of pearl music box. Next to it was a red access card. There was no sign of the source of the screaming. It ended as quickly as it began and Ianto sank against the wall until the pain in his head ebbed away. Then he grabbed the card off the desk. Ianto froze as he heard a clatter. The dominoes edging the bookshelf fell one by one, the last clattering onto the concrete floor at his feet. He turned and saw Ira standing behind him, watching him silently.

"Hello."

Ianto didn't reply, still clutching the card tightly.

"I can tell you anything you need to know. You don't have to steal it," Ira said.

"I don't want information," Ianto said.

Ira's mouth opened slightly, as he seemed to realize something. "You just want to see the rest of Lossit," Ira said softly.

"I don't want to be trapped here," Ianto said. "I don't want to be locked up, or have someone breathing down my neck. I don't want to be weird, and I'm not deluded."

"I know," Ira said to Ianto's surprise, before adding, "There's people who want to kill you out there, Ianto."

"They won't see me," Ianto said.

Ira smiled slightly, "You can come with me. Just give me back the card."

Ianto hesitated, then gave it to Ira, following him warily out of the office. Why was Ira willing to help him? He had to want something, people always wanted something.

"Your grandfather is doing well, I saw him recently," Ira said softly. "I can arrange for—"

"I don't want to see him," Ianto said flatly.

"What happened? After your parents died?"

"My grandfather saved my life, more or less," Ianto said, the memory of the fire returned to him so strongly, he could almost smell the acrid, burning smoke. "I don't remember much. He said I was...damaged. I just remember that he came inside and took me away. I passed out and woke up a couple of days later. He told me they'd been killed trying to escape the Capital. They were destroyed where they stood, there weren't any bodies. The funeral was already over when I woke up."

"I'm sorry," Ira said.

Ianto turned his head, his gaze lingering for a moment on Ira's face. When Jamie said those words, he could see the pity written all over Jamie's face. Ira was different. His voice was sympathetic, but his face was a mask. He was hiding something.

Ianto looked away and said, "I'm not. What does Johnson want with me, anyway? I'm the son of the protestors' heroic martyrs, aren't I? I expect any Defense officer to kill me on sight."

"Maybe she believes in second chances," Ira suggested. "Just look at her. The granddaughter of Samson Magler, the dictator Defense overthrew during the Plague."

"I don't think that's it," Ianto said skeptically. "She wants me for something. You know, don't you?"

Ira sighed, "She's looking for something. All of Defense is looking for something, something that's a danger to everything that was built here. I think she thinks you can find it for her."

"Why? What is it?"

"I don't know," Ira said.

"Is that a lie?"

They stopped in front of an elevator. "You can trust me, Ianto, no matter what. I knew your parents. Not well, but a little. They wanted young talent in their lab. So I know you, and you should know that I want to help you. I can assist you getting around Defense. I won't do anything to hurt you. I can get you anything you want-even freedom, but only if you trust me."

"What do you want?"

Ira smiled at Ianto's directness. "Your silence, when it becomes necessary."

"Silence about what?"

"Something."

"More 'somethings'?" Ianto said warily, though he felt the pull of the outside world and wanted desperately to escape Lossit.

"Yes."

"Okay, what if I trust you?" said Ianto. "What do you say I should do now?"

"Just follow orders," said Ira. "Listen to Johnson, but don't believe any of it. I can tell you more later." The doors of the elevator clanged open. "I'm your only friend here, Ianto. Believe that."

15

There was a single bored-looking guard, red-haired and young with a gaunt, skeletal face, waiting for them when the elevator stopped. Ira got out, Ianto followed behind him.

"Hey, Counta," Ira said and the guard nodded curtly without replying, an expectant look in his eyes.

"Nice day," Ira continued vaguely, as he stepped right in front of the guard.

Ianto saw a brief flash of metal as Ira slipped something into the guard's pocket, though he couldn't make out what was going on very well. The guard nodded again, before letting them walk on without a second glance. Ianto looked back at the guard who was staring back at the elevator blankly, stiff and robotic in posture.

"He didn't ask any questions. What kind of a guard...wait, did you bribe him?" Ianto whispered. "Was that money you put in his pocket?"

"We have to be back before midnight," was all Ira answered, but Ianto barely heard him.

In front of them was the atrium. Ianto crossed over. He held onto the railing and looked down at the floor below. Looking upwards, he could make out the whole story of the Nation of Steel in the stained glass ceiling.

"The colonists who built it," Ira said from behind him, pointing at a stain glass picture of a caravan of wide-eyed people in red robes. Beside it were images of people industriously building, putting together the Nation, and then the dark birth and rise of Samson

Magler, the only colonist not in red, but in black. His face was painted with grotesque, exaggerated features, as he stared down scornfully at all those below. Every picture depicting Magler's time of power was detailed by pitch black rivers forming around him. Lastly was the uprising that toppled him, creating Defense, and the rivers changed to ruby red.

"Incredible, isn't it?" Ira whispered, watching Ianto carefully.

"I suppose," Ianto said nonchalantly.

"You suppose?" Ira looked incredulous. "Not very easy to please, are you?"

Ianto ignored the comment, pointing at a picture near Samson Magler he'd never seen anywhere else, a picture of nine small indistinguishable figures, all clad in black with red-tipped arrows pointed at them from every direction. Ianto frowned, since he didn't remember a group of nine mentioned in Evita's history class.

"Who are they?"

"The council of Defense, the real rulers of the country. The Speakers are only mouthpieces when it comes to the biggest decisions."

"What...?" Ianto said, confused, and then he realized Ira was not looking at the same thing he was.

The atrium floor had filled with people below, and walking down an aisle formed by the crowd was a procession of figures shrouded in white and red cloaks. Their heavy footsteps echoed through the empty space, and then music began. The same as he'd heard on the train. If they knew he was just fifty feet above their heads, the son of Edwin and Lavender Ambrose, their supposed former worst enemies.... He stopped, realizing he didn't even have any idea who "they" were. Nobody ever spoke of them, and nobody ever saw their faces or heard their voices. The Speakers were their connection to the outside world. He started to ask Ira if he knew their true identitites when he noticed a strange change in Ira's face. Ira didn't look sad, or angry, not exactly. But there was something hard and cold about his expression that had not been there before. At that moment, the horrible, gut-wrenching scream erupted inside of Ianto's head, more powerful than before. A cry escaped from his lips as he fell to the floor, clutching his head. The music stopped and Ira tried to get Ianto onto his feet, but Ianto was lost in a blur of pain and a misery he couldn't understand. He felt himself being dragged away, and then the screaming stopped again. He realized what was going on as the sound of pounding footsteps echoed in the shadows all around them.

"Run!" Ira shouted at Ianto, but he'd already taken off.

Ianto heard the sound of barked commands behind him as the ground slipped away beneath his feet. He saw the red-haired skeletal faced guard that Ira had bribed glance at him ever so briefly before slipping away, then he was at the elevator, and threw himself in just as Ira came into view, managing to slip inside right before the doors clanged shut. Ira stooped over, gasping for breath, as Ianto stared ahead, still stunned.

"What happened to you?" Ira asked, finally looking up.

"I don't know, I got a bad headache," Ianto said. "I don't know why."

Ira didn't think he was deluded, now was not the time to change that, Ianto thought. Ira just shook his head in bewilderment. Now that he had caught his breath, there was a broad grin on his face.

"Well, that wasn't bad for your first day outside the walls," Ira said, sounding amused more than anything else, "It was fun."

Perhaps Ira was the real crazy one, Ianto thought.

****

The screams had to cease. She had to stop them. Melissa

Johnson stood in front of the second door in her office, her hands trembling. She stepped into a dim space lit only by a faint glow up ahead. Johnson followed the walls blindly until her hand hit rock, and she knew she was right beside the railing that kept her from falling down into a chasm that ran right to the heart of Defense. Light spilled upwards from it, but the screams did as well, ripping through her head. She forced herself to remain upright, to not collapse to the ground as she felt along the wall for a metal control box.

"Time to go to sleep," she whispered in a pain-stricken voice, flipping a switch in the dark. The screams ended instantly, the light from the chasm died, and all was well.

16

Alaska sat on the bed inside of her small room, holding the book Tarana had allowed her to keep. She wasn't sure what time it was as she turned the pages. Time seemed to pass without distinction inside of the facility. People slept when they were too tired to do anything else, and woke when they were needed again. She looked down at an illustration in the book, of a black river swallowing Lossit. No wonder Defense had wanted the book burned out of existence. She was about to turn to the next page when she heard a commotion and scrambled out of bed, opening the door of her room. One of the people working at the facility had set up a screen in the main room and everyone was assembling around it. She stepped forward, and Tarana noticed her.

"You can go back, you don't have to watch this," she said, but Alaska shook her head.

"We ought to have popcorn next time," Jakob said dryly from nearby, glancing at Alaska as she sat down beside Tarana.

The projector was turned on and music played, followed by a video. It was the news from earlier that day. They didn't mention recent problems at Defense, like Alaska's escape, but did mention the capture of a group of protestors who were caught plotting in a house, flashing their pictures across the screen. One of them looked vaguely familiar to Alaska; she thought she'd seen him before in school. Moving on, they talked of repairs being made to the highway, of tightened security in the center of the city. Then came the lists of deaths, births and marriages, followed by the list of executions of criminals. Alaska noticed everyone cringed except for Jakob, who didn't seem shaken at all as it finally finished. The screen went black, and slowly people left, Jakob first, disappearing down a corridor in silence. What had his family done to end up in Lossit, Alaska wondered.

"Is there any news from Ira?" Alaska asked Tarana, who shook her head, looking anxious.

"That's not abnormal," she reassured Alaska, but she sounded doubtful.

"Tarana...I've been thinking, if I hadn't been lucky, if Ira, Ginny and Owen hadn't saved me I wouldn't have stood a chance. Even if I'd been able to grab one of those weapons off the officers," Alaska said. "I couldn't defend myself. I couldn't even use a stun gun."

"So you want me to show you?" Tarana asked her, and she nodded her head.

"Well, I'm not the very best myself," Tarana admitted. "But come with me."

She started off and Alaska followed her past several rooms to a door at the very back. She put her hand to its cold metal surface, muttering a few words under her breath, and it slid away into the wall. They stepped into a huge circular room, with a low ceiling. Shelves lined the walls, most of them empty, but a fair number held various weapons.

"There's a lot of them," said Alaska, looking about in amazement.

"Oh, most are just models," Tarana said. "A last ditch resort. If Defense breaks in, we pretend we've got a lot more than we do. See?" She picked one up and fired it at the wall.

A holographic image of what would be the shot came from the end, bouncing off the wall, and then vanished. Tarana gingerly put it back on the shelf.

"Some of these are stunners, which, for the most part, cause little damage and are more of a fire-and-run device. Then there are lasers."

She took one down, showing it to Alaska cautiously. It was slender but long, a funny metallic color, that was neither quite blue, nor gray, nor green.

"Evil little things," said Tarana, her voice trembling slightly. "It was a cursed day they were invented. They've saved plenty of lives, but at the expense of many others. A laser is only ever meant for seriously maiming or killing, Alaska, without a sound, without a warning, there is only a bright white flash of light, and then the damage is done. Not very messy either, there's no gore like when they used the old weapons with bullets. No, it's a neat weapon, visually painless for its user."

Alaska turned it over, noticing a strange panel on the bottom with a dial.

"Don't touch it," said Tarana quickly. "Underneath that is the overload button, another last ditch resort. That," said Tarana, taking the laser away from Alaska, "is for a suicide mission. There is very little chance of escaping once the laser is set to overload."

Tarana put it back into place, turning instead to the stunners. "Let's try these for now."

Tarana turned to a small, silver weapon, handing it to Alaska. It fit perfectly in her hands, and to her surprise seemed to emanate a strange sort of warmth.

"Here you go, start with that," Tarana said, stepping back several paces cautiously as Alaska pointed it at the wall, found the button and fired.

There was an odd thrill as it charged and finally let loose against the wall. She tried it several more times before Tarana took it out of her hands.

"You're a natural. I've never seen somebody so proficient on their first try."

"But shouldn't I learn how to use it while moving?" Alaska said. "I'm hardly going to be standing still, am I?"

Tarana opened her mouth, looking unsure, then nodded her head, and clicked a button on the wall. A ring of metal silhouettes popped up from the floor, encircling Alaska in a sort of cage. Alaska fired at one of them, but it slid into the floor before she managed to hit it.

"Good try," said Tarana. "Don't expect to—"

Alaska spun around rapidly, firing at the same time, and one by one there was the sound of a pang as each and every one was hit, collapsing flat against the floor, before sliding out of sight.

"Wow, that's...that's very good, Alaska," said Tarana, looking shocked. "You've never done this before?"

"No," Alaska said, smiling at her, when she saw something in the corner of her eye. Jakob was standing in the doorway, an unreadable expression on his face.

"Just ignore him," Tarana said in a low voice when a gray-haired man who looked around sixty years old appeared, slipping past Jakob into the room.

"Everything is ready, it'll be here tomorrow," he said to Tarana, as Alaska stared at him in shock.

"Oh, Alaska, this is Gizel," Tarana said. "He's arranged an aerial transport for you. We won't know beforehand where it's headed, but the pilot will debrief you on board."

"I know Mr. Gizel," Alaska said, "He's my teacher."

Gizel nodded to Alaska. "I am sorry I couldn't help you. My hands were tied," Gizel said. "I couldn't have acted, but I am going to help you now."

Alaska didn't respond. She knew it was true, as much as she didn't want to accept his apology. She nodded her head stiffly.

She asked Tarana, "What if the transport goes to Pomander's Lid?"

Gizel and Tarana looked at each other.

"I don't know, it might," he said. "We definitely would not be told, though, if that's where it's headed. Pomander's Lid is kept in tight secrecy, few people know its location, though some say it is in the far north of the country, beyond the mountains. Only a few are allowed to leave after being there. It's said to be magnificent. I'd give anything to go there myself, but I have no idea how."

As he finished, Alaska saw Jakob listening nearby.

He spoke next, "All your little tin soldiers. Watch them fall," before going away.

****

"Where is Jakob?" Alaska asked, running up to Tarana later on.

"He works in the kitchens. Why?"

Alaska took off, following the rusty signs screwed into the walls at various corridors of the facility. She found the kitchens, a small, cramped and steaming hot space in a distant area of the compound. Jakob was alone, behind a metal tabletop covered in piles of dull, mud-colored fish. He was reaching for a cleaver, but froze as he saw her, a surprised and slightly wary expression in his warm hazel eyes. Alaska noticed he was still wearing gloves, and wondered if he ever took them off.

"You work here alone?" Alaska said, staring around the empty, desolate room, so isolated from everything else.

"Yes. What, you worried I'll poison you?" said Jakob coolly, moving a fish from the pile.

"No," Alaska said nervously. "I want to know about Pomander's Lid."

Jakob looked at her, one eyebrow raised, "Why?"

Alaska swallowed, saying more firmly, "If the people there really are everything you said, they can help my family."

"Tarana doesn't want us to talk about it," Jakob said, his eyes dropping to the fish as his grip tightened on the cleaver.

"I thought you didn't care."

"I'm in a good mood," said Jakob, bringing the cleaver down hard on the fish's head. "Maybe I do now."

"Please. Just tell me," Alaska said.

Jakob stared at her for a long time before he said softly, "I don't know anything more."

Alaska turned away to leave and he added, looking uncomfortable, "Except some say there's a weapon hidden in it—a weapon that could destroy Defense."

Alaska stopped and turned to face him. "Is that true?"

Jakob shrugged, "It's only another story."

17

Ianto stared at the wall of Ira's study where he had heard the scream before. The screaming had stopped suddenly. He hadn't heard any since that day outside of the department. "What's behind that wall?"

Ira looked up from where he was half-buried in boxes marked 'Cure Pill Mudflats.' Ianto scrolled down a list of civilian files he was supposed to sort, but the wall recaptured his attention.

"That wall?" Ira looked at it absently, surprised at Ianto's interest in it, before he frowned and said, "Actually...I don't know. Why?"

Ianto shrugged as he came to the record for someone named Alaska Donnel. The screams had stopped, but he wasn't sure he should discuss the sounds he was hearing in his head with anyone. Not Ira, not anyone. The answer would just be he was having hallucinations again, that he was suffering from stress, or nerves, or needed more exercise. *Or maybe*, Ianto thought, *I'm going stark raving mad in this prison.* If he was going mad, he'd be classified useless and Melissa Johnson would most certainly dispose of him. Best to keep quiet.

"I just want to know. It's sort of important."

"I'll find out for you," Ira promised.

Ianto quietly left the study and entered the rotunda. A screen was up playing the video of a new protestor capture. The faces flashed one by one, and he felt no pity. Suddenly, he saw a very familiar face—Jamie Campbell-Boyd.

18

"I'm going too."

The simple three word sentence made them all jump. Jakob stood in front of them, dressed in a heavy coat and carrying a small satchel.

"You sure?" Tarana asked him, startled.

He glanced at Alaska briefly, and she looked down at the floor, avoiding his piercing gaze. When she looked up, he'd turned to Tarana.

"Yes, I'm sure. I'm not staying here another moment of my existence. Sixteen hours a day preparing slop for the rest of my life. No way."

Tarana didn't say anything more to him. She handed Alaska a pack, "All the things you'll need."

Alaska nodded her head in gratitude.

"Let's get on, then," Tarana said. "The transport's waiting, but they can't stay out much longer. Six minutes tops they're giving you."

Hurriedly Alaska slung the pack over her shoulder, and with the guide of Tarana's light, made her way rather clumsily through the darkness into the tunnel that led up to ground level. The beam of Tarana's light flashed over several waiting figures, and she saw Gizel and nameless others from the facility.

"Got everything?" Gizel asked Tarana, who handed him a heavy looking box and a small emergency kit.

"Are you all going as well?" Alaska asked, joining them as they made their way towards the ladder.

"Dr. Bennett's coming in case we need medical attention, and a couple of the others are like you, ready to move on. I'm going to guide everything," Gizel said, and he added, in a soft, almost joking tone, "Besides, I've gotten too old for this place. Time to move on."

"You aren't going anywhere if you don't speed up!" Alaska heard Tarana snap, and they all ran, scrambling up to the ground level.

Cool air hit Alaska's face, refreshing after the tunnels, though she knew this went hand in hand with Defense officers and security cameras, so she felt nervous as well, eager to get onto the waiting air-ship. It was perfectly still in the midnight dusk, painted a deep blue to blend in with the sky and other aerial traffic. One of the hatches opened, and down from it came a ladder. Gizel went up first, stopping only to say a hurried goodbye to Tarana and shake her hand.

"You better take care of yourself!" she called after him, and Gizel nodded before leaving.

Jakob went up next and the others. Alaska was last. She waved goodbye to Tarana, knowing she'd probably never see her again, and Tarana ran up to her, handing her a leather pouch.

"It's not a stun gun, but it'll be helpful even if you don't need a weapon," she said. "Heaven forbid you'll need a weapon."

Tears came to her eyes, and she stepped back, waving, looking happy, but sad at the same time. The inside of the air-ship was bright white, a stark contrast to the exterior, with tinted windows and lines of seats facing the pilot's cabin. There was an area for cargo towards the back where Alaska stowed the pack. Everyone strapped down, so Alaska followed suit, and one of the pilots, a balding man of around fifty, came out to greet everyone.

"Fob McDonald," he said, shaking every hand. "Don't worry, I won't ask for names, I understand most of you will want to be anonymous. Okay, strap down if you haven't already, we're headed over the water, and there might be a bit of turbulence. If you see Defense air-ships coming to intercept, hold on to whatever you can for dear life, understood?"

Everyone nodded and he made his way back into the cabin. A silence fell across the air-ship as it took off and started towards the river, broken briefly only by Gizel's word of advice, "Always follow the water. It's the fastest, and surest way out of any large city in this country."

Alaska watched as the river passed beneath them, dazzling from a distance, instead of the sludgy darkness it appeared as close up. From above it was still very dark, but it also seemed to glimmer, like sheets of black glass running downward, beneath the vast metropolis above, which, like the water, was so much more beautiful viewed from afar. Looking at it from her vantage point, it was so hard to believe this was a place to run away from; Lossit looked like a grandiose glass tower, the people inside of it invisible.

"I hope they're alright," Alaska said, her voice trembling.

"Ira will save them," said Gizel reassuringly, following Alaska's gaze. "I've known him for many years. He's a good young man and true to his word."

Alaska tried to pinpoint where she had lived among the buildings, but she gave up after awhile, since from up above all the empty lots and houses seemed the same, so uniform and as a whole so magnificent, overlooking individuality, suffering.

"It's beautiful from up here. I never thought I'd ever see it in such a way..." Gizel's voice trailed off softly.

"What part of the Capital did you come from?" Alaska asked.

"No part," Gizel said immediately. "I was from a little village. I only came to the Capital to survive during the plague, when it was like a fortress, the safest place to be in the country. I was a scientist, and I tried many times to find a cure for the plague. I even offered to help Defense's team towards the end of the plague, but they rejected my offer. I always thought it strange, but perhaps they'd already found it by that time and didn't want anyone else coming in and taking credit. Then, afterward, when I realized it wasn't a real cure, I began to search for that, but they closed me down, said if I continued, I would be arrested." He looked out of the window, down at the city, down at Defense's headquarters, Lossit. "You can forget all about what goes on below, can't you, from this angle? You can forget what'll happen if we're found now."

Alaska watched him looking down sadly at the rooftops.

"Jakob said Pomander's Lid is a nation," Alaska said quietly to him. "What does that mean? How do you hide a nation?"

"Well, it is a legend, Alaska, and legends tend to be a bit... grandiose," Gizel said. "It may be very small, or very large, or maybe it's just a myth. Maybe it's just a little enclave of ten people somewhere on a lonely rock, telling Defense that they don't rule everyone. But I don't really care. It's a fair place, Pomander's Lid, and fair is enough for me."

19

"Jamie!" Ianto burst into Melissa Johnson's office. "Jamie Campbell-Boyd is not a protestor."

He was shocked by his own panic as he stood in the doorway, facing Melissa Johnson. The last time he'd felt this urgency was in a burning house, deserted. Johnson looked up from her desk, one eyebrow raised. She looked older than usual, dark circles around her eyes.

"So he does mean something to you," she said appraisingly, a pleased smile spreading across her face.

"No!" said Ianto immediately, seeing the danger. "No, he's nothing. I'm just sure he's not a protestor."

"Well, he was caught with them," said Johnson, turning back to her desk. "And since he's nothing, you won't care he'll be executed with them tomorrow."

"He's completely innocent, he...he won't even kill bugs. He thinks mosquitoes are precious."

Jamie was always too nice, too understanding about everything. Too interested in everything. *Dumb as as a doorknob*, Ianto thought. *But a protestor?*

"He attacked a Defense officer, Ianto. He resisted capture. That alone is worth the death penalty."

Ianto couldn't imagine mousy Jamie attacking a Defense officer. She was lying.

"Maybe he knows something," Ianto suggested. "Maybe he knows something valuable. That'll be lost if you kill him."

Melissa Johnson just smiled. "I've already thought of that, Ianto.

Don't worry, though, you'll be able to attend the execution."

"Johnson," Ianto stared at her cold face and saw clearly she wasn't going to yield.

"You should be grateful for what I haven't taken from you, Ianto," Johnson said in a very finalizing tone. "You are alive. Your grandfather is alive."

"Great," Ianto cried, a bitter edge to his voice. "I was only ever his servant."

Johnson searched Ianto's face, and he saw a look of disappointment on her own, but it passed quickly.

"You are dismissed," she said, looking down at her work and flicking her hand towards the door.

Ianto turned to leave, but she added without looking up, "You can see your 'friend' one last time, Ianto, and then you'll realize you aren't losing anything."

She slid an access card across her desk towards him. Gold—a gold access card! His name was stamped on it in red.

"This will let you into the Crypts, with security. But don't even bother trying to sneak out."

They had been traveling on the air-ship for several hours and most people had separated into groups, some sleeping, others talking in low voices. Alaska slipped away from all of it, finding a small, enclosed metal room in the back. She sat down on the floor and flipped open the pouch. Inside was a long, sword-like dagger with a leaf-shaped blade. She pulled it out, examining it in the dim light pouring in from the air-ship's now half-shuttered portholes. It looked antique, and there were silvery pictures engraved on the blade of nine cloaked figures. She had no idea what any of them meant, and began to slip the dagger back inside of its pouch when she felt she was being watched. *The cloaked figures*, she thought instinctively, but it was Jakob. *Don't be stupid*, Alaska told herself, *they can't get you, not anymore, not up here.*

"Do you know who owned that?" Jakob asked, nodding at the dagger.

Alaska shook her head. "It's old. Very old."

"It was Samson Magler's."

The dagger slipped out of Alaska's hand, clinking on the floor. She couldn't keep back her horror and disgust. The dagger was clean, but felt as if it was covered in blood now she knew its history. How had Tarana acquired it?

"People say he was really into ancient weapons. Your dagger was never used, anyway, too clean," Jakob said. "It's just aged from being old, not from use. Magler probably never even touched it."

Alaska still looked uncomfortable. Jakob came over and sat

down next to her.

"Alaska Donnel the runner," he nodded over his shoulder back at the main compartment, where the others were sitting. "You want to be one of them, then? All brave and heroic and noble? They never mention the end part, the part I can't help noticing. All of their heroes are dead."

Alaska didn't reply, but he didn't seem to expect an answer. "Welcome to the dark side, Alaska. Now you can be just like the rest of us." He spat out the words bitterly.

She still kept her mouth tightly shut.

"What did Ira tell you?" Jakob asked.

"What do you mean?" she finally spoke, staring at him in bewilderment.

"You still have hope," Jakob said, his voice almost angry as he looked at her from behind dark, narrowed eyes. "He must have told you something to make you believe you'd see your family again."

"He told me he'd get them out," Alaska said firmly. "He promised me he would."

"And you believe that, the word of a complete stranger?" he said, his voice shaking. Alaska noticed his hands trembling and he stuffed them into his pockets.

"You believe that?" he said, attempting to sound calmer.

"Yes," Alaska said, staring straight at him, even as she felt herself doubting, just a little, just slightly.

"Don't ever trust Ira Graye," said Jakob firmly. "I know what you probably think of him, what people always think of him, but I know Ira. I know him better than anybody else, and he's not trustworthy, or kind, and he's definitely no savior."

Suddenly, their conversation was interrupted as Fob shouted over the speaker, "Just picked up some other air-ships on the radar. Likely they've detected us too, perhaps ages ago, but they're not in shooting range, so for now we're fine. Just hang on, people."

Jakob got to his feet, and Alaska said quickly as she stuffed the dagger back into its leather pouch, "All I know, Jakob, is that I want my family to be safe. I haven't taken any sides."

He didn't reply, and she returned to her seat in the other room. Gizel sat down next to her, saying reassuringly, "It's okay. It's probably just cargo ships."

She didn't believe him, but she was willing to take any slice of hope that it wasn't Defense after them.

Silence fell, then Fob gave another report.

"They're picking up the pace, they probably are going to go for an intercept, and if they do it's better they don't see you lot, so be quiet and stay well out of view of the cabin doorway, understood? Good."

There was an agonizing wait for more news. Alaska ticked off the minutes on her fingers. Jakob made strange, low-pitched, impatient hissing noises under his breath. Dr. Bennett fidgeted, while several of the other passengers took to biting their nails. Gizel was the only person who seemed calm at all, resting perfectly still in his chair. Perhaps he was used to this type of thing, Alaska thought. *Was that why Marianne was so calm?*

"Hold on!" it was Fob's voice, half-screaming and Alaska instinctively grasped the bar on the back of the chair in front of her, but even this didn't keep her from being flung violently backwards as the air-ship shuddered, swerving sideways.

"You okay?" Fob shouted. "Anyone unconscious?"

Alaska's vision went fuzzy, and she felt dizzy as the air-ship's interior spun in front of her. She slid across the floor and made her way to a window where she could see what was going on. A gang of air-ships was attacking them. Their air-ship was surrounded. Then one of the Defense air-ships zoomed closer, there was the sound of a laser cannon firing and the whole vessel shook violently. She was thrown to the floor. Her whole body ached as she tried to raise herself up again to see what was going on. Then there was a huge blast of white light. Her eyes shut instinctively to block out the blinding light. Then she felt the sensation of falling downwards, out of the air. *We're lost*, she thought. There was a last, deafening bang and they crashed.

21

Alaska awoke to find herself in the dark. The sound of shots rang in her ears. They were in the truck again, ambushed, but this time she wasn't going to be able to escape. Leila was screaming. She fought furiously against hands trying to drag her away, and then suddenly a burst of dim light came out of nowhere and she realized her eyes weren't open. She had been dreaming. Alaska opened her eyes and looked around. There was a harsh morning light. Where was the air-ship? She looked around, but couldn't see any sort of wreckage. She was in some sort of room with a dirt floor and cinder block walls. Was she in a Defense prison? Alaska jumped to her feet, and then noticed Jakob watching her.

"Quiet," he hissed at her, then pointed out the window and she followed his gaze.

She could see the wreck in the distance and several air-ships surrounding it. People moved through the twisted metal remains. They were too far away for Alaska to tell whether they were Defense officers or not.

"They'll find us," she whispered, horrified.

"They already did. Searched the whole area. I paid them off."

"You what?"

"They're not Defense, just a bunch of bounty hunters looking for any source of income," Jakob said. "We got a lucky break, they thought we were just an illegal transport. It's not worth their time to turn us in now they've got the money, as long as we clear out in a day."

"Where did you get money from?" Alaska asked, trying to force herself into a sitting position.

"Some of the other passengers had money on them, all together it didn't add up to much, but it was enough," Jakob said.

"Where are they?" she looked around, but didn't see anyone else.

Jakob shrugged, "Gizel might be salvageable, but the others are all dead."

Alaska's mouth fell open, "Fob? Dr. Bennett?"

"Dr. Bennett threw himself on me," Jakob said flatly. "Used himself as a shield. Fob was probably the first to die along with the other pilot, the entire front cabin was torn off."

"You stole money off of dead people?" Alaska stared at him in horror.

"I didn't think they needed it anymore," Jakob said. "I got your dagger."

He tossed it over to her. Alaska stared at him incredulously before limping after him.

Gizel was slumped against the exterior wall of the building, his face badly cut and bruised, but he seemed conscious and able to walk.

"The others..." he whispered. Jakob forced him to his feet.

Gizel's face screwed up in pain, but he didn't shout.

"Easy," Alaska said warningly.

"No pain, no gain," Jakob hissed under his breath. "Can you walk?" he snapped at Gizel.

Gizel nodded, moving a few steps shakily, and then said, sounding somewhat panicked, "Where's my jacket?"

Jakob found the gray, white lined jacket nearby. Gizel snatched it out of Jakob's hands, breathing a sigh of relief.

"What happened?" he asked. Jakob didn't answer, so Alaska did.

"There was a crash. The others didn't make it."

Gizel's mouth fell open, "All of them?"

"They died," Alaska said and he shook his head.

"Only a few trips make it," he admitted. "It's always very dangerous, but there's no other way."

"You could have given me a bit of a warning beforehand," Alaska said, though gently. She turned to Jakob, "Where are we going now?"

Jakob shrugged, "Anywhere but here."

They started walking and she turned to Gizel, "Where was the air-ship going?"

He hesitated before responding.

"I really don't know, Alaska. They hadn't told us yet. Fob's route did seem to be taking us north, upriver, though, and I don't know where we'd be going that way. It's mostly desert and mountains."

The area they had crashed in was nothing like the Capital as it was woodsy and wet. All Alaska had ever seen of forests was through the barbed wire fence that encircled the city, or in storybooks. The provinces were a strange hidden world on the other side of the wire and now she was in the middle of them, and everything was completely and absolutely real. She could reach out and touch the rough bark of trees which showed through layers of thick, soft moss. The air was incredibly clear and damp, smelling of rain. Light, semi-translucent white beams, shone in between the trees. Alaska looked around in wonder, then stopped as the trees thinned and disappeared. They were on the edge of a field and in the distance was the high stone wall of a town with a rusty, twisted iron gate. Beyond the town rose a hill with a battered tower atop it.

Jakob looked about and said, "Cutter. I recognize this place. I was captured once, ten miles from here. We're a fair distance from the capital."

"Not far enough, though," said Gizel and he closed his eyes.

"Our best hope is to follow the water."

He stumbled straight towards the town, then collapsed on the ground.

"I'm fine," he said quickly as Alaska ran forward to help him, but she could see blood staining his clothes.

"Jakob, what's wrong with him?" Alaska asked, as Jakob stepped forward and examined Gizel's leg despite his protests.

His leg was severely cut, with a bloody wound in the center of it, lines of lacerations like veins running from it.

"It's bad," Jakob said simply.

He ran down to a small stream nearby, collected water and returned, pouring it over Gizel's leg. The excess water ran away, leaving the grass stained red. Jakob removed his overshirt, forming a crude bandage from it, which he wrapped tightly around Gizel's leg to apply pressure.

Gizel winced and shut his eyes. "Don't bother about me. Just go."

"Shut up," Alaska said, grabbing his arm.

Jakob wordlessly helped her support him and together they carried Gizel towards Cutter till it started to go dark. Alaska let out a sigh of relief as they settled down in an abandoned building on the outskirts of the town. It looked like it had once been a grand country house, but now it was only a ruin, with broken windows and a half-missing roof. Alaska felt far too exposed as she looked up the winding staircase covered in bits of red roof tile and saw the dark sky above. Alaska sat on the bottom step, not wanting to fall asleep despite the fact she felt as if she might collapse from exhaustion. She wondered about her family in Lossit's cells. She hoped they were in good hands, Ira's hands, but she didn't know him and didn't know if she trusted him.

"What are you thinking?" Jakob sat down on a windowseat opposite her.

"We can't leave Gizel like that," Alaska nodded at him as he rolled over violently on the floor.

Jakob nodded. "But there's something else you're thinking about."

"You said on the air-ship 'welcome to the dark side'."

"Yes."

"What is Defense then? Because I don't know right now what side I'm on, frankly, Jakob. Perhaps not any, none of this was my choice."

The look on his face softened, "It's all dark, Alaska, it's all ugly."

She looked down at the ground, "No, it isn't. I don't believe that. I believe there's more to it, Jakob. And I think you do, too."

He snorted.

"Why did you get the dagger out of the wreckage for me?"

"You might need it."

Jakob didn't elaborate. She watched him pull a gold chain out from where it was tucked beneath his collar and stare down at a pendant on the end of it.

"What is that?"

"I need to look at it, in times like this," he said simply.

"You're staring at it as if it is the key to everything."

"Hmm." Jakob held it up, where it caught the light and Alaska saw it fully.

It was odd, square, with a piece of black glass embedded in the surface, forming a slash across its otherwise pristine white surface. It was familiar. Had she seen a copy somewhere in the Capital before?

"Who gave you that? Was it somebody very important?"

Jakob nodded rather impatiently, "Yes."

"It's...it's nice," Alaska said, not sure what else to say.

A beam of moonlight touched it, and for a moment the slash

of black glimmered and seemed to come out from the stone itself like a projection. Alaska jumped back.

"It's just an optical illusion," Jakob said, sounding mildly amused by her reaction as he tucked it out of sight again. "I had to hide it very carefully every night because Defense did raids where I lived, and if you were caught with something not allowed, like this..." His voice trailed off. "They never found it. I retrieved it after I got away from the bastards. Did Tarana give you the dagger?"

Alaska nodded. "Who gave you the pendant?" she asked. Jakob turned away from her, looked out a window.

"Go to sleep, Alaska."

She wanted to protest, but she was finally too tired. She lay down on the floor, at the foot of the stairs, and watched him, his silhouette illuminated by moonlight, until she fell asleep.

22

The thing that first struck Ianto about the Crypts was the smell. A rank, nauseating, rotting smell. The security guards escorting him had masks, but they ignored him every time he asked for one as they led him down narrow, steep stone steps. Ira was waiting at the bottom.

"I'll escort him the rest of the way," Ira said. The guards didn't argue, immediately racing back up the stairs.

The Crypts were large and cavernous with several inches of dirty, foul water on the floor. Blood-sucking insects clung to every surface. Ira wasn't wearing a mask either, and his nose was wrinkled, but he didn't look like he was about to gag, like the expression on Ianto's face.

"You're more used to the Crypts," Ianto observed.

"I used to work down here," Ira said.

"Great job."

"Hmm. It's worse for the prisoners. It's a bit like a slow death, it breaks you down, sucks hope away. It's designed to be torture in and of itself." A shadow fell across Ira's face.

They crunched over the bones of rodents. Corridors were lined with cell doors, icy blue electronic screens above giving the names of the inmates.

"You talk about it as if you were a prisoner yourself," Ianto looked at Ira in surprise.

Ira shook his head. "Not me," Ira added very seriously, his voice slightly choked. "But I did know someone, Ianto. I lost someone to it, like you."

Before Ianto could ask who, they came to Jamie's cell, next to one marked "Donnels." There were two other people sharing it with him. Guards stood on either side of the door, and they unlocked it, pushing Ianto inside. The other inmates looked up at Ianto with dull eyes, grotesque skeletons following his every move expressionlessly.

"Jamie isn't here."

"He's been taken for exercise." The guard who spoke had a twisted smile on his face. "He'll be back. Just wait."

Then the door clanged shut. Ianto heard the lock click and felt panic. What if this was all a trick, what if...? But he still had the gold access card, they weren't trapping him. It wasn't likely Ira was going to desert him either, he thought, though he knew he could never be sure about anyone. Ianto sat down on the cleanest bench in the room, a narrow stone perch projecting out of the wall. He buried his head in his hands while he waited so he wouldn't have to look at the other inmates, though he could still feel their eyes boring into him silently. The cell was the same size as his grandfather's shed, where he'd awoken after the accident, after he'd been "saved."

He remembered opening his eyes and finding himself lying on the hard, cold floor, light coming in through a broken window. He'd started screaming, and Arthur Ambrose had burst in, roughly grabbing him by the arms and dragging him onto his feet, then putting a hand tightly over his mouth so he couldn't do anything but mumble indistinctly. After quite a bit of tussling, his grandfather had deemed him calm enough and had sat him down, telling him how his parents had left him in the house, how they were now dead, ambushed trying to escape the Capital and killed by Defense. He had refused to believe it, calling his grandfather a liar, among other things, but after several days in the shed, days which felt like weeks, he had realized they were not coming back for him. And his grandfather hadn't seemed to care, treating him as if he was something evil. He'd only moved Ianto from the shed to the house when Ianto escaped, and met....

"Jamie," Ianto looked up and saw Jamie standing in the doorway of the cell.

Jamie looked terrible, emaciated with dark shadows under his eyes, his hair in disarray. Cuts crisscrossed his face and arms, exposed under the torn sleeves of a gray prison gown. His mouth dropped open at the sight of Ianto.

"I never imagined you here," Ianto said, a bit stiffly under Jamie's pained gaze. "What did you do, Jamie?"

"You're wearing their clothes," Jamie managed to say, and Ianto looked down at his clothes.

The red and white Defense uniform had easily become a second skin to him. He didn't know what he had expected from Jamie, the usual wide-eyed curiosity and camaraderie, he supposed, but instead, Jamie looked wary.

"Just tell them what you were doing and they'll let you out of here," said Ianto urgently. "Explain yourself."

"Don't talk to me that way."

Ianto shook his head, puzzled. "What way?"

"That way, the way you always talk to me, like I'm a child, and you're my Dad."

"Sorry, never noticed," said Ianto. "But the point is—"

"How could you do this, Ianto?" Jamie's cold expression had suddenly melted away to a look of excruciating pain, and the look in his eyes only intensified.

Ianto knew what it was; he'd seen it before on other people's faces. His own. Betrayal. Jamie felt betrayed.

"What do you mean?" Ianto asked, though his tone suggested he knew perfectly well what Jamie meant.

"How could you go to work for them?" Jamie asked. "After all they did to you, all they took from you. I know about your parents, how Defense hunted them down for months and murdered them. But it wasn't enough for them, was it? They were going to kill you too because your parents were too loud, because your parents had an opinion! I don't know why they're sparing you now, Ianto, but you have to get out of here and run! They'll kill you when they're finished. Look what they've done to you already...getting you to inform on me."

"I didn't tell them about you," Ianto said quickly. "I'm trying to protect you. I'm sure this is just a mistake, if we—"

"I didn't do anything, Ianto, I didn't do anything! I told them again and again and again, but they don't care!" Jamie shook. "I don't want to help them. I don't want to be a Defense officer, Ianto, I don't want to grab kids off the street for doing nothing."

"Then why did you give me away?" Ianto shouted at Jamie before he could stop himself, and a puzzled look crossed Jamie's face, momentarily breaking his anger.

"What are you talking about?"

"You led them to me!" said Ianto, surprising himself with the accusation that had been at the back of his mind, but had never before surfaced. "Something you did made them find out about me. Being nosy about my past, instead of letting it rest!"

Jamie looked down at the ground, shaking, though it didn't seem to be from regret. "So you can't even face what you've done to yourself? To everyone who tried to protect you from them? Ianto, you led them to yourself. You were so reckless, it was bound to happen eventually."

"It's not my fault!" said Ianto quickly. He paced across the floor of the cell. "What did you do? What did they arrest you for?"

"I was at a meeting with a bunch of protestors."

Ianto stared at Jamie hard, "What were you doing there?"

"I was trying to find a way to save you!" Jamie said desperately. "I went to your grandfather's house looking for you. The neighbors told me you had been taken away. They're just grabbing people, Ianto, it's not just you. That house we saw burned, there was another—"

"Jamie, you don't know how evil protestors are. Defense has to go after them. My parents just left me without a second thought, and the rest of them are no better. I'm not saying Defense is wonderful, they're not, but they're better," Ianto said firmly. "You can't hang about with...murderers and traitors."

"Are you listening to yourself?" Jamie looked both angry and incredulous. He sank onto a bench, and Ianto heard creaking noises all around them, remembering there were other inmates.

They were all now casting him nasty looks.

"You shouldn't have come, Ianto," said Jamie, his voice hoarse. "You should have stayed in your comfortable, fluffy Defense bed." His voice broke as he added, "And forgotten I was being tortured under your head."

Ianto opened his mouth to respond and the door banged open, "Time is up," the guard snapped, flashing a warning look from Jamie to Ianto.

Ianto followed, but just before he passed through the door he called over his shoulder, "Just tell them, Jamie. Just tell them you made a mistake, just tell them you're not a protestor. Tell them anything you know about what the protestors were planning. They'll listen, they'll change their minds. They'll pardon you. That's all you have to do."

The guard forced him forward, pushing him ahead roughly, but not before he heard Jamie's response.

"Never."

Alaska woke up long before daylight to see Gizel leaning against a wall, a pained look in his eyes, though he forced a smile when he saw her worriedly watching him.

Jakob entered and turned to her. "I've been scoping out the town and there's a hospital. We can get something for Gizel from there."

"You and Alaska will be wasting time," Gizel said desperately. "You'll just have to come back for me. Just go and leave me here."

"I found a wheelbarrow," Jakob said. "We can carry you."

"We can't just march into the middle of a hospital," Alaska said. "We'll be seen."

"Not here," Jakob said and he pointed out the door.

Alaska followed his direction and stepped outside to look at Cutter. She hadn't been able to get a good look at it the first day, but now she saw a gray rotting hulk of worn streets and crumbling buildings. It looked like a war zone.

"What happened?" she asked as Jakob helped Gizel, leading him outside.

Jakob remained silent, but Gizel responded, "This place was a boom town, believe it or not, but the plague ruined that. When the recovery came, it didn't reach out to many areas further away from the capital. Everything became very capital-centric. Areas like this have become little more than ghost towns and pitched battlegrounds between escaping protestors and Defense."

They started into the middle of Cutter's core, and Alaska saw the empty shops, many half-collapsed and burnt out, while a small minority remained defiantly intact except for broken windows.

"There's been attempts to set up a different government," Gizel said. "They were too splintered, though, and easily crushed. One of them was here in Cutter for a year. These buildings didn't simply collapse. They were bombed by Defense."

"How long ago was that?" Alaska asked, and Gizel put up five fingers.

"I don't remember that," Alaska said. "I should remember that."

"Defense doesn't publicize its opponents," Gizel said. "Not until they're gone, anyways."

Alaska thought of the public funeral on television. *Not until they're gone.* Everything was eerily silent, and there was a strange smell on the wind, both gaseous and ashy. It was faint at first, but before long it filled Alaska's nostrils, forcing her to choke. She put a hand over her face, and saw Gizel's face had gone white, though Jakob looked unaffected.

"There's been a recent attack here. I can still smell fuel from a burning," said Gizel. "We have to get inside quickly, they may still be nearby."

They stopped in front of a hulking metal skeleton of a building, the glass from its windows lying at its feet. A sign covered in scorch marks hung crookedly above what was once double doors but now was just an opening. Someone had spray-painted "Magler Hall" in red across it. Jakob looked up at the sign for a moment, then pushed Gizel in the wheelbarrow inside. Alaska followed. She could hear scuttling in the shadows of the building.

"What's—"

"Rats," Jakob said before she could finish and he set Gizel down before running ahead of her. "They're normal ones. Come on."

Alaska followed him cautiously as they ascended a double helix staircase covered in creeping ivy to what was left of the glass floor upper level. A gaping hole in the side of the building illuminated the space as bright-eyed furry shapes scurried away from Alaska and Jakob. She shrunk back, but Jakob ran ahead and she forced herself to follow him. Jakob stopped suddenly, pointing at a nearby sign.

"Here," Jakob said. "There's a storage closet down this hall. Wait right here and I'll be back. There might be something useful, so look around."

Alaska watched him disappear into the shadows and looked around the space. There were frosted glass doors leading off to other rooms. Shelves and drawers lined the walls. There was one labeled 'Cure Pills.' In all the excitement, she had forgotten that they did not have any pills, and she was surprised that she did not find herself needing them as before. Yet, for how long could they survive without them? She did not want to find out.

She pushed a button on the drawer to open it, but there was nothing inside except dust. On the shelves were opaque glass vials. Alaska picked one up, staring at the cloudy, silvery liquid inside of it. The label read "Anesthetic." She put it back on the shelf and reached for another vial when she heard a clattering noise and turned, seeing a partially open door across from where she was standing. A sign hung behind the glass. Alaska took a step back as she saw her own initials staring back at her: A.N.D. Ward 5. She walked over to the door and pushed it all the way open. The room was empty and sterile, all the glass windows blown out. A heavy gust of wind blew in the room, ripping the sign from the door. Alaska heard a sound again and ran past hospital beds to the edge of a collapsed wall. Gaping through an opening, she peered out over the landscape to see a ghostly figure tearing away from the hospital.

"Alaska!" Jakob appeared in the doorway to the room, weighed down by a white satchel brimming with supplies. "I need you to carry some of this."

"There's somebody else out there," Alaska whispered.

"What are you talking about?"

"I just saw somebody running away," Alaska whispered, pointing, but the form had vanished.

"Were they wearing a Defense uniform?"

Alaska hesitated, trying to remember, then shook her head.

"Then there's no one, Defense wouldn't have left anyone alive," he said uncomfortably, staring past her. "Come on."

"I definitely saw something, Jakob," Alaska said, following him out. "I thought it was a rat or the wind at first, but...somebody was really there. They're following us. In the Capital, I was followed all the time. Something was always watching me."

"Come on," Jakob said impatiently, though his voice was also gentler than usual. "We can't afford to waste time. Explain it to me later."

Alaska followed him back, looking over her shoulder all the way down, but the hospital was silent.

****

"Are there ghosts?" Alaska asked, as they walked along the streets of Cutter. "I've wondered that, because that's what they're like. Nightmares. I don't know when it started. I must have been thirteen, or something. Maybe before. I have a sort of weird memory gap from when I was twelve. I can't remember much of my life from that year. Some things seem familiar, yet foreign at the same time from that period. Like déjà vu, or something. And that's when I became scared of cars, as far as I can remember."

"Were you in a bad accident?" Gizel suggested, leaning heavily on the crude cane Jakob had made for him out of a tall, gray branch.

"No, I asked my parents, they said nothing happened," Alaska said. "Besides, there's hardly ever any car crashes these days. There's loads of safety protocols."

"And these shadows just follow you?" said Jakob, frowning. "They just follow and watch, they never do anything?"

Alaska nodded her head, "Do they sound familiar?"

"Where I grew up, we had a rhyme, an old children's rhyme—" Jakob said.

"*The Parable of the Nightghosts*," Alaska said immediately, "I loved that when I was little."

"When children went missing, it would get blamed on the Nightghosts," Jakob said. "But I know it must have been Defense. The rhyme is just a stupid lie made up by fat-mouthed jerks to cover themselves."

Gizel flashed Jakob a very disapproving look. "I've heard the rhyme, Alaska. I can't see how it can have anything to do with you. Your case is most unusual, but you are far from the Capital now. Whoever you saw was probably only a poor soul trying to scavenge something, but they're gone now."

She wondered if she should tell him about the sign in the hospital, but she figured they wouldn't know about that either, and would probably say it was just a coincidence that the letters on the sign were the same as her initials. They passed by eerie, bombed-out houses. There was a house that if it hadn't been so burnt might have looked like the home she'd grown up in, with its latticed front porch and empty, muddy fishponds. She realized her own house probably looked like that now, a crumbling, blackened mess. She would never run up the walk of that bright, canary yellow house again. It was only a lonely, faded corner smelling of ash and dust and petrol now.

"Alaska?" Jakob turned around and saw she was staring at the house. "What is it?"

"Why can't we ask somebody outside of the country for help?"

Alaska asked, frustrated.

Jakob stared at her as if she was mad.

"The outside world?" He burst into laughter, "There's nothing left out there!"

"Gizel, what is it like?" asked Alaska, ignoring Jakob.

"From what I've read, there was a great deal of violence and wars," Gizel said. "They were immoral, cruel, primitive people for the most part, and they killed themselves off. You'll find nothing out there except bones and dust. Thank the gods we were spared from their inhumanity."

He noticed a group of buildings ahead and quickly hobbled over to them, disappearing inside one of the ruined shops, Jakob following after him. Alaska followed, noticing the blackened remains of a strange lantern by the door. She picked it up by its hook and carried it inside. The shop had once been an antiques store, with maps still lining the walls, somewhat faded and yellowed from exposure to elements and time, but still legible in most places. Gizel ripped one down from the wall, spreading it smooth on a dusty, broken table.

"What is this?" Alaska asked, holding up the lantern as Gizel scanned the map.

"Kerosene lamp," Gizel said with a brief sideways glance at it. "People use them all the time out in these little towns, some of them don't get electricity like the Capital. Unfortunately, the kerosene is highly flammable, and when exposed to dumped fuel they spread Defense's fires faster. We have no use for that, you can put it away."

Gizel jabbed at a spot on the map with his finger, as Alaska dumped the lamp in a corner.

"We're here, nowhere near any deserts, though close to plenty of water. There's the sea, the river, and the twin lakes, Savior and Valor."

"Edwin and Lavender," Jakob interjected.

"Lakes what?" Alaska asked, staring at him.

Jakob, who'd leaned forward to take a closer look, glared at her.

"You know them as lakes Savior and Valor. We changed their names from the ones Defense uses."

"Keep looking," Gizel said eagerly and as Jakob pulled down a few more maps Alaska looked around the walls for anything of a sand color, which might suggest desert terrain. Something caught her eye and she stretched, managing to just reach the edge of it and pull the map down to the floor.

"What about this?"

Gizel and Jakob bent over it, and there was the desert, right in front of their eyes, but Alaska couldn't make out Cutter in relation to it.

"Follow the water," Gizel pointed out a sliver of blue near the edge of the map, almost out of view, and the name Odyssey next to it. "It's the same river we've been following all this time, from the facility to here. That stream back there flows directly into it."

"Let's head there then," Jakob rolled up the map.

As he said this there was a rattling from above and the entire building started to sway dangerously. Staring cautiously out of the window Alaska saw a giant shadowy object above, almost invisible in the darkness. Gizel joined her at the window.

"Defense," he whispered under his breath as a beam of light flashed over the air-ship's surface, clearly showing Defense's emblem of a dragon biting it's own tail.

"They'll start scanning," Jakob hissed to Gizel. "We need to get o—"

Jakob's voice was broken off by an ear-splitting noise and a flash of brilliant light. They all dropped to the floor and then there was a—Boom! Alaska looked up over the bottom edge of the window and saw the explosion as the Defense air-ship disintegrated. Wreckage rained everywhere, sending the roof of the shop down on top of them.

"Alaska!" She made out Jakob's face through a cloud of plaster.

"I'm fine!" she coughed. "Gizel?"

He was already on his feet with his cane, by the door. "Hurry!" he said.

"What happened?" Alaska asked Gizel breathlessly, as she ran beside Jakob. "Why—why did the air-ship blow up?"

"Another air-ship," said Gizel. "Probably protestors."

"Well, that's good, isn't it?" Alaska said, "Why are we running away? They might land, help us..."

"The only way they are going to land is in splinters, same as the Defense air-ship!" Gizel shouted at her. "Defense is not going to rest until they find who is responsible and destroys them. The only thing we can do now is get out of here as quickly as possible before they find us."

24

The first thing Ianto realized as he rose out of bed was that there hadn't been any screams for a very long time. Then he looked at the calender on the wall and knew what was on the schedule for the day. A change of clothes sat outside his door, crisp and mourning white, like funeral attire. Johnson had left them there, to torture him further, he thought. He chucked them in the trash incinerator and dressed in his usual uniform. He repeated under his breath over and over again with his eyes shut, "Tell them, Jamie, just tell them."

But Jamie was no computer, there was no way of controlling him. Ianto started down a hallway but halted as he heard a soft screeching sound. He hesitated, but it wasn't the scream. Perhaps it was a much milder version? It was coming from a half open doorway, marked Lab 66. Ianto slipped inside, curious. It was empty, save for a few pieces of laboratory equipment and a cage of sandy-colored, tiny rats with abnormally large teeth atop a table. He walked up closer, realizing they were the source of the screech, but they weren't moving and seemed to be dead. He bent close to the bars, stared at them, and got a whiff of some chemical as he saw their beady, vacant eyes.

"Sand-rats," he said.

He heard footsteps out in the hallway, and looked over his shoulder as Evita entered. She looked surprised, but not annoyed to find a trespasser in her lab.

"Johnson is looking for you," Evita said.

"I don't care," Ianto replied. "Why do you have caged sand-rats? Why haven't they been killed?"

"Some people hate them simply because they're Magler's failed experiment, but I think they're fascinating and worth study," Evita said, her voice eager. Ianto watched in shock as Evita took a sand-rat and opened a panel hidden beneath the flesh and skull at the top of its head. Instead of a brain, there was circuitry and tiny pulses of light.

"You do know anything that was made by, or belonged to Magler is illegal according to the ten Commandments of Defense," said Ianto, one eyebrow raised. "The sand-rat robots wrecked nearly as much havoc as the plague Magler unleashed when he could sent a man into space. And now you have a stash of them in Lossit?" He shook his head disapprovingly and glanced at some electrical equipment piled on a table. "All robots resembling living creatures are banned, you know that."

"But he had good intentions," Evita said, and Ianto looked at her in surprise, clearly not expecting that response from a Defense officer. "He started the robotics movement of the 110s. It was the first step in the idea of combining organic and inorganic, once living and never lived. No boundaries." There was zeal in her voice as she spoke of her experiment. "Ira's been supplying me with specimens, and I've wanted to study the sand-rats, to run real experiments on them, instead of just keeping them caged like this. I know it could all lead to something, but I don't think anyone in Defense, especially Johnson, will give me a permit to do my experiments. The robot ban is a shame, really."

"Right," said Ianto, disagreeing completely as he looked down at the creatures.

Little abominations, he thought. Ianto was about to leave when he remembered what was waiting for him and stopped. Sand-rats were better than attending his best-friend's execution. With forced eagerness, he said to Evita, "I can help you if you want."

Evita looked at Ianto sympathetically, "That's nice of you, Ianto, but if you don't go willingly, you know Johnson will just force you to."

Reluctantly Ianto turned back towards the door, but before he could leave Evita called out a little worriedly, "It would probably be best if Johnson doesn't know about this. At least till I can convince one of the Speakers to give me a permit. Please."

Ianto hesitated then said, "Don't worry, I won't tell."

"Thank you," Evita said, the relief clear in her voice.

Ianto left the lab and shut the door. It looked like any other lab again, and nobody would know what illegal goings-on were taking place inside of it. Despite his hatred of the sand-rats, with their beady, watchful mechanical eyes, he couldn't help liking Evita for her miniature rebellion. It reminded him of himself when he would devise ways of beating his grandfather's security measures. He and Evita, in their own ways, wanted to be free. He started down the hall when the lab door opened again, and Evita poked her head out, saying in low voice, "Hey, Ianto, I'm sorry about your friend."

He turned around in surprise, but she'd already disappeared back inside.

****

Melissa Johnson was waiting at the entrance to the Crypts. She was dressed more solemnly than usual, in a pure white mourning suit with a red lace collar. A small, frightened boy stood beside her.

"Ah, Philip, this is Ianto."

The boy looked up at Ianto.

Ianto glanced at Johnson, "Why is he here?"

"He's my son. He's eleven years old, it's time for him to understand everything we do here. Boundaries off on my voice command." The newly installed electrical field cutting the Crypts off from the rest of Lossit switched off and they passed into the dark confines of the prison. "I thought you might want company in your friend's last moments," she added, with a false sweetness.

"I don't want to be here," Ianto said as he followed behind her and Philip.

Johnson didn't even turn around to face him. "We don't always get what we want, do we?"

As Johnson, Philip and Ianto walked down the corridor the shouting from the cells intensified, as if they could tell who was walking by. Johnson continued to look straight ahead, seeming completely unfazed. Ianto found himself looking at the cell doors though, trying to catch a glimpse of the inhabitants through the small windows on each of them.

"Ianto!" Johnson's sharp call made him jump. "Don't look at the cells, they don't deserve your attention."

"Fine then," he mumbled under his breath, but he obeyed.

Their walk didn't end at Jamie's cell; they went beyond it, into a vast room with a domed ceiling. It had windows but they all had heavy metal shutters over them, the only light source a giant glowing orb suspended from the ceiling, creating the effect of a dim sun shining downwards on the room. In the middle of the space sat Jamie, locked down in a chair. On the periphery, various machinery was being operated by Defense officers.

"What are you going to do?" Jamie was asking one of them, his voice shaking slightly, his face already deathly pale.

They ignored him, and Ianto turned to Johnson, "What are you going to do?"

"We're going to get the information from his brain," Johnson said smoothly. "Or at least, as much of it as we can, before the process kills him."

"Can't you do it without killing him?"

"If he does by some miracle survive this, you'll be wishing he hadn't," Johnson said coldly.

It was then Jamie noticed the three of them standing nearby, just inside the room. *Beg, Jamie!* Ianto thought desperately, *beg. Cry. Scream for your life.* But Jamie stubbornly just stared at Ianto instead, his expression hard, though Ianto could see fear as well.

"So you came to watch, did you?"

One of the officers moved to gag him, but Johnson held up her hand, "Stop."

They stepped back, and Ianto just stared at Jamie, not sure what he should say, or do. The officers took a metal cap connected to the computer and placed it on Jamie's head. Jamie struggled, looking terrified as he tried to prevent them from doing it, but restraints snapped out of the mechanism, securing him tightly. A blue light glowed from the cap as it turned on.

"Stop it," Ianto whispered, "Stop it."

He tried visualizing the computer console they were using, but he couldn't. Then he thought of something else, something easier. The restraints on Jamie were all computerized. Ianto shut his eyes. Where would he switch them off if he was standing by Jamie? There was a resounding click, and Ianto's eyes flew open as there was the sound of commotion all around him. Jamie had suddenly gotten loose. The guards flew after him, firing and Ianto dropped to the ground to avoid being hit by the laser blasts. Jamie ran faster than he'd ever done in his life, hurtling towards the doors. A shot flew past Ianto, hitting Jamie squarely in the leg. Jamie fell to the ground, screaming the worst scream Ianto had ever heard in his life. Ianto looked up, seeing Melissa Johnson standing nearby with a laser in her hand, a cold expression on her face. She walked across the room, dropped down beside Jamie and held the laser to his throat, as his eyes watered from pain. There was a long pause and then she rose to her feet again, kicking Jamie hard in his injured leg. Jamie screamed, rolling away from her across the floor to Ianto's feet, leaving a trail of blood.

Johnson looked directly at Ianto, "You can keep your pet. He's pardoned." Not taking her gaze off Ianto, she added in a high, cold voice to the guards, "Throw him back in the Crypts."

"Please..." Jamie started hoarsely, and the guards stunned him.

He twitched and fell still. The guards dragged him out of the room. Johnson roughly took the hand of her son Philip, silent, his eyes wide, his whole body trembling. She started to leave.

Ianto asked, "Why?"

Johnson looked over her shoulder at him briefly, "Whatever your parents told you about us, Ianto, is wrong. Defense is better than the protestors. Without us there would only be ruin, anarchy, untamed emotions and untempered violence. The Nation of Steel would crumble into dust. Don't ever forget that."

With that, she left.

"The Hill of Enders," Gizel said as they faced the rising mound.

It wasn't very tall. A gray tower stood at the peak, very nearly the same height as the hill itself. They hiked up the hill, Jakob and Alaska helping Gizel along. When they'd reached the top Alaska realized the tower was made completely out of gray glass. In the center of the glass swirled pieces of twisted metal and Alaska could just make out a metal door in the bottom of it, unreachable. Dried blood stained the area around the metal door, in a pattern as if somebody or something had been dragged to it, and through. All around were piled flat stones.

"What is it for?" Alaska asked as Gizel got down on his knees in front of it. "A bunker," he said. "It was once a bunker, during the Plague, but it became a mass grave. The monument was erected to permanently seal it, commemorating not only what was lost here, but everywhere."

Gizel began to murmur under his breath, staring down at the ground.

Alaska watched, unable to make out his words, shivering as a cold wind blew over the hilltop.

"There are old ghosts here," Gizel said solemnly, looking up. "Bodies not properly interned. Restless spirits."

Jakob rolled his eyes.

"I said a prayer for them, it's all I can do," Gizel said, getting onto his feet. Then they heard the sound of yells and screams, distant flashes of light illuminated the darkening sky.

"Defense officers!" Gizel warned, and the three of them ran for their lives, down the hill and into a field of wild roses.

"They're not after us," Alaska said, looking over her shoulder.

The air-ships flew right past them, disappearing into the forest. A second later Alaska heard loud, resounding thumps and the ground shook beneath her feet. "What are they doing?"

"They're a forestry team," Gizel said in relief. "They're reaping the trees which will be taken to the Capital for use."

The sounds grew more and more distant, before they faded altogether, and Alaska breathed a sigh of relief. Then she realized she couldn't see either Gizel or Jakob.

"Here!" Gizel called.

Alaska ran through the roses, their thorns tearing at her, and burst out into a clearing. Jakob was lying on the ground, thrashing wildly. His eyes were shut, his face screwed up into a look of incredible pain. Gizel stepped away, removing his jacket.

"Give me your dagger, Alaska."

Alaska stared in shock at Jakob and quickly handed him her dagger.

"What's wrong with him? What happened?"

"He hasn't had the cure pills for a long time, none of us have," said Gizel.

Alaska knew that, she felt the sickness gnawing at her insides, but forced the feeling to the back of her mind, knowing there was nothing they could do until they found other protestors with the cure pills or Pomander's Lid. She wondered why she was not thrashing on the ground in excruciating pain like Jakob.

"It's not the plague, it's withdrawal from the medication. It can cause pain, then brief blackouts," said Gizel, ripping open the inner lining of his jacket. "Then death."

Alaska felt nothing but terror at the thought of Jakob dying. Jakob could not die, there was no way she was going to let that happen.

"What do we do? What do I do?" Alaska asked.

"Nothing," said Gizel, as he pulled out a small plastic bag.

Alaska saw a flash of red, as he removed a cure pill from it. There were five inside.

"You've had..." Alaska said, bewildered, but Gizel was already leaning over Jakob and shoved the pill down his throat.

Jakob attacked him, and Alaska ran forward, pulling Gizel a safe distance away, as Jakob sat up, gasping and sputtering. Gizel shoved the plastic bag into his pocket, and looked Alaska in the eye with a hard expression.

"Don't tell him about the pills and don't ask questions."

Alaska opened her mouth, but then shut it and nodded, though she felt a thousand questions burning on the tip of her tongue. Jakob looked at the two of them, shaking. He looked embarrassed and frustrated, but most of all he looked extremely tired, dark shadows under his eyes.

"Come on, Jakob," Gizel said gently. "Let's find ourselves a campsite."

****

When they entered the forest it looked like carnage. Severed stumps were scattered among the few survivors, many of which had broken, ripped branches. Splintered bits and pieces of the trees that had been taken littered the ground, oozing with thick sap. The air was saturated with a strange, sharply metallic burnt smell. Small, wide-eyed rodents skittered over the ground, unsure what they had just witnessed. Jakob stood still, a sad look on his face. Alaska started towards him, but Gizel was faster and reached him first. He touched Jakob on the shoulder.

Jakob started off quickly, "Let's get the hell out of here before they come back."

"Is...is what happened to Jakob going to happen to us?" Alaska asked as she and Gizel walked out of earshot, behind Jakob.

"Yes, but not yet. He is particularly dependent on the pills," said Gizel. "Some...become very addicted to them. They cannot live without them for very long. He's not the worst. I knew of a protestor who died after only two days."

"What about those Cure pills in your jacket?"

"They're for emergencies, Alaska. I brought them with me from the facility."

"But whe ..."

Gizel shook his head, and Alaska saw they had come to an untouched clearing with a stream running through it. Jakob stopped, tasting the water.

"Brackish," he said, turning to face them.

Gizel sighed and turned away. He picked up a flat stone he'd found along with a much smaller oblong, sharpened stone. "Alaska," he called and she walked over.

"Where we've been traveling so far there hasn't been many people, but we're going to have to head into towns sooner or later," Gizel said. "If we get separated or lost, we'll need to be able to communicate. We'll need to be able to leave a quick message, which Defense can't decipher. The protestors don't always use standard language to communicate. Too easy for Defense to read. Sometimes they use a much older language called Desertpic."

"I've never heard of that."

"It's not taught in the Capital. It's not recognized or known by Defense." He started to etch with the oblong stone against the flat stone. "This is your name. That can be your calling card."

She watched as he carved a small winged creature.

"A bird," Alaska said. "Some say they aren't just mythical, they actually existed once, long before Defense's time."

"Aye, and some say Pomander's Lid is a castle floating in the sky," Gizel said. "Air-ships are the only birds, Alaska. That symbol stands for your first name. It's the same symbol as winter."

"What's Jakob's?" she asked suddenly, looking up at him, and then frowned. "Jakob, what's your last name?"

"It doesn't matter," Jakob said, his voice suddenly dark and wary.

"I'll show you Jakob's and mine," Gizel said.

They went through them and then settled down. Alaska could hear nighttime sounds, but it was too dark to see anything. *A Defense air-ship could be above our heads now blending in with the stars and the clouds*, Alaska thought. *We wouldn't know until it was too late.* She froze, hearing footsteps behind her. She turned her head, and saw Jakob. He still looked uncomfortable and on edge after what had happened earlier. She wondered if she should say something to him about it, tell him it was alright, or nothing to be ashamed about. Or tell him about Gizel's hidden Cure pills. She glanced towards Gizel, already asleep, the bag still safely hidden in his pocket. She felt the gnawing pain again, sharper than ever. She wouldn't steal them, she thought firmly. Jakob sat down beside her. She turned her head, smiling at him and Jakob stared back with a conflicted expression. Alaska could still see pain in his hazel eyes, still lingering from earlier. There was something else there though, something that she didn't know, but left her unable to speak and unwilling to look away.

"What did you two do anyway?" Jakob asked suddenly, breaking their long silence, "How did you bring me back?"

Alaska looked down and lied, "Nothing. You just sort of woke up again."

Jakob was silent, but she doubted he believed what she'd said, and knew he was probably wondering why she was lying. There were only three of them. It seemed wrong to keep secrets from one another, especially about something that big, but then again, Alaska thought, if she was thinking about stealing the Cure pills, even for a second, what would Jakob do with that knowledge?

"Do you think there's anything out there?" Alaska asked, quickly changing the subject and pointing up to the sky, a dark swirling blue above them. "I don't mean air-ships, but beyond that, beyond the dome."

"Alien viruses, obviously," said Jakob.

Alaska shook her head, "I mean people. Or...or someone watching. I wonder if anyone tried to leave the dome after Markus Walker. Not go up into space, but just go outside and see what it's really like."

"It's impossible to leave if you don't go up," Jakob said. "There's the sea and the desert, and you know it's impossible to cross either far enough to reach the wall of the dome."

"I wish there was someone who could help us," Alaska said. Jakob looked at her silently.

"I'll do lookout tonight," he said finally.

Alaska shook her head, "It's my turn."

She sat by the edge of their makeshift camp, thinking of the times they'd had, Jakob's incident, Pomander's Lid somewhere out there. But most of all she thought of her family in Lossit.

"Ira, if you're out there, please save them."

"There's a mole in Defense," Melissa Johnson said. "I want you to find them."

Ianto looked at her in surprise. "Excuse me?"

Johnson rose from her desk, walking in circles around the chair he was sitting in, facing the second door in her office. "So far, I haven't given you a challenge, a real task. I want to see how effective you are, before you're given something...larger."

"So this is a test?"

Johnson smiled widely. "Someone has been attempting to release prisoners from the Crypts. All of their attempts have been thwarted, of course, but their identity is still unknown. I want you to find them."

"How am I supposed to find them?"

"Just keep your eyes peeled, most likely they'll be right in front of your nose. They might even try to recruit you. Report to me at the end of the day. If I'm satisfied, I might even consider moving Jamie to a better part of the Crypts and lightening his...exercise. You would like that, wouldn't you?"

****

Ianto walked down the halls in Lossit, watching people going in and out of their offices with slightly hunched backs and blank stares, communicators glued to their ears. He turned a corner and heard whispering, agitated voices: Ira's voice, and one of the other officers, Ginny, he thought her name was. They were whispering rather urgently, and he slowed down, walking softly to try to overhear what they were saying.

"...the Donnels," he heard Ira say.

"We have a plan, don't we?" Ginny replied. "Wait, I hear somebody coming."

They both stopped speaking and Ianto walked past.

"Hey, Ianto!"

He turned as Ira ran to catch up to him. There was a wary look on Ira's face. "You okay?"

"Yeh, I'm fine," said Ianto nonchalantly, wondering what the snippet of conversation he'd just overheard meant, as he saw a brief flicker of relief on Ira's face.

"I have some information for you. I found out what's behind the wall," Ira said. "The floorplans say it's part of Johnson's office. She has some sort of storage area. That's it."

The second door in Melissa Johnson's office must be the entrance to that storage area, Ianto thought. *Where the screams came from.*

"Thanks," said Ianto quickly, ideas racing through his head at a thousand miles an hour.

"Evita's waiting for us in lab 966. Tell her I'll be right there. I just need to do something," Ira said hurriedly as he sprinted away.

Ianto spotted Evita, standing in the doorway of an office sipping coffee and talking in a low voice to a fairly young, red-haired man. Ianto recognized him as the guard who had accepted Ira's bribe and let him and Ira out of Melissa Johnson's department. Ianto walked slowly towards them, listening.

"I'm not sure, but I think that might be what she's planning—"

Evita stopped as the man nodded, gesturing for her to look over her shoulder. She turned around to see Ianto watching.

Evita quickly went over to him.

"I'm sorry. I forgot we had work to do in the labs. 966 right, with Ira?"

"Who was that man?" Ianto asked, as they headed towards the lab.

"Oh, just a coworker. Why? Are you jealous?" Evita asked teasingly.

Ianto ignored her question. They got into an elevator and went down several levels to the labs. The one they were using today was in a dark, dusty space that looked as if it hadn't been touched for years.

"Should we wait for Ira?"

Evita snorted, "Johnson's pet and chief spy? I wouldn't. Don't get too close to him, he'll just use you. Treat anything nice he says or does like poison."

Ianto looked surprised. "Why are you telling me this? You're getting illegal specimens from him."

"I don't really have any other choice if I'm going to continue my experiments," Evita said. "He's just as interested in the sand-rats as I am, so he won't say anything. But I know I can't trust him with anything else. You have a choice to not trust him. You're the new kid. I don't want you to get hurt. Anyway, I don't know if Johnson will last long. It's better to be neutral, not too much on her side."

Ianto stared at Evita, taken aback by her boldness. First the unauthorized experiments. Now her blatant statement about Johnson's possible ouster. Was she the saboteur trying to release Crypt prisoners?

Evita half-smiled at him over her shoulder, "Johnson knows her position is precarious. That's why she hangs onto it with talons. She's desperate. That's why she has to find Pomander's Lid."

"Pomander's Lid?" Ianto didn't know why, but the name sounded familiar.

"Some sort of protestor Eden. The council is getting more and more desperate to find it. They say there is a weapon hidden inside that'll destroy us all and the trigger-happy savages are going to use it."

They stepped inside lab 966. Evita set a flask of almost clear, slightly grayish liquid on the metal lab table and quietly said, "Just don't forget Johnson doesn't care about anybody except herself. That boy Philip she drags after her, that boy she calls her son, he's not. He was the child of some Mudflat residents who got too brash. She renamed him and pretended he'd been hers from the beginning. She even took him to his parents' execution in the main square with her and slapped him when he started crying."

Evita paused, letting her words sink in, "She's not going to protect you if you aren't useful. The moment you are no longer useful, you'll meet the knife, and that time comes without you even realizing it. Ira...Ira has much the same method, in his own way." Evita went silent for a moment, a wistful look on her face, before saying, "I think she's going to ask you to do something for her."

She already has, Ianto thought. *To find traitors like you.*

Evita was about to say more, and then stopped, raising her hand. Ianto heard the muffled sound of screaming from beyond. There was a metallic, rattling noise from outside the room, a scraping across the floor.

"Sand-rats," Evita said.

"Sand-rats?" said Ianto, confused.

Suddenly one of the vents in the room near the door burst open, and they swarmed into the room, their eyes glowing in the shadows. Ianto jumped onto a table, along with Evita, as the room was flooded.

"They're mine!" Evita said, horrified. "No, wait, not all of them."

"Not all of them?"

"No," Evita said.

"Then whose are they and why are they out?"

The grotesque things began to scrabble up the table legs. The only way to the door was blocked.

"I'm going to have to jump down to get to the door and open it," Evita shouted above the squeaky din of the rats.

"They'll eat you alive!" Ianto yelled, seeing their many sets of bared, sharp teeth.

They were up on the table, moving quickly, much faster than normal rats. Ianto kicked one away with his boot, but four more followed.

"The chemicals, one of them should corrode them," Evita said desperately, jumping off the table.

She waded through the horde of sand-rats to the shelves, and grabbed a bottle. She screamed in pain as they crawled up her, biting. Ianto jumped off the table, trying to knock them off her. She threw the bottle and it shattered on the floor, a thick gray liquid pooled on the ground and spread. The sand-rats shrieked in panic and ran from it, except for the ones on Evita. One sank its teeth into her neck. Ianto grabbed it, tearing it free from her neck. The thing thrashed in his hands, biting him once before he crushed it and tossed it to the ground. He looked down at his arm, looking for where it had bitten him, but there was nothing. It was as if he had never been bitten. Evita collapsed on the ground, thrashing about, unable to speak, choking on her own blood. Ianto tried to move her out of the room, but the chemical created horrible fumes which made him sick, and he sank to his knees. A horrible, gut-wrenching pain filled his body, as he lay among the defunct sand-rats, gasping for breath, feeling as if every bit of him was being slowly burned and melted away along with the sand-rats. As his sight began to fade, Ianto made out an image of the lab door suddenly swinging open and Ira entering, before everything turned black.

"**W**e will never forget."

He remembered sitting by the window of a house and seeing his parents talking in the garden. He'd risen to his feet, crossed to the door even though he knew it would be locked. It was locked. Everything was always locked...

"We will never forget."

One day he'd risen to his feet and crossed to the door, expecting it to be locked as usual. It wasn't locked! Somehow, miraculously, his parents had forgotten to lock it. He'd gone to the second door in the living room and turned the doorknob. There in front of his eyes was a stairway to a room in the attic, a secret room his parents had never told him about...

"We will never forget."

A room he no longer remembered. The only shard of memory he could recall was turning the doorknob, climbing halfway up the stairs and the sound of his father's shout. Then he remembered he was suddenly back in his room again, locked away and not let out until that last day, that day...

"They will be remembered!"

Ianto opened his eyes, and found himself in Johnson's office, slumped in a chair. How in the world had he gotten there, he wondered, when the last thing he remembered was falling unconscious on the lab floor. There had been sand-rats and a heavy, choking cloud of chemicals. He still smelled it, even though it was gone. He rose unsteadily onto his feet and walked over to an unshuttered office window. He stared out at a crowd of officers, chanting in high voices. He decided to join them and entered the rotunda. He caught sight of Melissa Johnson, addressing the crowd beneath white and red banners.

"Whoever is responsible for this attack is not a human being. They are an insane monster. Only a creature bent on destroying us and everything civil in this world could have created these monstrosities and unleashed them," Johnson said. "The sand-rats were designed to kill, they had a poison in their bite that breaks down their victim's vital organs. If you have seen anything suspicious, report it immediately. I know we are strong. We cannot be broken. The monster will be hunted down and pay until their blood stains the main square red."

The crowd dispersed and Ianto made his way to her. "What happened?"

She turned, surprised to see him. "You were with Evita during this sand-rat attack."

"I was," Ianto said. "How—"

"Ira brought you to me. You were unconscious, but uninjured, and I thought it best not to send you to the hospital wing. There was too much of a risk of your identity being discovered and leaked. We both know that would be your death."

"Yes," Ianto said, relieved he hadn't been taken there.

He'd never been to a hospital, having never fallen sick or been seriously injured, but he'd heard enough about them to not want to go. "So where's Evita? Is she still in the hospital wing?"

"She's dead," said Johnson coolly.

Ianto stared at her in shock, "What?"

"Were you not listening? The sand-rats were designed to kill," Johnson snarled. "She was a very efficient worker, too," she huffed. "It will be difficult to replace her."

Johnson scowled at him. "And I suppose you are no step closer to finding this monster. Whoever did this is also responsible for the attempted Crypt break-outs."

With that Johnson walked away. Ianto's eyes scanned the crowd. There was one conspicuous absence. Ira Graye. Ianto slipped away, going in search of Ira. Ira had something to do with all of this, Ianto was sure of it. He remembered Ira whispering with Ginny in the hall as he passed and his strange reaction, as if he hadn't wanted Ianto to overhear their conversation. What had Ira been up to? What was Ira hiding? Ianto sped up, running down several corridors past bewildered workers until he reached the elevators going down to the cellar. He stepped inside, and immediately a light switched on, then flickered out. He waited for it to flicker on again and then pushed the down button. It hurtled downward, shaking dangerously on ancient cables. He clung to the bars lining the wall. It stopped, but the doors didn't open.

"Let me out," he told the computer.

"Access denied. The cellar has been temporarily sealed because of a chemical spillage."

"My name is Ianto Ambrose and you will let me out!"

The doors clicked open.

"Thanks," he said, still unsure what to make of the computer's strange compliance. He stepped out, finding himself in front of three people in bio-hazard suits.

They whipped around in unison. One of them pulled out a stun gun, pointing it at him and firing. He ducked just in time, stumbling backwards into the elevator and punching the up button. The doors quickly shut as the elevator hurtled upward. He got off on the ground level and ran. He heard the dinging sound of the elevator next to his as it too reached the ground level, and he quickly looked around for a hiding place, spotting a door. He threw it open and slipped inside to find himself in a cramped, dark closet. He listened, holding his breath.

"It's okay, he's with us," Ira's voice pleaded.

"You trust him? I saw him. He was at Boyd's execution!" said a young man's rough voice.

"You're one to talk," Ira's voice, speaking very icily.

Silence fell for a moment, before he heard a female voice for the first time, "So that was you, Owen, that let the sand-rats out?"

"I thought both of you did it, Ginny," Ira said, sounding puzzled.

"I thought it was both of you," said Ginny.

"I had no part in it!" said Ira quickly.

"No part in it?" Owen sounded incredulous. "Didn't you say you needed a distraction to get the Donnels out?"

"I didn't mean a slaughter!" Ira said angrily. "I didn't want those people to die, Owen!"

"What do you care about their deaths?" said Owen, also sounding angry. "Are you starting to feel compassionate, or something else? Or is this about your ex-girlfriend? Was she worth more than the lives of all the protestors she interrogated and executed?"

"Don't talk to me about Evita," snapped Ira. "They're human beings, Owen. They're you and me. I don't have to like them."

"Oh, please, Ira, don't go on about moral high ground again, or I'll be sick." It was Ginny. "They were killers."

"Okay, they're just like Owen, then," snapped Ira.

Owen said something in a low tone Ianto couldn't understand, and when Ira spoke next, his voice shook with rage. Ianto half-expected to hear the sound of Owen being punched next, but that didn't come.

"Don't ever say that to me again, Owen! Don't you dare!"

"We're wasting time." Ginny was clearly trying to calm things down. "Where's the boy? We should stun him and take him to the facility before he gets a chance to report us."

"He's hiding. I saw him go inside a closet," Owen said. "He's just some gutless newbie."

"Well, what are we waiting for?" Ginny asked.

"Ginny, he won't tell," Ira said. "Leave him be."

"How do you know that? How can you keep telling us that?" Ginny asked, "How can—?"

"Let me get a word in edgewise," said Ira calmly. "His name is Ianto Ambrose. Ambrose."

A silence ensued, finally punctured by Owen. "Is he their son?"

"I think he's more than that," Ira said. "The point is we can not kidnap him, or hurt him, and we definitely CAN NOT KILL HIM. Understood, Owen?"

"Still, can we trust him?" Ginny sounded uncomfortable.

"Ginny, he's their son."

"I nearly shot him," Owen said. "How do we know if we let him walk out of the closet, he won't go straight to Johnson?"

"I'll talk to him," Ira promised. "No more killing, understood?"

He was talking to them as if they had only made a small mistake, Ianto thought. Like kids who had been playing with their food and now had to stop.

"Only if I can avoid it," grumbled Owen.

"I mean it," Ira said, a threatening edge to his voice, though it remained calm.

"It was wrong of Owen, Ira, I know that," Ginny said, "But aren't you being a bit harsh? They were mon—"

"Ginny," said Ira, in a very finalizing tone.

"They killed everyone, Ira, everyone," she said firmly.

"I know, and I'm sorry, I'm so sorry, but we've got to think about the other people trapped here, the other people who could die," said Ira. There was the sound of receding footsteps.

A moment later Ianto jumped back as the door of the closet was opened and Ira peered in, no sign of Ginny and Owen.

"What are you going to do now you know?" asked Ira, letting Ianto out.

"Evita's dead."

"I know."

"You killed her," Ianto said.

A funny look passed across Ira's face before he said, "No, I didn't. Defense provoked Owen, and I...I assisted." Ira sighed deeply. "I should have told him what sort of distraction. Sometimes I forget how vulnerable Owen is."

"Vulnerable?" Ianto held back a snort. "You talk about them so nonchalantly, when your "friends" are a pack of psychopaths."

"No, they're not," Ira's voice was very defensive. "War paints things in black and white. They're just fighting on their side, but they went too far."

"There's no war."

"There is for us," Ira looked at Ianto for a long time. "I asked you to keep silent when it was necessary, Ianto. Do that now. Don't tell Johnson. You know what she'll do if you tell."

Ianto wanted to object. He hadn't known what "silence" meant at the time, and never thought it could mean this. But he didn't object, just stared back at Ira with an annoyed expression.

"You won't tell Johnson," Ira said firmly, before turning the corner, and disappearing out of sight.

In the morning they left the forest. The terrain changed
to desert, a long expanse of dry, mountainous land and
scorching heat that seemed to suck all the water out of Alaska.
Eventually the land began to change with bushy undergrowth and
sparse groves of trees surrounding the edge of a settlement ahead
with the river snaking through it.

"I'll see if there's a way around," Jakob said.

Gizel yelled after him, "We shouldn't split up!" But he didn't
stop. Alaska started to run after him as he disappeared around a
boulder, but Gizel called her back.

"Let him go," Gizel said.

"He's so maddening! He better take care of himself," Alaska
said, gritting her teeth. "If he gets himself caught..."

"Jakob may be maddening, but he's not an idiot," Gizel said.
"He's been out here before, he knows the land."

"He said he was captured out here," Alaska said.

"Yes. He ran away from the Capital after his house was attacked
and his parents killed, but Defense caught up with him again.
After that, Ira saved him from the Crypts."

"Why did they go after his parents?"

"That is all Jakob ever told any of us, Alaska. Well, besides the
fact Ira couldn't save his sisters who were also imprisoned in the
Crypts."

Gizel paused, then opened his mouth to say something
else when there was a soft rustling and the sound of branches
snapping. Gizel went perfectly still, and Alaska stared out into

the undergrowth, trying to see the source of it. A strange creature lunged out of the undergrowth. It was a small, squirrel-like animal with a disproportionately large, triangular head. It charged towards them. As it moved, it ballooned out its body, expanding to the size of a human before leaping forward and nearly bowling Alaska over. She immediately ran, hearing Gizel pounding through the brush behind her. She swerved around several trees, and then stopped, spun around and realized Gizel was gone.

"Gizel?" she whispered, but the world was deathly silent.

Then she heard a sound, the sudden snap of a branch behind her. She turned around and saw the creature standing fifteen feet away from her. It began to charge towards her, and panic filled her. She looked into the animal's glassy eyes, and saw only a frantic mania.

Stop! she thought manically. *Please, stop!* She held up one hand. The creature skidded to a halt seven feet away, and turned abruptly, leaping into a tree and catching a mouse. It ripped the mouse apart in a spray of blood and she turned away, finding herself face-to-face with Gizel.

"Get down," Gizel said quickly, "Get down before it sees you."

"It already did," Alaska said, mystified about why it had chosen to go after the mouse instead of her, but she dropped down to the ground, watching it make quick work of its prey.

It was still in the tree when suddenly it fell off the branch onto the ground, dead. Alaska stared at the downed creature in shock. Then she heard voices and a group of people emerged from the undergrowth holding lasers. They all seemed to be quite young, dressed in Defense uniforms. Gizel glanced at Alaska briefly, holding his breath as one of them kicked the creature's body.

"Thought it was a protestor. Is this a good spot? Give them a good show?"

"Maybe we shouldn't do this..."

"Don't be a girl, Yuri Evers. Besides, Hemming said we could do whatever we liked with Vermin, didn't he? Get Vermin out of the car, Asher."

Gizel's eyes grew wide. "Alaska, get out of here," he whispered.

"What?" Alaska asked, watching as one of them disappeared back into the undergrowth.

More people were coming, mostly women and a few small children, not dressed in Defense uniforms, but in dusty, worn civilian clothes, picking through the foliage and talking in gossipy voices.

"Get out of here now," Gizel said. "I'll create a distraction."

"This better be a good one," said one of the newcomers, a woman who looked to be in her mid-twenties in a pale blue dress, sitting down on a stump. The officer who had ordered Asher away winked at her.

"No," Alaska whispered under her breath. "I'm not leaving you, especially not to them."

Asher returned, leading a disheveled hand-cuffed man in a shabby lab coat. There was a metal cap in one of his hands.

"Don't look, Alaska," Gizel tried to shield her view, but she forced him away, watching as Asher chained him to a tree and placed the cap on his head as he thrashed about.

The one who objected, Yuri, turned his head away as Asher snapped several buttons on the cap and it tightened around the man's head till his face was contorted in pain. Then it started to glow. Gizel weakly repeated for Alaska to look away, but she didn't as the man's screams reverberated around the forest. She felt sick.

"Alaska..." Gizel said, but he'd given up.

The chains broke, and like a matchstick, the man snapped and fell to the ground in a heap. The cap cracked and fell away, taking his head with it, leaving a blackened stump behind. A small scream escaped from Alaska's lips as the watching crowd began to clap. Asher whipped around, staring into the undergrowth.

"I thought I heard something."

Alaska held her breath as Gizel froze beside her. *Don't look. Please don't look*, she thought.

"I just thought..." Asher stepped towards where she and Gizel were hiding.

"Boys!"

Alaska turned her head to see a red-haired man, also in a Defense uniform, walking towards them.

Her mouth fell open as she recognized the man as the same one who had killed Mr. Robinson and been in the alleyway after her escape from the Defense truck.

"Come on," the red-haired man said. "You've had your fun. Hemming expects you to do some work, too."

Asher reluctantly turned away, following the others who had already disappeared in the tall undergrowth. The red-haired man lingered for a moment, his eyes scanning over Alaska and Gizel's hiding place, and then he followed the others until he was out of sight. Cautiously, Alaska and Gizel rose and ran. She knew how close they'd come to being caught. What had happened to the man in the lab coat was what they would have done to her, and could still do to her family if she couldn't get them out. She was more determined than ever to get to Pomander's Lid and get them help.

"Wait," Alaska stopped briefly, "should we bury him?"

Gizel vehemently shook his head. "They'll know then somebody was here. Most likely they'll come back to burn what's left later."

She looked back at the figure. He was barely visible now. "He was wearing a lab coat," Alaska said. "He seemed to be...some sort of scientist, or something. Why did they kill a scientist? He could help find a permanent cure."

Gizel looked incredulously at Alaska, "Do you still really

think Defense is interested in finding a permanent cure? Why fix something that helps maintain their control over us? I don't think Defense is interested in scientific innovation unless it gives them more control. They have said a cure is impossible, and they will make sure that is so."

Alaska remained silent and a funny look crossed Gizel's face.

"You seemed to know the red-haired officer."

"Not really."

"Who is he to you?" Gizel asked, and she realized the look was suspicion.

"Gizel!" Alaska said shocked, "You don't think I'm a spy?"

Gizel sighed, settling down on a tree stump to rest his leg. "You don't live as long as I have, Alaska, by assuming anything."

"Well, if you really must know, I saw him...murder someone I knew," Alaska snapped. Gizel's eyes scanned her face, as if x-raying her.

Then he finally said apologetically, "I'm sorry, Alaska, but I had to make sure."

"You two!"

Alaska whipped around and saw Jakob running towards them.

Blood soaked his sleeve and a feeling of dread overwhelmed her as she wondered what had happened now.

"Damn spider-snake-rat thing," said Jakob in an irritated voice. "Mouthful of little teeth."

"Never mind that," said Gizel, looking relieved it was nothing more. "What did you find?"

"We can avoid most of the towns, but there's no way of avoiding Enders, and if we go that way we'll have to cross a mountain range."

"I'll take that option," Gizel said, adding under his breath, "I've had enough close calls for today."

Ianto stood outside Melissa Johnson's office. *I don't have to say it is Ira, Owen or Ginny,* he thought. *I can tell her it's somebody else. One of the other officers.* Maybe it would give him some time to figure out a way to free Jamie...with Ira's help. Ianto swiped his ID bracelet across the entrance panel, announcing his arrival, but there was no answer. He slid his access card in a slot by the door.

"Access denied."

He paused and then remembered his encounter in the elevator. "Computer, let me in. Ianto Ambrose."

The door slid open. Ianto stepped inside. The room was empty. On the desk was an empty white metal box. It should have held Evita's ashes, but they had been discarded immediately by the hospital wing. The box would only be a symbol, with Evita's name engraved on the bottom. He glanced at the second door. For once it wasn't covered up. The screams had stopped. What had stopped them? Why had they begun? He moved towards the door, and it suddenly opened. Melissa Johnson stood in the doorway. She glanced at him, looking surprised.

"I would say come in, but you seem to have done that already."

The door slid shut behind her as she slipped past him, clicking a button on the white metal box on her desk.

Panels slid out from the sides, clicking across the top of it like a puzzle box. Johnson put it away on a shelf, for the funeral later.

"What's behind that door?" Ira asked, pointing.

Johnson's eyes narrowed, before she replied, "Maybe when you return, I'll tell you."

"Return from where?" Ianto looked at her in confusion.

"Walk with me."

He fell into step with Johnson, following her down the hallways of Lossit. He realized where they were going.

"The Crypts," Ianto said. "Why are we going to the Crypts?"

"I thought you might want to see Jamie," Johnson said with a wide, mysterious smile.

Ianto frowned, trying to figure out what she was doing.

Before he could respond she said, "I have an assignment for you, a more permanent assignment than any of the jobs you've been doing recently. If you do this, nobody will ever want you dead again. You will be free to walk around Lossit as you please, or leave it, if that's what you want. You'll be a hero to the Defense council, a testament to your country."

Ianto remembered Evita's warning before her death. They descended the steps of the Crypts and Johnson flashed her bright red access card for several loitering guards to check, then stopped in front of the door to Jamie's cell.

"Ira Graye," Johnson said, turning to face him.

"What?" Ianto stared at her. Johnson just smiled.

"Did you think you could keep your little meeting with Ira from me? He's been responsible for all of this, hasn't he? And you decided to keep him secret. You had no intention of telling me who the real mole was when you came into my office. I can see it all over your face. How touching."

"I—"

"Don't worry, you're not in trouble," Johnson went on sweetly. Ianto gave her a quizzical look.

"No," Johnson said. "I was only testing you. I've been using him for years, nearly since he first came to work for us as a young child. Usually no harm comes out of it. I pretend to give him a lot more power than I do, but sometimes things slip through the cracks," Johnson's face twitched. "Ira hunts down the traitors and corruptible in Defense. He works better than any secret agent. He and his mother are one and the same, both two-faced, the very worst type of protestor."

"So he doesn't know you're using him?"

"Of course not," Johnson said impatiently. "He has no willing part in it. And he won't know when you do the same."

"What do you want me to do?"

"Ira trusts you," Johnson said, smiling slightly, "and there's something I need you to convince him to do *outside* of Lossit. If you ask him, he will do it."

Ianto was silent, and Johnson tapped the door. A panel opened in it, revealing a small window. Jamie was lying asleep on the floor. He looked small and battered, his skin hugging his bones. Somebody had crudely chopped his hair. The back was buzzed, revealing dark bruises on his neck.

"Everyone thinks he's dead, including his parents," said Johnson softly. "It doesn't have to be this way. If you do what I ask, I will release him."

"Winter!" in Alaska's dream she had flown off the slope and been trapped in the dark shadows which were now screaming the name in her head with one voice, over and over again.

She tried to force the voice back, but it repeated, growing more and more shrill. She saw a tiny, rounded door painted bright white, with the initials A.N.D emblazoned on it in black. It seemed to be expanding out of the wall, trying to swallow her, trying to pull her...

"Winter!" the voice shrieked.

"No!" Alaska screamed, but she couldn't escape the door.

She awoke, and jumped to her feet, sweaty and shaking. There was no sign of Gizel or Jakob. She didn't dare call their names for fear a Defense patrol might hear her. Instead, she fought her way through thick undergrowth, looking for them. She soon saw them ahead of her, talking.

"You must know if she finds out it changes everything," said Gizel. "She is from the Capital, you know."

"I don't care," Jakob said, a little too sharply and quickly. Alaska knew whatever they were talking about, Jakob did care.

"It doesn't matter to me. I'm not going to hide who I am, I'm not ashamed of it."

"Of course not, I only meant..."

A branch snapped beneath Alaska's foot. Jakob and Gizel turned suddenly.

"Hello," Alaska said, emerging from the undergrowth.

Gizel turned to her, but Jakob stocked off, adjusting the makeshift bandage he'd wrapped around his injured arm.

"Is something wrong?" Alaska asked.

Gizel just smiled weakly at her, shaking his head, and she thought of the secret they both were keeping from Jakob. Could he and Jakob be keeping secrets from her as well? The idea annoyed her, and as she and Gizel caught up with Jakob, she watched the two of them suspiciously, analyzing every glance they shared. A mountain range came into view up ahead, beyond the high stone wall of a city.

"Larchhuller Mountain Range," Gizel said, pointing.

"Maglerite," Jakob countered and Gizel flashed Jakob a wary look.

"Only some very extreme protestors call it Maglerite, Jakob. This is not about returning to the old days of Magler, this is about freeing ourselves of Defense."

They stopped in front of the twisted and mostly useless open gates of Enders. Beyond them Alaska could see a bit of the streets and houses, and rising above them, a mountain range that seemed miles away. The river ran straight past through a canal, splitting the city in half as it did the Capital far behind them, but it stopped at the mountain's base, forming a small lake in its shadow.

"Won't we be breaking away from the water if we cross the mountains?" Alaska asked Gizel, who shook his head.

"Not very long ago the river cut straight through. There were no mountains," Gizel said. "That's a man-made mountain range that cut the river short, stemming it here in an artificial lake. It was supposed to be a territorial boundary, though there's long been speculation that there is a more sinister aspect to it," Gizel added darkly. "Whatever it's meant for, the public can cross over, though there'll be security cameras and a heavy Defense presence."

"What's our plan then?" Alaska asked.

Gizel said regretfully to her, "I'm sorry, but I honestly don't know. It's risky, but I doubt people this far out from the Capital will recognize us on sight. We just need to avoid Defense."

"That'll be easy," Jakob said sarcastically.

They walked through the gates and were stopped briefly by a group of guards. Alaska held her breath, acting as normal as she could until the guards let them through. It was a battered city and Alaska was struck immediately by the oddity of the buildings. They were so different from the ones she was accustomed to in the capital, the high, towering monoliths of the city center, the shanties of the outer neighborhoods, and the elaborate mansions of the Goldcage. Here every outlandish building looked as if it had been made out of rusty metal wicker, forming oddly spiraling and curving towers. Bridges of the same strange material linked certain buildings together, running high above brick streets inset with gold. Alaska noticed that in many places were empty crevices, where there should have been gold, but it had been pried up. The buildings were dirty and laundry hung on cables beneath the bridges. They passed by the hulking remains of a train station once fashioned totally out of glass. Several of the panels had been broken, and mice seemed to be using it as an ideal nesting spot. Jakob looked about as they passed through the streets, a wistful expression on his face. Alaska watched him silently, wondering how someone could look so fond of such a nightmarish place. He was walking a bit ahead of her and Gizel. He seemed as if he knew where he was going.

"Have you been here before?" she asked.

"Yes..." Jakob said guardedly. "I grew up near here, and sometimes my parents and I would visit. It hasn't changed at all."

Alaska looked at Jakob in shock. "You're a...how did you end up in the Capital? This place...this doesn't seem..."

She looked about, at the people, who seemed very disinterested in them, and had a horrible air about them of rot and brokenness. She could see a few small children playing in a pit of dark water by the side of the road below bathroom windows where people were throwing out buckets of more water, containing things Alaska didn't really want to think about. Broken glass lay on the streets, people swerving around it, or crunching over it. The decay was part of life.

"How did a provincial like me end up among you capital brats? Is that what you're wondering?" asked Jakob sharply, and Alaska quickly struggled to assure him that wasn't what she meant, which he quickly interrupted by saying, "Don't apologize. I know that's what you were thinking. You won't hurt me, I'm used to it. I was "lucky" enough to have an uncle who was a Defense officer. He got my family permission to move to the Capital when I was twelve."

"Oh," said Alaska. "So you've lived in the Capital for a long time."

"There's more of me here than there will ever be in the Capital," Jakob said rather coldly as his accent changed to match that of the voices all around them, and he took off one of the fingerless leather gloves she'd never seen him remove before, holding up his hand for her to see. The skin was a patchwork of cuts and old burns, but most prominent was a deep, U-shaped scar in the center. Alaska stared at his hand with a mixture of horror, anger and pain, remembering what the Speaker had done to her and wondering how many times they'd done the same to him, and worse.

"They made sure I never forgot I didn't belong."

"I'm sorry," Alaska said quickly, but he didn't reply.

He turned around to look for Gizel and she realized Gizel wasn't near them anymore. He had gone off and was talking to the children who'd been playing in the water.

"Do you know where I can find a guide?" he was asking one of them.

Jakob ran over, looking at Gizel as if he'd just gone crazy, his expression mirrored on the children's faces.

"I thought we were trying not to draw attention?" he hissed angrily in Gizel's ear. "Or should I just shoot a big giant flare into the sky screaming 'Fugitives, Come and Get Us'?"

"We can't get over those mountains on our own," Gizel said, sighing heavily. "Besides, I think Defense will think us less conspicuous if we have a good reason for wanting to cross. There's nothing on the other side except for barren desert as far as they're concerned, why should an old man and two teenagers want to go together there? If I tell them I'm an archeological enthusiast and you're my students, they'll understand that."

"But you saw what they did to that scientist back there," Alaska said, horrified.

"He was an independent scientist, working outside of Defense, and that's illegal. I'm not pretending to be a scientist, just an old enthusiast. Besides, the scientist you saw die was interested in something a little different than I would ever pretend to be," Gizel said. "I don't think Defense has much of a problem with artifacts hundreds of years old, Alaska. I know you've been to museums on school trips. The far-distant past, and the Plague are safe topics as far as Defense is concerned."

"I don't like the idea of working with somebody," Jakob said and Gizel stared at him rather sadly.

"You've never liked that idea, Jakob."

One of the children, a girl of about twelve, strode over.

"My uncle is a guide, but he'll want something in return," the child said solemnly.

Gizel grabbed Jakob's arm, dragging him out of the child's hearing. The three of them huddled together and Gizel said, "I need that pendant of yours."

"What?" Jakob said, taking a step back as his accent changed back to the Capital.

"The chain is gold," Gizel said. "It's all we can offer them for a guide."

"The pendant doesn't come off the chain," Jakob said and Gizel sighed.

"I know, Jakob."

Jakob gave Gizel a murderous look. "I'm not giving it to you," He hissed.

"Then we can all stay here," Gizel said harshly. "Defense will find us and we will be killed. Is that what you want? To come all this way to die...for Alaska to die?"

Jakob glared at him.

"Jakob, just give it up, please," Alaska said. "You don't need it."

He whipped around, turning on her, his eyes huge. "Why don't you give up something then? That dagger maybe? Sweeten the deal?"

"Leave her alone, you know that's worthless to these people," Gizel said. "But they could do with the gold from the chain."

"I'm not giving it up!" Jakob said to him. "Don't you get that, old man?"

Gizel stepped away, facing the child. "We can't give payment until we know you can deliver."

The girl nodded, seeming to have expected this. "This way."

They followed her to one of the tallest buildings and up a winding narrow stone staircase to a short door at the top. There was a doorway with a metal shutter and the girl knocked, before the metal shutter was briefly slid back, and an emerald green eye appeared.

"Tourists, uncle," the girl said.

The door opened and they all entered into a tiny set of rooms. Through a doorway Alaska could see a makeshift kitchen and a woman bending over a stove-top. Two children were sitting on the floor, playing with an old television set, switching between a Defense news broadcast, and some sort of reality TV show, with mace-wielding madmen chasing each other across the Capital's marina. A boy of around thirteen watched them wistfully, perched on a wooden chair and dressed from head to toe in mourning white. Alaska noticed Jakob watching the boy silently, an odd look in his eyes.

"Billy, Jolene, stop doing that!" the woman yelled from the kitchen-bath, sounding irritated, "You know that uses up way too much electricity. The blackouts have only just stopped."

"Blackouts?" Alaska said, turning to the girl in bewilderment. "Why are there blackouts? That's rare these days."

It was only after the words had left her mouth she remembered the kerosene lamp, and what Gizel had told her about electricity outside of the Capital, but it was too late.

The girl stared at Alaska as if she was crazy. "Where are you from, the Capital? We get them all the time. Punishment from Defense whenever we do anything wrong. It happens one time or another in all of the settlements. Where are you...?"

"Excuse me, is that your uncle?" Gizel said quickly, distracting the girl and she followed his gaze to a gaunt, hawk-like man watching them.

"Oh, yeh, that's him," she said, nodding her head. "Uncle!"

The man got up and walked over, looking at all three of them with a cold expression on his face. "You want to go over the mountains?"

"Yes, we're looking for a good mountaineer," Gizel said.

The uncle stared at them, sour-faced, before responding, "All of us are mountaineers here. But why over? That's obsolete. Most people use the tunnels through the mountains these days. The Defense officers can lead you through there."

"No, I'd prefer to go over," Gizel said and the man's eyes narrowed suspiciously. He quickly added, "We prefer the scenic route."

"No one else will go with you, then. This is a dangerous whim you're suggesting, especially in this season, when temperatures are sporadic. I will only do this as we have a funeral to arrange for my son's wife," he said as he nodded towards the boy. "I will expect a great deal in return."

Gizel nodded his head, "I expected nothing less."

"Then wait the night at the tavern," he said, jabbing a finger out the window in the direction of the street outside. "I'll meet you there tomorrow morning."

"I really would like to go tonight," Gizel said and the uncle stared coldly at him. "Then you shall be going up that mountain on your own," he said, turning his back on them.

Gizel stared at Alaska and Jakob warily, then turned back to the man. "We don't have money for a room."

The man looked surprised, "You are tourists with no money?" He laughed, and then something caught his eye, and his laughter stopped, as he jabbed his finger at Jakob, "What is that? Hanging around the little boy's neck?"

Jakob's hand curled around the pendant protectively.

"I'll take that as payment," said the man immediately. "For over the mountains and for a room at the tavern."

Jakob opened his mouth, but Gizel was already nodding his head, "Very well. But we'll give it to you in the morning. The room first."

The uncle handed Gizel a few coins, "All yours." He grinned at Jakob, "I'd be careful if I were you, with an object like that hanging around my neck."

Jakob tensed, and Gizel put his hand on the teenager's shoulder.

"Thank you," Gizel said to the uncle.

The man's niece showed them out and just before the door shut behind them, he called out, "Watch yourselves, you can get lost here...so easily."

31

Ianto looked for Ira, and finally found him sitting in the hushed rotunda at a desk. He was watching as people walked past, carrying boxes of items that had been cleared from the quarters of the deceased officers, to be returned to families, or burned. Ianto walked up to him.

"How are you?"

Ira looked at him in surprise. "You were wondering how I'm doing?"

"I don't know, I thought it was the sort of thing you ask after someone's died," said Ianto. "Isn't it?"

"No, no, it was...it was only human," said Ira, a strange expression still lingering on his face. "And I'm fine."

"I want to help you," Ianto said.

Ira looked startled for a moment, then said, "Let's go down to the labs then."

Ianto followed him into an elevator and down to one of the usual labs, now eerily empty. Ianto sensed a change in Ira as they entered the room for the first time since Evita's death.

"It's safe to talk here," Ira said once they'd stepped inside, his voice calm, though he still seemed different.

"I want to help," Ianto repeated.

"You can, any time," said Ira, looking pleased.

"She knows it's you," Ianto said and Ira stared at him, shocked. "What?"

"She knows it's you. She thinks you might be involved. She's talking about interrogating you, about prosecuting you."

Ira whirled around, surveying the room, a shocked expression on his face, "But I'm not finished, I can't go back to the facility..."

It was going perfectly, all Ianto had to do was say the words. Or not, and side with Ira.

"There's a place," Ira said suddenly. "A place where we could go, and both get out of here."

****

Ira joined Ianto in the middle of a field. He examined Ianto's arm where Johnson had put the ID tag that first day, and slipped it off his arm.

"That's funny," Ira said. "Usually they meld deep into your skin before now. This one's barely clinging to the surface. It rejected you." He pulled off his dark backpack and pulled a small laser knife out of it, "Borrowed it off a friend."

Ianto eyed it distastefully. "What sort of friend? Those things are temperamental, Evita told me once."

"I completely trust the friend, I assure you," Ira said, seeming unfazed by the reference.

"Like you trust Owen?" Ianto said, and Ira's face darkened.

It had not been an easy goodbye for Ira, Ianto knew that. Why Ira felt so deeply for Owen and Ginny, he didn't know, but he remembered the goodbye in the basement of Defense. There'd been tears and hugs, a brief, hushed talk about some sort of plan, in which something called the Mariner was brought up and then he'd reminded Ira they had to go. Pulling Ira into a hug, Ginny had said over his shoulder to Ianto, "Take care of him."

An hour later, Ianto was most definitely sure Ira was going to chop his arm off.

"If I just hold it steady, nothing bad will happen, I promise," Ira assured him, switching on the fire orange line that formed the knife's blade. "There, I'm done."

Ianto stared down at the tiny flake of skin Ira had removed. He could barely make out the tracker Johnson had embedded in it.

"Come on," said Ira, starting off towards the road. "I'll throw it on a moving truck, and then we can go to the house. I have to warn my mother."

****

They entered a shabby, dark building that looked as if it might collapse with a single touch. Ianto watched as Ira's nose crinkled at the smell. A group of cloudy-eyed, skeletal figures followed them as they made their way through to the living room. Ira rested a hand on Ianto's arm just before they entered.

"Whatever happens, it's alright, just stand back and wait for me."

Ianto gave him a quizzical look.

Ira hesitated, before saying, "Sometimes she's fine, and sometimes she's not."

They had to climb a set of stairs to a small, dark room before they found her, a gray, glum, haggard woman sitting alone on a battered, overstuffed sofa beneath a large window. Ianto took in the room, bedraggled and clearly uncared for, with yellowed volumes of books lying across the dusty floor. The woman herself matched the room perfectly. A funereal image, dressed from head to toe in crisp mourning white, her stringy hair hanging around her sullen face, eyes cold and piercing as they stared down at a photograph she clutched with her thin, spindly fingers.

"Mother?"

She didn't look up, her hands continued to clutch the photograph.

"Mother, it's Ira," he said as he stepped up to her and gently tried to remove the photograph from her grasp.

"Mother, it's Ira, it's Ira, it's Ira," the woman snapped bitterly, looking up into her son's face. Ianto saw Ira cringe. "Is that all you can say, coming again and again. Fired from every job. All you can keep is a half-year position at Defense." Her hands shook violently and the photograph fell to the floor. "Sixteen years and that's what you can keep. Nothing! You're never going to be a Speaker. Sixteen years! I expected more of you, your father expects...expected more of you! Useless, stupid boy. What have you come for now? Money, is that what you want?"

"No, mother..."

Sarah Graye rose to her feet.

"Of course that's what you want, it's what you always want. Then you'll say you've met the love of your life and you're relocating together somewhere. A day, and you'll be gone, never asking me for anything again. Never seeing my face...isn't that what you're going to say to me? Who is it?" She looked past Ira, jabbing a finger at Ianto, who took several steps back. "Spit it out, you useless boy."

"Mother, I don't love..."

"Don't even say that word to me. Not again. Love my foot. It'll be a different stranger the next week, you can tell this love that from me, from your poor mother. Yes, that's what you're here for. What is it now? How much do you want?"

Ianto glanced at Ira.

"No, it's not any of that, I..." Ira shut his eyes. "I'm...leaving."

"I knew it," his mother said venomously. "Who is it? Who is it that you are leaving your mother alone for, wasting here? To leave me like your father did? Do you not care for your mother at all? Who is—"

"It's not...not like that," Ira opened his eyes, taking his mother's hand. "This isn't about one person. It's a lot of people. And I'm not leaving you. I'm leaving Defense."

"What...?" his mother froze, staring back in wide-eyed horror at her son's calm face.

"I can't do this anymore, after father died, after..." He stopped himself. "Well, you know what happened. What I did. What I made myself do. I felt...so terrible afterward. But I was set right. Defense can not continue, they're terrorizing people and driving them to violence. So several years ago, I started spying on them for the other side. For the protestors."

His mother listened silently, caught in a stupor.

"I think they've found me out," he continued. "I'm running away to officially join the protestors, but I know you'll be in trouble, even though you didn't know, so I'm asking you to come with me."

"Oh, my David..." Her voice was dreamy, absent, horrified. "David, he doesn't know what he says, does he? He doesn't mean to kill us, does he?"

Sarah Graye's stupor suddenly broke and she flew in a rage at her son. Ira scrambled backward until he was flattened against the wall.

"Get out of my house!"

"But mother..."

"You're not my son! Get out!"

"You have to come with me," Ira insisted.

She picked the photograph up off the floor and threw it at his face. He ducked, but not quickly enough, and the photograph clipped his nose. He winced in pain, clutching it. Blood dripped through his fingers.

"Please just come," he cried faintly.

"How could you? You have killed your father all over again!" she said, slapping every unprotected inch of him. "I'll skin you alive. After what the protestors did to your father...you...little..." The last word was drowned by Ira's change from pleas to screams. Ianto grabbed Ira's arm, pulling him away from the woman. As they ran back down the stairs and into the kitchen full of bewildered persons.

Ianto saw her limping weakly after them, sobbing, her eyes following them out as she shrilly screamed, "Wait, come back here...Ira, come back here!"

Out of the dark house and down several roads and alleyways, Ianto finally let go of Ira, sitting him down on a rock in the middle of an empty field by a set of train tracks and checked his face. Though his nose was still bleeding, it didn't look broken. Ira attempted to wipe his nose off on his sleeve, but mostly just smeared the blood along the side of his face.

"Here," Ianto fished a tissue out of his pocket and Ira took it gratefully.

"I have to go back," Ira said, a dazed look on his face. "I have to get her out of there. They'll kill her."

"She nearly killed you."

"No, she wouldn't have," Ira said. "She never means to hurt me. She's just angry, she's upset, she's not listening to reason. Let me go back." Ira jumped to his feet, but Ianto pushed him back down.

"You have to take me to the place," Ianto said. "If we go back and waste time, we'll be late for those people we're supposed to meet up with. Besides, what if Defense shows up? We'll be captured." Except he knew they wouldn't. Melissa Johnson wanted this to happen, to succeed.

Ira sighed, looking back in the direction of his house then got to his feet and started off away from it, mumbling, "She...she'll be alright. She can take care of herself. She'll get herself out of there. She's probably on the run now."

"That's right," Ianto said, relieved. "She'll understand she has to keep herself alive."

"Yes, yes, you're right, she'll be okay," Ira seemed to be saying more to himself than anyone else. They walked in silence, then suddenly Ira stopped. "What have I done, Ianto?"

****

Melissa Johnson stood on the glass bridge, staring out at the night. From where she stood one could see all of the city, all the way to the dark, black river that cut through it, though she wasn't looking at that. Instead she looked down at the prison a couple of streets away, the light of the dying sun illuminating the metal fortress.

"You've sent him away."

Johnson looked over her shoulder as Clement came limping down the bridge, supported by a cane. "Ianto Ambrose. Where is he going? Do you really think it's safe to let him loose?"

Johnson didn't respond.

"Is there any word on Pomander's Lid?" Clement asked and Johnson warily looked about before leaning her head close to Clement's and whispering between nearly closed lips, "No. But I have an idea."

"Do you ever think we're too harsh?" Clement asked as he too turned to stare out the glass wall at the city below.

"No. What does the Speaker of Health & Education always say? A contagion must be bled out. That is my favorite part, Clement, the bleeding," Johnson's voice was even, but her hands shook slightly.

Clement frowned. "You've been flipping the switch, haven't you, Melissa? You heard the screams? You shouldn't have put that implant..."

"I can handle hearing them," Johnson said coldly. "It's only a little pain. I know you think the Chasm and the Crypts are cruel, Clement, but both are justice plain and simple."

"Ianto is a different matter, I'm guessing, now you've incorporated him into your team?"

"Yes," Johnson's voice was even again.

"Do you think he'll lead us to it? Is that why you've sent him away?"

"You always see into my plans," Johnson smiled ever so slightly.

"How do you know he's not an imposter?" Clement asked.

"I highly doubt he is," said Johnson, "Whether he is their child biologically, or adopted is another question, but it doesn't vastly matter as long as Ira accepts him. Still, I'm running a DNA test on him all the same, using the old Defense databases to match it to that of his parents."

"And if he is their son? If it's found out you've been secretly..."

"There are many secrets in Lossit. The Council, the Chasm... this would not be the first. And when this is all over, I'll be revered, Clement."

"How will you stop Ianto from falling into the hands of other departments? All of them will want him. Some to use him, some to keep him as a sort of trophy, some to kill him." Clement stared at her pointedly.

"I'm quite sure he'll be safe," Johnson said. "My security is never lax."

Clement snorted, "I wouldn't be so quick to say that if I were you. Look at the Crypts. There's a mole somewhere, no doubt."

"You tutored me," said Johnson, smiling slightly. "If I am ineffectual, it's your failure."

"What about Hemming?"

Johnson's smile vanished from her face. "They haven't let that madwoman out again, have they?"

She looked back at the prison in the distance, her eyes wide.

"They believe Oxsana has recovered from her insanity, and I am afraid the offense of hanging Defense's flag upside down could not keep her in prison indefinitely. They released her nearly a week ago, though I'm sure you'll devise another excuse for keeping your stepdaughter locked up," Clement said.

Johnson's eyes narrowed, "I can deal with her. Don't worry."

32

The only tavern was on the other side of the city. As they walked quickly and inconspicuously as possible, Alaska saw a bright white Defense vehicle with the words Mining Company emblazoned on its side in red. A group of gray, washed-out men and women dressed in rags were crowded around it. A Defense officer looked over each member of the crowd as if they were animals, choosing a few who were then roughly hauled inside of the truck. Alaska craned her neck, trying to see better and caught a glimpse of the vehicle as it moved on, towards the twisted gates and out of the city. The crowd of people who hadn't been taken chased after it, stumbling over each other in desperation, their voices a harsh, indistinguishable chorus. The Defense officers tossed small red pouches from the windows of the vehicle, and a fight broke out as the crowd scrabbled for them. A security officer ran out of a small white cubical building that stood out amongst the wicker constructions all around it. Gizel looked around warily.

"Jakob, hide the pendant well. Make sure no one steals it."

Jakob reluctantly took off the gold chain and pendant, placing the object in his pocket. He kept one hand around it. He quickened his pace, walking a little ahead of Alaska and Gizel.

"What is that pendant?" she whispered to Gizel who shook his head.

"I don't know what it is. I suspect whatever it is, it's on a Defense black list," said Gizel. "Very valuable in illegal markets, no doubt, but very dangerous to be walking around with so obviously."

Jakob's pace slowed and they caught up with him.

"This person who gave you the pendant, Jakob, do you know where they got it from?" Gizel asked.

"No," Jakob said harshly.

They left behind the fighting and reached a dark, grimy alleyway packed with an array of people, many in strange, shabby, washed out garments. There was a tavern called the Red Wolf at the end of the alley. They entered, and a bell went off somewhere far within the building. A fat man dressed from head to toe in scarlet, with a slightly darker red skullcap and long white leather gloves ran to assist them. His accent wasn't like the other people; it was closer to the Capital. A pendant hung around his neck, bearing an odd symbol, much like Defense's ouroboros, but superimposed on the image of a dagger.

"What is that?" Alaska whispered to Jakob, as Gizel gave the man half their coins.

"The symbol of the M.O.D. He must be a servant," said Jakob.

"Who is the M.O.D?" Alaska asked, frowning in confusion.

"Overseer of the provinces, makes sure all of the towns are toeing the line," said Jakob. "Nobody you want to mess with."

The man pocketed the coins distastefully, slipped a key into Gizel's hand and pointed up the narrow, stone stairs vaguely, saying, "Room thirteen."

They climbed the stairs, reaching a wide, dusty corridor with black wallpaper hanging off the walls. Loud, rambunctious voices came out of a room across the hall where a group of shabby, shady-looking travelers were gambling. Through a grated window Alaska could see a glimpse of the entire city, and the imposingly tall mountain range beyond.

"Our room," said Gizel, inserting the key into the lock of a door that had a sloppily painted red number '13' emblazoned on it.

Room thirteen was tiny, barely eight feet by six feet. Beige paint flaked off the walls and ceiling. The only window in the room was broken and boarded up from the outside, plunging the room almost completely in darkness. Beneath the window was a metal cot with no sheets, only a worn mattress.

"We can sleep on the floor," Alaska said immediately to Jakob, "Gizel should have the cot."

"No..." Gizel started, but Jakob shook his head.

"Don't even try to change our minds, old man." Privately, to Alaska, he added in a whisper, "The bed's probably full of bugs anyway."

There was a small bathroom off of the room. It was in much the same state as the room; the lock was broken, there was little light, and all the fixtures were old and rusted, though when Alaska switched them on, they worked.

"I'm going to wash up. Don't come in," Alaska said, shutting the door.

The shower was undeniably grungy, the once white tile now a dirty brown or missing altogether, but she couldn't turn down the possibility of a shower after days trekking endlessly through forests and ruins. She found a ragged towel in a worn cabinet above the sink, and pulled a thin white curtain across the shower. As a thin trickle of dark water came out of the showerhead, she wondered what was happening in the Capital with her sister, brother, parents, Marianne. Had Ira rescued them yet? If none of this had happened, what would she be doing now? Still worrying over that stupid early acceptance letter from Defense probably, she thought. She jumped, nearly slipping as she heard a loud banging on the door.

"I need to come in. My arm's bleeding again," Jakob yelled from the other side of the door.

"Leave her alone, Jakob!" she heard Gizel say.

"I need a new bandage," Jakob yelled back. "You want me to

bleed all over the floor? I know the room could use a bit of color, but..."

"It's fine," shouted Alaska quickly, and she heard Jakob enter, ruffling through the contents of the cabinet.

"If you're not from the Capital, where are you from?"

"Winter's Gate," said Jakob. "A dark, exotic place where they cut off people's heads every Saturday."

"Really?" asked Alaska listening close to the curtain, horrified and bewildered but also mesmerized by the image.

"No, but that's what people always want to hear, isn't it?" Jakob said, and his voice grew slightly wistful as he went on. "Truthfully, we didn't cut off someone's head *every* Saturday. It was gray, glum and quiet. A mining town by the sea. Don't use up our whole water allowance, Alaska."

Alaska shut off the shower, still listening as Jakob continued.

"When I was a child, I'd go down to the water. There was something about the sea...I dunno, I can't explain it. When the waves crashed it was so forceful it nearly knocked me off my feet, but all I wanted to do was run into it, and never stop. My parents screamed at me not to go out into it because of the sharks. But I did anyway. I was just a stupid kid. I thought it'd be cool to see a shark."

She could tell by Jakob's voice that he'd loved Winter's Gate, that he missed it, no matter how gray or glum it had been. It was his home, after all, as the Capital had been hers. Was the Capital still her home? The thought had never occurred to her before it might not be. Yet now it suddenly appeared, inescapable and unnerving. She hesitated, then poked her head around the side of the curtain to see Jakob shut the cabinet. A rag-like towel was wrapped tightly around his arm wound. He looked up and froze, seeing her watching him.

"I can't ever go back to the Capital, can I?"

"When Defense is gone, nobody will stop you from going home," Jakob said firmly.

He quietly left and Alaska wondered if his answer was any better than never.

****

"Do you trust the guide?" Alaska asked Gizel, though she could already see the discomfort written on his face as he sat on the edge of the cot. Jakob paced around the room, twisting the chain of the pendant in his hands.

"Not much point to doubting him, is there?" Gizel said, sighing and staring out of the window.

"I'm starving," Jakob said finally, stopping and tossing the pendant back into his pocket.

Gizel handed him the remaining coins, "I trust you'll use it wisely."

"Coming, Alaska?" Jakob inquired. Alaska stared at Gizel with concern, but he nodded his head.

"I'll be fine. Go on."

As the door shut, Alaska heard Gizel call, "Make sure he doesn't do anything stupid, Alaska!"

"Don't worry, I won't let him out of my sight!" Alaska called back with a smile. They walked down the cobbled streets of Ender. She noticed Jakob had put his fingerless gloves back on.

"Nobody's going to mind you being from the Provinces here," she said to him and Jakob shook his head.

"No, but they'll mind I've been to the Capital. They know what the mark is, the people in my town used to call it the 'Fork.' They sometimes killed people who had it. They don't trust anyone from the Capital out here, so don't talk. Just let me."

Alaska looked around uncomfortably, half-expecting all of Ender to be staring at her menacingly, but no one paid any attention to her, and her eyes drifted instead to the commanding presence of the mountains in the distance, as she tried to think of something other than how vulnerable they were.

"We're crazy to try to cross that," Alaska said, nodding towards the mountains. "But I've always wanted to go to the top of a mountain range. When I was a little girl, I read all those legends about huge mountains, like Mt. Everest."

Jakob didn't respond and she saw a grim procession passing. People scrambled out of its way as it moved through the city, a line of white-clad mourners, bony and gray-faced. Borne atop their shoulders was a rough wooden coffin.

"Eloise Lavigne, taken from us by the Nightghosts, beasts of shadow, smoke and curiosity," a man in red was saying at the front of the procession, an ouroboros symbol hanging around his neck on a chain. "May she rest in peace."

"Wasn't it really Defense?" Alaska asked in a low voice. "Or are there Nightghosts?"

Jakob didn't respond. Alaska strangely felt a sense of tremendous pain that didn't emanate from the procession. She turned and glanced at Jakob's face. He looked stricken. She reached for his hand for a moment, then stopped herself, sticking her hands in her pockets instead.

"You didn't...you didn't know them at all, did you?"

Jakob shook his head as the last mourners passed and Alaska saw the boy who'd been at the uncle's residence, sitting alone in a chair. His head was down as he walked along in the procession.

"Is that the boy's wife?" Alaska gasped. "But he's only...thirteen or something."

"Could be younger. That's the way in the outer cities and towns. Life is all very quick," Jakob said quietly. "You never know how long it'll be. We have to bow now, Alaska."

"What?"

"Just bow."

Alaska bowed her head as a strange vehicle rolled past at the end of the procession, like a carriage from a fairytale, Alaska thought, but distorted and skeletal. It was a dark shade of gray, nearly black, its dark ornamentation hanging off its sinewy frame like drooping skin, the initials M.O.D engraved on its door. It was powered by two mechanical objects that roughly resembled horses, but sharp-edged and crude, dragging the entire contraption after them. Alaska caught a glimpse of a hunchbacked figure shrouded in a red cloak inside the carriage, attended to by a very familiar red-haired Defense officer. She quickly bowed lower, only standing up when the carriage had passed, the air ringing with the peculiar sound of clockwork long after the horses had disappeared out of view.

The crowds lining the procession rejoined into a great mass.

Alaska turned to Jakob and asked, "What about you? You're provincial, does that mean—?"

"Look, an open market," Jakob said, pointing and he quickly took off in that direction.

Alaska ran to catch up with him until they were surrounded by stalls. All sorts of items crowded them: books, food, jewelry, clothing, in a bright smorgasbord of color and sound.

Alaska stood in awe, turning in a circle to get a full view of everything. Jakob stared about cautiously as several people clad in red passed by.

"Come on, Alaska."

They worked their way through the crowd, looking at all the different items and Alaska wandered over to one stall with pendants.

"You could always get another one at some point," she said to Jakob, who watched her eying them.

"It wouldn't matter," Jakob said somberly. "And didn't I tell you about talking so much?"

Several children were clustered around the stall next to it. Alaska looked over their heads, and saw a silver-haired woman juggling white, opaque glass balls.

"I know her," Jakob said in surprise. "I saw her when I was a child."

"Let's go and see," Alaska suggested, disregarding Jakob's warning about revealing her Capital accent. She moved over to the stall while Jakob followed hesitantly.

"Who knows what we'll get?" the silver-haired woman asked the curious children surrounding her stall.

She tossed the glass balls higher and higher, until she finally let them go and they hit the ground, cracking in half neatly, an explosion of miniature air-ships with paper sails bursting from them, flying through the air above the children.

"There's a fortune in each of them," the woman announced, looking past the children, at Jakob. "Proceed if you dare."

The children reached up and caught them before they hit the ground. Alaska caught two and tossed one to Jakob.

The silver-haired woman spoke suddenly, pointing at Jakob, "You! I've seen you before. You look so familiar."

"I'm not," Jakob said gruffly.

The woman shook her head as if to clear it, stroking a tabby cat. "Perhaps not. Perhaps it was somebody else. Children come and go so quickly now. I used to see that poor girl who died so often, before the Nightghosts got her. So they say."

Alaska's eyes widened immediately, and though she knew she shouldn't speak, she couldn't help it, "Nightghosts?"

"The heartless demons," said the woman, nodding her head slightly as she leaned against the counter. "They only ever take the children."

Alaska ignored the warning look Jakob cast at her.

"Have you ever seen one?"

The silver-haired woman's eyes widened and her voice took on a low, haunted tone, dropping to a whisper. "They say only children can see the Nightghosts, Miss. They come for the children, they don't want no one else to see them."

"So...do you know of any children who have seen one?"

"Any child seen a Nightghost is marked. They'll be dead or scissored in a fortnight," the old woman whispered, barely audible.

Alaska felt a shiver run down her spine, and opened her mouth to ask what "scissored" meant, but the woman had turned away to tend to a child who wanted to buy one of the opaque glass balls. Jakob pulled Alaska away from the stall. She followed him, thinking about what the woman had told her and then noticed Jakob crumbling his fortune in his hand. She looked down at her own, which simply read: *You Will Discover The Power Within Yourself.*

"What did you get?" she asked him.

He stopped, looking at her strangely. "Just stupid rubbish. It doesn't mean anything."

"Come on, what does it say?" Alaska asked, forcing an insistent and probably far too cheery smile. Jakob sighed and tossed it over to her.

"Go on, read it. 'You will find your heart's desire.' Rubbish." Alaska looked down at the crinkled piece of paper as Jakob asked a little sharply, "Why did you ask that woman about Nightghosts?"

"I was wondering about what I saw once," Alaska said.

"Nightghosts don't exist," said Jakob, coldly. "Only Defense does. I told you not to draw attention to yourself."

"If you want to be grumpy about it, be grumpy, but I have to find out what they are," Alaska huffed. She waved the piece of paper in her hand. "Anyway, what is it?"

Jakob stared at her. "What?"

"What's your heart's desire?"

Jakob's mouth fell open and he stared at her incredulously, before starting off, shaking his head, muttering "stupid" several times under his breath. As they moved further through the crowd, the stalls changed. Now there were white and red banners bearing Defense's insignia and flags of the Nation hanging everywhere. Alaska shrunk back.

"Just act normal," Jakob whispered in her ear. "Nobody will recognize you. These people are cut off from the Capital."

Alaska stepped back, pointing over his head at a TV screen hanging in the town square. Her own face flashed back at her, though the image was grainy.

"Okay. Stay here, keep your head down," Jakob said quickly. Before she could protest he sprinted away to a food stall.

As she waited for Jakob to finish, she noticed a little girl walking by who looked slightly like Leila. She was holding up a white coat at one of the stalls and laughing as she draped it over herself. Alaska wondered where her sister was now, whether she was nearing the same fate as the man in the woods.

"Alaska?" she turned around and saw Jakob behind her, holding a package in one hand.

"Oh, you're done," Alaska said, forcing a smile. "Great, let's go back before Gizel starts worrying."

She started forward, keeping her head down.

"Wait, Alaska!" he ran, catching up with her as she walked at an abnormally fast speed. "You're crying. Why are you crying?"

"I'm not!" Alaska snapped, a little too forcefully, wiping tears away with her sleeve.

"See, you are crying."

They were interrupted by a shout. "Wait, you're that girl!"

Alaska froze as she saw an elderly man staring at her from across the street. Simultaneously the crowd of people around him stopped, looking straight at her. Then something incredible happened. There was a burst of white light, like a flash of intense sunlight in the sky. It ripped across the sky, striking the tavern like lightning. The windows of the tavern shattered and glass flew everywhere like deadly raindrops. She heard screams and started to run as the building crumbled to the ground and the open market turned into pandemonium. She cut through narrow, dark alleyways, trying to escape, trying to find Jakob who had vanished. Gizel had been inside the tavern. Was he dead? She wound through the streets, yelling out their names, though her voice was drowned out by the voices of every other desperate person calling out for their loved ones. She reached the canal and saw a narrow wooden footbridge that crossed to the other side. Perhaps Jakob had gone across to escape the chaos. She ran onto it. Suddenly it creaked and swayed dangerously, knocking her off her feet. The bridge disintegrated, half of it falling into the canal, the other half with her on it precariously suspended in the air above the dark waters. She pulled herself up onto the remaining part of the bridge and crawled along until she got to the other side of the bank where she felt confident enough to stand on her feet. That's when she saw it. A hooded cloaked figure, face hidden stood a few yards ahead of her, blocking her way.

"Go away," Alaska trembled, unable to keep the fear out of her voice as she stepped back, her hand flying to her pocket where she carried Magler's antique dagger.

The hooded figure stepped towards her and she stepped back slightly, onto the edge of the bridge. She braced herself, gripped the handrails on either side and stared about for some means of escape, but she couldn't see any.

"You were the person following me before."

"We are not people," the voice was mechanical, computerized. "We follow the trail of our own flesh, watching and waiting."

"Who are you? Just tell me who you are!"

"We are you. We come from the same."

It had nearly reached her. There was a flash of blinding light and Alaska collapsed on the ground, her head hitting it hard. She could see the ebb and flow of water around her, the bridge's metal handrail the edge of a gurney, the darkening blue sky beyond a ceiling.

"No!" Alaska screamed, scrabbling hard to keep herself conscious against the invisible force pushing hard against her.

At the same time, she heard a woman's scream, "Don't take her, please don't take her!"

The scream was somewhere nearby. Someone was trying to help her, if only she could get free. Alaska tried pinching herself, tearing at the ground, but she was immobilized. A flash of metal appeared briefly in her vision as she scratched her fingernails against the metallic surface of the bridge in a final attempt to keep herself grounded, and then, for a moment, she saw a ring of demonic, steel faces staring at her before all light faded from her sight.

"Wearing yourself out won't wake her up any faster, Jakob."

Pacing feet. The sound came distantly, as if through a tunnel, but it was growing louder and clearer.

"This is my fault."

"She's waking up."

"Alaska?"

Alaska woke up sprawled on the ground, the sun shining down on her face. Jakob was kneeling on the ground beside her, his face paler than she'd ever seen it.

"Gizel!" Alaska said immediately, sitting bolt upright. She saw Gizel nearby, propped against a tree, and realized he'd been the second voice she heard.

He was coughing badly, but he seemed fine otherwise.

"What happened? We just found you unconscious on the bridge," Jakob said.

"I don't know...something attacked me." Alaska struggled to remember, but she couldn't. "I just sort of faded out. I think there were...faces. Why was there an explosion? It was like really intense sunlight, but all over the place, coming from the sky. What happened? Was it that man? Did he tell Defense?"

"No, Alaska, it wasn't him," said Gizel tiredly, easing himself onto his feet. "He got me out alive and helped me find you two. I don't even know if that explosion had anything to do with us, but it's time we leave. He's waiting for us on the outskirts of town."

The girl's uncle was waiting by a battered truck which might have been green, or brown, its paintwork was so aged and chipped. He stared warily about before crossing over to where they were standing.

"Payment?" he said soberly. Gizel turned to Jakob who removed the chain with the pendant resignedly, and handed it over.

The man bit into it, then satisfied, pocketed it.

"Ready?" he said, and Gizel nodded.

They got inside. Alaska felt a sickening feeling in her stomach, but reminded herself quickly that it wasn't a car but a truck, a completely different sort of vehicle. Still she was glad when they reached the end of the winding, bumpy road up into the mountains.

"No more road. We'll have to walk the rest of the way," the man said, and smirked before adding, "unless you can pay for a cable line across."

"No, we'll walk," Gizel replied.

They slipped around a sign saying 'Continue At Your Own Risk' and crossed on foot, stumbling around the rocks and sheer slopes in the blazing heat.

"Hot day," the guide said. "They say on hot days, you smell all the travelers who've fallen in the mountains. Then you don't smell anymore."

He gave them a wide, toothy grin and Jakob flashed a murderous look at him. "I'd shut up if I were you."

Jakob got gradually more and more ill-tempered, cursing under his breath with every step and glaring at anyone who spoke. Alaska felt his surliness ought to annoy her, but to her surprise it didn't. She couldn't help feeling a nagging fondness towards him while they traveled, but she guessed running from Defense and traversing through dangerous places could make friends, or whatever they were, out of any two people.

"What are you thinking? Why are you looking at me?" Jakob

snapped at her suspiciously. "You think I'm disgusting, that my skeleton ought to be hanging in the Glory of Defense museum? You can say it, I can take it."

"I'm not thinking that all," Alaska said, immediately taken aback.

Jakob laughed bitterly, "Right."

"You're not disgusting," Alaska said.

"Thanks, neither are you," Jakob replied.

As the sun rose to its highest point they took refuge in the shadow of a broken, twisted old tree. Alaska looked around and saw a set of crumbling old steps climbing up the mountain, to a narrow ledge in its side.

"What's that?" she asked pointing and the guide glanced at the set of stairs disinterestedly.

"Who knows?" he said darkly, before turning away to speak to Gizel.

Alaska hesitated, then cautiously ascended the narrow, steep stairs. At the top of it she stopped, gasping for breath, and looked around the ledge. The ruins of a building stood near the edge. The building itself still looked completely intact, though there were gaps in the stone walls and it had an air of having been abandoned for a long time. She stepped between two Doric columns standing on either side of its doorway. A heavy wooden door was on the ground. The space inside was vast and dark, with a high ceiling. She could see a mural painted on it, some kind of battle scene. In the center of the space was a square hole in the ceiling, below an altar. A tunnel of bright sunlight came through it, illuminating a lightning rod in the center of the altar. She skirted around it, crossing the room. A crumbling, twisting set of stairs at the back led downwards to other rooms.

"Are you really going down there?"

Alaska turned sharply, and saw Jakob standing across the

room, in the doorway of the temple.

He stepped inside, looking about distastefully, "Lightning rod. I heard about a nutter cult that was big on lightning rods."

"For some reason they abandoned it," said Alaska, taking a tentative step down the stairs.

They held up beneath her feet, and she found the rest of the complex as rundown as the upper rooms. She heard Jakob's footsteps on the stairs as he followed, and called up, "There's four rooms here. We could stay here and keep traveling when its cooler."

An inscription had been spray-painted in black on the wall above a door that read, 'We stand hand in hand with Tristan and Oxsana.'

"Oxsana Cathar Hemming," said Alaska.

"Some protestors must have been squatting here, and painted that," said Jakob, crossing over to stand beside her, looking up at the giant words. "You know the story, right?"

"My mother wouldn't let me forget it," whispered Alaska, feeling a lump in her throat, as she shut her eyes, and remembered. "She was the daughter of a top Defense officer and engaged to our Speaker of Health & Education. A prov..." she stopped and glanced awkwardly at Jakob, who nodded his head, before turning back to the inscription. "A provincial man named Tristan worked as a servant for her father. They met and he made her lose her mind."

"How did he do that?"

"I don't know. People say she was normal before she met him, and then she went insane. She decided she didn't really love the Speaker, she wanted to marry Tristan. They tried to secretly run off, were caught, and brought before the Defense's assembly of Speakers. Everyone thought they'd both be executed, but the Defense council gave her clemency because of her madness.

People...people thought the council favored her father, Vladimir Hemming and did it because of that."

"Probably. What about Tristan? Did anyone talk about him?" Jakob's jaw tightened.

"He was executed," said Alaska slowly. "Publicly. They made her watch. My mother said that's when Oxsana saw he was just a monster that needed to be slain."

"Do you think they should have been arrested? That Tristan should have been killed?"

Alaska froze. She remembered when her mother had asked that very same question after telling her the story.

"No."

The answer rushed from her lips in complete honesty. She almost felt the sting of her mother's hand slapping her hard when she'd given the same answer, six years before. Jakob was silent, watching her. She looked back at him, but there was a strange intensity in his gaze that made her turn back to the walls. She moved away from him, towards the door.

"My mother didn't like that answer. She said he was dirty and manipulative, like all provincials, and if he'd really loved Oxsana, he wouldn't have said anything. She said he was jealous of Oxsana and wanted her dead no matter the cost because she was better than him, because she was from the Capital."

Behind her, Jakob didn't speak and she wondered if she'd said too much, but she didn't stop. Her voice shaking, she continued.

"She took me and my brother Malcolm to where they executed Tristan and there was this giant, ugly device with a neck-clamp and a blade. There were still old bloodstains on the concrete. There was a haggard old woman crying in the square. My mother pointed down at the bloodstains and then at her and said, 'That's what you'll get for disobedience. Now some poor mother is crying.'"

"Your mother sounds lovely," said Jakob, his voice dark and sarcastic.

"She was, she really was," said Alaska, her voice breaking. "I was angry at first about it, but she cried afterward and she hugged me. I'd never seen her cry before, not like that. She didn't mean to hurt me. She was...she was terrified..."

The moment had been so disarming, to see her mother, who'd always been so distant and composed, terrified like a helpless child, clinging to her for support. Where was Amina Donnel now? Trapped in the Crypts or...the second thought, the thought of her mother dead, made Alaska feel utterly sick, alone and desperate. She heard Jakob step towards her, and quickly turned the handle of the door to another room. A scream tore from her lips when she entered. Every single wall was covered with Nightghosts, phantasmal, dark cloaked figures closing in around her. They projected out, reaching for her with long, spindly fingers. She backed away, and nearly slammed straight into Jakob who'd run into the room.

He froze at the sight of the Nightghosts, and then said, "They're not real, Alaska."

She had already realized that. They were only flat, three-dimensional cheap painted illusions.

"It's a torture chamber," Alaska said.

Jakob frowned. "Let's go back, before Gizel starts worrying."

Alaska followed him out, noticing as she walked along the walls there were a few first names inscribed on them, snaking upwards from the floor to ceiling. One stood out. ~~Helen~~. Then, just as she was about to step out into the harsh sunlight again, she noticed a dusty object lying on the ground in a corner, not far from the altar—a metallic mask, with a strange, grotesque face.

****

Night fell and climbing became treacherous. The merciless heat had given way to a bitter cold, but the border wasn't far away. Soon, they would have to deal with the border guards and get across. Alaska had been lost in reverie when she stared concernedly in Gizel's direction, wondering how he was doing, but she stopped, unable to see him.

"Gizel!" Alaska called worriedly. "Gizel!"

"Here!" his voice rang out and she veered off the guide's path. Jakob noticed and followed her. Gizel was lying on the ground breathing heavily. He managed to get onto his feet when he saw them, but Alaska could tell he wasn't well.

"A bit much for an old man like me," he said weakly. "Just give me a moment, and I'll catch up."

Alaska turned to Jakob, "He needs to stop. All of us do."

Jakob turned to the guide, "Hey, Uncle, time to let up a little."

He stopped, staring at the three of them and shook his head disapprovingly. "Lazy bottoms! You are almost there to the border!" he said over and over again pointing to an electric wire fence in the distance.

They settled down in the spot Gizel had found, a rock outcropping which partially sheltered them from the harsh wind. Even though Alaska was exhausted, it was nearly impossible to fall asleep here. She dozed in and out of sleep. It always seemed to be cold when she wished it was hot and hot when she wished it was cold, and every time she awoke she found herself tired and windswept with a massive headache from the temperature changes. Sunrise, the end of misery when she could start walking again, was still some hours away. The seventh time she awoke, light was just beginning to appear, casting the sky in a pinkish-purple color. The wind had died down a bit. Alaska looked around and realized there were two people missing, Jakob and the guide.

"Jakob?" Alaska said, getting to her feet.

Gizel stirred, staring up at her. "Something wrong?" Then he looked around sleepily and realized they were gone, too.

"Perhaps they went to get water," Alaska suggested, though Gizel looked unconvinced, but nodded his head.

"They should be back soon. I just don't trust—"

"The guide?" Alaska interjected.

"No, Jakob."

"Jakob?" Alaska said, startled.

Gizel nodded. "I've known him since he was fourteen years old. Jakob never did anything wrong exactly, but something always felt wrong about him. He was unnaturally quiet, like so many provincial children. I remember when Ira brought him to our unit; he was worried about Jakob, asked me to look out for him. I feel fatherly towards Jakob sometimes. He lost his parents after all, it didn't matter where he came from. But I wonder, I wonder sometimes what I'm a father to."

"I trust him," Alaska said.

Gizel smiled slightly. "Well, then I guess we needn't worry."

"Gizel, what made you decide not to work with Defense?" Alaska asked. "I know what they did, because you were an unauthorized scientist, but why didn't you just get authorization?"

Gizel sighed, "In everyone's life, I think, there is a turning point, a moment everything changes, that can never truly ever be forgotten. For me, that was the children."

"The children?" said Alaska, confused, and Gizel nodded.

"My son, Hamnet. Died in the plague, and that got me interested in defeating it, of course," Gizel said. "My daughter Holly was forced to enter a Defense school. They never told me which one, they just took her away. I realized then they already had enough power, they didn't need me to give them more."

"Is that why you were pretending to be a teacher? Did you find her again?" Alaska asked.

"By the time I found her, Holly had already been transferred somewhere else. Too rebellious, they said, keeps biting teachers." Gizel smiled a little, then his smile vanished as he said, "She was only three years old when they took her away, and it's been ten years." Silence fell, and Gizel jumped to his feet. "It's been long enough. I don't think they went for water." He stumbled out onto the path.

"Jakob!" Alaska called out.

Gizel quickly covered her mouth and whispered, "Shhh! There might be Defense patrols. They might hear you."

"A bit late for that," a sharp voice said.

34

A laska and Gizel simultaneously turned around to see two uniformed Defense officers approaching them, both armed.

One of them was holding Jakob, his wrists chained. Alaska and Gizel stared at them open-mouthed when there was the sound of a bomb overhead, and Gizel screamed, "Get to cover!"

Alaska immediately ran for the wire fencing in the distance at the summit that marked the border, but she couldn't cross on her own; she knew it had electricity coursing through it. A shot was fired, and it flew just above her head, narrowly missing her. Alaska threw herself down to the ground and saw Jakob had managed to break free of the officer's grasp. But he didn't run. Instead, he tried to wrestle the officer's weapon away, while Gizel ran for cover in the opposite direction further along the fence. Overhead a protestor air-ship started shooting near the officers and Jakob.

"Jakob!" Alaska screamed. "Get over here, forget it!"

He wasn't listening. Alaska started towards him when she heard Gizel's scream to stay put. She watched in horror as an explosion sent flying debris everywhere, exactly where the Defense officers and Jakob had once stood. She flattened herself to the ground, shielding her head from the debris. She heard screams all around her, though she couldn't tell if they were the guards', Jakob's or Gizel's. She could hear through all the chaos, the sound of more air-ships approaching, though friendly or not she couldn't tell. Shots were still being fired, but the combat was airborne now. Alaska got to her feet and ran over to where the Defense officers and Jakob had been. She saw Jakob first, lying nearby, but couldn't tell whether he was still because he was dead, or injured, or keeping down. She glanced towards what was left of the Defense officers, pools of blood surrounding them. She knelt down beside Jakob.

"Alaska?" He tried to sit up, his low whisper laced with pain, but he was definitely alive. "Help me," he gasped, spitting out blood. "Help me."

"Just a minute." Alaska looked towards the fence where Gizel was. A gigantic hole had been ripped in it, the edges sizzling. Gizel was slumped nearby. She couldn't tell his condition. More and more air-ships were arriving. She heard a voice boom out, "Surrender and line up along the fence."

Alaska looked up, wondering which of the air-ships the voice had come from. She stayed still. A moment later, a couple of them fired down again, barely missing the spot where she and Jakob helplessly remained. Seconds later the air-ships that had fired upon them burst into flames while being attacked by a contingent of protestor air-ships. Alaska tried to remember the protestor air-ships out of the crowd. She hoped they could help, but then they slammed into the remaining attacking Defense air-ships directly above them and all were decimated in a flash of orange fire. The debris rained down while Alaska tried to pull Jakob out of the way. Gizel was exposed by the fence. She started towards him, but Jakob shook his head, "Stay here. I'll go."

"Don't be ridiculous," Alaska said hoarsely, but he was already dragging himself across the ground.

Alaska saw people emerging from the rocks all around them. Alaska and Jakob were surrounded by an unarmed crowd of dusty, haggard refugees. Their faces were sweaty and barely distinguishable under grit. Several of them wore crude bandages around their legs and arms. Severe gashes were covered with gauze patches. They all seemed exhausted and several of them shook as they moved, looking up at the battling air-ships some distance away above their heads. Even more protestor air-ships had joined in the fray now, though they were smaller and older than the Defense attackers. It amazed Alaska how they could keep fighting despite their disadvantages. One of the protestor air-ships was knocked by a more powerful Defense vessel. The Defense air-ship sustained barely any damage, while the protestor air-ship went crashing down and slammed into the mountainside. There were only two Defense air-ships left, and the remaining group of protestor air-ships closed in. One of the two Defense air-ships swerved to avoid a shot, but miscalculated, flying within the range of two of its enemies. They fired in unison, destroying it. There was only one Defense air-ship left, and Alaska ducked instinctively as something soared overhead, crashing squarely into it and smashing it in midair. There was a fireworks of red and orange. The battle ended and the crowds surveyed the wreckages on the ground. One of the surviving older protester air-ships landed and people ran towards it immediately. Alaska had to scramble away to keep from being trampled and made her way to Jakob by the fence.

"He's dead," Jakob said flatly. "Gizel's dead. We have to get out of here on that air-ship."

Tears ran down Alaska's face. She felt as if something was stuck in her throat, as if she was going to explode, but somehow she managed to say, "We can't leave him here. We can't leave him for Defense."

"We have to." Jakob saw the crowd thinning as people made it onto the air-ship. "Come on."

He struggled to rise to his feet despite his injuries, but only collapsed again, letting out a scream of frustration. "I can't walk."

Alaska knew the air-ship would be gone before he could drag himself over, and she couldn't carry him. She ran towards the crowd, yelling at them, "Wait! Someone help me, please! My friend is injured!"

Several eyes turned towards her, but nobody stopped.

"Stop, please, there's somebody injured here!" Alaska screamed. "He needs help or he'll die! Hasn't there been enough deaths today?"

"We all need help," somebody yelled back at her.

"Please, he'll die! I don't want anything else, just get him safely from here."

The person who yelled at her boarded. Everyone else followed suit. She could feel Jakob's desperate eyes watching her attempts hopelessly. Alaska broke through the crowd and pummeled her way towards the air-ship. She'd block the entrance if she had to. She reached it and scrambled up, blocking the doorway. A woman tried to push her away from inside the ship, "Out of the way, girl!"

Alaska turned and removed the dagger from her pocket with trembling fingers. "No! You have to help me! There's somebody... he's going to die if you don't." Alaska pointed desperately towards where Jakob was lying on the ground. "Jakob's one of you. A rebel. He worked at a facility in the Capital. He saved countless lives and fought everyday for your people. You can't abandon him now."

Alaska hoped the woman would believe her and not see through her desperation that she was exaggerating things.

A man stepped forward from behind the skeptical-looking woman. "Help her and her friend," he ordered.

The woman nodded her head reluctantly and went out with a group of people to where Jakob lay on the ground. They carried him back to the air-ship. Alaska breathed a sigh of relief and followed. She collapsed against the wall of the air-ship. The moment Jakob was laid down on the floor the hatch was shut and the air-ship took off again. She accepted a blanket and packet of

Cure pills from a man in a torn olive green coat who bent over Jakob and removed his shredded shirt to examine the injuries. She watched silently as the man diagnosed Jakob's injuries through the mess of blood. Then she realized something. The gold chain and pendant were around Jakob's neck once again.

"Very bad bruising, several lacerations, but no broken bones, thank goodness," the man said.

"Where are we going?" Alaska asked the man.

"You'll know when we get there," he replied and then moved on quickly to help the other injured passengers.

35

oments before the air-ship had landed to take on its bedraggled cargo of refugees including Alaska and Jakob, Ianto had been sitting at a window, watching the carnage below. Johnson clearly hadn't been counting on a border skirmish in her plan. A hit from a Defense air-ship clipped theirs, sending them spiraling out of control. Ira hung on by the arms of his seat as if for dear life, looking as if he might vomit. Ianto wondered why he had ever let Ira convince him to go on an air-ship called the Hurdler that was salvaged from a junkyard. Suddenly there was an explosion of orange fire outside the window as one of the air-ships was shattered to pieces, though he wasn't sure whether it had been a Defense or protestor air-ship.

Ira looked up. "Is that the end of it?"

Somebody nearby nodded and Ianto cautiously moved towards the window, peering out. There were still air-ships in the sky, but they were protestor air-ships; the Defense ones lay in ruins below. Their air-ship lowered towards the ground and the hatch opened. For the first time Ianto noticed all the people standing outside, a crowd of dusty, starving strangers, many of them wounded and bloodied. He also noticed they seemed to have no doctor, only members of the crew trying to help the injured, though none of them seemed to know what they were doing. A child who looked no older than thirteen or fourteen with dark hair was carried inside, her clothes soaked red, and Ira sprang to his feet, "I have medical experience!" he said. "I can help."

"This girl is Gizel's daughter," said the pilot, apprehensively looking out of the cabin. "Do what you can for her."

Ira dropped down next to the child. Then a shout came from the crowd.

"What are they saying?" the pilot asked.

"They're yelling for help, they say somebody is hurt," Ianto said, noticing a growing look of apprehension on Ira's face.

"I know that voice," Ira said, and he jumped to his feet. "Help them," he said to the pilot.

"I don't know..."

"I know who she is. If you want my help, let them on board," Ira said sharply.

"All right, Ira," the pilot said with a sigh and he left.

"You know who's shouting?" Ianto asked. Ira gave a quick, slight smile that didn't quite extend to his eyes.

"Alaska Donnel."

"Who?"

Ianto saw a dark-haired girl and a battered teenage boy covered in blood being hauled through the hatch. The boy was laid on the floor of the air-ship as the pilot reentered the cabin and the air-ship took off again.

The dark-haired girl was talking to a man in a tattered olive green coat, asking where they were going, then she was pulled away to be searched for bugs.

"Why is she here?" Ira asked, his brow furrowing.

"Is there something wrong with her being here? She's alive, isn't she?" Ianto asked, puzzled by Ira's reaction.

"She's not supposed to be here," Ira said. "But who knows what's happened? It's been awhile since my last contact with the facility, all I know is she got there." Ira turned away as she looked in his direction. "I told her I'd make sure her family got out okay."

"And you didn't," Ianto said, as Alaska's gaze lingered on him for a moment before she looked elsewhere.

Jakob was moved from the floor to a set of seats folded out to form a bed. Ianto nodded at him as he passed and then asked Ira, "Do you know who he is?"

"Huh...?"

Ira was still staring at the girl, but he hesitantly shifted his gaze to the boy.

"Oh," Ira seemed even more uncomfortable than before. "Yes, he was also at the facility. Why did he leave?" Ira got up and walked over to him. When Alaska made a beeline for where the boy was, Ira quickly dodged out of the way and disappeared in a crowd of other passengers.

"Is he going to be okay?" she asked the green-coated man.

"I don't honestly know, we're very low on equipment," he said. "If I had medical supplies, I'd say he'd do just fine, but..."

Alaska nodded grimly before he could finish.

"We left somebody back there. Gizel. I don't know what his first name was. He died when one of the bombs hit."

Ianto noticed Ira's eyes widening slightly in horror.

The green-coated man nodded and sadly said, "I knew of him, he was widely respected. He left us before his time, and he'll be remembered for everything he did."

"I take it you knew Gizel?" Ianto moved over to Ira, who was still staring at Alaska in disbelief.

"He could have died a million times before, but he didn't," said Ira in a low, reserved voice. "The Immortal Gizel, a lot of protestors called him."

"Ira?" Alaska stared in his direction. "Ira Graye?"

Ira froze as Alaska looked straight at him. It was impossible for him to escape now. Ianto expected her to yell at Ira, or punch him, and stood well away, preferring to stay at the periphery of any conflict with a girl. He wondered what to do if Alaska tried to murder Ira and was completely taken aback when the girl hugged

Ira.

"They're alright?" she asked breathlessly. "Are they here?" She looked around frantically for her family and Marianne.

Ira looked desperately apologetic and Alaska stepped away from him, a growing look of dread on her face as Ira remained silent, before he finally said, "I had to leave Defense. I was going to be found out, but I left instructions for Ginny and Owen to help your family escape."

"I should have known when Tarana wouldn't promise," Alaska said, her voice angry and distressed, glaring at Ira before she pushed past him and disappeared out of sight.

"Y ou really shouldn't be so surprised."

Alaska jumped at the sound of Jakob's voice.

He had heard her toss and turn, punching the seat several times to try to stop from yelling out in anger and frustration. Everyone except for the two of them and the crew was asleep, though she suspected some of the still figures stretched over the air-ship's seats were just lying down with closed eyes, too scared and paranoid by now to sleep properly. Like herself.

"What shouldn't I be surprised about?" Alaska whispered hoarsely to Jakob.

"That Ira deserted your family," said Jakob. "I've seen it over and over again. He lies, he gets away with saving one person, and he can feel good about himself. He never thinks of consequences. To him, just being alive should be good enough for you."

Alaska didn't respond right away. She listened to the sound of people snoring.

"Gizel said it was your sisters."

"Excuse me?" Jakob said, bewildered.

"Gizel said Ira rescued you, but left behind your sisters. That's why you're upset with him, isn't it?"

Jakob shrugged, "That's part of it...doesn't matter anymore, does it?"

He toyed with the pendant around his neck.

"How did you get that back?" Alaska asked, watching him. "You and the guide disappeared before...before Gizel and I were found. What happened?"

"I got it back. Then those Defense officers found me."

"How did you get it back? You didn't...you didn't hurt him or...?"

"He was alive when I last saw him," said Jakob. "The Defense officers might have changed that. I can't say I didn't hurt him. He wouldn't let go of it otherwise."

"Jakob!"

"Well, I can't say I feel sorry for him. He was well enough to run after me screaming his head off and attracting the Defense officers."

Alaska sighed and went silent. As time passed, thoughts of her own home, her own family came back to her. Had the house been completely destroyed? Or did someone else live there now?

"Don't just sit there being quiet," Jakob snapped at her.

"Scared?" Alaska asked him, not mockingly, just interestedly.

Jakob snorted in response.

"I want to know," Alaska said. "About before."

"About the pendant, or my family?"

"Both, but especially the latter."

"If you tell me what you left behind," he said.

Alaska shut her eyes, thinking back. "Lifetimes ago there was a girl who agonized over friends and her stuck-up sister-in-law-to-be and school, and she had a sister who she fought with all the time over everything, and she thought she hated it all, but...she loved it," she heard her own voice breaking, "She loved every single minute of it and she loved all of them." Alaska swallowed, steadying herself. "She never said that enough, how much she loved all of them. She...she knows if she ever gets a chance to see someone she cares about so much again, she won't make that mistake, she'll tell them, because she knows there might not be another chance. And now, the girl feels completely lost in the dark."

Alaska swallowed and turned away from Jakob who watched her silently. Someone nearby got up, and she recognized the figure as the boy who had been standing next to Ira, watching their earlier exchange. There was something very strange about him, but she couldn't put her finger on it. Alaska watched him attempt to get across the air-ship to the one bathroom, trying to step through a sea of people lying about on the floor, and finally giving up and fighting his way back. It seemed odd to her he'd give up so easily if he really needed to use the bathroom. He would have kept fighting, like so many others over the past few hours, but if he didn't, why bother in the first place? And what was it about him that made her skin crawl?

"I don't like him," Jakob said under his breath, following Alaska's gaze.

"Do you know him?"

"No," he said bluntly. "It's just something about him. His eyes, maybe. They don't look human...more like glass. I've seen that before. They should chuck him out somewhere."

Alaska gaped at him.

"You want to chuck somebody out for the way their eyes look?"

"Want to and would, if I could walk," Jakob spat. "People like him leave trails of blood behind them."

"He looks fine to me," Alaska said defensively, not liking the way Jakob was talking.

"So did the Defense officers who killed my parents, got me imprisoned," Jakob said. "One of them knew my family. Did that make any difference?"

"But you don't know him!" Alaska said in exasperation. "What if I looked like him?"

"You don't," Jakob replied, turning over and shutting his eyes, clearly done with the conversation while Alaska sighed in exasperation. Sometimes Jakob could be downright infuriating, she thought. She got up and made her way to the window. They were over a stretch of indistinctive desert now, the ground an endless expanse of deep tan and soft pink. Where were they going?

"They're alive."

Alaska didn't have to turn around to recognize Ira's voice.

Despite the fact he really did look very similar to Jakob, enough to be mistaken for Jakob's brother, he had a very different voice, and there was something in that voice that kept her from storming away. Still, she didn't turn around to face him, just stared intently out of the window.

"Everyone except Marianne and your brother were moved to the deepest part of the Crypts before I left," he went on. "It'll be hard there, but it's highly unlikely they'll be called for execution. Ginny and Owen will have time to save them. I tried to break them out before I left, but the plan went wrong."

"Went wrong how?" Alaska asked angrily and he didn't answer. "Ira, they're all I've got..."

"I know, I know, I'm sorry," Ira moved to hug her, and she moved away, so he stood still instead, following her fixed gaze out the window. "I knew your brother and sister-in-law a bit. They're strong. They can hold out for a long time, both of them. We can save them, Alaska. Together. At least you're safe now, right?"

Alaska glared at him and Ira sighed.

"I promised you your family would be saved. I don't go back on my promises. There is a plan."

He smiled at her, lightly patting her hand that rested on the edge of the window. "Trust me."

He let his hand linger on hers for a moment before he walked away and left her alone at the window. Alaska frowned. Her hand felt cold where his fingers had touched it, as a vague ghostly impression of a memory crossed her mind. She didn't know what it was, bad, good or neither, but she had known Ira Graye before, in that year she couldn't remember, when she was twelve. Had he been a friend? Had she trusted him then?

I anto knew immediately when things began to fall apart. The day had passed, a hot, confined day inside of the slow-moving, clunky air-ship, and tempers were beginning to fray. Hours slipped past accompanied by symphonies of shouting matches. Ianto watched it all distantly. Then, in the early morning hours of the next day, as he was walking across the air-ship somebody crashed into him, nearly bowling him over and he realized fighting had broken out. People were screaming and shouting, throwing punches randomly, as the crewmembers fought back the angry mob in front of a pile of Cure pills and food bags.

"I found them!" a woman screamed. "I found them when you were trying to hide them from us! Trying to starve us!"

"They're for the people at our destination," one of the crew yelled, and the woman held up her child's bony arm.

"Look at this!" she screamed at them. "He's starving!"

Ianto quickly tried to get out of the way as the crowd grew more agitated, throwing anything they could find at the crewmembers, but somebody shoved him back into the fray. He was hit by a flying arm and fell to the ground.

"Stop it! Get off him!"

He found himself face-to-face with the girl he'd seen Ira conversing with before, Alaska Donnel.

"Here."

She reached out her hand to help him up and he accepted it, startled, as they freed themselves from the tussle.

"Thank you," he said curtly.

Alaska nodded and smiled, before stepping away. Ianto heard Ira's voice and saw him struggling through the fighting crowd to the crew.

"What's the idiot doing now?"

Ianto turned and looked to see who had spoken. It was the boy who had accompanied Alaska.

"Stop!" Ira yelled, waving his hands, half to get people's attention, half to fend off blows. "These people saved your lives and are taking you to safety. Does it seem right, to attack them? To bite the hand that feeds you?"

"Except we aren't actually getting fed, are we?" somebody yelled at him, when a voice boomed over the loudspeaker.

"This is the captain. Ready for landing. Our destination's in sight!"

Almost everyone ran to the windows, the fight forgotten, except for the mother and a few others who tried to break into the food stores. They were quickly overpowered by the crewmembers and hauled out of the way. Ianto ran over to the window, looking out to see a gray-brown, angular mountain range facing the air-ship. The air-ship began to lower. Ianto wondered why as there was nothing in view, just desert sand and rocks.

A crewmember yelled out, "We're landing here for all those without injuries, those with injuries should remain on board and they will be attended to by the doctor. Take out any luggage that belongs to you. Take off any coats, scarves, anything that might be uncomfortable in a hundred plus degree heat. I suggest shoes on your feet, if you don't have shoes, protect your soles as best you can."

Everyone followed the orders. Ianto didn't have any luggage, so he sat by watching and waiting until finally they were lined up and marched out through the hatch, going down the ladder two at a time. Even in the pale light of morning, it was boiling, a giant oven with no escape.

"Move it!" Somebody shoved Ianto in the back and he started walking, following the crewmembers lugging several bags ahead of the passengers.

It wasn't long before the collapses started. The first one happened after only half an hour, a woman sank to the dusty ground. Somebody stayed behind to take care of her, but neither they nor the woman ever rejoined the rest of the walkers. It felt like hours before the mountain's base was reached. After clambering a few feet up the mountainside, the procession stopped. The crewmembers, slightly up ahead of everyone else on a ridge, were engaged in something. Ianto couldn't see over the heads in front of him. Then there came a soft clicking noise. An opening appeared and the crewmembers stepped inside the mountain, gesturing for the others to follow. There was a cool, dark cave. Paintings and carvings adorned the stone walls. Ianto recognized it immediately and told Ira walking beside him, "They're pictograms, an old language. I read that somewhere."

Ira, out of breath, just nodded.

"Keep moving!"

The crowd was pushed ahead by the crew through to the back of the cave, where there was a solid stone wall.

One of the crewmembers spoke to it in a foreign language.

"Open," Ianto translated and suddenly the wall rose, revealing a transculent one behind it that looked like a slightly off-color, distorted glass. Two guards stood on the other side of the glass.

The two guards took one look at the crowd pressed into the cave, then the crewmember in front said in a harsh voice, "Come in."

The wall slid upwards with a bang and everything became clear, revealing a long dark tunnel.

"What you see must be kept in the strictest confidence," one of the guards said, leading them down it. "If you ever have the privilege of leaving on a mission, speak of this, and you will meet the same end as the people you tell."

They kept walking in silence, and Ianto saw a pinprick of light up ahead. The light grew stronger in intensity as they walked closer to it, exploding into brilliant light surrounding them, engulfing them, swallowing them...

"What is it?" Ianto heard Ira ask from behind. "What do you see?"

****

Alaska opened her eyes. It took some blinking to regain her vision, and then she saw it and felt her breath leave her. Spreading up the sides of a gigantic cave was an endless village, a collection of brightly painted thatched buildings that sprawled upwards over the stone sides. There were several suspended levels accessed by lifts that glided up and down above strings of light bulbs and power lines. It looked as if it had all been snatched straight from the pages of a children's tale. A storybook village, a nation within a mountain.

"Welcome to Pomander's Lid."

PART

TWO

Nation of Steel: The Capital
January 23rd, Year 137 A.C.

Alaska Donnel looked up at her distorted reflection in the mirrored ceiling of the immense room. It spun, dancing from left to right as she was jostled by the suffocating wave of giants on the dance floor swirling around her, an ocean of red suits and ballgowns. Some of the dancers wore wolf masks which stared down at her leeringly. A deafening anthem was piped into the room from massive speakers inset in the lacquered, ruby-colored walls.

"It's okay."

Her small hand was caught by a tall young woman with a round, doll-like face. She appeared tired with shadowy eyes, her ebony hair twisted into a single loose braid. Alaska saw one of her eyes was covered with a brass and glass eyepiece that was secured by a leather band that wrapped around her head.

"I'm Oxsana Hemming. Are you lost?"

"She's my daughter!" a tall man in a bright red suit cut his way through the crowd towards Alaska and relief flooded through her as she saw her father's face. "Step away from her, please."

His tone was more of a warning. Oxsana Hemming quickly let go of Alaska's hand and awkwardly walked away. The crowd parted as the dancers all glared after Oxsana with distaste.

"Where's your mother?" Benjamin Donnel asked Alaska. She shook her head, indicating she didn't know and he nodded, "We better find her, aye?"

There was something grim in her father's expression that made her relief falter as they worked their way to a long table with a 'Happy Glory of Defense Day' banner hanging above it. The table was covered in a bright gold tablecloth, glittering with crystal and silver dishes laden with mouthwatering chocolate tortes, rich sauces, salads and what seemed like a hundred main courses. Her brother Malcolm was heaping food onto a gold-rimmed plate, but Mrs. Donnel was eying it all hawkishly, adding a proper dollop of this and that on her own plate.

"Amina," Benjamin Donnel said urgently, tapping his wife's shoulder. "They've caught Edwin Ambrose."

Amina's eyes widened. "And Lavender?" She turned to Malcolm, saying in a rushed voice very unlike her usual one, "Malcolm, watch your sister."

Then she and their father were gone, disappearing into the crowd. Malcolm looked at Alaska, none too eager about watching his younger sister, before handing her a plate and wishing her, "Happy Defense Day," in a gruff, sarcastic tone.

"Happy Defense Day," Alaska forced out, the words nearly sticking in her throat. She managed a little salute, and then began forlornly shoveling orange ice cream onto the plate.

Malcolm frowned, but didn't comment, and then a tall teenage girl with pixish, short-cropped dark hair and a pretty, mischievous face materialized out of the crowd. She was wearing a pinstriped suit in a dangerously dark shade of red. Marianne Poesy, Alaska realized. She'd never seen Marianne before, but Malcolm had described her enough times.

"Do you want to dance?" she asked Malcolm. Then she saw Alaska.

"It's okay," Alaska said quickly as Malcolm opened his mouth to refuse.

Alaska didn't like the thought of being alone again, in the middle of all those people, but she could see the expression on Malcolm's face as he looked at Marianne and knew she'd already lost her older brother. Malcolm would probably just glare at her and be nasty all afternoon if he was forced to watch her. He never wanted to spend time with her anymore anyway, she thought. Malcolm shook his head, looking at Marianne regretfully, "I'm sorry, Marianne, but I can't."

"Come on," said Marianne. "She's gotten so old. She can take care of herself. And besides, what's going to happen to her here? At worst she'll get a stomachache from too much ice cream."

Alaska reddened and clutched her heaping plate of ice cream closer to herself. Malcolm looked uneasy, but finally nodded yes. Looking thrilled, Marianne grabbed his hand immediately and dragged him away. Alaska heard him call, "I'll be right back!" to her, before he disappeared into the crowd.

Alaska slumped into a chair with her plate of ice cream. Then she heard a low rustling noise behind her and turned just in time to see a little boy jump, withdraw his hand quickly from a plate of biscuits and duck back under the table. She rose to her feet, setting her plate on the edge of the table. She grabbed three biscuits from the plate and lifted up the tablecloth. The boy was huddled underneath, his bony arms wrapped around his legs. He was incredibly thin, thinner than beggar boys she'd seen on the streets as her mother rushed her past them. A black and white pendant hung around his neck. He briefly looked back at her, fear in his hazel eyes, then down at the ground. She tossed a biscuit towards him and he grabbed it, tearing through it in seconds without wasting a crumb. She gave him the others, and he devoured them just as quickly.

"Why are you so hungry?" she whispered to him under the table.

He didn't speak, just eyed her suspiciously.

"It's okay," Alaska said. "I'm not going to tell anyone anything."

"Defense officers broke into our house," he whispered. "They said it was an example. They took everything. My parents...my parents are dead."

Alaska stared at him, confused. "Defense doesn't do that. They saved us. They don't house-break or kill people, unless they're bad."

"They killed my parents," the boy said insistently.

"No," Alaska said, confident he had to be wrong. "Your parents must have done something very wrong."

The boy glared at her, opened his mouth to retort but then Alaska's arm was caught in an iron grip and she was dragged backwards out from under the table and onto her feet. She looked up at her mother's angry face.

"What were you doing on the floor?" Amina Donnel saw the boy, as he scrambled out from under the tablecloth and screamed, "Why is this little rat here!"

The boy ran and the room descended into chaos until one of the Defense officers roughly grabbed him. The boy cried out, and the officer hit him across the face. Alaska saw blood.

"No, don't hurt him! He wasn't doing anything bad! Don't hurt him!" she cried out.

The officer dragged him out of the room, ignoring her, while the crowd began dancing again. Alaska moved without thinking, wrenching her arm free of her mother's grasp.

"Alaska Nasrin Donnel!" she heard her mother scream, but she ignored her and flew across the room. When she reached the door there was a guard standing in front of it.

"Excuse me..."

The guard did not move, he stared. Oxsana Hemming appeared behind Alaska.

"She's my charge. She forgot something," Oxsana said.

The guard gave Oxsana the same hateful expression every other person in the room had, but nodded his head and let Alaska run out into the heavy rain. She ran through a foggy field, mud pulling on her shoes, dragging her downwards, but she fought back. Her dress clung uncomfortably to her small frame. She was freezing cold which made her teeth chatter, but she heard screams and quickened her pace in that direction. Then she saw the Defense officer standing over the boy. The officer had a split lip. The boy's face was bloodied and she saw a laser gun in the officer's hand. The boy's eyes widened when he saw her, and he shook his head.

"Go," he managed to whisper. "Run away."

"Shut up, you dirty little thief!" the officer growled. Then he saw Alaska, staring, paralyzed. "It's okay," the officer said, kicking the boy in the side as he quickly moved towards her. "Where are your parents? Where's Ben?"

The boy rose quickly onto his feet and bolted away. The man raised his laser gun. Alaska screamed, "No!"

The officer was startled and hesitated before firing. The boy escaped out of range.

"You hurt him," Alaska said, stumbling away from the officer.

"He was bad, he had to learn his lesson," the Defense officer said impatiently.

"He didn't steal anything. He was hungry. I gave him the biscuits," Alaska said.

The Defense officer got down on his knees so they were face-to-face. "That was very bad of you. But don't worry. Nobody's going to hurt you. What happened to him isn't going to happen to you. Not now."

They walked back to the red room, full of joyful, oblivious voices and the sickening, choking smell of the banquet, growing cold and rotten. All she could think of was what the Defense officer had said—what happened to that boy wasn't going to happen to her. Not now. But he hadn't promised not ever.

"I told you I made the best choice," Oxsana Cathar Hemming said as the door to the dance hall shut behind Alaska and the Defense officer. Oxsana and two cloaked, ghostly figures stood in the shadows. With arms crossed and a determined expression on her face, Oxsana stared at the closed door.

"You are always right, Oxsana," the mechanical voice of the figure standing next to her concurred. "Mir Counta will approve. She is perfect."

Alaska knew it was only a dream, yet it felt real. The smell of wet grass beneath her feet, the sky above clear and placid gray. She reached the edge of a cliff, and took off into the sky. All of it felt real until the shadows filled in, drowning the world, then she saw the white door awaiting her. The dream had her in its grasp, and she could not tear herself free of it.

"Winter!" The scream was so loud it felt as if it was shrieking in her ear. She tried to put her hands to her ears to block the sound, but she could not.

"I won't go in!" she screamed at the voice. "I won't go through the door!"

With a gasp, Alaska awoke and stared around in confusion. She was in a bed. She was surrounded by windows from which the came the sound of voices. She remembered. This was her second day in Pomander's Lid. After med checks yesterday, today would be orientation. She rose to her feet. A set of fresh clothes had been left for her at the foot of the bed on a low chest, the same eccentric patchwork clothing she'd seen everyone in Pomander's Lid wearing. Alaska looked around the room she had all to herself. She'd never lived alone before. Somehow, it felt empty and hollow despite its cramped size. There was a kitchen, bath, and bed. Lanterns hung from the ceiling and bookshelves filled with copies of texts similar to what she'd seen in the Capital facility lined the walls. Alaska crossed over to the sink and poured herself a glass of water, then heard a tapping sound on the window. Alaska opened the window above the sink and saw a firefly sitting on the windowsill. She'd noticed them everywhere the first day, messengers like in the Capital. These, however, were pieced together from scrap metal and didn't seem to come apart to reveal a screen. She tried to figure out where its screen was, and then noticed a tiny black button on the bottom of it. Cautiously she reached out and pressed it.

A deep woman's voice issued out of the tiny messenger, "This is councilor Cassandra Prince. You will learn more about me at orientation. I have been made aware of the fact that you, Alaska Donnel, knew Fernando Gizel. Please join us before orientation for a short memorial to be held in his memory."

Alaska went down to the main square. All around her she heard people talking, sharing memories of Gizel, and felt oddly apart from it all. Until a few minutes before she hadn't even known his first name.

"They say you were there when he died," Alaska turned in surprise to see a girl walking up to her.

The girl looked around thirteen, with several bandages on her arms and face. She was a scrawny waif, with a vicious-looking scar on her pale cheek and soot black, doe-like eyes that had become red and puffy from crying.

"Did you know him well? I'm Holly," the girl introduced herself, smiling at Alaska. Alaska realized who was standing in front of her—Gizel's daughter.

"You escaped and got all the way here," Alaska said, shocked, before she added quickly, "I was there, but I didn't know him well. We traveled for a short bit, he helped me and my friend but I wish...I wish I'd known more about him."

"I never knew him at all," Holly said in a soft voice. "He was a legend among the protestors. I wish I had known him better, but I heard he rarely said anything about himself."

Alaska nodded. Just then, a bell went off.

"The work bell," said Holly. "And for you, that'll be orientation."
She pointed towards a pink building across the square. "They'll be
waiting for you there. Good luck."

Alaska nodded gratefully, and Holly limped back towards the
hospital.

****

Orientation started with Alaska being ushered into a tiny, closet-
sized room in the town hall flooded with soft blue light. A cool,
even female voice came from a grated opening near the ceiling.

"The Nation was founded by brave, good men and women,
fleeing the cruel and evil wars of the outside world. Unspeakable
horrors had torn their homes and lives apart. They envisioned
a paradise where they and their descendents would forever find
peace. Defense has ripped apart that dream, but though it may be
bloodied, it is not dead. It is our mission to continue the dream,
here in Pomander's Lid."

The voice died, and with it, the blue light. The door behind
Alaska opened, and she stepped out. She saw a crowd of other
newcomers that had previously emerged from the room gathered
around four figures.

"I am the head of Pomander's Lid's council, Cassandra Prince,"
said a woman in her mid-thirties, her dark hair in small braids
pulled back into a ponytail. "Beside me are the other members
of the council, Lymir Bastion, Hawk Pluange and Temple Blue."

To her right was a short, overweight man of similar age, a
pompous look on his double-chinned face, while on her left was a
thin, elderly man with bushy eyebrows leaning on a thick, metal-
tipped cane. Standing off to the side fiddling with his eyeglasses
was a sandy-haired young man who looked like he was eighteen
at the oldest. The crowd all reached out, shaking the hands of the
council members. Alaska reached to shake Lymir's hand as he

passed, but he moved away as if he hadn't seen her.

"We use first names here," said Cassandra. "You can refer to the four of us as Cassandra, Lymir, Hawk and Temple. Temple is the junior advisor. Unfortunately two councilors and three advisors were killed only a few days ago in a grave accident involving a tunnel collapse. We will be looking for new recruits and perhaps some of you newcomers will pass muster. First, you must be officially registered."

Alaska stepped forward at the head of the line but Cassandra pulled her away, "You're already registered, Alaska Donnel."

"How...?"

Alaska turned and saw Ira with Ianto following behind him, looking perplexed.

"You and Ianto Ambrose. Ira told me about both of you."

"You know these people already?" Alaska heard Ianto ask Ira.

"Ira has been a trusted ally of the protestor movement for years. He is well-known to all of us," said Cassandra as they stepped through the doors of town hall and stood on the steps, looking out over the center of Pomander's Lid. "Alaska, you're very unusual here in Pomander's Lid. Few protestors are Capital-born and many are going to judge you differently because of that. But in your motivations, you are like all the rest of us. You fear for your future, for your family. Your work, your contribution to the community will earn your family's rescue in time. And you will learn everything you need to prevent others from feeling the same fear. Ianto, you want a home, after losing your parents. Edwin and Lavender Ambrose...it was a great loss for all of us. Pomander's Lid is happy to give you a home, a welcoming environment with everything you could ever need. Both of you have the potential to be anything here. It all depends on what you choose."

She removed two pieces of paper from her pocket, handing one to Alaska and the other to Ianto.

"These are lists of jobs open."

"Why don't I get one?" Ira asked.

Alaska looked down at her paper. There were only two things left available, everything else was scratched out.

"We need your help here at town hall," said Cassandra to Ira. "You'll be an unofficial advisor."

"I'll do safety checking," Ianto offered and Alaska glared at him.

"Tunneling then," said Cassandra, taking Alaska's paper she'd been about to hand over.

Safety checking was clearly circled on it.

"You can't have her do that," said Ira, shocked.

Alaska glared at him. "I can take care of myself."

Ira glanced away in silence.

"Come on. I'll go over the basics very quickly. Pomander's Lid is the only permanent shelter for refugees of Defense's rule in the Nation of Steel. We have special coins you can earn through your work and commitment. Everything is based on this currency. You can pay for anything with it," said Cassandra as they walked along the streets of Pomander's Lid. "The hospital wing is to the right."

Alaska stopped, feeling like she was being watched. She turned around and looked in the direction of a narrow, dark building along the street. For a brief second, she thought she saw a face in the window, but then it vanished out of sight.

"Coming, Alaska?" asked Cassandra while she, Ianto and Ira waited several yards in front of her.

"Yeh, sorry." She hurried to catch up to them, but the image of the face in the window stayed with her.

"Ah, the new safety checker!"

Ianto was greeted by a garishly dressed man of around fifty, with a washed-out face, shoulder-length gray hair, and a goatee with a handlebar mustache. He dragged Ianto into the town hall by his sleeve, talking quickly and sharply.

"Never can get a hold of any safety checker in Pomander's Lid these days...been asking about the crack for days...the whole ceiling could collapse on me and then splat! Who would be translator?"

The man pulled Ianto through an open doorway. Ianto saw the name Nigel Mcavoy on a card taped to the door's window, before he was lined up facing a stone wall. The man, Mcavoy, jabbed a finger at the wall. Ianto squinted and finally saw the crack, the size of a single hair.

"I don't think..." Ianto started.

Mcavoy snapped, "Don't think you're getting out of here so easily, boy! Do you know how precious the contents of this room are? I'm not taking any risks. Look properly!"

He finally released Ianto's arm and took a seat behind a desk on the opposite side of the room. Ianto sighed and scanned the room. He saw a small, intricately carved stepladder leaning against the desk, and walked over. Mcavoy barely noticed him, poring over a photograph. Ianto took a quick look at it, then grabbed the stepladder, and leaned it up against the stone wall. He pretended to examine the crack in great detail as his mind went over the photograph.

"I'm done," he said finally, jumping down off the ladder.

Mcavoy looked up fearfully, "Well?"

"You'll live."

"You're useless, just like all the others," said Mcavoy angrily. "Get out of my sight, boy."

"Can I see your photo?" Ianto asked.

"What?" Mcavoy stared at him in bewilderment, one eyebrow raised. "What are you talking about?"

"The photo. It's of an air-ship, isn't it? An air-ship in a desert?"

Mcavoy crossed his arms. "I asked you to examine my wall... hey!" He jumped back as Ianto's hand suddenly flew out and snatched the photo out of his hand. Ianto examined it closely while avoiding Mcavoy's attempts to snatch it back.

"Are you trying to decipher the writing?" he asked Mcavoy whose mouth fell open in amazement.

"Writing? What are you talking about?"

Ianto laid the photograph down on the desk and picked up a gold magnifying glass, ignoring Mcavoy's exclamation of outrage.

"Now look," he said, placing it over the air-ship in the picture. Mcavoy bent close, and his eyes widened.

"You're right, something is written there. Can you..." Mcavoy said unsurely, "can you decipher it?"

"It's the same language as the pictures on the walls of the entry cave," Ianto said.

"Desertpic," said the expert, his mouth falling open once again. "But how do you know all of this?"

There was a knock on the door-frame and they both turned around to see Cassandra.

"Any progress?" she asked Mcavoy. She noticed his perturbed look and Ianto holding the magnifying glass over the picture on the desk. "What's going on?"

"It turns out our young new addition has quite a keen eye."

Mcavoy held up the photo. "He noticed there's writing on the air-ship, in Desertpic."

Cassandra immediately relaxed, a relieved look on her face. "It can't be Defense then?"

"It is most likely on our side," said Mcavoy, nodding his head. "But I would still recommend caution."

Cassandra nodded her head in agreement and started to leave, but Mcavoy called out, "Councilor, is it possible for this young man to be reassigned to me? I could do with an assistant."

Cassandra nodded. "I think he has already shown he is more suited with you, Nigel," she said, before leaving.

Mcavoy turned to Ianto. "What's your name, boy?"

"Ianto Ambrose," Ianto said.

Mcavoy's eyes widened, "You're not by any chance related to Edwin and Lavender Ambrose?"

"They're my parents," Ianto said unenthusiastically.

Mcavoy stepped back in amazement. "Ianto Ambrose! Ianto Ambrose in my office! I'm Nigel Mcavoy, but you can just call me Nigel," he said with a warm smile as he reached out and vigorously shook Ianto's hand. "It is an honor to have you here, among us, in Pomander's Lid."

Ianto saw a hungry look in Mcavoy's eyes as the man asked, "How extensive is your knowledge in Desertpic?"

Ianto shook his head, "I don't know."

"Let's see," he pulled out a tablet covered with images. "I'll give you anything you want if you can read this for me."

Ianto looked at the pictures on it, and then said, "A pool of water symbolizes an oasis and can be taken less literally for hope. The scratch in-between is the connecter. I believe the next one is future, the sun rising over a setting sun. They're close, so it all translates to 'hope in the near future'." He looked at Mcavoy. "Where did you get this piece of rock from?"

"It was in one of the far caves of Pomander's Lid," Mcavoy said impatiently. "Keep going, now."

Ianto turned back to it, "Now it's talking about some sort of weapon and a plague," Ianto said. "And...a giant computer?"

"That doesn't make any sense. Sometimes we use Desertpic to send messages Defense won't understand, but I found this in a far tunnel," said Mcavoy, his brow furrowing. "It would have to be original to the caves, written by people long before the modern age. How could they be talking about computers?"

"Maybe I'm reading that last one wrong," Ianto said.

"Well, that's still excellent," said Mcavoy happily. "I told you I'd give you anything you wanted. Just say the word."

"How do you get to the far tunnels?" Ianto asked Mcavoy. "Cassandra took us on a tour. I don't remember her taking us there."

"It's off-limits, really," Mcavoy looked slightly sheepish. "They installed a locked door to prevent people from wandering there. Ancient tunnels...must not be disturbed...rules and nonsense. This," he said, patting the tablet, "can be our little secret."

"I want to go there," Ianto said.

Mcavoy looked at him hesitantly for a moment, then disappeared into a back room. Ianto shut his eyes. In his mind he saw an empty, dark room. Three figures, two shrouded in the darkness. He watched as a communicator dropped from the pocket of the third figure, falling onto the ground. He had forgotten the memory, locking it away in his mind till now.

"Ianto?"

He opened his eyes and saw Mcavoy standing in front of him with a black key. Ianto hastily accepted the key from Mcavoy, and started to leave, when Mcavoy called to him.

"Ianto!" Ianto turned around, facing the translator, who looked bemused. "You look just like your father."

"Yeh, I know. My grandfather used to say that all the time," Ianto said uncomfortably.

"They were wonderful, charming, clever people, your parents. I was good friends with them, before their deaths," said Mcavoy softly. "They laid the foundation for the resistance against Defense. We owe them everything. They told me about how they were both very close to Magler before his death. Your mother was his chief scientist, even at her young age at the time. But..." Mcavoy shook his head, "I don't remember them ever mentioning a son."

Ianto sucked in his breath as he felt a dull pain in his chest.

"No, they wouldn't have," said Ianto, before he exited out the door.

Clement ran through the thickly falling snow to the steel backdoor of the Glory of Defense museum, holding on tightly to the handle of a red box. He heard a snapping noise and looked around quickly, apprehensive, his eyes searching for any sign of movement through the thick fog hanging over the city. There had been rumors and whispers of Capital protestors plotting an attack, and though he knew Melissa Johnson felt the rebels incapable of plotting their way out of a paper bag, he knew one could never be too cautious. He quickly slipped inside the museum and relocked the door, then walked rapidly down the cavernous corridors of the building, painfully aware of the loud clicking of his shoes against the cold, marble floors. He jumped several times, thinking that he'd heard a noise, but it was always the mere scuttling of rats, or drip-drip of melting snow seeping in through the leaky, arched glass ceilings. He glanced sideways as he went, eyeing the exhibits fitted into grottoes on either side of the central aisle.

The first was simply dark empty space, marking the beginning of the Nation, a time few knew much about, despite the fact it had happened only a hundred and forty-one years before. The next was of the colonists' air-ships flying in, and people on the ground settling and building the foundations of what would soon be the Nation's oldest concrete skyscrapers and mansions. The colonists had owned drone robots in those days, humanoid, faceless machines which dutifully stacked bricks and fitted glass. The next exhibit was of Samson Magler's time and Clement stopped in front of it despite himself. Something seemed wrong about it, though he couldn't quite put his finger on what it was. As always, there was a life-size statue of Magler in his heyday, brash and young and all-powerful, towering over smaller, metal figurines of men and women, but something wasn't right at all. He leaned forward, squinting and then realized a black flag, a symbol of the protestor movement, had been placed in the statue's hand.

"Yes, that was me."

He froze. The voice came from right behind him. It was a young man's voice, but unnatural, masked to conceal his real voice. He felt a strange pressure against his neck.

"You sound familiar," Clement said. "Who are you?"

"Give me the box. I have an identical one for you to take back to the Speaker."

"I got a message that Johnson was going to meet me here, but it was you, wasn't it?"

"You will go to Melissa Johnson in Lossit, and you will lie to her. Tell her Ianto Ambrose is their son, there is no doubt, the evidence is clear."

"How do you know what I have in this box? Why do you want this hidden?"

"Inside the box I'm giving you are results of a DNA test that says Ianto Ambrose is their son. If you tell the truth, if you reveal that these results are false, you will die."

"I'll do as you say, I promise."

"Good. Do not turn around until I tell you to. I have a laser, don't think yourself safe until then."

The stranger released the pressure on his neck and Clement stood perfectly still, his eyes fixed on the black flag as he heard receding footsteps.

"If you are a protestor," Clement called out suddenly. "You'll know it doesn't matter whether Johnson knows the truth about

Ianto Ambrose or not. It doesn't matter if he's dead or alive. Lavender and Edwin Ambrose never built a weapon. It's only a hopeful fairy tale. The boy knows nothing."

"The weapon is real! There is a cure for the plague. It's safe where Defense will never get their hands on it. Not while I'm on this Earth. Watch yourself, Clement. Shut your eyes, leave not a trace, for the Nightghosts have come to chase."

The footsteps were nearly gone, as the voice said in ending, "And rock you to sleep in their embrace."

Clement turned around. There was no one there. He stood alone in the empty museum, the black flag fluttering behind him as an icy breeze came in through an open window.

41

Alaska found pieces of paper among the books in her room. A pen was in a kitchen drawer. She sat down with all of it at the breakfast table. She attempted to write something but kept putting the pen down. Tap. Tap. Tap. Alaska tried to ignore the sound, but the metal insect was merciless. She rose to her feet and crossed to the window where it sat in waiting. She clicked the button and heard Jakob's voice.

"I'm fine. Horrid place, isn't it? Doctors everywhere. It's like some sort of nightmare. You'd think I was an invalid. There is NO WAY IN HELL I'm staying here. I feel so stupid talking to a bug as if it were you, so if you've got the time, drop by. Jakob."

Alaska shook her head, a smile passed across her face, and then there was a loud chiming of bells. The work alarms. She grabbed a bag off the floor, ran out the door, and raced down the narrow, clogged walk paths of Pomander's Lid towards the entrance to the tunnelworks. It was dark and dank, and only got worse as she went further underground, feeling her way along the walls into the pitch-blackness until she found a LED lantern. Pomander's Lid was built over a jumbled maze of tunnels that had been, for the most part, carved out long ago, perhaps thousands of years in the past. The new tunnels were much higher than the older ones, with their own separate entrances and exits from the main space, though they seemed to somehow always worm their way to intersect with the old ones. As she went further and further in, the entire area become coated in a thick layer of sticky muck, and she felt herself sinking with every plunge forward, struggling to keep from being pulled under until she managed to reach an outcrop of dry rock where a large group of people were assembled with shovels and pickaxes, chiseling away at the cave face in front of them.

"I wish I had a goring bull," one of the diggers said, ignoring Alaska's arrival, brushing several strands of grimy hair out of her face.

Alaska tried to remember what a goring bull was. She'd heard of one before when for a summer her brother got a construction job to help pay for his college tuition. He hadn't managed to hold onto it for long, like all the jobs he tried before. For years he'd been quiet and average in everything. No one had thought he'd amount to anything and called him lazy. But he had amounted to something, Alaska thought, just by going to one protestor rally. He and Marianne had gotten themselves, her parents and even her little sister branded as rebels and arrested by Defense. She took a deep breath, knowing it wasn't fair to blame Malcolm for everything that had gone wrong. Much of it was the work of Defense, not Malcolm, she thought forcefully.

Swallowing, Alaska asked, "What is a goring bull?"

The diggers all stopped their work and turned at the sound of her voice. They stared at the girl who stood in front of them with an awkward look on her face, covered in muck.

"I'm Alaska Donnel," Alaska said quickly.

"You're late," said a digger, her voice cold, before turning back to her work without another word.

"I'm sorry," Alaska said quickly.

"That's understandable, new kid in school, and all that," said one of the other diggers, stepping forward. "Just get to work, and nobody will hold it against you."

"Um...sorry, what am I supposed to do now?"

One of the group handed Alaska a chisel and Alaska swung it at a patch of the wall above her head. Immediately someone grabbed her arm, stopping the chisel inches from the rock.

"Do you want the whole thing to collapse on top of us? Follow the lines we made!"

Alaska looked closer and saw a thin line had been etched around the wall, showing the opening they were supposed to make. Alaska swung in the middle, and the chisel hit, making a small, barely visible dent. She turned to see the others' work, wondering if she was doing something wrong, but they had hardly made any more progress.

"Are we supposed to do this whole wall?" Alaska asked, bewildered.

"It'll take a bit of time," was the response from the nearest digger.

Alaska shook her head, "Can't we just blow it out?"

"Do you have explosives?" one digger snapped. "It'll take longer if you talk, you know."

The hours of work seemed to drag on and by the end of it Alaska felt aches racking her body as the group filed out into the dimly lit square. Night was closing quickly, Alaska could tell, though the volume of the lights was the only indicator of time. She rested on a bench in the main square, watching people go by, just as fast as people in the Capital, but with a life and vigor and resolve she didn't remember anybody in the Capital having. It was hard here, but she already felt an odd, safe sensation, like nothing bad was going to happen here. She wished the rest of her family was with her, sitting on the bench, enjoying this life free of fear and anxiety. She imagined their responses to Pomander's Lid, how awestruck they'd be by all of it. She looked in the direction of the town hall, a slightly imposing building standing tall against the low-slung landscape of the village. She had to talk to the council about rescuing them, maybe Cassandra wouldn't talk about it with her before, but perhaps now...

She forced herself to her feet, heading there. It was nothing like the Defense kiosks she had sometimes gone to with her mother whenever they needed passes or permits for something. By the reception window, manned by a gangly, crooked-toothed man, was a sign marked "complaints." She didn't remember Defense ever asking for anyone's complaints, or any sort of opinion, for that matter. Walking down the hall, she saw the name labels of the offices. There were council members, but also other people. Nigel Mcavoy, translator. Inspectors' Offices, where a single bored office worker milled about. A bloodcurdling screeching noise came from 'Lost and Found.' Inside, Alaska thought she saw something fluffy, orange and fanged in a cage. Eventually Alaska found Cassandra's door, but there was a sign hanging from the doorknob turned to 'Out.' She went further down the hallway, up a set of stairs and past several corridors, including one with a door marked 'Communications' until she came to Lymir's office. Alaska knocked, and the door swung open.

"Come in."

Alaska stepped inside and saw Lymir was at his desk, looking down at papers. She looked around for who opened the door and saw Ira standing in a corner. What was he doing there?

"What is it?" Lymir asked, looking up.

"My family was arrested by Defense. They're prisoners in Lossit," Alaska started.

"I'm sorry...Alaska Donnel...that is your name, isn't it? I'm very sorry, Alaska, but we can not—"

"If you don't, Defense will kill them," Alaska pleaded. "They were going to kill me. I only just got out."

"Perhaps because you're the daughter of a Defense officer, from the Capital, you think you're supposed to get special treatment," Lymir's voice was cold. "But everyone in Pomander's Lid has the same sad story, everyone knows someone who was thrown into the Crypts. We can't get everyone out."

"But they'll die if you don't! How can you let that happen if there's a chance to save them?" Alaska turned desperately to Ira. "Tell him. Tell him how close I came to being thrown in the Crypts. If you hadn't come, they might have executed me. I can't sit back and dig tunnels all day while my family is in Lossit!"

"We can't do everything, Alaska," Ira's voice sounded slightly exasperated. "We're only human."

"Only human?" Alaska stared at him incredulously, "That's easy for you to say, your mother is a Defense plant. She's *safe.*"

"I'm a traitor, Alaska. She's on the run," Ira said softly and Alaska gaped at him.

"Excuse me," Lymir said sharply. "Alaska, all I can give you is the same promise I give every new resident of Pomander's Lid. Any special treatment you had in the Capital is null here. Here you prove yourself and how important you are. Put your heart and soul into Pomander's Lid and then we will review your case." He turned to the contents of his desk, clearly finished. "That is all."

Alaska didn't want to move, but Ira dragged her out, shutting the door behind himself.

Alaska shook angrily, "I'm not asking because my father—"

"I know," said Ira gently. "It was wrong of Lymir to bring it up. It doesn't matter."

"I'm sorry about your mother," Alaska said. "I didn't know."

"Never mind," Ira said, as they both walked to the exit out of town hall. "Why is Jakob here?" he asked her suddenly, an edge to his voice.

"Jakob?" Alaska asked in surprise. "He came with me and the others from the facility, but—"

Ira nodded his head, "Gizel didn't make it. So you two are friends now?" he said, a sarcastic smile playing across his face.

"Funny, isn't it? I never would have guessed either of you would have anything in common."

"How would you know? You don't know me. You only really met me at your mother's house," Alaska said, watching Ira for some sort of reaction, a giveaway he'd known her before, but there was none. "Defense went after his family, too. I can understand that."

"He's from the provinces, Alaska. You can't possibly begin to understand him."

Alaska stopped walking and glared at Ira. "How is he any different? Is he different because he's got a scar on his hand? Is that why, Ira Graye?"

"No," said Ira. "I...you know what I mean, Alaska. Besides, he's a bitter, jealous person. He doesn't care about anyone except himself, he doesn't like people."

"He's not like that at all," said Alaska firmly.

"Perhaps not. Maybe I'm wrong about someone I've known for eight years."

Ira slipped past her and she called after him, "You just don't like him, like he doesn't like you. He doesn't dislike other people, he's not just "bitter." He's angry with you! If you actually listened to him for five minutes, you'd realize that!"

Ira looked for a moment as if he was going to respond, but then he walked out of sight down the corridor.

Alaska turned to leave when she noticed someone watching her. It was a wild-haired, bare foot woman, wrapped in a crazy-quilt shawl. Her eyes were large, hooded and a violet blue color, but strangely flat and cold.

"Alaska Donnel?" she said.

"How do you know my name?" Alaska asked startled.

The woman turned away and merged into the crowd.

Alaska followed her, just managing to see her before she

disappeared out of sight. Alaska plunged out of the crowd, sidestepping people until she spied the woman getting into the glass elevator to go to the second level. Alaska sprinted to catch up to her and managed to catch the elevator before it went up.

"Who are you?" Alaska asked, but the woman looked away from her and stared out over the crowd below until the elevator reached the second floor.

The woman got off. Alaska cautiously followed her until she stopped in front of a narrow, tall building with a bell-topped tower that resembled an old church.

"Come inside," she said.

Alaska shook her head. "Who are you?"

"I know why the Nightghosts are following you."

42

The woman opened the church building's rounded door and disappeared inside. Alaska remained on the step outside, waiting for her to return, but she didn't, and finally, unable to bear it, Alaska hesitantly followed her inside. The woman was waiting and Alaska started towards her, but stopped suddenly as she noticed the interior of the space for the first time. It was small but seemed cavernous with a high, arched ceiling. Naturally formed stone pillars created a sort of central aisle through the space and makeshift pews were arranged on either side of that aisle. The whole space had a warm, suffocating musty damp smell that made Alaska's head swim. She put her hand to her head and dizzily looked up to see very old, threadbare tapestries hanging from the walls. Each and every one of them seemed to depict the same group of people in cloaks astride ebony horses, sometimes in a meadow, or on a quiet hamlet, with a forest rising in the distance.

Alaska stopped as her eyes fell on the last and largest one of the tapestries that depicted a bloody battlefield about to be overcome by a wave of black water. Alaska stepped closer to get a better look, and the woman grabbed her hand.

"This way, dear," she said, leading Alaska away from it, to a small, closet-like back room with a single window. Alaska stared at the walls and realized they were covered in photographs. She stepped back as she saw herself, younger, a small girl of ten or eleven, her hair pulled back in two fat, dark pigtails smiling for the camera. Happy.

"Why...?"Alaska began, when she saw the other photographs.

Her parents. Leila. Malcolm.

"You've seen them, haven't you? Things that aren't really there," said the woman. "Nightghosts."

"How do you know that?"

"The last time I saw you, you were very young, Alaska Donnel, and I am sure you no longer remember me," said the woman. "But my name is Helen. I was a friend of your mother, Amina, and I used to be a part of an order called the Nightghosts, an order that was wrong. They've been following you."

"Why? What are the Nightghosts?" Alaska asked, frustrated. "What do you want with me?"

"Not me, I'm not one of them anymore," said Helen. "I joined them because I was against Defense. Defense took the most important people in my life away from me, as they've done to you. But I didn't realize the cruelty and mania of the Nightghosts. I didn't realize how far they'd go to achieve their goals. As soon as I did, I left them."

"What were they doing?"

"Experiments," said Helen. "Some of them involving children, especially provincial children, who are easy to take. Defense doesn't care if provincial children go missing. That is where the term "scissor children" comes from. The children the Nightghosts experimented upon were often killed in the end, rendered dangerously mad, or severely disabled to the point of being little more than Stills."

A chill ran down Alaska's spine, "Why are they following me, Helen?"

"They took you," Helen said.

Alaska froze, staring at Helen. She tried to speak, but couldn't find her voice.

"Don't worry, I see no sign they did anything to you," said Helen. "Sometimes they reject children from their experiments for various reasons. When they do that, they wipe their memories of the abduction and safely return them home. The families rarely speak of it, as it's considered a great shame to have been taken by the Nightghosts. A contamination..."

"My parents would never think I was contaminated!" Alaska cried out. "There's nothing wrong with me."

"Of course not, Alaska," said Helen quickly, her voice kind. "I have no explanation for why they didn't tell you. But I know you were taken. I saw it happen and tried to stop it. I know this is a lot to accept, Alaska, but I'm telling the truth."

Alaska saw the earnestness in Helen's face. *I have a year missing from my memory and I'm being followed by cloaked figures,* she thought. *that isn't coincidence.*

"If they didn't want me..." Alaska said slowly, "why are they following me?"

"They keep tabs on all their children, wanted or unwanted. It sometimes drives children mad, and they start seeing Nightghosts even when they aren't really there."

Alaska swallowed, remembeirng all the times she'd seen the Nightghosts and nobody else had. Were those real appearances, or hallucinations? They had to be real, Alaska thought fiercely. She wasn't crazy.

"The whole thing is mad," said Alaska, shaking her head and Helen nodded.

"Mad, but true," Helen said and she clasped Alaska's hands in hers as Alaska stood still, a look of shock on her face. "I want to help you, Alaska. I couldn't stop what happened to you before. I couldn't stop them from taking you, but I can help save your family."

Alaska looked up into Helen's face in surprise, "How?"

"When I left the Nightghosts, I wasn't alone. There are more of us, some inside Defense itself. If you help us find something, we will get your family out of Lossit."

43

That night all Alaska could dream of was the dark-haired young girl, flying down the hill and then being caught in shadows. This time she never reached the door, never heard the screams because the shadows became wolves, surrounding her and tearing her apart, carrying what was left of her away into their dens to devour. Alaska awoke in a sweat, her mind racing and got out of bed. The square was dimly lit as she crossed it in the early morning. There were no lights in the church's windows when she arrived, but when she turned the knob the door was unlocked. There was an icy chill inside of the building as she entered and she heard a noise in the shadows. She stopped, looked around and saw Helen emerge carrying a pile of books in her arms.

"Goodness, child, you scared me," said Helen, smiling warmly. She dropped the books on a pew. "Is something the matter?"

Alaska shook her head, "I just couldn't sleep."

"It's my fault, isn't it? I'm sorry," said Helen, walking up to her, and pulling her into a warm embrace. "There's things I have to explain."

Alaska didn't know quite why, but there was something familiar and reassuring about Helen, even though she could not remember anything about her. Alaska decided it was like how she felt about Ira, that somehow Helen, too, had been there during her missing year, but she didn't remember anything of it except ghosts of feelings and wispy impressions. Helen disappeared into the back room, and returned with a cage filled with loudly twittering, small aqua blue, white and black creatures. Alaska's eyes widened in shock as she realized they were birds. Helen unlocked the cage, pulled one out, and then quickly locked the cage again and set it down on top of the book pile.

"They're called blue-masked love birds, friendly, but selfish. They never give me any peace," she said, placing the bird in Alaska's hands.

"They're not supposed to exist," Alaska said, staring down at it, and then she realized it was completely cold.

"Why is it so cold?" Alaska asked in horror. "It's like it's dead."

"It was never alive," Helen said, smiling fondly at the bird. "It's a machine, made to look like the mythical little creatures. There used to be lots of machines like these, of all varying shapes and sizes. You may have heard of sand-rats, though they are even more primitive than these creatures. Many of the machines were far more complex, some even looked like humans."

Alaska accidentally let go of the bird. As it tried to flee, Helen caught it with a forceful grip that would have crushed an ordinary bird, but did no damage to the creature. She pressed a button hidden in the feathers, then violently twisted the bird. Alaska knew it wasn't real, but watching it twist, crack in half and fold open was still strangely grotesque. Inside was clockwork, wires and a tiny black box where its heart should have been.

"The box is its brain, small for a bird," said Helen, pulling the black box free from its wires. "Disconnected from its brain, it is only a fancy plaything." She slipped the black box in her pocket and clicked the body back together. "You can keep the bird, if you like," she said and set it down beside Alaska. "It was a simple contraption. The ones the Nightghosts pledged to protect were far more complicated."

Alaska tried to ask a question, but found it stuck in her throat like a hard lump. She looked down at the bird, and finally managed to say, "What were the Nightghosts pledged to protect?"

"Defense lied when they said the dome was created by the first colonists. The Nation was created as a safe haven, a sort of paradise, by Samson Magler's father, a former inventor and soldier who was tired of the endless wars. He ruled it while nine beings, machines that looked and acted like humans, guarded and protected it. Their kind had been treated in the outside world like cogs in a great machine, worthless and replaceable, but Magler's father felt differently. He took them in. He treated them like his wards, and they all took his last name, Magler. Because of that they were called Magler's children by the colonists and were revered, until Defense rose up and decided they were a threat.

"Some say they could change faces and manipulate the dome in ways no one has been able to since, creating lightning out of thin air, or sudden rainstorms at the click of a finger. They were loved like gods, but they were also feared like anything people don't understand is feared. The Order of the Nightghosts was created to protect Magler and the Children. Defense usurped the Nightghosts' name, turning them into evil child-hunting beings. They also painted Magler's Children as demons to be destroyed and people listened. Since then, the Order of the Nightghosts has sworn to obliterate Defense, no matter the cost. The Nightghosts and Magler's Children have both become the monsters Defense said they were from the beginning."

"Machines that look like humans? Like androids?" Alaska's eyes widened in disbelief. She had heard of robots made to mimic living creatures existing during Samson Magler's time, especially about what menaces they were, but had never dreamt of any quite so complex.

"No, not exactly. They were part machinery, part biological. The mixtures varied, each a different blend."

"Did Defense destroy all of Magler's Children?"

"Defense says they did, but Magler's Children had the ability to change names and faces and had guardians to pretend to be family, so they were difficult to trace. Some might have escaped. I believe the Nightghosts have a Magler's Child among them. I have long suspected the identity of one Magler's Child. It's important to know when one is near. Magler's Children were kind once, but Defense's prosecution of them turned them rotten to the core. If there are any alive, they are very dangerous, Alaska. More dangerous than their guardians."

"More dangerous than the Nightghosts?"

"The Nightghosts are often pure evil, so blinded by their hatred of Defense they have become hardly better. If they have marked you as theirs, you are in grave danger. But even so, a Magler's Child following you is far more frightening."

"But I'm in Pomander's Lid now," Alaska said hopefully. "They can't possibly—"

"I believe there is a Magler's Child in Pomander's Lid, and I know his name...Ira Graye."

44

Ianto let go of the key and like a moth to a light, it stuck to the wall. There was a clicking noise and the wall slid away, revealing an old labyrinth of hidden tunnels going down beneath Pomander's Lid. He shut his eyes and followed some instinct that drove him to wander down several of the tunnels in the passageways which all looked the same, trying to remember the exact spot. The space was so familiar to him, every step felt as if it were simply walked from some journey only moments before. He felt along the walls and then stopped suddenly, turning around to face a door. He put his hand to it, then sprang back as it burned hot. The door slid away and he stepped inside into the almost complete darkness. There was a rustling noise.

"Hello?" his voice echoed through the space.

"Hello?" the voice replied, sounding familiar, yet distorted. He wasn't sure if it was an echo, or another voice, and his brow furrowed in consternation.

A dim light showed at the end of the space and he saw the edges of a figure in the dark, moving. He pulled a flashlight out of his pocket, switched it on and illuminated the space in an eerie glow, but there was no one. The entire space was empty. There was nothing but stone walls. Completely and utterly empty, he was sure of it. Then he stopped. He remembered something, irrelevant till now and locked away in distant memory. He'd come here before, to this very space, holding the hand of a person whose face he couldn't see, whose voice had only been a buzzing sound. Someone had taken him to Pomander's Lid before as a young child. But who? He cast the glow of his flashlight across the floor, but it was not the right place, it had to be further in. He was about to leave when he heard the soft sound of feet behind him. He whipped around, staring into the darkness but saw no one. Again he shone the light, but the room was empty, then a voice called.

"Ianto?"

It was Jamie's voice. Jamie Campbell-Boyd. Ianto quickly backed out of the space and shut the door, his hand shaking as he continued to clutch the knob. He let go of the door and slowly stepped away. He had to be only imagining it all, he couldn't have heard Jamie's voice.

"Ianto?" It was the voice again, coming from down the passageway now. Ianto turned around, but he could see no one.

"Hello?" he called, his voice reverberating against the tunnel walls, and then he heard the sound of running footsteps.

He followed, speeding up but the footsteps sped up with him, matching him exactly, until they were both pounding down the narrow passageways, the phantom steps always ahead. Then the sound suddenly stopped and Ianto found himself in front of a high, stone staircase.

****

Helen picked the lock on the door and discreetly slipped inside. Inside, the rooms were silent and meticulously arranged. Small stones were lined up like dominoes on the windowsill by the bed and on top of a nearby nightstand was a rusty lantern and a mother of pearl music box. Helen picked up the music box, flipped open the lid, and her eyes widened at the name inscribed there, as she smiled weakly, whispering under her breath, "The thing you love most."

There was a clatter from a nearby closet, and Helen spun around, dropping the music box on the bed. She removed a mother of pearl-handled dagger from her pocket, gripping the handle. A slip of paper fell from her pocket at the same time and settled partially under the bed on the floor. The door of the closet swung open, and Ira Graye peeked out, a laser gun in his hand.

"Oh, it's you, Helen! You know, you look older, what have you been doing to yourself?"

"I haven't forgotten what was done to me." Helen's eyes widened further at the laser, her voice suddenly fearful. "I know what you are. Others may pretend, but I won't."

"The council of Pomander's Lid must know your secret too, Helen, or you wouldn't still be alive." Helen didn't reply and Ira went on seriously, "I'm sorry for what happened to Winter. I didn't have a choice."

He casually dropped into a chair by the closet, though he was gripping the laser tightly as he looked up at Helen, a look of innocent curiosity on his face. "I knew you were going to try to kill me but a dagger...why a dagger?"

"Because the council doesn't dispense weapons to me so freely," said Helen coldly. "And because this is personal. You wronged me."

"I didn't do anything wrong," Ira said fervently. "My death... what'll that solve?"

"She's not alive, not truly alive!" Helen screamed at him, "Because of you, I'm never going to get her back!"

"I did what I could for Winter," said Ira evenly, getting to his feet. "I don't regret that and I never will, Helen. If that's what you're so mad about, you need to think about it some more, and decide if I'm really so wrong."

"She was ready to die, Ira," Helen's voice choked. "She had lost everything and all she wanted was for it to end. Now she is trapped, not dead or alive, because of you, with what you've done haunting her forever."

"Stop. I did everything because I couldn't see her die." Ira halted a few feet away from Helen, a troubled look passed across his face. "I never meant—"

"So you condemned her to hell," spat Helen. "For yourself! For yourself! Don't pretend you did it for her. I don't care if she isn't dead, Ira, because what you did to my daughter was worse than death—"

"She wasn't your daughter, Helen. You were Winter's guardian, nothing more!"

"I will never forgive you! You will regret what you've done!"

Ira's gaze fell on the music box.

"I've seen you near Alaska. Stay away from her," Ira exclaimed, glaring at Helen. "Don't you dare touch—"

"Don't worry, I would never hurt her!" Helen said viciously. "The Nightghosts hurt her. I tried to save her!"

Helen slammed the dagger down onto the table in the middle of the room and picked up the music box off the bed.

"This is not yours," she said, holding up the box.

Ira didn't move as Helen left with it, slamming the door shut behind her.

Helen had told her Ira wasn't human. It all seemed too incredible. He seemed completely human. But hadn't his hand felt strangely cold, now that she thought of it? Hadn't he always seemed off, like there was something hidden she couldn't quite see?

"Alaska!"

She turned and saw Lymir and Cassandra approaching.

"We need another person for a mission. We thought you would be suitable," Lymir said.

"It is dangerous," said Cassandra. "I won't blame you if you turn it down."

Alaska heard Cassandra's doubtful tone and saw the skeptical looks of those standing nearby.

"I'll do it," Alaska said firmly.

Her eyes scanned the crowd and she saw Helen standing amongst them, watching.

****

Several hours later she met with the others, including Lymir, Ira and Ianto, who looked very unwilling to be there. Ira glanced at her and she looked away. She would talk to him, she would ask him outright, she thought. She couldn't bear wondering if the person standing next to her was some sort of monstrous clockwork spy or not.

There was an argument over whether or not to wear fake Defense uniforms. They finally decided to do it, pulling them on over their clothes and boarded a battered air-ship spared for their mission. The air-ship shook as it took off and the moment they left the ground, Alaska could see why it had been long since decommissioned as it moved through the air with a frightening lack of aerodynamics, rocking to the point of throwing Alaska from her chair several times. They finally half-landed, half-crashed in the valley and suddenly the landscape looked familiar; it was the place where they had first arrived before taking the long walk to Pomander's Lid.

"Is that it, just below?" asked Holly, who she'd found out worked in the agriculture unit.

Alaska looked down below into the valley and saw the hulking dark vessel. It looked perfectly intact, bearing the blood red insignia of Defense's aerial force. The only reason it hadn't been destroyed yet was the writing on its underside. Even from this close it was hard to see. She couldn't believe the council had detected it in a grainy long-distance photograph.

"We should go down here," Lymir said to the rest of the team. "Don't let them see you."

The team clambered down, Holly handing Alaska a pair of binoculars on the ladder. Alaska saw Holly's hands shaking, despite her effort to hide them.

Alaska whispered in Holly's ear, "Are you alright?"

"I'm fine," said Holly quickly, though she sounded terrified.

Alaska looked at the air-ship through the binoculars and was sure it hadn't been downed in a fight. There were scratches on the bottom indicating it wasn't a smooth descent, but no signs of a battle. She didn't see any signs of occupants either. If there was a survivor, they hadn't left the air-ship. Maybe it was an ambush...

"One person should go and investigate," Lymir said. "We don't want to reveal we're a group. Whoever goes, you should act like you're alone." Lymir looked around at the many faces in the group. His eyes rested on her. "Alaska, why not you?"

Alaska stared back at Lymir incredulously and Ira opened his mouth to protest immediately.

"No!" Ira started, but Alaska was already walking towards the air-ship.

Prove yourself, Lymir had said to her. Well, she could do that. She could show him she wasn't a spoiled Capital brat. But the closer she got, the more and more nervous she became. *The others are nearby*, she thought as she forced herself onward. *The others are waiting.* They'd help her if something happened. But there was an all too familiar coldness in Lymir's eyes and she doubted he'd take the risk of saving her if something went wrong. *He is like a Defense officer*, she thought. Every step felt as if she were being sucked further and further into a trap. As she got closer to the air-ship, she couldn't keep herself from trembling, despite the desert heat. She was right next to it, close enough to touch its hot, metallic sides and she heard a noise from inside. Perhaps it was just an animal, she thought hopefully, moving towards the entrance hatchway. *Keep walking. Don't think too much.* She reached for the button to activate the door, but before her fingers could touch it, the door slid open of its own accord. Was someone inside? Biting her lip and forcing herself not to look back at the others for help, in case she might betray them, she stepped inside alone, to face whatever waited. It was completely empty. She stepped a little further inside and the door slid shut. There was no sign of anyone, so she decided a motion sensor had activated the door. Without the open door the air-ship felt darker and more closed in, the heat was drowning, her hair was already stuck to her face with sweat. Then she heard a noise again, this time to her right. She looked around and saw a doorway left ajar, a strange light streaming in from another room. She held her breath and approached it, her heart beating unnaturally as she entered. Plain, nondescript walls and plain nondescript cabinets. She looked down and saw a figure sprawled on the floor, facing away from her, clothes hung off an emaciated, skeletal frame. She wasn't sure whether the person was dead, unconscious, or faking. Finally, looking over her shoulder and making sure she could run for it if she had to, she went over and rolled the figure onto their back. She gasped when she saw the face staring back at her.

Alaska ran back to the group yelling, "It's Tarana! She's hurt, come quickly! Bring water!"

Ira started out first, a look of shock on his face. Ianto and the others followed him to the air-ship where the skeletal woman was slumped against its side, sun-burnt and battered. Her eyes were barely open as she squinted in the harsh light, then her mouth fell open as she seemed to recognize Ira.

"Alaska said you were here. I wasn't sure whether or not I was imagining it," she said, relieved. "She said Pomander's Lid and I thought she'd gone crazy."

"No, she hasn't," Ira said, giving her some water. He helped Tarana to her feet and supported her as they walked to the group's old battered air-ship. While they walked, he asked her several times how she had ended up in the air-ship in the middle of the desert, but she wouldn't respond, her eyes always looking on the ground.

"Who is she?" Ianto asked Ira, and only then did she speak.

"I was at a facility. Ira worked there as well. They all died."

A look of horrified shock passed over Alaska's face, but there was no surprise on Ira's, only resignation. Had Ira expected this, or was he only hiding his feelings? Sometimes people were puzzles he couldn't solve, Ianto thought. They got onto their air-ship and Ianto watched as Alaska gave Tarana her seat, and Lymir handed her the water. Ira sat next to her and tended to her.

"Where did this cut come from?" Ira asked, pointing to a bad, fairly fresh scar on Tarana's upper arm.

"A desert creature," said Tarana in a shaking voice. "It was like a demon."

"You must tell me what happened," Ira commanded her.

Tarana gulped down some water, then let the flagon drop on the floor. She regretfully watched as drops of water leaked from the cap onto the floor.

"Tarana, *listen* to me," Ira stressed. "I need to know what's happening. I have no link to the outside world here."

A pained look came across Tarana's face. "I don't want to remember," she whispered.

"Take your time," said Holly gently, but Tarana shook her head.

"No, I have to tell Ira," Tarana said. "Ginny and Owen don't know yet either, we haven't had any contact with them since you left. Owen told us you'd gone into hiding, that was it, last contact... Are they here as well?"

"No, but your story first," Ira said.

Tarana closed her eyes briefly, "Defense burned us out of the facility. Some got trapped inside. I barely got out myself. You could hear the screams everywhere, just chasing us down the hallways. We knew where Defense was in the compound, from the screams. Some of us, including myself, managed to find another facility, and ask for help, and they had that air-ship," Tarana nodded in the direction of the one she'd just been rescued from. "They also had fake uniforms, so we disguised ourselves, and made it through to here pretty untouched. The others began to die, though. I thought I would too. Every time I buried one of them I wondered whether anyone would be there to bury me. I found some desert vermin and I had some water, but it all ran out."

Ira opened his mouth to question her further, but Holly interjected, "Don't you think she should rest, Ira?"

Ira looked ready to protest, but he kept his mouth shut, and Alaska got more water for Tarana. She accepted it gratefully and asked, "Gizel, he was with you, Alaska. How is he doing at Pomander's Lid? He and I always heard all these wondrous stories about it. It's breathtaking, isn't it?"

Alaska swallowed and quickly glanced at Ira, who lied, "Gizel's fine."

"Pomander's Lid is amazing," Alaska said with false cheeriness. "You'll love it. It's just as fantastic as all the stories you've heard about it."

Ianto looked from Alaska's to Ira's face. Neither of them revealed they were lying. What other secrets were they keeping?

Tarana reached out and clutched both of Ira's hands in her own. "You're very good, Ira." She looked at the whole group. "You are all very kind."

Not all of us, Ianto thought. He couldn't care less about Tarana and her troubles. Melissa Johnson had given him a mission and he felt closer to completing it everyday.

"I'm so glad you're okay," Alaska said, clasping Tarana's hand in the hospital wing.

Tarana gave her a weak smile and leaned back on her pillow, letting out a tired sigh. "I thought I was going to die so many times. I can barely believe I'm not dreaming. It is so good to see you, Alaska."

Alaska smiled back at her and then saw a dark shadow pass quickly by the window. She was sure she knew who it was and hastily said goodbye to Tarana. Alaska walked out onto the darkening streets of Pomander's Lid and heard her name called.

"You're supposed to be in the hospital," she said immediately as Jakob walked over, leaning heavily on a cane.

"Hello to you, too," he said. "I sent you a messenger about where I was hiding but I think it got lost. I think most people ditch the blasted things for word of mouth."

"Don't change the subject," Alaska said.

"Nobody can tell me what to do," Jakob said snappishly. "I was suffocating in there. Bloody doctors talking to me like I'm some sort of cripple. Do I look like a cripple?"

"Well..."

"Don't answer that," Jakob said, the slightest, vaguest hint of a smile playing across his lips.

"We found Tarana today. The facility was attacked but she escaped and made it all the way here," Alaska said.

Jakob nodded his head, "I heard about that. Come on, I'll show you the place I found."

They took the elevator up to the highest level. As they walked, Jakob pointed to a nearby crowd. "Who is that woman?" he asked, suddenly stopping.

Alaska followed Jakob's gaze. "Helen. Do you know her?"

Jakob frowned and shook his head. "No, not really, she's one of Ira's friends. Her eyes are exactly like Ianto's."

"No, they're not," said Alaska in a rather defensive voice, remembering the coldness of Ianto's eyes. "They're nothing alike."

Jakob shrugged. They continued walking.

"Jakob..." Alaska started slowly. "Have you ever heard of machines that look like humans?"

Jakob's expression darkened and he said, "Magler's children. People are banned from talking about them, but sometimes people do. I heard about them once."

"How can you tell if someone is one of the Magler's children?"

Jakob stared at Alaska. "If you're trying to find one, Alaska, they're all gone. Defense executed all of them. There's stories that a few escaped, but that's just stories."

"But...if they weren't all dead, how could you tell if someone was real, or a Magler's child?" Alaska asked.

Jakob shrugged. "There's lots of theories, most of it trash. Some say their blood is blue or black, or that they have a hidden third eye, or smell like roses, but there's no way of knowing without chopping the person to pieces. A lot of people died when Defense was searching for them right after the plague ended. If you did anything "weird," you were a candidate and executed before you could say 'Magler's Child'."

Alaska felt a chill run down her spine. Jakob looked at her.

"Why are you asking anyway? Is something wrong?"

"Everything's fine," said Alaska hastily. "It's just horrible, all those people getting executed for being something they weren't. I don't think I could ever let that happen, if I was a Magler's Child.

I'd turn myself in."

"They aren't you, Alaska," said Jakob gently. "They aren't human."

And what was Ira, Alaska wondered. She still had no proof he wasn't human, except for Helen's suspicions which could be wrong. She suddenly felt ashamed of herself.

"We're here," Jakob said, breaking her train of thought.

They reached a strange, cave-like structure. Shelves crammed the space, seeming to grow organically out of the stone floor. Alaska glanced at Jakob.

"Is this a library?"

He nodded his head.

"You've been hiding in a library...what do you do?"

He stared at her. "What do you think I'd do in a library?"

"Oh, you can read th..." she stopped, reddening. "Sorry."

"I may be a Provincial, but I can read, Alaska," said Jakob, his voice cold, a hateful expression on his face. "Teach anybody, give them a book and they can read. I'm sure I'm a hell of a lot better at it than some people in the Capital."

"Yeh," said Alaska, still embarrassed. "I'm sorry."

Jakob's expression didn't soften, though the coldness disappeared from his voice. "You really are?"

"Of course I am," said Alaska quickly, desperate that he understand. "When I lived in the Capital...well, I heard things about people from the Provinces, things that weren't true. And I feel ashamed now, but I sort of believed some of it. But I shouldn't have and I'm sorry now. About all of it. I'm sure I must seem like some sort of ignorant, nasty Capital brat."

"You do, but I forgive you anyway," said Jakob, his anger and coldness from moments before dissipated. "Race you."

He tore off much faster than she ever thought someone on a cane could move, weaving his way through the stacks. Alaska sped up to rejoin him.

"Jakob! Stop, you'll make yourself worse! Jakob!" Alaska called after him, but he didn't.

Laughing, she followed him to a lift. The moment they stepped inside they were enclosed in a tiny, rusted cylinder with a single window covered in thick wire.

"Where are we going?"

"You'll see," Jakob said.

The elevator stopped and they got off and walked into a small room lined with books. There was a door directly in front of them and Alaska ran ahead of Jakob, opened the door and stepped back, stunned.

"You said someday you wanted to go to the summit of a mountain," Jakob said.

In front of them was an open-air observation deck, a thousand feet above the ground, at the very peak of the mountain range. A lighthouse turret containing a kerosene lamp cut through the center of the space. Three walls in the room were lined with metal but directly across from where they stood was a glass railing. Alaska walked over and stood directly in front of the railing. She leaned over and noticed that the ground fell away at the edge of the footing. She stepped back, dazed.

"Go on," Jakob said daringly, and she glanced at him, hesitating, then stepped out until she was standing on the very edge, the glass the only thing keeping her from falling down the cliff face. She pressed her hand to the cold surface of the glass railing and looked down. Below her, she saw a place untouched by the plague, preserved so far away from the Capital. It was far more stunning than anything Alaska had ever seen before, far more stunning than the mansions of the Goldcage. She shook for a moment from a feeling of dizziness. Jakob caught her hand and steadied her.

"I know, it's a bit unnerving," he said. "But you get used to it.

You're not going to fall over."

"It's beautiful," said Alaska, before she realized he'd touched her hand. She felt the scarred edge of the U that had been constantly cut into his hand over time in the Capital. Jakob didn't seem to realize what had happened as he sat down and stared out. She sat down on the floor beside him, following his gaze as he watched the skies in front of them, but she found herself chancing a glimpse back at him every few seconds. He looked truly at peace for once, more like the seventeen year old he was suppose to be, despite the strands of gray hair, wary eyes, and that bitter expression nearly always plastered on his face, though it was softened now.

"What do you think they're doing down there?" Jakob asked.

Alaska looked down and saw air-ships far below on a platform of rock that jutted out from the mountainside. The air-ships would regroup, over and over again, each time a pair of them disappearing off into the dusk.

"Some sort of practice," Alaska said. "I'd like to do that someday, be a pilot."

"I could teach you."

"You know how to fly air-ships?" Alaska looked at him in utter surprise.

"No, you see, we'll both sprout wings and flap around," he said sarcastically. "Of course I know how to fly air-ships. Outside of the Capital, you can learn at any age. I learned at ten."

Alaska felt a lump form in her throat at the mention of the Capital. She looked back down at the air-ships. Less than half of them remained.

"I want to go back home someday," said Alaska earnestly. "I wish everything could just be normal."

"You want to forget?"

"No!" said Alaska immediately. "No, I don't want to forget. I don't want to sit around the Capital pretending Defense is benevolent and wonderful again. But I don't want to be a rebel, either."

"But you already are," said Jakob. "Neither one of us has a choice anymore, Alaska."

Alaska looked down at the ground. "I hate Defense. I wish they were gone. I wish I could break every single one of their stupid Commandments, and they would just disappear."

The passion in Alaska's voice brought a look of surprise to Jakob's face as he turned to look at her.

"I don't think you could have ever been anything else than a rebel."

Uncomfortably Alaska remembered all the rules she'd broken in the Capital, the stash of stolen books she'd hidden under her floor. She had seen her house burning, but had everything burned? Was there a chance Defense had found the books and would also use that against her family trapped in the Crypts? She pushed the thought aside as a lump formed in her throat. She reached out her hand and placed it over Jakob's. He looked down, surprised, and his surprise only grew when she hugged him, at first delicately, and then more naturally.

"Gotcha," Alaska said.

It was like hugging anyone, she thought. Completely normal. Yet if she was at home, she'd be in the back of a Defense truck right now, and Jakob...she shivered at that thought, nearly letting go of him, but he was smiling at her, not a half smile, or a smirk, but a full, happy smile. She was so shocked, she froze. It was a beautiful glowing smile and she couldn't help but smile herself just at seeing him finally looking happy and knowing she'd caused it. The overwhelming power of that feeling frightened her. It's silly to be so giddy because he's smiling at me, Alaska thought furiously. She must be going mad. She pulled away from Jakob, looking up into the sky just to look at something else, and for a moment she thought she saw a strange white light and...

"Did you see that?"

Jakob reluctantly turned away from her, looking upwards. "No, what did you see?"

"I thought...I don't know. I thought I saw a rip in the sky, like the dome broke, just for a second," Alaska said, knowing the moment she said it, how silly it sounded, though she was sure she'd seen something exactly like that before, when they had been traveling with Gizel.

"A rip in the sky?"

"I don't know, it was strange," Alaska said quickly.

"Probably just far-off lightning," Jakob suggested.

"Yeh," said Alaska doubtfully. "Probably."

48

Melissa Johnson tapped the wall of her office, pulling up a screen listing six names. There was a spot for three more, but it was blank. She stared at the names warily, then tapped the wall again, and they disappeared. She made her way out of the office and was stopped by Clement.

"Capital rebels are growing restless," said Clement. "There's rumors of a threat—"

"I'm terrified," Johnson said, with sardonic impatience. "Find them and get rid of them. I have more important things to do than chase after a bunch of disillusioned idiots."

She descended a set of stairs to the Crypts. She waded across floors flooded with black water until she came to a cell marked "Poesy, Marianne." Through a glass viewing window she saw the young woman's interrogator, a red-haired young officer with a strange, gaunt face Johnson had never seen before. Marianne looked tortured, her eyes bloodshot with bags under them, her scraggly hair hung in her face, but her expression remained defiant. *Was she a Nightghost?* Johnson wondered. Johnson stepped inside of the cell, putting her hand on the officer's shoulder. He looked up, startled, and she thought there was something familiar about him though she couldn't put her finger on it.

"What is your name?" she asked him.

"Mir Counta," he replied politely.

"You may leave us," Johnson said, her voice cold. The officer nodded and left the room. "My name is Melissa John—"

"I know who you are. Everyone knows who you are. A murderer.

You're sick. You disgust me."

"Don't tell me you haven't killed," Johnson said coldly. "I have your file, Marianne Poesy. I know you killed a Defense officer."

"I never touched—"

"You can lie all you want, Marianne, but I have more time than you. What you're part of, what you support, is the merciless killing of Defense officers, of innocent people, of children."

"I want to stop innocent people from being murdered, from being hurt," Marianne whispered through cracked lips. "You are killing! For your Council. Do you even know who they are? No one else seems to."

"Yes, I know who they are," Johnson said softly. "They're the same as me, Marianne. They realized who Magler was, who my grandfather was, a brutal, selfish, power-hungry man who was going to destroy our world. You want to return to that? You want another Magler? You want to provoke a war and destroy us all? If you succeed, if you topple Defense, what do you think you'll get in our place? All you'll get is another Magler, and death."

"Maybe I want another Magler," spat Marianne. "Maybe I don't care if I have to die for it."

Johnson's eyes widened, "Do you know what you're saying?"

"He was a good man, better than Defense," Marianne slid down the wall she had been leaning against. "He was more human than you'll ever be."

Something in Melissa Johnson snapped as her eyes bulged to seemingly inhuman proportions. She ripped her laser from its casing, aiming it between the bars at Marianne. "Don't you dare say that to me, you foolish little girl!"

The young officer reappeared and pulled Johnson back before she could fire.

"You don't have to do that, I'll interrogate her again!" he said quickly.

"Don't you dare!" Johnson spat, and she fired at his leg.

The officer crumpled to the ground as Clement came running down the hall. Then something strange happened. Johnson's face contorted in pain as a scream uncontrollably ripped from the young officer's lips. She clutched her head as she stumbled backwards and the man scrambled onto his feet. He ran quickly down the hall and past Clement.

"Stop him!" Johnson screamed.

Clement tore down the hallway, Johnson behind him, but the red-haired Defense officer had already escaped.

****

"Let's take a little break," Nigel Mcavoy said, reaching for a dark, unlabeled bottle as Ianto peered over several tablets containing more of the old writing.

"We've just begun," Ianto said in surprise and Nigel's eyebrows rose in astonishment.

"Really my boy, you're far too serious. Go on then if you like, but five hours of work is enough for me," he said. "I'm going to find myself a nice late night snack."

He left and Ianto was about to turn back to his work when he saw Ira and Lymir walking outside of the office. They stopped, speaking briefly in low voices before Ira ran off in a different direction. Ianto frowned, got to his feet and went into the hallway.

"What's going on?" he asked Lymir.

Lymir jumped, whipped around and then calmed down. "Ianto Ambrose?"

He nodded.

"You've certainly been making yourself well-known. You are all I hear people talking about these days, Ianto Ambrose's arrival, Ianto Ambrose's magical skill with languages. Your discovery of that small discrepancy in the photo, that tiny writing—"

"You're changing the subject," Ianto pointed out.

Lymir smiled. "You are as sharp as they say," he said flatteringly. "I am changing the subject, but only because what you asked me about is far less interesting and important than what I asked you about. Never mind that. Are you really as good as they say at languages?"

"Yes," said Ianto bluntly.

Lymir's smile widened. "I've got something to show you then. I saw Nigel on his way to dinner. Nigel Mcavoy...well, he enjoys his dinners."

One of Ianto's eyebrows rose as he looked at Lymir, and thought, *so do you*, but he refrained from saying that. He followed Lymir out of the town hall and towards the entrance to the new tunnels.

The new tunnels were surprisingly dry and rocky, but there were still damp, boggy portions, and everything stank of mold. It was easy keeping up with Lymir, who said, "I heard you've deciphered twenty dialects of Desertpic already," as they turned a corner of the tunnelworks.

"Yes," Ianto said.

Lymir nodded, "You know all the dialects?"

Ianto shook his head. "I don't know," he said honestly. "I didn't know I could speak half the ones I can. I suppose my parents must have taught me...but I don't remember."

Lymir stared into his face curiously. "I am curious, where did you go after the tragedy?"

"My grandfather saved me," Ianto said bitterly. "I don't know why he decided to save me. Maybe he thought he'd get something for it. We hate each other."

"Hmm. I was raised by a rather unpleasant uncle myself, when I became a young orphan. His name was Tiberius, and he used to threaten to gut me and turn my bones into chess pieces if I ever disobeyed him. I never doubted he would."

Lymir turned the corner and asked, "What about non-Desertpic languages?"

"I know them all."

"Do you know what this is?" Lymir asked and Ianto looked ahead at the blank wall, except it wasn't blank. Ianto looked at the letters and symbols and they slowly formed some meaning.

"Some of our tunnelers found the space we are now standing in. It's old. It's part of the labyrinth Pomander's Lid was built upon. They thought it was only scratches. But I realized it was lettering of some sort. I just couldn't decipher it myself."

Ianto stepped closer, looking at the writing. "Why didn't you go to Mcavoy?"

Lymir smiled knowingly. "Mcavoy is enjoying his dinner."

"I've deciphered much of this," Ianto said to Lymir, and a look of excitement passed across Lymir's face. "I don't know what language it is though, just that it says approximately 'Storage Closet.'"

The look on Lymir's face quickly changed to one of clear disappointment. "Are you sure?" he asked.

Ianto nodded.

"Why do you need a whole wall to write 'Storage Closet'?" Lymir asked, irritation in his voice.

"This language they used needs many symbols to form each sound. It's strange they didn't use a more common language, though, since I see that on all the other public areas of Pomander's Lid. Is there anything stored in Pomander's Lid that they wouldn't want to be public knowledge?"

Lymir shook his head, frowning. "Pomander's Lid is an open place with few secrets."

"I don't think you believe that, Lymir."

Lymir looked at Ianto fondly. "You have your parents' perception. I am afraid I can't tell you what I think this 'storage closet' was used for, Ianto, but it's no concern of ours. Let's go back."

Lymir started down the tunnel, and Ianto called out to him, "Everybody keeps bringing up that I'm the son of Lavender and Edwin Ambrose as if that's supposed to mean something important. What did they do? I know they 'built the foundation,' for the protestor movement, but what does that mean? What did they really do?"

Lymir stopped, a look of true shock on his face. "You don't know? Your grandfather never told you? Ira?"

"Told me what?" asked Ianto, frowning.

"The Ambroses founded and built Pomander's Lid."

"Alaska, we have tried to do the best we can for you." Alaska looked up from where she sat in the back room with Helen, poring over maps of the Nation.

"We're very close to finding out where your family is being held in Lossit." There was a strange, sad smile on Helen's face. "I want to give you something."

Helen rose to her feet and crossed over to a weathered cabinet from which she pulled out a mother of pearl music box. She set it in Alaska's hands.

"This belonged to my daughter, Winter," said Helen, pain in her voice as she looked at the box in Alaska's hands. "I lost her... when she was about the same age as you."

Winter. She had heard that name many times recently, Alaska thought briefly as she looked down at the box in surprise.

"Helen, I'm sorry—"

"So am I, but that changes nothing," said Helen, putting her hand on Alaska's shoulder. "Take it."

"I couldn't."

"Take it, please. Besides, it's your birthday, December 1st, is it not?"

Alaska realized it was. She'd lost track of days and her birthday had completely slipped her mind.

"Alaska, would you leave Pomander's Lid if we asked you to?" Helen asked gently.

"Of course. I'd go anywhere to save my family."

"But would you hesitate? It is safe here, comfortable here. You have friends here," Helen said.

"I'd leave. I'd have to. But I'd miss my friends here," said Alaska. "And you. You've helped me and been so kind to me."

Helen just smiled. "What about that girl Holly, and that child of the provinces, Jakob? Would you miss them?"

"Yes," said Alaska.

"But you would still leave?"

Alaska nodded her head.

"That's good," Helen said, taking the map away from Alaska.

A red path was marked on it, crossing through the places Alaska remembered going through with Jakob and Gizel to get to Pomander's Lid. "You chose nearly the best route."

"Why are you testing me?" asked Alaska. "Why did you need me to mark a route?"

Helen just smiled. "You should go now. I will see you later."

"Helen..." Alaska began. "I don't know if Ira is a Magler's Child."

"He is," said Helen forcefully, her eyes narrowed. "He must be."

"I'm going to ask him," Alaska said and Helen shook her head vigorously in protest, horrified at such an action.

"Ask him? You think that's going to get you an answer, Alaska Donnel? He will merely lie, and perhaps hurt you."

"He's never tried to hurt me," Alaska said.

Helen sighed. "You don't know what Ira Graye is, Alaska Donnel—what he has done before. He is dangerous. Stay away from him."

****

Alaska saw Ira go into the hospital wing. She stopped and remembered Helen's warning, but curiosity got the better of her and she decided to go in. She didn't want to be perpetually paranoid about Ira. She wanted answers. She entered the hospital wing, but saw no sign of him and walked over to Tarana's bed.

"How are you?" Alaska asked as she settled next to Tarana, who looked extremely tired.

"A bit sore," Tarana said. "But I'm fine, I truly am, Alaska."

Alaska looked at Tarana skeptically.

"I'm fine, really," Tarana said, looking slightly flustered. "I should be free to go. That boy doesn't have to stay."

"That boy?" asked Alaska, looking across the hospital, and she saw Jakob's empty bed.

"*That boy* keeps running away," the doctor commented wearily from nearby. "He really shouldn't be putting so much stress on his leg. I keep trying to find him, but never can."

"I'll look around and see if I can find him," Alaska said knowingly. "Have either of you seen Ira? I saw him come in here."

"He's in the back in my office," the doctor said. "He injured himself, but it's nothing serious. I promised he could look at some of my antique book collection while he waited for me to finish with these patients."

Alaska saw an open doorway at the back of the hospital wing. She peered in and saw Ira sitting in a chair by a stack of dusty volumes that looked like they had been printed and bound hundreds of years before. She watched him turn the pages, his eyes skimming over them. It seemed impossible that he wasn't human, absurd. She almost turned around and walked out, but he looked up over the top of the book and saw her.

"Alaska?"

She took a deep breath, before asking point-blank, "Are you human, Ira?"

Ira stared at her in confusion. He looked as if he wanted to crack up laughing, but couldn't, seeing the seriousness on her own face.

"Yes, I am human. What else would I be?"

"I don't know. It's nothing," said Alaska quickly, "Silly…"

"Alaska," Ira rose to his feet, "Have you been talking to a woman named Helen?"

Alaska didn't respond.

"You have!" said Ira. "What has she said to you?"

"She said you were a robot," Alaska said.

"You believed that?" Ira looked incredulous. "Would you believe her if she said I was an alien with three eyes or breathed fire?"

"This isn't silly, made-up stuff. They existed, didn't they?" said Alaska sharply. "Robots that looked like humans?" She wanted him to say no. She didn't want to believe that such things could have existed, that they might still exist, sending henchmen after her. But Ira nodded his head.

"Yes, they did exist, I won't deny that. But I'm not one of them, Alaska. That woman hates me, whatever she's said about me, it isn't true." He saw the skepticism in Alaska's gaze and sighed, "Look at me." He pointed at a cut on his arm which had bled. "If I was a robot, could I bleed?"

"She said they were human and machine," Alaska said uncertainly.

"Well then, you can't know," Ira said, standing straight and stiff, his eyes not meeting hers. "You'll have to decide for yourself."

"Everything alright?" Alaska heard the doctor behind her.

She quickly nodded and pushed past him out the door. She passed by Tarana as she left the hospital wing.

The young woman called out to her, "Can you ask Gizel if he can stop by? It's been a week now, and he's not come to see me. I do miss him."

Alaska looked at her guiltily. "I'll try."

The work bells rang across Pomander's Lid and Alaska hurried back to her rooms to get her equipment for tunneling. As she pulled out the key to unlock the frontdoor, she felt something wasn't right and stopped. She turned the doorknob. The door was unlocked and as she entered she saw a piece of paper sitting on the table.

Alaska,
There is something you need to know, a development. Meet us as soon as possible. We need you to come NOW.

Helen

laska rushed into the back room of the church, gasping for breath, and saw Helen had laid out diagrams and maps of Pomander's Lid everywhere.

She looked at Alaska and snapped, "You're late."

"You didn't give me a time. I came as fast as I could."

Helen's face softened. "Forgive me, Alaska. Just run faster next time."

"What's all this for?" Alaska asked when suddenly the door behind her banged open. She jumped back as a scruffy, pale teenage girl entered.

"Gloriana Davies," Helen introduced her. "Gloriana, this is Alaska."

Gloriana stepped forward and looked Alaska over silently before nodding her head.

"So, you have not backed out?" Helen asked Gloriana.

"Of course not," Gloriana said reassuringly.

"What is going on?" Alaska asked. "What is all of this about?"

"The council will not have said a word of this to you. Pomander's Lid has always been much, much greater than even Defense could dream. The original mythical accounts of Pomander's Lid include a weapon. But that is no myth."

Alaska remembered Jakob telling her about a weapon, back in the facility when Pomander's Lid was still only a just a legend to her.

"Hidden somewhere inside of Pomander's Lid, it is said," Helen went on, "is something that can end Defense permanently.

Hidden deep within Pomander's Lid. We've looked for it. We've never found it."

Helen tossed the maps aside and began drawing on the desktop in chalk. "This is a map of the labyrinth below Pomander's Lid. We'll retrieve this mysterious weapon, and then use it against Defense and break out your family. We've procured an air-ship and using the map route you drew, we can get to Lossit."

"So when do we go get it?" Alaska asked, looking down at the map Helen was drawing. "Will the council help?"

"I tried to find this object before and the council stopped me," said Helen. "The council doesn't want to take action; it abhors action and favors bureaucracy. Lymir is here only because he is so corrupt and lazy not even Defense wanted him. Hawk was once great but now he's old and dusty, no more useful than a Still. That little mouthpiece of theirs, the idiot, is only in place to give Lymir more power. He'll agree to anything if properly threatened. Cassandra, meanwhile, is weak and everyone with half a brain in Pomander's Lid knows that, and exploits it for their own vile goals. Her life will be short and the council leadership will go to Lymir, anyway. Weaklings often die young. There's already been several assassination attempts against her. She survived only by luck."

"Assassination attempts?" said Alaska, stunned. "In Pomander's Lid?"

"This isn't paradise, Alaska," Gloriana sneered.

"Be gentle with the child, Gloriana," said Helen. "The council keeps Pomander's Lid's precious name pure by not mentioning the uglier side of it, but nothing's hidden from us. Look, this is the place I reached, before I was stopped."

Alaska leaned over and with her eyes, followed the path Helen traced from the entry of the tunnelworks to a marked spot.

"Wait, I know that spot," Alaska said, pointing. "It's not far from the gates—"

"There is a hidden door. You'll need a key, which I have." Helen reached into a desk drawer, removed a black key, and handed it to Alaska. "There was a blockade. It took me too long to figure out how to get around it and the council found me. But I have faith you can get through. You are clever, Alaska Donnel. I have watched you. You let nothing stand in your way. Nothing."

Alaska nodded her head uncomfortably.

"Gloriana will go with you on several trips to familiarize you with the area before searching for the weapon itself. Until you find it, Alaska, do not speak of us or this place to anyone. Do not trust anyone outside of this room. And most of all make sure the council trusts you. We cannot have another interference."

51

I anto returned to the wall marked Storage Closet. He put his hand to its surface and searched for a memory, any memory. Suddenly a vague image came to the forefront of his mind, a dark space with the outline of a figure standing very near to him. His father, Edwin Ambrose. He had brought Ianto here once before and whispered words. If only he could...

"The wolf is hiding in the rabbit-hole," said Ianto, in a voice deeper and not quite his own.

At first he thought nothing would happen, but then the wall covered in writing creaked inwards, and he entered. Every surface of the room was covered in a thick layer of dust and cobwebs. Dead spiders littered the floor and crunched under his feet. There was a rickety three-legged table and two broken chairs in the center of the room below a wrought iron hanging candelabra. On one side of the room was a low wall and he crossed over, looking over the side. All he saw was a dark, bottomless chasm with no apparent way up or down. But he knew he had been in the room before. What had Edwin done next? He searched his memory again and found the answer. He crossed over to the opposite wall. Edwin had spoken to a woman here, his mother Lavender, he was sure of it.

"If they try anything, if one of them tries to hurt you—" he could hear Edwin's voice in his head, almost as if he was standing directly next to him.

In his mind's eye, he saw their movements, the motions of ghosts.

"I will be safe, Edwin. This is what I do," Lavender said,

touching her husband's arm gently.

Edwin said...no, first he reached into his pocket and removed something. Ianto tried hard to remember and a small, blocky metal device came to the forefront of his mind. It rested in the palm of Edwin's hand as he held it out towards Lavender.

"Take it. It's a metal beeper, a simple communicator. It only gives off an SOS signal, but one of our friends will pick it up. If anything happens, go to the Hall of Remembrance. These walls are thick, you won't be able to get the signal out properly, but it'll work there. Set it off and help will come."

"Edwin, I can't, what if Defense..." Lavender shook her head, rejecting the beeper.

"I don't care, Lavender. I don't care about any of this anymore if one of those monsters kills you."

"But *I* didn't matter! You didn't care about *me!*" Ianto whispered, shaking with rage at the memory.

"I can't take that, Edwin. It's too dangerous," Lavender said.

"Then I'll leave it here for you, at least give you a chance," Edwin replied stubbornly as he got down on his knees, removed a hidden panel in the wall, and put the beeper in the nook, before covering it up again.

Ianto ran over to the exact same spot where his father had knelt years ago and felt along the wall, until he found a small, hidden release button. He pressed it and a section of the wall popped out slightly, allowing him to pry it loose. He threw the panel onto the floor. The nook was empty.

Alaska stood in front of the ship-holds, knowing the plan for that night. She and Gloriana would go in the tunnels in search of the weapon, find it, and give it to Helen, who said she had an ally who could get a Pomander's Lid air-ship. Then she and Alaska would leave, Helen had promised, to rescue Alaska's family. She didn't know if she would ever return to Pomander's Lid. She didn't know if they'd let her come back after what she was about to do. There was no choice, though, she thought. She had to do it to save her family. Ira, Cassandra, Lymir—they had all let her down. Now it was up to her and her alone to try to save her family, but she wanted to say goodbye first. She couldn't leave without doing that. Jakob was standing in the ship-hold with Cassandra, talking. The councilor seemed so easy-going and comfortable, not like someone who had just barely escaped two assassination attempts against her life, as Helen had revealed to her. Alaska wondered how anyone could be so comfortable in public after that.

"You want to be a pilot," said Cassandra, not as a question, but as a fact.

Alaska was startled for a moment. She had been lost in her thoughts as she approached them and was surprised at Cassandra's sudden acknowledgement of her presence. She saw Jakob also looking at her and wondered what he and Cassandra had been talking about.

"Yes," said Alaska immediately.

"She can be your first student then," said Cassandra to Jakob.

"If I do give you the pilot instructor position, however, you will be required to follow the doctor's orders and return to hospital wing for further rehabilitation."

"Okay," said Jakob. "First lesson starts now. Come on, Alaska."

"What?" said Alaska, her eyes widening in shock.

"However," said Cassandra, ignoring Alaska. "We do not have a fleet of air-ships, we are not Defense. If you crash..."

"I'll make sure she doesn't crash," Jakob said, eying Alaska.

"And you are sure you're well enough?" Cassandra asked Jakob uncertainly.

Jakob leaned his cane up against the wall away from himself. Alaska had seen enough of his progress to know that he had to be in excruciating pain, but he gave none of it away as Cassandra approvingly nodded for him to follow her up a ramp to where the air-ships were docked.

"Who taught you?" Alaska asked Jakob as they walked up the ramp.

"My father taught me when I was ten. He was a zeppelin pilot for bored Goldcage brats. I'm nowhere near as good, though, as the glorious Ira Graye—"

"Why do you dislike Ira so much? I feel like there's something else. He did something else, didn't he, besides not saving your sisters?" Alaska asked.

"...But I'm a decent flier," Jakob ignored her, finishing the sentence she'd interrupted.

The ramp got steeper which made it difficult to climb; Jakob slipped several times. Alaska reached forward to help him, but he staggered away from her, a fierce look on his face.

"Don't help me. I'm not an old cripple, understood, Donnel?"

"Understood, whatever your last name is," Alaska replied frowning. "What is your last name?"

"Do you want to guess?" Jakob asked, with a wry smile.

"Dylan," Alaska suggested.

"Nope."

"Datchery."

"Definitely not."

"Rumpelstiltskin."

"Not bad, only took you three guesses."

At the top Cassandra showed them the air-ship they could use. It was the worst of the lot, its cobbled parts seemingly hanging together by a thread.

"She has faith in us," Jakob said sarcastically.

Alaska and Jakob climbed inside and worked their way to the cockpit which was barely large enough for two people. Jakob took the pilot's position first and steered the air-ship up into the air. It rattled dangerously at first, swaying from side to side, then settled smoothly out of the ship-hold into the early night sky, still fairly bright over the desert. He went up higher until they were above the lower clouds. Alaska couldn't see most of the mountain range sheltering Pomander's Lid anymore, except for the mountain's highest peak where the glass room sat at the top of the Records, the room where she'd seen that strange light in the sky.

"Your turn," Jakob said suddenly, jumping up and pushing Alaska into the pilot's seat.

She grabbed the controls before the air-ship spiraled into the peak.

"You don't have to do much of anything on the newer air-ships," Jakob said wistfully as she tried to operate it, jumping from control to control to keep it from rocking violently, and nodding quickly as Jakob blathered on, wishing he would be quiet. "It's less work. Pilots get dumb and lazy. Careful, Alaska." She managed to turn the air-ship, but one of its wings still clipped the mountainside, rocking the vessel.

As soon as Alaska pulled out of the turn the air-ship jerked upward suddenly, and she felt the urge to vomit, but forced it back.

"Maybe I should take a bit of a break," Alaska suggested to him. "Will you—?"

"No," he said firmly.

After more minutes of turning around and around in a circle in midair she pleaded with him, "Please, Jakob, just take over."

"No," Jakob said for the umpteenth time.

Finally, after frantically flipping switches and pushing buttons in trial and error, she got the air-ship to fly straight.

"I've got it to work!" Alaska exclaimed, thrilled as it glided through the air, still rocking from side to side, but not as badly as before. She turned to Jakob and saw his calm expression.

"Careful of that green control, it'll dump the fuel," Jakob replied. Alaska quickly moved her hand away from a large, florescent green button.

"I'm not very good, am I?" Alaska asked, frustrated.

"No."

"I know," Alaska said, not sure whether she was annoyed or relieved by Jakob's candidness.

"You're brilliant."

Her hands froze on the controls and the entire air-ship shuddered in midair.

"You're burning fuel," he said and she quickly started the air-ship flying again.

"You're not just saying that?" Alaska asked, though she knew Jakob wouldn't.

"My first time I nearly crashed seven times in half an hour. You only managed to do that twice. And I think Ira Graye crashed his first time flying, suffered several broken ribs and a concussion."

Alaska's eyes widened. "Really?"

A machine could not have several broken ribs and a concussion, she thought with relief.

"Well, the ribs might have been from his instructor kicking him afterward," Jakob said coolly. "If you look at it, though, he was lucky. He nearly crashed into Lossit. They would have had his head for that. He's always been more interested in medicine than flying, anyway. He probably needs a legit reason for his ghoulish interest in body parts."

Alaska stared out of the window. The light was starting to change, the crisp dim semi light of evening turning to full darkness.

"It's time to go back," Jakob said quietly. Reluctantly Alaska turned the air-ship around, but for a long time she maintained their altitude.

She didn't want to return to the ground. Somewhere beyond, Nightghosts and Defense still waited. They couldn't reach her here in the sky. Right now Defense held her parents. *They have Leila, Malcolm and Marianne*, she thought, the thought that made her take the air-ship back down, towards the ship-hold. She glanced at Jakob as he stared out of the window, his brow furrowed. She wished she knew what he was thinking. She wanted to say something to him. Somehow put words to the odd feelings she had. They felt slightly crazy and she wondered if she was losing her mind. *Oxsana Cathar Hemming lost her mind*, Alaska thought, remembering the warnings her mother had given her and the bloodstained square. She pushed these thoughts away. Her fear and discomfort had nothing to do with his Provinical status, she assured herself. *I'm over that.* The real problem, she decided, was that she barely knew Jakob. How could it be sane to fancy him when she still didn't even know his last name? How could she feel as if she'd known Jakob all her life, as if being around him was the most right thing in the world?

"Alaska...you're a fast learner," Jakob said, oblivious to her thoughts. "In a couple of lessons you won't need any help.

Cassandra will see that, she'll want to use you, to make you part of her fleet, just another soldier on the front-line. I would say that's a bad idea, but...I know you won't just take someone at their word, you won't just do that. That's not you."

"How do you know that?" Alaska asked, staring straight ahead.

"Rumpelstiltskin," Jakob replied. Alaska stared at him in bewilderment.

"What?"

"That story, it's not in any Defense issue books. I haven't seen you around the library, so I'm guessing in the Capital, you were reading illegal books. That's against the Commandments, it's treason, but you did it anyway. The protestors, Pomander's Lid, the council, they haven't changed you. You've always done what you know is right. Just...just keep doing that."

Alaska wanted then to tell Jakob what she was planning to do. Everything about Helen, everything about the plan. But she couldn't. Instead she reached out and put her free hand over his.

"I will," Alaska said reassuringly, even as she felt more uncertain than ever, and she landed the air-ship.

Cassandra walked up clapping her hands in congratulations as Alaska and Jakob alighted from the air-ship. "That was very good," she said to Alaska, pulling her aside. "A few more lessons and we'll make you a full-time pilot."

"I—" Alaska started, but Cassandra cut her off and gave her a big hug.

"Go on, it's late, you're probably tired." Cassandra let go of Alaska with a bright, encouraging smile, before stepping away and nodding towards the exit.

"I can't stand fake smiles," Jakob whispered as he slipped past.

Alaska followed him through the ship-hold exit, feeling Cassandra's eyes on her all the way out. Silence fell between them as they walked towards the main square, and suddenly Jakob asked,

"Is there something you want to tell me?"

There's a lot of things I want to tell you, Alaska thought. Starting with Helen and the fact she would be gone the next day, and not see him again...maybe ever. She knew Jakob would understand if she told him why. He might not even care. He'd probably forget all about her in a few days, she thought, although the idea caused an uncomfortable tightening in her chest.

"No," she replied. "Goodbye...goodnight."

"Goodnight, Alaska," Jakob said hesitantly and then he walked away. She went in the opposite direction back to her room.

She looked over her shoulder and saw that he had stopped and turned to watch her leave. She'd seen it before in his eyes, a flash of some overwhelming emotion, and for the first time she realized she had seen that expression on another person's face as well. Malcolm had looked like that on Glory of Defense Day so many years ago, when Marianne Poesy had walked over to them at the banquet table.

I anto remembered being in a dark, dank room when he was a child. Peeling wallpaper covered the walls and there was a cot in a corner. A chandelier missing most of its crystal pendants hung high above, covered in rust and cobwebs. He knew it must be cold outside and was soaked to the skin in a heavy dampness as he sat huddled atop an antique chest, his face pressed to the grimy glass of a window. He could see figures moving on the street below, figures whose lives he never thought he would touch. Another young boy was being dragged by his mother down the street.

"But I don't want to!" he heard the child's cry through the thin glass and his mother's reply, "Jamie Campbell-Boyd, you will come with me right this instant!"

Ianto heard the door of the room creak open, but he didn't move, seeing his father's reflection.

"Look at me," Edwin Ambrose said insistently.

Ianto didn't move. Edwin crossed the room and pulled the moldering curtains across the window, before he caught Ianto's hand and dragged him to his feet. Ianto finally looked up at Edwin and saw he was just as soaked. There was a bandage across the side of his face.

"What happened?" Ianto asked.

"You acted very badly, Ianto," said Edwin as he dragged Ianto towards the door. "We told you not to leave the house, and you did anyway. Bad people could have come and taken you away from us. You should be glad we were able to rescue you. You should be thanking us."

Ianto turned his head away and Edwin slapped him, forcing him to turn around.

"You're going to be punished, do you understand? You're not to do that again, ever again. And you cannot leave this room unless we take you out. If you leave again, you'll be locked up in the Room."

"You said I could go downstairs," Ianto replied, his voice shaking. "You told me, in the other house, I could always go downstairs."

"Not anymore," said Edwin coldly. "Bad children like you don't get to leave their rooms. Now thank me."

****

Ianto opened his eyes. He was splayed out on his bed, and someone was knocking fervently on the door.

"I know you're awake, Ianto!" he heard Ira's voice on the other side and quickly got to his feet and opened the door. "Tarana's doing well—" Ira started, but Ianto cut him short.

"Why didn't you tell me my parents were the founders of Pomander's Lid?"

Ira stared at Ianto. "Who told you?"

"Lymir," Ianto said. "He told me they founded and built this place."

Ira nodded uncomfortably. "Come on, I'll explain while we walk."

Ianto followed Ira out the door. "Well?"

"I didn't know how you'd take it. How do you feel?" Ira asked, a look of curiosity on his face.

"It doesn't matter, it doesn't change anything," said Ianto bluntly, though he knew it was a lie.

It did matter to him. It changed everything. If he destroyed Pomander's Lid, Ianto thought, he would destroy Edwin and

Lavender's dream. He would destroy what they had thought more valuable than him. It no longer felt just like something he was doing to save Jamie, now it felt only right, like proper justice.

"They built this place in only six years," Ira said, waving his hands around as they maneuvered through the crowded streets. "The blood and sweat of hundreds of volunteers, fighting for a better future, working without rest for days on end. It's all in Pomander's Lid. It's beautiful, isn't it, Ianto?"

Ianto took in every detail, every laid stone, every wooden house, every smile on every oblivious face. And hated every square inch of it.

"It's alright," he lied to Ira, who shook his head, laughing lightly.

"What do I have to show you to impress you, Ianto?"

Ira stopped in front of a set of black gates Ianto had passed many times before. He tried to remember what was beyond them, but the first time he had come here, whenever that had been, he was sure this had either not existed, or he'd never entered it. They walked inside and Ianto saw it was a park. Green blankets carpeted the stone ground while trees, real, living trees, were laid out in a grid, pathways formed between them. They all seemed to link to one central spot, which Ira led him to. There stood a black heavily scratched stone monolith, an odd sort of glow coming off of it. As Ianto approached he realized the odd glow was from the deactivated bodies of failing messenger flies, who'd flown to that one spot to die. They lay scattered across the ground. He bent down, looked at one blankly, and saw water trickling off of the monolith in short, steady droplets like tears. Beneath the water the scratches looked magnified and became tiny letters to him.

"Jamie Campbell-Boyd," Ira said. Immediately a few letters near the top highlighted, forming Jamie's name. "There he is," said Ira. "He's not the only one."

Ianto turned away from the name, knowing the truth. "So this is a monument? Of everyone whose dead on the protestor side?"

Ira nodded grimly and Ianto knew he'd been staring at hundreds, maybe thousands of dead people's names.

"How does it work?"

"It's crude, really, this may only be one percent of the deaths. They're reported here to Pomander's Lid, then entered into our computer, which updates the monolith. Its facets are just plain stone, with a hologram of the names over it. This is only one facet. There are eight of them."

Ianto nodded, he'd already noticed. Thousands times eight...

"Look."

Ianto looked towards Ira and saw him pointing at the very bottom of the monolith. There was a thick band of steel with names engraved into it.

"Those are the names of the people who built Pomander's Lid," said Ira. "The people who died building Pomander's Lid."

Ianto looked down at the steel and frowned as it flashed in the light. For some reason the band and the names bothered him. He got down on his knees and reached out to touch it. He felt the cold metal against his fingertips and remembered. He had stood on the top of a steel ladder leading to the second level, before the elevator had been built.

"Come on, Ianto!" Lavender had said at the top, a bright smile on her face. "Come see your room."

Such a bright smile, he'd never seen a smile like that from her before or again. He'd turned his head, taking one last look back. And there was the expanse of Pomander's Lid, the foundations of wooden houses, of the town-hall. Stones were being laid in the main square, cables were being hung. But not by humans. By faceless, mechanical men.

Alaska's dream was different that night. She dreamed of a little boy under a table in a field of grass, softly crying. She tried to help him, but every time she did a red river materialized, and when she tried to swim across it, the water clung to her, thick and sticky and not like water at all, pulling her under, drowning her. She woke with a start, breathing heavily. The alarm clock in her room went off, marking midnight. It was pitch dark outside and everything was perfectly silent. Time to go. She rose quickly. She'd fallen asleep fully dressed and only had to slip on her shoes before leaving. She ran quickly, darting past a set of tall gates. She saw Gloriana first, then Helen beside her, a shawl pulled close around her so her face was hidden.

"You look happy, Alaska, but don't forget this will be dangerous," Helen said sternly when Alaska joined them. "Be extremely careful."

Alaska nodded.

Gloriana glared at her, before saying, "Yes, ma'am."

Helen's gaze dropped down to a dagger protruding from Alaska's belt.

"What is that?" she asked, and Alaska handed it over.

"Tarana gave it to me, before I came here," Alaska said. "I think it was Magler's."

"Yes, it was," said Helen, astonished. "This is very precious, Alaska, you wouldn't want to lose this."

"If there's danger—" Alaska started.

Gloriana snorted, "Yes, killer rocks."

Helen looked disapprovingly at Gloriana. "Alaska is taking precautions, a very smart thing to do. I advise you to listen to her." She turned back to Alaska, as Gloriana looked crestfallen and jealous. "Gloriana's pack contains a few old lasers I could scavenge. There is no need to risk this antique dagger. I'll hold onto it for you."

Alaska nodded uncertainly.

"Come, there's not much time," said Helen. "Go. We will meet with both of you afterward."

Gloriana led the way, Alaska behind her. They came to a stone wall and Alaska pulled the key out that Helen had given her before. To her surprise, the key flew through the air, attracted to the stone wall like a magnet. The wall moved and revealed an opening which they entered. Gloriana turned on her flashlight and handed Alaska another one.

"This way."

The walls were rife with empty spots where slabs of stone bearing various inscriptions had been pried loose, and she doubted the Pomander's Lid council had sanctioned the removals. Alaska followed Gloriana as she passed multiple open tunnel entrances. The sounds of her own footsteps and the soft drip of water coming through the rock formations echoed all around her.

"Are you Helen's daughter?" Gloriana asked sharply, more as a demand than a question.

"No," Alaska said, startled by the question. "Why would I be?"

"She talks about you like you're her daughter," said Gloriana bitterly. "Alaska said this, Alaska did that. You must notice."

Alaska shook her head.

Gloriana sneered, "Come on, then!" She sped off and Alaska had to run to keep with her until Gloriana stopped abruptly and Alaska nearly crashed into the back of her.

They were in front of a solid wall of steel.

"This is what stopped Helen before, but she found the answer," Gloriana said, reaching out one hand. She ran her finger across its surface in an odd pattern and Alaska realized she was spelling something.

"What—?" Alaska started to ask, and then she heard a resounding scream from somewhere inside of the tunnelworks. "Did you hear that?"

"Hear what?" Gloriana didn't turn around. She was still writing with her finger.

Alaska heard the soft approach of footsteps. She knew who they were before they came into sight, wraith-like, cloaked and hooded. They leered at her in the dark. She backed away, towards Gloriana, who had stepped back from the wall as the sound of churning mechanisms came from somewhere inside it.

"Gloriana, we've got to go," Alaska said. "Look, look right now."

"Just a moment," Gloriana snapped.

"No, look," Alaska said, but Gloriana didn't.

They were closing in.

"You can't be here," Alaska whispered. "You don't belong here."

But they stood unwaveringly, reaching out spindly ghost fingers for her. At the same time the wall shot upwards and Alaska ran through, past Gloriana. She heard the wall clang back down after Gloriana followed, cutting them off from the rest of the tunnelworks.

"Did you see them?" Alaska asked gasping for breath.

Gloriana glared at her, "See who?"

Alaska shook her head. There was no way they could get to her now, as long as the solid wall of metal stood between them. "Never mind."

They walked down a pathway, which eventually split, but Gloriana knew exactly which way to go. Alaska smelled a strange, earthy odor as she walked forward and found herself on a ledge, below her the bottom of a huge cavern, filled with water though to what depth she couldn't tell. Red dots covered the ground between her and the edge, where Gloriana stood.

"They set off alarms," Gloriana said. "The council will be alerted we're here if you step on them. Go around very, very carefully."

Alaska cautiously maneuvered around them. Gloriana dropped a rock into the pool and it sank out of sight.

"Can you swim?"

Alaska nodded and Gloriana jumped off the ledge and plunged into the water. Alaska followed her a moment later, shivering the minute she hit the ice-cold waters. Alaska waded forward, but it only got higher until it swelled to nearly over her head. As she made her way back up towards the light, she saw a tunnel ahead, from which a soft glow emanated. She had to keep going, she thought, it was just a little further. There was no sign of Gloriana.

"Gloriana!" she yelled, her voice reverberating off the stone walls, but there was no reply.

She struggled to keep above the ever-deepening water. Then it was far above her head, and she was beneath its surface, in a strange, murky, distorted world. She could see the bottom even further below, dropping off into darkness, though she could just make out polished squares of black and white. Underneath all of the water, the ground was checkered like a chessboard. That had to be man-made, Alaska thought, and then she broke through back to the surface, gasping for breath, and swam onto the sandy shore. She lay there, collecting herself, teeth chattering and then scrambled onto her feet. She looked around for any sign of the other girl, but there was none. Had she gotten lost, been washed out into some other passageway? Alaska looked down the tunnel. It concluded in a dead end, but in front of the blank stone wall was a pedestal. Alaska walked towards it, and saw there was a bare, dirty wooden chest sitting on top of it. She reached out, and suddenly a figure burst out from nowhere, sending her flying against the wall. She saw Gloriana grab the chest.

"I wasn't going to run off with it," Alaska said indignantly. "Is it there?"

Gloriana didn't respond as she scrabbled at the lock. Alaska looked around the tunnel, and saw a metallic glint from a dirty corner. She glanced at Gloriana, still struggling to open the chest. She walked over and pressed away the muck to find a small, gold key on a frayed ribbon.

"I found something!" Alaska called out, just as Gloriana threw the lid of the chest open.

A horde of sand-rats emerged. Gloriana screamed and backed away from the chest as the sand-rats crawled across the ground towards her, their glowing electronic eyes forming pinpoints of light in the darkness. Alaska grabbed the paralyzed girl's arm and dragged her back towards the water.

"We have to get out of here, we have to swim!" she screamed into Gloriana's ear.

Finally Gloriana seemed to snap out of it. Gloriana leapt into the water, and Alaska put the ribbon with the key around her neck before following. She remembered the stories she'd heard about Samson Magler's deadly failed experiments. Sand-rats were waterproof, and could easily swim, much faster than a human being. Alaska forced herself to paddle hard, her heart beating fast. She looked back and saw the shore was empty. The chest lay empty on the ground, and there was no sign of the rats, which meant they could only be in....

"Alaska!" she whipped around, hearing Gloriana's scream.

She was bobbing a little ways away in the water, and Alaska could see the sand-rats biting her. Alaska knew she couldn't do anything in the water to help her. She looked towards the ledge and remembered the red alarms. She swam towards them.

Alaska felt the first bite most painfully. She could see it out of the corner of her eye; a stray sandrat had latched itself onto her leg. She threw it off with a powerful kick, but the water around her leg began to turn red and she felt a paralyzing pain spread through her injured limb. More rats were coming, scenting the blood like piranhas. She felt the stone wall with her hands and hauled herself out of the water, but the world was becoming floaty, a haze of pain. Her hands and feet felt boneless and flabby, slipping and sliding over the wet rock as she tried to climb upwards. Then she heard a terrible, gut-wrenching scream from Gloriana, and she forced herself to keep going, until she could see a single red dot swimming in front of her eyes. She slammed her fist down onto it, and saw the cavern bathed in blood red light before she fell unconscious.

Alaska opened her eyes. She was drenched but wrapped in a thick, warm blanket. Cassandra stared down at Alaska with a hard expression on her face. She was dressed in a slightly darker patchwork uniform with a stun gun attached to her leather belt.

"Cassandra."

Alaska turned her head to see who'd spoken and saw Gloriana, covered in cuts but looking as composed as ever.

"Go to hell."

They were both just outside the entrance to the tunnelworks, surrounded by guards.

"The second girl is coming to," one of the guards said.

"They're going to try and arrest us, like they did to Helen," Gloriana said in a barely audible whisper to Alaska. "Then they'll chain us in a cell, and let us live half-starved in the dark, while they pretend we're being treated civilly."

"Where did you get this key?" Cassandra asked coldly, holding up the black magnetic device. "What were you doing in the labyrinth? Both of you should know it's off-limits."

"Off-limits, but not illegal," said Gloriana, before Alaska could speak.

"That depends on what you were doing," Cassandra snapped. "What were you doing?"

"We were curious, that's all," Gloriana said. "Weren't we, Alaska?"

Alaska felt dazed but managed to quickly nod her head, feeling around her neck. The ribbon was still there and she felt the cold, wet metal surface of the key against her skin.

"Wait, here's something."

Alaska saw Gloriana jump as one of the officers suddenly unclipped something from beneath her collar.

"S.O.S beeper. It's an outside communication device. That's illegal in Pomander's Lid!"

"I just found it on the ground in one of the tunnels!" said Gloriana, her voice angry. "I was going to give it the council!"

"Check her pack," Cassandra said, swinging over the dark rucksack she'd apprehended from Gloriana.

"Run," Gloriana whispered to Alaska. "When I tell you to."

"What are you going to do?"

"There's lasers," said the guard examining the rucksack, "Powerful ones, though they're very old. They must have been stolen from armory."

Gloriana yanked off her boot and pulled up a red lever on a metal device sewn into it.

"RUN!"

There was a flash of white light.

Alaska ran, throwing herself sideways, as there was a deafening blast. She saw the officers and Cassandra caught in the light. They fell to the ground. The light finally vanished and Alaska scrambled onto her feet.

"You killed them," Alaska gasped.

"It won't kill the idiots," Gloriana hissed. "Come on."

Alaska ignored her and ran towards Cassandra's fallen figure.

Gloriana chased after her and caught her arm, "Come with me!"

"I'm not leaving Cassandra," Alaska said as she fought Gloriana off and freed herself.

She dropped down on the ground beside Cassandra. Blood

soaked her clothes. Her eyes were open wide in shock and her breathing was ragged.

"Go for help!" said Alaska frantically. "She needs immediate help, Gloriana!"

"No," Gloriana said. "If I do, they'll say it was our fault. They'll say we did it on purpose. Both of us. Do you want to go to jail, Alaska? We should tell Helen what happened."

"I won't leave her, I won't let her die," said Alaska, desperately trying to stop the bleeding.

"Alaska," Gloriana's voice was right beside her ear. Gloriana tightly grasped her bloody hands and pulled her away from Cassandra. "There's nothing you can do, unless you want to take the blame for this. We need to report to Helen. She'll get us out of this, okay?"

Alaska rose to her feet and nodded her head as Gloriana led her away to Helen's place.

"Are you sure she can help us?" Alaska asked, but Gloriana was already knocking. The doors opened immediately and Helen ushered them inside with, "Where is it?"

"It wasn't there..." Gloriana started, but Alaska cut her off.

"Helen, we were caught. Gloriana set off an explosion and she nearly killed Cassandra. Cassandra's really hurt, you have to help her."

Helen looked from Gloriana to Alaska with an unreadable expression, and then said flatly, "Well, then, you better go help her, Gloriana."

Gloriana's eyes narrowed, and she looked as if she was about to protest, but Helen put her finger to her lips and nodded her head in the direction of the door. Gloriana bowed her head and left.

"I better help..." Alaska started after Gloriana, but Helen caught her arm.

"No, not you. This is Gloriana's mess, she will clean it up. I need you to tell me exactly what happened."

Helen walked to the back room, and Alaska followed beside her, telling her every detail of what had happened, except the scream and seeing the Nightghosts.

"Let me see the key," Helen said.

Alaska removed it from around her neck and handed it to Helen. Helen looked at it curiously, then gestured at a small, grimy sink where Alaska could wash.

"I don't know what this goes to, but it's a start. We will have to make a new plan."

She looked pensive for a moment, and then crossed over to Alaska who was rolling up her sleeves, lightly touching a spot on her arm where a sand-rat had bit her.

"We don't put you through too much, do we, Alaska?"

"No, I want to do this," said Alaska, washing her hands. "If this will save my family."

Helen's gaze dropped down to a long, thin, jagged scar near the sand-rat bite. It was several years old, but still vicious looking.

"Did someone cut you?" Helen asked with concern.

"No," said Alaska. She turned off the taps and stared at the scar. She had never thought about it before, but now she realized she had no idea how she'd gotten it. It didn't look natural.

Helen shook her head, a sad look on her face. "Have you been happy, Alaska?"

Alaska looked at Helen, unsure how to answer the question. "I...I'll be happy when I know they're safe. That Defense can't ever get them."

"But you'll never truly be, will you?" Helen leaned in closer, looking carefully at Alaska's face. "I can see it in your eyes. When I see you smile, it looks like a mask, covering up so much sadness. You are young, Alaska, you shouldn't be so sad."

"I'm...I'm fine now, Helen," said Alaska, her voice shaking. "I think I should see if Cassandra..."

"Follow me, Alaska."

Helen crossed the room and pulled back a tapestry, revealing a hidden door. She turned the doorknob and stepped through. Alaska hesitated, then followed her. A short set of cracked steps led into a room with a low ceiling and a single shuttered window. The only light came from candles lining the room. There was a screen hanging in the center of the room and cushions on the floor. Helen went over to the screen and pressed a button. It switched on, and Alaska nearly cried out as she saw her old home. There they all were, immortalized on film: her mother, her father, her sister, her brother. It had to be from only a year ago.

"I remember recording this," said Alaska, a smile slipping onto her face as her sister waved at the camera. "I got the camera for my birthday. How did you get it?"

"It was saved from the wreckage of your home."

On the video, Malcolm Donnel said with a wide smile, "Let's do it!" and in a off-tone chorus, they all began to sing "Happy birthday, Alaska."

Tears ran down Alaska's face. She turned to thank Helen and saw the woman was leaning against the wall, tears in her eyes as her whole body shook.

"Helen?" Alaska said in bewilderment. She stepped towards the trembling woman. "Helen, are you alright?"

"I lied to you," Helen said, her voice hoarse. "There are things I need to tell you, Alaska Donnel..."

Helen was cut short by a bang outside the room, and then the door flew open. A battered Ira appeared in the doorway, laser in hand, a furious look on his face.

"I told you to stay away from her!"

Ira locked the door behind himself and aimed the laser gun at Helen. Alaska threw herself in front of the woman.

"Ira, what are you doing?"

"Get away from her, Alaska, she'll kill you."

"She wouldn't..." Alaska started. She felt the cold blade of Magler's dagger press into her throat and froze.

"You will turn around and go immediately. You will never threaten my life again," said Helen, her voice like ice.

"There's three of your people waiting outside to rip me apart," Ira said. "And I know if I turn my back on you, you'll kill me."

"Then she dies," Helen said. Alaska felt the dagger nick her neck.

"You would put your life over hers," Ira said, glaring at Helen. "You're a worse monster than I thought you were, Helen Magler."

"Helen Ma—" Alaska said in horror and disbelief. "Helen, please don't do this."

"The Nightghosts made her a weapon!" Helen ignored Alaska's plea and spoke to Ira. "They've claimed her, they'll never let go of her. What life is that for anyone to lead? Death would be kind."

"You said they didn't do anything to me!" said Alaska.

"I lied," Helen responded and she looked at Ira. "To kill me, you'll have to lose her."

"You won't kill her," said Ira, not lowering his laser.

Alaska's eyes widened. She was sure she was dead, any second Helen would kill her. Instead, Helen's grip relaxed, the coldness of the dagger blade disappeared, and Helen shoved her away.

"I can't kill her," Helen said, her voice breaking. "But I can kill you, Ira."

Helen threw the dagger. An involuntary scream escaped Alaska's lips. The dagger flew through the air towards Ira, who threw himself sideways, but wasn't fast enough to avoid it grazing his arm, before embedding itself in the wall behind him. Blood stained the sleeve of his shirt. Ira hit the floor and the laser gun spun out of his hand. Helen made a dive for the laser gun, but Alaska beat her to it and snatched it off the floor. She remembered Ira had said there were three followers of Helen's outside the room. She helped Ira onto his feet and ran to the shuttered window.

"Alaska—" Helen started pleading, but Alaska pushed aside the part of her that wanted to listen, that wanted to give Helen a chance to explain herself.

Helen was beyond forgiveness. Alaska managed to force open the shutter, then the window, and shoved Ira through. He cried out as he hit the ground on his injured arm.

"Don't go, Alaska," Helen said. "Don't follow him."

Alaska jumped out the window. Ira was already on his feet again, and they ran to the end of the narrow alley they'd fallen into.

"She's crazy," Alaska said when they stopped at the end of the alleyway. "You were right. I shouldn't have listened to her. It was all a lie." It was then she remembered. "Cassandra!"

"What?" said Ira, startled.

Alaska ran towards where the explosion had happened, Ira close behind her. Cassandra and the guards lay on the ground abandoned. There was no sign of Gloriana. Alaska dropped onto her knees beside Cassandra. The woman was still, her eyes shut.

"We have to get her to the hospital wing, Ira, and tell the council about Helen."

Alaska heard footsteps behind them and turned around. She saw Helen's figure approaching, half in shadow. She scrambled to her feet, but Helen had already reached them, Alaska's dagger in her hand. Helen fixed her gaze on Ira, but when she spoke, it was to Alaska.

"Alaska, I'm sorry I frightened you. I never would have killed you. But Ira has to die. He is one of them. I know he is, he means to hurt you. I am doing you a kindness."

"He's not a Nightghost, Helen," Alaska said, but she knew Helen didn't care what she thought as the woman raised the knife grimly, "And you're not hurting him with my dagger."

Alaska did the only thing she could do. She had never let go of Ira's laser gun. She fired it at Helen's arm. Helen hit the ground, a look of utter surprise on her face as she looked up at Alaska. The dagger flew out of Helen's hand. The woman tried to rise to her feet and Alaska fired the laser gun again, at her leg. Helen collapsed against the ground, groaning in pain. Alaska stared at her in utter shock, not noticing at first when Ira stepped forward and gently eased the laser gun from her immobilized hands.

"Are you okay?" Ira asked Alaska, who merely nodded, dazed.

"Cassandra," Alaska whispered. "Cassandra needs to be taken to the hospital wing."

"Take her," Ira said coldly, to Alaska's bewilderment.

"Ira—?" Alaska started, but he had already upped the settings on the laser and fired it again at Helen's leg.

A horrible scream escaped from between Helen's lips. The air filled with a burnt, metallic smell. The scream made Alaska freeze. It felt as if something ice cold had just been poured down her spine. Then she saw the wound the laser shot had left behind. While at first it looked like any nasty injury, Alaska saw beneath the blood a sliver of brass clockwork poking through, and a tangle of wires and tubes running through the mechanisms like veins.

"She really is one," said Alaska, her eyes widening as she realized what she was seeing. "Helen is a Magler's child."

Ira got down beside Helen. The woman was gasping in pain, her face contorted and ash white. She stared up into Ira's face, a hateful, but strangely fearful look on her face.

"I've done nothing by your human standards to deserve this. You lied to me, Ira Graye. You said you wouldn't hurt Winter, and you did. Tell her. Tell Alaska what you did."

Ira pointed the laser at Helen's heart.

"No!" Alaska said desperately, taking a step forward. "Ira, we'll tell the council. They can decide what to do with her. She can't hurt anyone now, Ira, don't kill her!"

"You can't stop destroying, can you? Not even for her," Helen spat. "It's the only thing you're good at. You're too proud and stupid to get what you want any other way. You're a murderer, Ira Graye. You're the very worst kind of human."

"Don't kill her, Ira!" Alaska shouted.

He fired.

Alaska was twelve years old and everything was right with the world. Everything was wondrous, with a strange, bleary magic, and all of her family was around her. Then she was running through a muddy field and everything whizzed past her, the world a blur, the skies overcast and gray. Rain fell. There was a ledge. She flew like a bird. Then darkness encompassed everything and suddenly there was silence, then shadows. And Helen's voice screaming, "Winter!"

Alaska opened her eyes. The memory of what happened earlier slowly began to come back to her as she realized she was in her room in bed. Ira had fired the laser gun, Helen had screamed, a horrible scream that echoed throughout Pomander's Lid, piercing through the calm. Alaska had felt a splitting pain in her head before she'd grabbed Cassandra by the shoulders and dragged her away to the hospital. The doctor had tried to get her to stay, but she refused, and left for her room. She had tried to harden herself, had sworn not to cry, but when she reached her room and collapsed onto her bed, the tears had come, and they wouldn't stop. Even when she had pressed her face into her pillow, trying desperately to suppress the tears and all the emotions, to bury it all deep inside of herself behind locked doors.

She didn't remember falling asleep. As she raised her head, she realized someone was knocking at the door. She got up and looked out the window. Ira was standing outside her door. She didn't move, but he kept knocking and finally she opened the door. He barged in, carrying a steaming mug.

"How are you doing?" was the first thing he said as he sat at the table.

Words came to her mouth, stiff and in a voice very much unlike her own. "I'm fine."

"Alaska..." Ira started, setting down the mug, then seeming to decide against whatever he was going to say, pulled Alaska's dagger out of his pocket. "I got it back for you."

He held it out to her and she took it immediately. For the first time, Ira noticed the music box on the kitchen table.

"Did Helen give you that?"

"Yes," Alaska said, gripping the antique Magler's dagger in her hand a little more firmly.

He eyed the music box. "You don't have to be scared of me. I'm not going to hurt you, you know," he said as he flipped open the music box.

A melancholy, sharp sound came from it. The sound filled Alaska's ears and made her head hurt.

"I know that," said Alaska.

Ira watched her for a moment, then pushed the mug towards her.

"Hot chocolate. It might be a little burnt," said Ira quickly. "I'm still learning." He flashed her a small smile she didn't return, before saying, "I was worried about you. The doctor said you just ran out of the hospital wing."

"I said I was fine," said Alaska. She placed a hand tentatively on her still aching head and pointed at the door, "You can go."

"You have no reason to be scared of me," Ira said, sounding hurt. "Cassandra's alright, you know. I told her what you did, carrying her to the hospital wing on your own. She realized you were only a victim too, and she wants to thank you personally. She...she asked me to tell you Helen's true nature has to remain a secret. Nobody but the council and the two of us can know she wasn't human."

Alaska stared at the mug. "You didn't have to kill Helen."

"I don't believe bad people should be allowed to live," Ira said coldly. "She wasn't even human, Alaska. Is destroying a machine murder?"

There was a silence between them filled by the sound of the music box, before Alaska nodded at it.

"Turn it off, Ira," Alaska demanded.

Ira immediately obeyed, shutting the lid. "Helen was a lying creature who tried to use you and would have killed you when you weren't useful anymore if you didn't remind her of her adopted daughter. There's no weapon in Pomander's Lid, no panacea. She told you what you wanted to hear and you believed it. She used a little g—"

"I'm not a little girl!" Alaska snapped, and he nodded quickly.

"No, you're not," he said, staring into her face. "You were desperate, I understand how badly you have to get your family out of the Crypts. Helen was very dangerous. Helen was suspected of trying to kill Cassandra before and she was in Pomander's Lid's prison several times."

"She knew you," Alaska said. "She was afraid of you."

"I haven't done anything wrong," said Ira.

"She could have been locked up. She didn't have to be killed!" Alaska fumed. Ira leaned back at the fury in Alaska's voice as she collapsed on the edge of her bed and buried her head in her hands. "I heard her scream. I know she was evil, I know she wasn't even human. But it felt wrong, Ira, and it sounded wrong."

"It was a terrible thing to see," said Ira, grimacing. "I wish you hadn't seen that."

"I didn't see her die. I didn't look. But I saw you. You looked like a Defense Speaker."

"I'm not anything like a Defense Speaker," said Ira, sounding shocked. "I didn't enjoy it, Alaska. I don't make a habit out of killing. Afterward, I didn't know what to do, I was angry and terrified. I was angry at what she did to you, terrified she might try and hurt you again if I let her go. Her mind is not like ours, she could have done anything, she could have changed her mind about you."

Ira's hands shook and he gripped the edge of the table. "I'm sorry she's gone," he said. "I truly am. I didn't want to kill her."

Alaska didn't speak, her anger numbed by Ira's words and her memory of being chased by Helen, of her own fear.

"I have a memory gap from when I was twelve years old," Alaska said, realizing something. "Helen told me I was taken by an order that swore to protect the Magler's children machines and defeat Defense—the Nightghosts. She told me they didn't do anything to me, but then...she said that was just a lie and they did. But she told you that, Ira, as if you knew I'd been taken."

"I do," Ira said and Alaska looked up at him in surprise. "Four years ago, in 137, I was frequently put on Defense curfew patrol. One time, there was a car crash. Helen and a little girl. The little girl was you."

Alaska looked at Ira, wide-eyed. "I did know you before."

"Did you think you knew me?" said Ira, surprised. "It was quick. I did the best I could to help you, but you were seriously injured, so I went back for help. When I returned, Helen was battered, mumbling something about trying to stop the Nightghosts and you were gone. Nearly a year later you were found on a bridge in the Capital with the rhyme about the Nightghosts pinned to your sleeve. It's a rather twisted way of marking a child as theirs."

So the Nightghosts did take me, Alaska thought with dread. *And they did something to me.*

"Do you know what they did to me?"

"I don't know, Alaska."

Ira watched her sympathetically and she hated that expression.

She did not want to be pitied. She wanted to know what was wrong with her, but then again, a part of her didn't. What if it was something terrible?

"Helen took a small gold key from me before...before she died," Alaska said, her voice shaking slightly. "It was on an old ribbon. I want it back."

"The key belongs to Pomander's Lid. The council confiscated it along with all the other things in her apartment. I just barely managed to get your dagger from next to her body without them noticing. I can ask if they'll give the key back to you, but I doubt they will," Ira replied. "There is no weapon, Alaska. Only a plan."

She felt his hand touch her face and jumped, grabbing his arm. While she had been looking down, he'd managed to cross the room soundlessly. He was standing next to her, and had been reaching for a strand of her hair when she grabbed him. She let go of him and he stepped back at the look on her face.

"Don't touch me," she said, getting to her feet. "In fact, get out. Tell the doctor I'm fine."

"You can trust me. I'm not the one who tried to kill you," Ira said impatiently.

"I don't think you'd ever try to kill me," said Alaska, and she quickly added, "But I don't know you, and I don't trust you one bit, Ira Graye."

"Alaska..."

"This plan, what is it? Don't I deserve to know something? I'm always the one being kept in the dark. It's always 'mind your own business Alaska, while we conduct our brilliant plan.' Well, that didn't work so well with Malcolm and Marianne, did it?"

Her voice was full of venom.

"I'm sorry, Alaska, but I can't tell you anything," Ira replied.

"If you can't tell me anything, leave."

Ira walked to the door and opened it to leave. A shout came

unexpectedly from the doorway.

"Ira!"

Alaska saw Ianto stop in the doorway, looking between the two of them. She noticed his strange face again, so blank and unmoving with cold, glassy gray-blue eyes. "Coming, Ira?"

Ira nodded his head and to Alaska's surprise said, "Just a moment." Ianto hurried away, and Ira turned back to Alaska.

"I can tell you something, Alaska. If you want to know who I am, I'll tell you. I'm Ira Julian Graye, born January 1st, 117 in the Capital, son of Sarah and David Graye. I started working for Defense the moment I turned eleven years old. When I was nineteen, not much older than you, I was told to execute a protestor. I was told I had to do it, or my mother and I would take her place. The protestor was Helen's adopted daughter, Winter. I...I shot her, but she didn't die. She was let go and put in a mental hospital. She's like a Still now, nearly comatose. She can't speak, or write. I never wanted to...I never wanted to hurt her."

Alaska realized Ira was crying. It was strange, the first time she had ever seen him cry.

"I was scared and Defense used me. Helen didn't understand. She swore to get me back for what I did someday, to take revenge on me. She always said I'd taken from her the thing she loved most and she'd do the same to me. I would have died a thousand times, Alaska, instead of do what I did, but my mother...Winter isn't dead, but I know I murdered everything she was and I can never forget that."

Alaska didn't speak for a long minute, and then when she did, her own words surprised herself.

"You didn't have a choice," she said, though she wasn't talking about Winter at all. "It's not your fault."

Ira looked over his shoulder at her, a grateful expression on his face, before he shut the door behind himself.

58

Lossit

Melissa Johnson ran down the corridor and stopped at a heavy metal door. There was a sign on the door that read simply 'The Box.' Johnson entered, briskly walked down to a stage and found a control-pad in the wall. She picked up a set of headphones and inserted a round, peg-like key into a panel on them. As soon as the key turned the panel came loose, revealing a red button, which she pushed. The room filled with voices, strange, strangled, mechanical voices, all talking over each other.

"I've given you time," said Melissa Johnson coldly. "Have you found the name?"

A perfect silence fell. Then the air all around began to pixelize and form a shape in front of her. A moment later, she was staring into the face of Ianto Ambrose.

****

Clement stood on the glass bridge. Heavy smog, a gray which bled into the dark red of the sky as the sun set, blanketed the Capital. The Capital clock tower managed to break through the opacity of the blanket, the clock-face stained a pinkish color by the odd light. The hands ticked stoically on.

"Johnson!" said Clement cheerily as she appeared, clicking down the bridge towards him, the expression on her face giving away no emotions.

"Was Mir Counta found?"

"I'm afraid not," Clement said.

They stood side by side in silence, before he said, nodding his head towards the view of the city, "It's beautiful, isn't it?"

"If you think that is beautiful, Clement, you have seen very little," said Johnson coolly, as some Goldcage tycoon's ridiculous, rainbow-colored, fish-shaped zeppelin passed by. "The provinces, they are truly beautiful."

Clement's eyes widened in surprise. "The provinces?"

Johnson nodded her head. "When Defense was first created, I was the council's favorite, head of the science team, head of the militia. They would have stationed me anywhere I liked, and I loved the provinces, but I did not choose the provinces."

"Why?"

"Because the Speakers have grown into fat, slow and lazy backstabbing bastards. If I had chosen what I wanted, the others would have whispered poison to the council about me and forced me out so they could claim the council's favor for themselves. I would have become nothing but another grunt. So I stayed in the Capital. One day I'll be shed of this choking bureaucracy, Clement, one day things will be simpler, but until then I would rather reign in hell, even if it means destroying heaven."

Clement looked at her sadly, but also curiously. "Why are you telling me all this, Melissa?"

"Because you lied to me," said Johnson turning to face him, her voice low and vicious. "And though you are very dear to me, Clement, I will execute you."

Clement stumbled backwards, looking shocked, "Johnson..."

"I got a very interesting message from the Chasm, Clement," Johnson said coldly.

"You said you were going to shut it down. It's a pointless experiment. It only hurts you. The screams..."

Johnson ignored Clement. "They gave me a name. Ianto Ambrose. You told me he was Lavender and Edwin's son."

"Ma'am," there was a fearful expression on Clement's face and his hands shook. "I gave you the findings from his DNA test. It said he is their son."

"He is not," Johnson spat. "He is not their son. You lied to me. It's Vladimir Hemming's stupid little mad daughter, isn't it? The girl has hated me since I refused to push for her clemency. She wants her father, the Speaker for nothing more than Forestry and Mining, to get to the prize of Pomander's Lid, to get the council's favor! Oxsana made you do this, Oxsana is after it. Oxsana!"

Johnson quickly removed her laser gun, and Clement held out his hands desperately. "They threatened me, Johnson. Don't kill me."

"You ask for a great deal considering you haven't caught that red-haired imposter and now have two strikes against you. Tell me who threatened you." Johnson didn't raise her voice when she spoke to Clement, but the quietness made it seem all the more dangerous, her expression like a madwoman's.

"I didn't see...a face," Clement gasped. "Just a voice. But it wasn't Oxsana, Johnson. It was a young man's voice. I don't know who, but the voice was familiar. He said something about Nightghosts, just children's rhyme gibberish. Please don't kill me."

Johnson pointed the laser gun at him. He shook, wheezy pleas spilling out of his mouth, before she dropped the laser. He looked up in shocked relief, unable to believe she hadn't killed him.

"The young man was undoubtedly Mir Counta," said Johnson coldly. "He may have fled to the provinces already, but I have a friend there who can hunt him down."

"Thank you, Johnson," Clement said, staring up into her face. "For forgiving me."

Johnson frowned at him, puzzled. "I didn't forgive you."

She raised the laser gun again and fired. Clement slumped to the floor as two guards came running.

"Clean up this disgusting mess," Johnson said coldly as her heels clicked across the glass bridge and out of sight.

"Who did you lose to the Crypts?"

Ira looked at Ianto in surprise. They were in Ianto's room, Ira in a chair, Ianto on the edge of his bed, staring across at the kitchen cabinet in which he'd hidden the SOS beeper, behind several canisters of salt. He had heard an explosion on his way to the old tunnels and seen Alaska and Gloriana run away. When they were out of sight he'd taken the beeper off an unconscious guard and hid when Gloriana came back for it. Ianto had seen Helen die. He collapsed the moment her scream began, so short, yet so much worse than even the screams he'd inexplicably heard in Lossit. He'd been overcome by a massive headache. Some of the pain still lingered, but he barely felt it, knowing he now had everything he needed. The beeper was safely in his pocket, and he knew where the Hall of Remembrance was.

"Somebody very close to me," replied Ira simply to Ianto's question.

"Did you try to stop it? Did you try to get them out?"

"Of course," said Ira. "I tried everything."

Something in Ira's expression was silencing, saying he wanted to answer no more questions on the subject.

"I'm worried," said Ira confidentially. "The incident with Helen...that disciple of Helen's, Gloriana, still hasn't been found. I always strive to make things better. To fix things. But in the end I sometimes make things worse for people, don't I, Ianto?"

Ianto didn't respond.

Ira sighed and turned to him. "I was hoping you'd disagree."

Ianto almost told Ira he did, but swallowed his words. It was a lie he was unwilling to tell, not when Ira had brought him to Pomander's Lid, and he had every intent of destroying it.

Ira went on, "Lymir wants to meet you. They like you, the council..."

"Ira, who really built Pomander's Lid?" Ianto interrupted.

Ira stared at Ianto. "I told you."

"You either lied to me," said Ianto. "Or told me the lies you'd been told yourself. I remember being here when Pomander's Lid was built, and it was machines that built Pomander's Lid."

Ira hesitated. "Yes, I suppose they used machines as well. Well, they must have, to build something of this scale so quickly."

"They looked like humans," Ianto said. "Machines built to look like humans. Defense never would have approved that. What happened to them? Why aren't they still here?"

"They weren't humans," said Ira evenly. "They were probably only drones. And when drones aren't useful, they're deactivated."

"What does "deactivated" mean, exactly?"

"In the case of the Pomander's Lid drones it means their systems were stripped down and the shells of their bodies were thrown down a chasm."

"So they're dead?"

Ira sighed as if Ianto had asked something incredibly stupid. "If a thing isn't alive it can't die."

"So they're dead. Good. I hate robots," said Ianto darkly. "More things my parents thought were more important than me."

"Ianto, I know how you feel about them..."

"I hate Lavender and Edwin Ambrose, and I'm tired of hearing about them," said Ianto. "Now I know the truth, of what they were really doing, I'm finished with them."

"No you aren't!" said Ira. "You don't hate them, you just think..."

"You don't know what I think," Ianto snapped.

"I'm sorry," Ira said quickly. "I understand why you're angry..."

"No, don't," Ianto said.

"What?"

Ianto turned on him, looking furious. "Don't pretend you understand why I can't forgive them. You don't know anything about us, Ira. You don't know anything about me. You don't know they never cared about me, why they never loved me. Why they didn't want me. Why they just left me to die, so they could spend the rest of their lives with a bunch of ragtag revoluntaries and tin-men."

Ira started to respond, a funny look on his face, but he seemed lost for words. Ianto rose to his feet and threw open the door. "I want to be alone, Ira."

"Ianto, I'm sorry..."

"I'm not mad at you. I only want to be alone." Ianto looked at Ira pointedly, and Ira hesitantly rose to his feet and opened his mouth to say one last thing, but Ianto shook his head, and Ira left.

Ianto locked the door behind him, crossed over to the cabinet and pulled out the beeper. He stared down at it, cradling the device in his hands for a long time, lost in thought. Hours later, he entered Lymir's office. Lymir was bent over his desk.

"Sit, please."

Ianto sat down and Lymir looked up at him. "You remind me so much of your father. I never saw him when he was fifteen, but I imagine he would have looked exactly like you."

"Everyone says that," said Ianto.

Lymir smiled slightly. "Of course. I'm sure you're tired of it. Anyway, we have another junior advisor and two new council members. We still need a senior advisor. We need a fuller staff in light of the problems we face. We have just sent out a fleet of air-ships and will have less than usual at our disposal. We'll need to find new ways of making do."

Ianto nodded. "Yes, sir."

Lymir watched him rolling a stray pencil back and forth across the desk. "Your father used to do that," he said. "The same as you, roll thrice and let go, roll thrice and let go. You get that from him, don't you?"

Ianto looked Lymir in the eye, letting go of the pencil till it slid off the desktop. "I barely knew him. He decided that was best."

Lymir smiled again, the same empty smile.

"Actually, we should have automatically promoted you to the council," Lymir continued. "However, we didn't want to seem to be nepotistic, of course."

"Right."

"As the son of the founders of Pomander's Lid, a council position was a given for you, but it wouldn't seem proper, would it, to make you a member of council before you'd even been a senior advisor?"

Ianto stared at him expressionlessly.

"You really do remind me of Edwin Ambrose as a boy. It's strange...like I'm talking to a ghost. Appearance, mannerisms, even your voices are nearly the same. As a man I only saw him once, before he and your mother were killed, but he made quite an impression...intelligent, devoted, thoughtful. He'd be so quick to learn sometimes I felt he must have been born a genius." Lymir laughed lightly, "I know you feel uncomfortable. You want to prove yourself, not rely on your parents' legacy. But it's good having you and Ira here. We need more people like the two of you."

Ianto remained silent.

"What I'm saying is..." Lymir took a long pause, "will you be senior advisor to the council?"

Ianto needed them to trust him, to not have any doubts, to

have no idea he was about to betray them all.

"Yes."

Alaska found the memorial, in the middle of a vast, makeshift park. She watched through the black gates as an old woman called out names. Some highlighted on its surface, and others not. Hesitantly, Alaska slipped through the gates and walked towards it slowly, unsure if she really wanted to do this. Finally, she got down on her knees beside it, and said the names, "Benjamin Donnel. Amina Donnel. Leila Donnel. Malcolm Donnel."

None of the names highlighted, and she breathed a sigh of relief. "Mari..."

"Alaska!"

She jumped, startled, and saw Jakob walking towards her swiftly with his cane, a look of enormous relief on his face.

"It's alright, it's only me. How are you doing?"

She rose to her feet and ran over, hugging him.

"I've been attacked by sand-rats and chased by a crazy woman," said Alaska. "I'm just glad to see you again."

"Tarana's been worried about you," said Jakob into her ear.

"Just Tarana?" Alaska asked and Jakob looked thoughtful.

"Well, and Holly, I suppose. What happened?" Jakob asked, trying and failing to sound nonchalant.

They walked back towards the black gates, and Alaska told him everything, leaving out Helen's secret.

At the end Jakob shook his head, saying, "You're insane, do you know that, Alaska Donnel?"

"The Nightghosts are real," Alaska said. "I saw them in the

tunnels when I was with Gloriana."

"Did Gloriana see them?"

"No, she wasn't looking," Alaska said, shaking her head.

"Or maybe they aren't real," Jakob suggested bluntly. "Have you ever considered you might be imagining them, Alaska?"

"I'm not imagining them, Jakob. I know they're real," Alaska said in a low, sharp voice. "I was kidnapped when I was twelve, Jakob."

Jakob halted, stopping her. "What?"

She didn't want to tell him what had happened, she wanted to keep it a secret, to forget it had ever happened, to move on, but after Helen and seeing the Nightghosts in Pomander's Lid, she knew it was impossible to forget, and she needed to tell someone, someone she trusted.

"Like those scissor children you were talking about only...only I don't know what they did to me," said Alaska, looking down at the ground. "I don't remember anything, but it really did happen. And these Nightghosts...these people won't leave me alone. They'll follow me forever, Jakob."

She had to ball her hands into fists to keep them from shaking. She didn't want to look at Jakob, worried at the expression that might be on his face. Did he think she was wrong and disturbing now, like everyone in the Capital had always seemed to, though none of them could have possibly known the full truth of what disturbed them? If he did, she thought, she'd just have to face it. She looked up and saw that he was staring at her with a mixture of sadness and distress.

"Alaska, the Nightghost people are evil," Jakob hesitated, before he said, "But I'm not going to let anything happen to you. We'll both look out for them, and you'll be fine."

Words burst out of her mouth, "I know they did something to me! I know I'm...I'm some sort of freak."

Jakob stared at her in surprise, "No you're not. You snuck me three biscuits under the table and then ran into the rain when that Defense officer was going to kill me. You're kind, beautiful, brave. You're brilliant, Alaska Donnel."

His gaze dropped to the ground.

"Three biscuits?" Alaska barely heard the other things he'd said as she was hit by a revelation. "You...you..."

"Yeh, me," Jakob said awkwardly. "I never thanked you for that. I pretended I didn't recognize you in the facility because I figured you'd probably changed, and if you did recognize me, you'd hate me just for living."

"I don't hate you at all."

"I'm glad to hear it," said Jakob, his tone dry but underneath the sarcasm she heard a relieved honesty. "Don't call yourself a freak, Alaska, because you're not."

"People in the Capital always said there was something about me that wasn't right. They said I was crazy, like a wild animal, or too imaginative," Alaska said. "I tried not to care what they thought. I pretended I didn't, but I couldn't help feeling like...like there was something wrong with me, the way people would just stare at me. As if there was something bad in me only they could see. Maybe they were right."

"No, they weren't. 'They' want you to feel like that," Jakob said fiercely. "All those people in the Capital never doing anything. Morning to night, it's work for Defense, curfew at one, cure pills at six. They're dead as zombies and can't stand to see someone whose actually living and thinking. You're alive, Alaska, that's all. You're not one of the zombies following the crowd. They don't really like me either, do they?"

Alaska knew he earnestly believed everything that he said, and she loved him for that. She stepped towards Jakob, till they were standing directly in front of one another, and reached up towards his face. She was going to kiss him, she thought, and warning bells went off in her head as images flashed, of stories she'd been told as a child, of Tristan and Oxsana, of a blood-stained square, of a crying mother, and a terrible, aching pain ran through her. She froze, her hands dropped to her sides. Then, suddenly, she hugged Jakob, something she could do without fear or guilt.

"You're suffocating me," Jakob said in a funny, exaggeratedly strangled voice and she loosened her grip.

"But now that you know everything about me you have to tell me more about yourself," Alaska said smiling.

"There isn't much to know," Jakob said.

"Seriously? I don't even know your last name, Jakob."

His expression darkened. "Graye. I'm Ira's cousin."

Alaska realized why Jakob and Ira looked vaguely similar, why Jakob had refused to say his last name for so long.

"We were never close, or anything," Jakob continued. "Most people pretend like they don't have provincial relatives, so I didn't see him very often. And then his father invited my family to move to the Capital out of the blue."

"What happened to your parents?" Alaska asked.

He hesitated, and then said, his voice full of anger, "They were murdered in a Defense raid. A Defense raid headed by Ira's father."

****

Watching by the gate, Ira looked away. He removed the mother of pearl-handled dagger Helen had left with him from his weapons belt. He glanced at the crest on it, the image of a dragon biting its own tail. Magler's old symbol, before Defense usurped and twisted it for their own purposes. He pulled the note out of his pocket that he had found on the floor near his bed and read:

Ira Julian Graye,

You will read this before you die. You will never be forgiven. Winter will never forgive you. You are a liar and a murderer like your father. I will make sure you are remembered in disgust and hatred. People will spit on your grave and curse at your name. Then they will forget you, the thing you fear the most. The Nightghosts may have forgiven you for Winter's execution.

But I never will.

Helen

61

Ianto entered Nigel Mcavoy's office. The translator was in the middle of lunch, and enough food for a banquet was spread on the desk in front of him. He jumped when he saw Ianto.

"Oh, Ianto!"

Ianto's gaze swept over the food.

"Gifts from my many friends," Mcavoy said quickly and he added hesitantly, almost painfully, "Did you want some?"

"No, I'm not hungry," said Ianto. "Where is Gloriana hiding?"

Mcavoy jumped up, looking affronted, "I have no idea..."

"You gave Helen keys to the old tunnelworks. You must know something," Ianto said, unperturbed by Mcavoy's anger.

Mcavoy banged the desk, "Me, give a key to that woman? Your accusations hurt me, my dear boy! I thought you had a higher opinion of me!"

Ianto picked up a rectangular slab of stone leaning against the wall. "This says 'Go tell the wolves from whose den I escaped.' I found a place in the old tunnels where an engraving was missing, the exact same size as this. The rest of the inscription is still there."

Mcavoy's face contorted, "Ianto..."

"So the question is, did you ask Helen to get it for you, or did you take it yourself? I don't think you do any dirty work, so I'm guessing the former. I'm guessing she's been working for you. Tell me, and if you lie, I'm going straight to the council. I know how happy they'll be to find out you've been stealing from the old tunnels," Ianto's voice and expression were cold as ice.

Mcavoy sunk back into his chair. "Perhaps...I did speak to the woman. I asked her for help, and promised her a key in return, the same as with you. Why should I know where her disciple is?"

"I don't know, but I'm kind of hoping you do," said Ianto, shaking the slab of stone. "Because this relic is heavy, and I'm going to drop it if you don't."

Mcavoy looked stricken, "Ianto Ambrose, your parent's legacy, their flesh and blood..."

"It would be a shame, wouldn't it?" Ianto said, wobbling the slab in his hand. Mcavoy cringed as a flake from the corner fell off on the floor.

"Gloriana Davies is hiding in the old tunnels!"

Ianto nodded his head, "Okay." He set the stone on the floor and ran out the door, leaving Mcavoy to stare after him in bewilderment.

Ianto grabbed a backpack and ran to Ira's rooms, knocking fervently on the door. It was awhile before it opened.

"Come in," said Ira.

He looked tired, his usually immaculate hair a wild halo of dark curls around his head. One hand was wrapped in a bandage, and looking past Ira, Ianto saw bloody shards of a mirror on the floor.

"Something wrong?" Ianto asked and Ira laughed at the ceiling before dropping his gaze back to Ianto.

"Life is horrific, Ianto," said Ira. "Sometimes I hate having to take part in it. Sometimes I wish I could have just been born a god. I'd watch on the sidelines forever." He dropped into a chair, burying his head in his hands. "What am I doing here, Ianto?"

Ianto slipped past him and scanned the room quickly. "What you have to," Ianto said absently.

Ira nodded. "Yes, of course."

Ianto opened the night table drawer, masking the sound by very loudly saying, "I believe, Ira, that whatever is bothering you, you're more than smart enough to work it out."

"Damn right," said Ira confidently. "I mean, it's completely ridiculous. He's dull, stupid, a provincial, for gods' sakes! Half the capital would be better. Half the Mudflats! It must be a seventeen year old girl thing, don't you think?"

"I have no idea, Ira. I've never been a seventeen year old girl," said Ianto, who had no clue what Ira was talking about, but he'd found Ira's laser gun in the drawer.

"The council announces your appointment tomorrow, but you don't actually have to be there," Ira said, rising to his feet.

Ianto quickly took it out, slipped it into his backpack, and gently closed the drawer.

"Ira, I want a real name. I want to know who it was you lost to the Crypts."

Ira stopped, and when he turned around, Ianto saw he looked stricken, but Ianto couldn't tell if it was real or fake.

"Why?" Ira said, forcing a confused smile.

"I just want to know," Ianto said. "I don't know anything about you, Ira, when you know so much about me. Seems only fair."

"Winter," said Ira. "Her name was Winter Magler."

"Would you have put her life before someone else's, if it would save her? Let someone else die for her to live?" Ianto asked.

Ira hesitated, then looked into Ianto's face before he said with an honesty Ianto had never heard before in Ira's voice.

"Yes."

****

It took the entire day to find Gloriana. It was dark, and he had to follow the dim illumination of his flashlight. He saw lamplight up ahead, and walked up as silently as possible. There was a makeshift bed and a few supplies, but no sign of anyone. As he looked around the space, he saw slabs of stone leaning up against the wall, newly chiseled out. *So Mcavoy found a new collector to replace Helen*, he thought.

"What are you doing here?"

He looked up and saw Gloriana carrying a jug of water.

She removed a knife. "I'm not letting that council witch kill me, like she did Helen."

"I'm not here for the council," Ianto said.

"Right," said Gloriana disbelievingly. She advanced towards him. He removed the laser gun from his backpack and pointed it at her.

She stopped and took a step back.

"I'm not here to turn you in, or hurt you," said Ianto. "I don't care for the council either. I want you to help me blow something up."

laska woke up the next day. Light streamed into her room. She felt oddly light for a moment, then saw the music box sitting in the middle of the table across from her. She had never opened it. Only Ira had and the music that had issued from it had made her head feel funny. She lifted the lid. Inside, she saw the clockwork mechanisms turning as the tune played from it, melancholy and cold. She looked at the lid and saw a name written there in the large, messy print of a child.

Winter.

The name seemed to follow her everywhere, Alaska thought, and then she was reminded of Leila, who had liked music boxes; Leila trapped in the Crypts while she was here, safe now, with a bed and kitchen and all of Pomander's Lid surrounding her. She slammed the lid of the music box down and pushed it off the table. It hit the ground hard and a corner broke off. She forced herself to calm down, rose to her feet, and left behind the room for the square.

There was a tremendous bellow from the new tunnels. She turned her head and saw a cloud of dust rising from the mouth of them. A crowd assembled there, and Alaska could hear screams from inside.

"Twelve people are trapped down there!" someone screamed. "Does anyone know the tunnels? Anyone a tunneler?"

Alaska shut her eyes and plunged forward into the tunnel. She ignored yells for her to stop. It was almost impossible to see. She doubled over, hawking horribly at the dust, feeling the walls as she stumbled along in the dusty gloom until she found a lantern which somewhat improved visibility. The tunnels grew hot, till it felt like she'd been thrown into an oven and she saw flames ahead. She tried to keep moving, but they held her gaze, an orange dance. Flames like in her house. Her house burning.

"Help!"

Alaska forced herself to look away from the flames and saw a group of people huddled on the other side of the trench of fire. Nigel Mcavoy and three others were standing there, all looking terrified.

"Just a moment!" Alaska said, forcing herself to move closer, but she couldn't reach them. "Can you jump over it?"

One of them judged the distance, then jumped. Alaska shut her eyes, afraid for a moment they'd missed, but when she opened them they'd safely landed on the other side and collapsed on the ground.

"Okay," Alaska said, grabbing the stranger's hand, easing them onto their feet. "The rest of you, come on."

One of them seemed to have a broken leg; he had to be hauled over carefully by Alaska and the already rescued tunneler, Mcavoy lifting him on the other side. Once he'd been safely moved Mcavoy was next, but he was holding a heavy bag.

"Mcavoy, drop it!" one of the tunnelers called to him. "You can't jump across with it."

"I can't leave it!" Mcavoy said, looking terrified. "This is important. A precious part of history will be lost if I leave it all to burn."

"Come on, Mcavoy!" Alaska called impatiently, and Mcavoy threw the bag across the flames.

It landed just outside the ring of flames and Alaska dragged it away from the fire. "Now you!"

Mcavoy shut his eyes, steeled himself, and jumped. He didn't quite make it across and Alaska and the other tunnelers put out the flames on his clothes.

"Come on!" Alaska ran forward as fast as she could, relieved when they exited out into the light and cool air.

She saw Ira standing at the exit. All the color was gone from his face, but some of it returned at the sight of the group.

Alaska turned away from him to Lymir, who approached with the doctor. The doctor hurriedly went over to the survivors.

"Is that all?" Lymir asked Alaska, who shook her head.

"I don't know. There's a fire down there."

Lymir nodded, a strange, cloudy expression on his face. "There was a collapse, but it wasn't a natural tunnel collapse. There was an explosion. It was sabotage. The water pipeline's been destroyed along with the tunnel."

"Do you know who the saboteur is?" asked Alaska worriedly.

She spoke at the same time Ira asked, "Are we going to run out of water?"

"We won't, we'll repair it and collect what we have," Lymir said in reply to Ira's question, before scurrying off.

Lymir doesn't know anything, Alaska thought. If there was a Defense mole in Pomander's Lid, the council had no idea who it was.

"You're okay?" Ira asked her.

Alaska sank to the ground, "I'm fine."

"Don't ever do that to me again," Ira said, breathing heavily. "You scared the life out of me."

To her relief he ran away to help, as Lymir yelled, "Ira!"

Alaska watched, coughing, as people went into the tunnels to put out the fire. The doctor came over to her and tried to convince her to go to the hospital wing, but she refused.

"I'm fine," Alaska said. "I wasn't in for all that long. I don't want to take up anyone's bed."

He didn't argue with her and walked away. Eventually the people who went in the tunnels came out, carrying those who hadn't survived. People were wailing everywhere, filling the usually semi-quiet square with a mournful lament. The dead were laid by the town hall. Alaska went over to where they were and looked at the dust-covered figures. In this new world of Pomander's Lid she felt so very lost, navigating blindly through a sea of unfamiliar faces. She knew the Capital and her life before. Here she didn't know what would come next.

She saw Nigel Mcavoy scurry past. For a man who'd been through such a tremendous shock, he was moving with agility and purpose. As he passed her she caught a glimpse of stone with writing on it inside of his precious bag. It had been removed from a tunnel wall somewhere. She remembered seeing missing pieces of inscription on the tunnel walls when she and Gloriana had been searching for the mysterious hidden weapon. An idea popped in her head. She had always wondered where Helen had gotten her key from. She had gotten it working for Nigel, illegally lifting ancient inscriptions from the restricted area in the tunnels. Alaska was sure of this now as she watched Mcavoy disappear in the chaos.

Ianto streaked past her, nodding briefly at Nigel. She saw a flash of black following him. A Nightghost. Alaska ran forward immediately. It trailed right behind Ianto, stalking him. She followed carefully, weaving in and out of the crowds, until Ianto and the Nightghost reached a wall. Ianto let a magnetic key fly to its surface, unlocking the revolving wall and he slipped inside, the Nightghost managing to slip in right behind before the wall slammed shut. A few moments later, she followed them both.

Alaska heard Ianto's footsteps echo on the stone floor of the underground maze. She had come this way with Gloriana and it was strange being back. She kept expecting to see the strange mutated sand-rats that had attacked her creep out of a dark corner, but there was nothing but the sound of Ianto's footsteps and the drip of water off the walls. Why was the Nightghost following Ianto, Alaska wondered. Was he a marked child as well? Ianto quickly climbed a steep, narrow staircase roughly hewn from the rock by hand, that seemed impossibly long. Alaska had never come to it before.

There was another corridor at the top of the stairs, which seemed to stretch forever, and Alaska wondered for the first time how long it had taken to create all of this. It felt like centuries of work, and yet was still mostly intact, as if it hadn't been done so long ago. She stopped as Ianto and his shadowy ghost turned a corner and disappeared through a set of metal doors. She saw light flooding into the dim maze from the doorway. Sunlight. She stepped forward and crept as quietly as possible until she reached the doorway and cautiously looked around the edge. They were definitely no longer underground. There was a wide ledge, probably a hundred feet above the desert floor below. A giant, engraved stone was in the middle of the space. She could see Ianto, but not the Nightghost. There were doorways leading off of the ledge. It might have gone through one of them, or merely disappeared. She wondered if she ought to go back, and then she noticed the small metal beeper in Ianto's hand, and a tiny gasp escaped her lips. It was not loud, but Ianto whipped around and saw her by the doorway.

"Why are you following me?"

"I wasn't following you," said Alaska. "There was something behind you. I was following it."

Ianto stared at her, puzzled. She nodded at the beeper, her tone dark, "What are you doing?"

He didn't reply. She looked more carefully and saw that it was the same SOS beeper the Pomander's Lid guard had taken from

Gloriana's backpack.

"You can't," Alaska said quickly. "If you set that off, Defense will pick up the signal and find Pomander's Lid."

"Why should I care?" asked Ianto, his voice quiet and flat.

Alaska stared at him in shock. "Because everyone will die!"

"Maybe I don't care," Ianto said. "I'm a Defense officer. I don't care who my parents were."

"I'm not talking about your parents," said Alaska, looking confused. "Nobody in Pomander's Lid has done anything to you, Ianto. There's little kids. You used to be one once. You couldn't control where you were or whose side you were on. Do you want them to die?"

Ianto stared at her in a stupor as if she'd just said something incredibly profound. Alaska quickly went on, taking advantage of his confusion.

"You know you don't want to do this. What about Ira? He's your friend, isn't he? Do you want him to die, because of you?"

Ianto hesitated, and a hint of relief crossed Alaska's face as she continued softly. "Just put the beeper down."

Ianto's gaze quickly shifted away from Alaska's face. "You don't know anything about me," he said. He turned away from her.

"Ianto!" Alaska cried out, charging across the ledge to knock it out of his hand.

Ianto swallowed, "I already set it off."

It took two hard whacks from the laser gun to knock Alaska Donnel out. Ianto stared at her unconscious figure slumped on the ground. She had been in pain and shock when she collapsed, he'd known that. For some strange reason the pain had reached out to him as well. But he pushed those thoughts aside. He knew what he had to do, what he had come here to do. There was no turning back now. He looked back one last time and his eyes rested on the damaged, half-missing inscription above the edge of the Hall of Remembrance: *I will slay goliaths, I will find the Cure, and at the dying of my day's light, I will be perfected.*

"Why?" Ianto wondered aloud, with an old ache he'd felt for years.

They had left him, a defenseless child to die. There were no good answers to why. But now he wasn't defenseless anymore, he thought. He had a weapon in his hands and he had used it against them. Three deadly beeps were all he had needed. Three beeps to change the world. Three beeps to bring Defense with a fleet. Jamie would live. In his mind's eye, he saw the buildings, the town halls, all crumbled into dust and rubble. Everyone would die, Ira would die. Hundreds of voices silenced in flame, like his had nearly been. He forced that image away immediately, feeling suddenly sick, and ran.

64

laska awoke, plunged in darkness. She moved her head and a shot of pain ran through it. Alaska groggily scrambled to her feet and looked around. Beyond the ledge, she saw stars in a midnight blue sky. It was very late at night and she didn't know how long she had been out, but it was too long. She looked down and saw the beeper, discarded on the ground. Beside it was a flashlight. Bemused, she picked it up and switched it on, before running. She found the stairs and rushed down them as quickly as possible in the dark despite the narrow steps barely large enough to fit her foot. The flashlight began to die as she moved through the corridors, and soon it was so dim she was feeling her way along them, hoping she'd had enough experience in the tunnels to find her way out. Then a horrific thought struck her. Ianto's key had unlocked the revolving wall. Would it still be unlocked from the inside if Ianto had taken it with him? When she reached the wall and pushed on it, however, it opened easily. She saw Ianto's key was still there on the other side. He'd left it, like the beeper and the flashlight. She wasn't sure what that meant, but it only made her more panicked, as she tore the key from the magnetic wall, shoved it in her pocket, and ran. She'd have to tell the council about Ianto. They had to listen to her about this, they had to. She started towards town hall and saw Holly coming from that direction. A crowd was assembled around the steps and Cassandra was speaking.

"Alaska, there you are!" said Holly, looking relieved. "Everyone kept saying they hadn't seen you for hours, and there were five more explosions and I thought..."

"I need to talk to them," Alaska said to Holly as she barreled her way through the crowd, but they pushed her back indignantly, pressing together as they tried to hear what was being said.

"There's an announcement being made..." Holly started.

Alaska shook her head. "I have to say something. It can't wait. It's an emergency!"

Holly frowned. "What—" she began to ask, but Cassandra started talking.

"...And we are very proud to announce the new senior advisor will be Ianto Ambrose, son of Pomander's Lid's founders!" proclaimed Cassandra proudly. "I'm sure nobody will have any objection."

"Wait!" Alaska screamed, but her voice was lost in the sound of applause and jubilant discussion.

Several people nearby cast her confused, annoyed glances.

"Let me help you."

Alaska turned around and saw Jakob. He took her hand. She looked at him in astonishment as he hobbled forward on his cane.

"Crippled old man coming through!" he called out to the people standing in his way, who stepped aside, looking completely taken aback.

Alaska followed him up front and repeated, "Wait!"

Cassandra looked down at her, startled. "What is it?"

"Ianto can't be made senior advisor. In fact, somebody should be figuring out where he is right this moment." Alaska fished the beeper out of her pocket, and there were gasps. "He's the saboteur! He's betrayed us!" she said and held up the black magnetic key as well. "I saw him with this as well. He went into the old tunnels and found an open air ledge where he could broadcast a signal. He told Defense where we are. He's one of them! He has been from the start."

She expected Cassandra to act immediately, to go after Ianto and arrest him, but instead Cassandra asked coolly, "Do you have any other witnesses?"

"No," said Alaska, shocked. "But I'm telling the truth! He...he knocked me unconcious!"

Cassandra's expression was sour, as she said, "Alaska Donnel, Ianto is the son of Pomander's Lid's founders, a respectable individual, a senior advisor. You, quite frankly, are—"

"Shut up," Jakob said angrily, "You have no right to say that, when Alaska—"

"And you have connections to Defense," Cassandra finished, ignoring Jakob's interjection. "How do we know you did not get that key and beeper with the intent of signaling Defense?"

Jakob shook his head, before yelling, "This is trash! Ira was a high ranking Defense officer who you know was involved with countless murders of innocent citizens. Yet you trust him with all kinds of top secret information about this place. And do you forget that Ira's father was one step away from becoming a damn Speaker? And Defense didn't care Alaska's father was a Defense officer, they locked him up. Why should she care about Defense?"

"I didn't!" Alaska looked at them open-mouthed. "I would never..."

"Arrest her."

Alaska spun around as guards emerged from the crowd and closed in around her.

Jakob blocked the guards with his cane and glared at Cassandra. "She saved your life, you stupid—"

"You will be quiet unless you want to go to prison as well, Jakob Graye," snapped Cassandra. Jakob flinched.

"She was desperate to get her family out of Defense's prison," Lymir looked down at Alaska hatefully. "Maybe she thought she could strike a bargain. Now, if she has done what she says she has, she is the murderer of us all."

"Alaska didn't do it!"

Alaska looked out over the crowd and saw Ira standing in the back, at the edge of the mass of people.

He looked straight at Alaska. "She didn't," Ira repeated.

"And how do you know this, Ira Graye?" snapped Cassandra impatiently.

"I've seen Ianto go into the tunnels numerous times, I...I suspected he was up to something but I never believed it would be this," said Ira.

"You complete idiot," Alaska whispered under her breath.

Ira went on, "He was closer, I think, to Defense than to his parents. He had a lot of hate."

"And you never thought we should know this?" Cassandra stared at Ira in shock.

"That doesn't mean he did it!" said Ira quickly, glancing at Alaska, whose eyes widened. "Perhaps Alaska didn't understand what she was seeing. I know Ianto, he would never have—"

"That is for us to figure out," Cassandra said coldly. "But Ira, you better hope he didn't. I want him brought in front of the council, immediately."

"He's gone," said Ira. "I already looked. He must have slipped out during the commotion over the explosions. He's missing."

****

Ianto looked all around, but there was only desert and the distant mountain range hiding Pomander's Lid. How long had he traveled? It felt like days. Seconds, minutes, hours, they had all slipped away from him. Ianto dropped down onto the sand and covered his face with both hands. Then he heard a soft, whirring noise. He tried to see, but was blinded by the harsh sunlight.

"On your feet, officer."

He recognized the prim, overly sweet voice as a figure stepped forward and reached out a red gloved hand. Ianto took it and rose to his feet. He found himself face to face with Melissa Johnson.

"I'm taking you back to where you belong," Johnson said, pointing towards a small, armored air-ship waiting in the distance.

"Is Jamie fine?" Ianto asked and Johnson nodded.

"He is. But I can't say the same for the people over there," Johnson turned her head and stared in the direction of the mountains. "They'll be dead soon enough."

Ianto followed her gaze, his eyes widening.

"You're not having second thoughts, are you, dear?" Johnson asked, watching him carefully and Ianto shook his head. "Ianto, you made the right choice and you can't go back. You should be proud. You have brought the end to a very long war."

Nation of Steel: The Capital
January 24th, Year 137 A.C.

"What story do you want tonight?"

Alaska sat cross-legged on her bed, a dark-haired, cheery twelve year old girl with bright youthful eyes full of life, dressed in a royal blue nightgown and slippers. A glass of orange juice and small plastic cup of medicine sat on her night table. In a chair opposite the bed was Tarana, a book balanced in her lap.

"The one about the Nightghosts!" Alaska said eagerly. "I like that one."

"But it gives you nightmares," said Tarana, with a slightly disapproving smile. "I'm not even supposed to be talking to you, let alone scaring you. Besides, don't children like you want happy things when they're sick? Your parents won't like it if they return home and you're hiding in the bathtub again!"

"Please," said Alaska, clasping her hands together and Tarana hesitated, and then sighed, nodding her head.

"Alright, alright, just one more time. Curiosity killed the man from space, curiosity stopped the clock by the staircase, hear their steps as they walk with grace—"

Tarana was interrupted by a banging at the front door. She frowned, giving the book to Alaska, and left the room. When she returned, there was a look of sheer terror on her face.

"Alaska, come with me quickly."

"What?"

"You have to hide Alaska. Just like the children in the story, understand? Now!"

Alaska followed Tarana, her heart pounding in her chest. There was a closet near the staircase landing. Tarana opened the closet door.

The banging at the front door grew louder.

"You have to hide now, Alaska!"

Alaska hesitated, then nodded her head, clutching a mother of pearl music box tightly in her hands. Tarana pushed her into the closet, threw several blankets over her, and shut the door. Alaska curled up in a corner, shaking. She heard the banging on the front door and Tarana's scream, "She's not here! She's not here!"

There was a tremendous blast. Alaska dropped the music box as she covered her ears, trying to shut out the sound, but she couldn't. Tarana's screams filled the air as a strange female voice bellowed, "Where is she? What did you do with her, you piece of scum!"

"I don't know!" Tarana cried. "Please, stop!"

There were more screams and a horrible crash. Tears ran down Alaska's face and she scrambled to her feet, shoving open the door of the closet. She stood alone on the stair landing, a tiny twelve year old. She could see Tarana lying on the ground unconscious, a wild-eyed woman stooped over her.

"Leave her alone!" Alaska screamed. "Leave her alone! Leave her alone!"

Helen Magler turned and looked at Alaska with her piercing violet gaze. She started up the stairs. Alaska ran to the bathroom which had a lock on the door, but as she grabbed the handle she was caught by the woman and dragged back.

"No, let go of me! Let go of me!" Alaska screamed, kicking and clawing at the woman, as she was violently pulled down the stairs.

"I'm trying to save your life, you little beast!" the woman hissed in her ear.

As Alaska struggled, she saw Tarana's crumpled, bloodied figure lying by the fireplace in the living room. A clock on the mantel had been knocked over onto the floor, and broken shards of glass were tangled up in the carpet.

"Your maid is one of the bad people," the woman said. "Your parents should never have left you in her care. I'm saving you. Someday you'll thank me."

"Let me go!" Alaska screamed again, her voice hoarse, but she was powerless as she was shoved into a waiting bright red car.

As they drove away from the house, she fought uselessly against the seat-belt holding her down. There was a key lock on it, and she had no way of freeing herself.

"Let me go!" she screamed. "Let me go, or I'll bite you as soon as we get out! My father is a Defense officer and if he doesn't kill you, Defense—"

"SHUT UP!" the woman screamed, turning her attention away from the road. The car swerved and hit something hard. The world turned upside down, topsy-turvy and everything was wrong. The air was driven from Alaska's lungs. She was sure she was dying, if she wasn't already dead. She blinked, dazed, feeling nothing but pain throughout her body. Her vision was blurred and fading out.

"Hold tight, it'll be okay," she vaguely heard a young man's voice say and then he was gone.

A loud, gut-wrenching siren blared in her ears and all she could see was red everywhere. Was that the strange, evil woman lying in front of her? Cold, still, bloodless. Alaska realized there was blood all over her, and she screamed, tears flowing out of her eyes. Maybe it was her screams, or maybe it was the blood that attracted them, like wolves. Faces appeared all around, closing in around her. The woman lying so still in the front of the wrecked car snapped to life, and screamed, trying to pull Alaska away from them, but they flung Helen out of the wreckage as easily as if she was a ragdoll. Ghastly, nightmarish faces appeared out of the shadows. They were half-obscured by thick, hooded cloaks, but Alaska still saw them, grabbing for her with claw-like hands, pulling her away, dragging her into their darkness.

She couldn't scream anymore. Everything faded to black.

"Bastion, Lymir," Lymir called out, to suspicious glares from the crowd and calls of cronyism which Lymir ignored.

Alaska Donnel watched Lymir call out names from a list that she knew contained only a hundred names. A hundred names out of hundreds. She looked at the assembled crowd, her stomach tightening with each name called. Nearby, Holly's eyes were red and puffy as she bit her nails. Beside Alaska, Jakob was silent. He had barely spoken to her since Ianto's betrayal had been revealed and the council had begun their agonizingly long deliberations about what to do, recalling every aircraft Pomander's Lid had to spare. Today the evacuations would begin.

"Darzi, Gregori."

Alaska watched the man go up to get a black slip and took a deep breath. Out of the corner of her eye she saw Jakob glance at her. She reached out and gripped his hand tightly.

"Graye, Jakob."

Jakob looked up, startled, seeming as if he couldn't believe his name had been called.

"Graye, Jakob," Lymir repeated. Jakob finally let go of Alaska's hand and went up the steps of the town hall to receive his black slip, then rushed off.

Alaska watched him go. She stood alone in the middle of the square until the last names were called.

Lymir rolled up the paper. Nearby, Holly finally couldn't contain herself and burst into tears. All around Alaska she saw the faces of those who hadn't been called. Those who would stay and fight, instead of being evacuated. The crowd shouted abuse at Lymir as he hurriedly left the stage, directing the chosen towards the ship-hold. She saw a mother run forward and snag Lymir's shirt sleeve.

"Please, just let my daughter go," the woman pleaded and Alaska saw a small, black-haired girl beside her, who couldn't be older than six years old, peering wide-eyed and scared at what was going on around her. *She could be Leila*, Alaska thought. She fought her way over, just as Lymir beat the woman's hand back, and removed a stun gun as she tried to reach for his arm again.

"Your daughter can't go," Lymir said harshly, pointing the stun gun at the woman.

"There must be room for one more," said Alaska, but Lymir shook his head, his eyes narrowing.

"Maybe you're used to getting what you want, Miss Donnel, but if we let one in, then every one of these people will be clamoring for us to let them in."

"I'm not asking for myself!" said Alaska angrily. "And they already are, by the way!" She pointed a finger at the outraged crowd, being kept back by guards.

Lymir glared at her, "We're not yielding, not to this person, or to any of them. Go make yourself useful somewhere else!"

A pair of guards reached Alaska and dragged her back. She tussled with them, freed herself, and marched off, the woman's desperate pleas still ringing in her ears. She kept walking until she reached the hospital wing. There was no sign of Jakob, but Tarana was sitting up in bed, staring blankly at the wall adjacent to her bed. Alaska watched her silently for a moment, wondering if she should tell Tarana about the strange dream she'd had. It was the first time Tarana had ever appeared in any of her dreams, and it had seemed so real and detailed, more like a memory than a dream.

"You okay?" Alaska said, walking over and sitting down beside her. Tarana smiled at her, but Alaska noticed how empty the smile was.

"I heard what happened," Tarana said, not answering Alaska's question. "I'm sorry, Alaska," her voice trembled.

"It's not your fault," Alaska said gently, grasping Tarana's hand.

"We're both going to be just fine, Alaska, we're going to be fine," Tarana whispered. "Gizel...Gizel is dead, isn't he?"

Alaska had lied to Tarana, told her a million stories of how he was busy, of how he wanted to come visit her in the hospital wing, but was always delayed. Tarana had always accepted them with a smile and nod, though Alaska knew she didn't really believe any of it, only wanted to. Now that she had finally asked, Alaska found it impossible to lie to her.

"He died before we made it to Pomander's Lid."

Tarana nodded, looking down at the blankets, her voice low. "I hoped he would get to see it at least. He had done so much for the protest movement, but I knew in my heart he might never."

****

As Alaska walked back to her room she heard the fevered, terrified commotion all around her, the talk of the evacuees, or "survivors" as they were already being called. *At least Jakob is getting out*, she thought, and that thought brought her some relief. Jakob Graye. She reached the door of her rooms and froze. A cloaked figure stood in front of her. She stumbled backwards and the figure looked up. Her mouth fell open when she saw it was Ira.

"Alaska."

He held a gold key on a ribbon in his hand, and she knew immediately it was her key, the one she'd found in the old tunnels when she'd barely escaped with her life.

"What are you doing here?"

"Let me in, Alaska, before someone sees me."

Alaska grabbed Ira by the arm and pulled him inside. He dropped the key onto the table. She snatched it off the table and looked at it closer. She'd barely noticed before, but now she could see a symbol engraved on it. She squinted and jumped as she made out the Desertpic symbol for her name. What had Gizel said it was also for? *Winter.* Ira coughed. She looked up and saw he was looking at her with an annoyingly knowing smile on his face.

"Ira, you're supposed to be in prison. How did you—?"

"I broke out of prison. I needed to talk to you, and I doubted Cassandra would let me."

Alaska stared at him incredulously. Then she looked down at the key in her hand. "How did you get this back from the council?"

"The council never had it," Ira admitted. "I lied."

"You lied?" Alaska's voice faltered. "You had it all this time? The weapon...the weapon's real, isn't it?"

"Alaska, I couldn't just give the key to you," said Ira. "I needed to confirm what it was—"

"All you do is lie," Alaska said in a low voice. "You were never going to help them, were you? I thought...I really thought you would get them out of the Crypts," Alaska's voice trembled. "But you were just lying."

"No, I wasn't!" said Ira. His voice shook as he shouted so loudly Alaska stepped back. "You can think anything you want of me, Alaska. I don't care, but don't you dare think I wasn't trying, because I did everything I could, and I would have done more. You have nothing to blame me for! How dare you blame me!"

Ira quickly dropped his voice and glanced towards the window, afraid he had been overheard. "I'm sorry. I shouldn't have yelled at you."

"No, you shouldn't have. You brought Ianto here! You refused to believe he might be bad, even when you suspected him! You let him betray Pomander's Lid," Alaska angrily spat back at him. "I should tell the council exactly where you are. Maybe while you're in prison, you'll start thinking about how wrong you've been."

Ira looked at Alaska, his eyes widening further. She hated his expression, like a scientist watching an unusually interesting specimen.

"Do you really hate me so much?" he asked, in a pitiably sad voice. "I've lost a home, my father, nearly everything I cared about because of Defense. I've risked my life a thousand times for this place, for these people. I love them, Alaska. I love Pomander's Lid and I love...I would never have done anything to harm Pomander's Lid. It pains me more than you know how Ianto betrayed me. The idea of you hating me—"

"I...I don't hate you," said Alaska. "I don't really think you didn't try to save them. But I wish you'd just tell me the truth, Ira. That you wouldn't hide things from me."

"That's why I came to see you. That's why I gave you back your key."

Alaska felt the cold gold surface of the key in her hand and nodded her head.

"There is a cure for the plague," Ira said. Alaska stared at him incredulously. "At least a prototype vaccine. Ianto's mother was developing it when she and his father were captured by Defense. She stored the prototype somewhere. People thought it was in Pomander's Lid, but if it ever was, it was moved long ago. That key isn't to anything here. It's old, far older than Pomander's Lid. I think it may come in handy somehow, but I don't know how. There's writing on it, Desertpic. It says—"

"Winter," Alaska finished. Ira nodded, smiling slightly.

"Right. The vaccine was going to be called the Winter Cure, after Winter Magler, Helen's adopted daughter. I believe that key will help us find it. You'll need that key," said Ira. "You need to find the vaccine. If you want to make sure no one else ever gets hurt, like your family, then you need to find it."

"How do you know all of this?"

"I've been trying to...fix the mistakes I made," Ira said, looking her in the eye. "I was helping Lavender Ambrose on the Winter Cure project, but...we were stopped. I was lucky nobody found out how involved I was."

Ira worked on a cure for the plague? Alaska stared at him in shock. How many things was he hiding about himself?

"How much do you know?" Alaska asked, astonished.

"I try to know everything."

"Then you know where she hid it?" Alaska asked, folding her arms across her chest.

Ira faltered, shook his head. "I did say try. I was only there at the beginning. I don't even know how far she got. But people who knew Lavender told me the rest after the Ambroses' capture. I know you can find it, Alaska."

"How can I?" Alaska asked. "I have no idea and I'm sure others have looked."

"Because you're not 'others'," said Ira gravely. "What the Nightghosts want more than anything is to bring down Defense. For some reason, Alaska, you became their best hope. They wanted you specifically."

"I'm not any different," Alaska said a little forcefully.

"Something about you is. When I found you deserted on the bridge with the rhyme pinned to your sleeve, you—"

"Wait, you found me?"

Ira nodded. "You were really dazed. I think you barely noticed me, but I got you home. Your parents didn't want anyone talking about the incident. You didn't remember anything and they didn't want you to be hurt more than you already had been. And I think they were afraid of what the Nightghosts might have done."

A siren blared outside. Alaska ran to the window and saw

guards. They dragged a handcuffed Holly after them, her face tear-stained. One of them yelled, "Find him!"

"She helped me get out. I didn't want them to catch her," Alaska heard Ira say behind her, his breath on her ear.

Alaska turned to find him standing right behind her, unnervingly close. How did he manage to creep across rooms so silently?

"You have to get out of here. Hide."

"Do you forgive me now?" Ira asked.

Out of the corner of her eye she saw one of the guards approaching and turned away, pulling the raggedy curtains shut.

"Ira, get out," Alaska whispered.

Ira nodded hesitantly and ran for the door, then stopped, his hand on the handle. "How much do you care about Jakob?"

"Ira, get out!" said Alaska, impatiently.

"How much?"

"I...I don't know!" Alaska snapped, her face growing hot. "Why does it matter?"

"Holly told me Jakob got a black slip. If he offers it to you, say yes, Alaska. He's a coward, he'll only ask once, so no matter how worried you are about him, say yes. I'll take care of him. I'll help him, I promise. You don't want to be here when all hell breaks loose. You can't die. You have the key. Find the Cure. Get that slip and don't let anyone take it away from you."

With that, Ira was gone.

****

In an empty alley, Ira watched from the shadows as the lumbering guards passed, dragging Holly after them. He smiled, sure they were far too stupid to ever find him. Then he saw Jakob following close behind them. His smile disappeared, leaving a dark expression on his face. He slipped away to the morgue. It was unguarded. He easily entered and crossed the small, dimly lit room to Helen's coffin that was wedged into a stone alcove in the back. The coffin was a plain wooden box roughly nailed together, the lid fastened beneath a dirty white sheet. A slash of red paint on the side marked it for a private burning. The council was going to make sure Helen's secret was not revealed to the rest of Pomander's Lid. He removed a handkerchief from his pocket, got down on his knees and began to pry it open with a small crowbar. The lid lifted up little by little until he managed to force it off and dump it down on the dusty ground. Helen's body was wrapped in a shroud, and he carefully unwrapped the top of it, revealing the mangled mess of skin, blood, skeletal steel structuring, brass clockwork and wires. Her face was undamaged. Her eyes stared up at him eerily. There was a black box, its wires disconnected and melted by a laser shot. Ira picked it up and pocketed it, wiping his hands clean on the handkerchief. He set the mother of pearl-handled dagger in the coffin. Then he replaced the lid, draping the sheet back over the coffin, hiding any signs of his tampering.

"Rest in peace, Helen Magler."

"Why is the clock broken?" Ianto remembered asking Lavender, looking out of the window, where passersby lingered to chat joyfully on the snow-powdered streets of a beautiful, unreachable city.

Lavender Ambrose had looked up from the armchair where she sat in his bedroom. *No*, he corrected himself. *The room assigned to him.* A storybook was open in her lap. She'd insisted on continuing to read it to him, even though he was far too old for storybooks.

"What are you talking about?" she had asked, in that calm voice of hers that had always reassured him, but now irritated him.

"The clock is broken," Ianto had repeated. "Stuck at eight-fifteen. But it's not always eight-fifteen, is it? There are more seconds and minutes and hours. Days and days. How many days? How old am I?"

"Ianto..."

"And why are there no mirrors?" Ianto had asked. "There used to be mirrors. The clocks used to work."

"Ianto, listen to me."

"You don't want me to know what time it is, or how old I am, or what I look like!" Ianto had screamed. "Because I'm not your son, am I?"

Lavender had risen to her feet as he had run for the door, wrestling with the handle that was always locked. She had stepped back in alarm, the book falling from her hands.

"Ianto, don't try to run away again! You can't get out. You'll upset Edwin."

"I broke into the room upstairs and there were masks and a long, steel table and weirdo stuff. I saw a letter, from someone named 'Oxsana.' It said you're part of some group called Nightghosts. It talked about taking children. That's what you did to me, isn't it? You kidnapped me?"

"Of course we didn't kidnap you, Ianto. We're your parents!"

"I don't believe you!" Ianto screamed at her.

"Ianto, you know I'm your mother."

He had stopped screaming for a second, took a deep gulping breath and then spat out, "Then let me go outside. Just once!"

"No," said Lavender Ambrose firmly. "It's not safe."

"I need to go outside!" Ianto had given the handle a ferocious yank and the entire room shook.

"Ianto, there's nothing out there! Remember the picture of that nasty woman, the woman in red I showed you, remember Ianto?" said Lavender, a desperate urgency in her voice as she had stepped closer. "She is very dangerous and she runs the world outside for some very bad people. If she caught you, she would kill you. That is why we have to keep you here, because we love you..."

"You don't love me!" Ianto had snapped. "If you loved me you wouldn't lock me up in this room and hurt me. I haven't forgotten any of the things you've done to me. I know you come in at night, when you think I'm sleeping, and run experiments on me."

Lavender had stepped a little closer, but Ianto had warned her.

"Get away from me! You've never cared about me. You don't care about anything except your stupid cause."

He had given the door one last yank, and it burst open. He had peered through the open doorway. In just a few steps he could escape the room and head down a set of wide stairs to the front door.

"You're right," Lavender had said.

He remembered turning around, staring at her in shock. She had never told him he was right before.

"We haven't been the best parents. We've messed up, Ianto, I know I certainly have." Tears sparkled in Lavender's eyes. "But don't say we don't care about you, don't believe that, Ianto, please. I love you, always. You're my son, Ianto. I know sometimes we do things you don't understand, but we would never do anything to hurt you and the things we do...we do them because you're special."

Ianto had remained silent.

"I love you, Ianto," Lavender had said with tears trailing down her face. "I will always love you."

Ianto had stared into Lavender's face as she smiled weakly, and when he had spoken, his voice choked, "I can't believe that."

"Yes you can," Lavender had assured him, nodding her head. "Don't ever say you can't."

"I can't."

He bolted out the door and Lavender had tried to stop him, grabbing his arm. He had fought her back, and she let out a scream as he yanked his arm free, followed by a cracking noise. He had gasped in shock as she stumbled away from him, clutching her arm. He remembered her hitting a wall and sliding to the floor.

"Mother?"

A door had violently swung open and Edwin ran out, his gray-blue eyes scanning the scene, from a confused Ianto to a half-unconscious Lavender.

"My gods!" Edwin Ambrose had exclaimed and then he had grabbed Ianto roughly, pressing a stun gun into his back. "Don't you dare try anything on me."

"I'm sorry," Ianto had whimpered, still looking at Lavender, a mortified expression on his face. "I didn't mean to hurt her! Please don't put me in the Room!"

Edwin Ambrose had tossed him in the Room with a tall metal door and then slammed it shut. Ten locking mechanisms had clicked into place and then he had been perfectly alone, in total darkness. He had curled up in the corner, dissolving into dry sobs.

****

Ianto rose unsteadily from the floor of the steel closet he'd locked himself inside. He was unsure for how long he'd been sitting there on the ground, his head resting on his knees as he listened to silence. He felt nothing akin to satisfaction, only a hollow emptiness. He left behind the closet and his rooms, going out to the glass bridge of Lossit. He could see the Capital festooned for the coming New Year holidays. During his absence it had changed completely, ashy snow covering the city in a heavy blanket. Some of the murky fog lifted, leaving the streets clearer so he could see a good half mile forward. The last air-ships were taking off from the launch pad en masse, like a flock of incredibly fast, ugly, misshapen metal birds, headed for an uneven battle that would be nothing more than a massacre.

"Mr. Ambrose?"

He turned and saw Melissa Johnson approaching him in a furry, bright red coat. She looked out of the glass windows at the army of air-ships departing.

"Defense has taken far too long, but that is our style, I'm afraid. I guess I should be glad I'm still alive to see any decisions made," she said in a concerned and slightly resentful voice.

"When do I get to see Jamie? When will he be released?" Ianto asked in a rushed voice.

"Soon," said Johnson, smiling slightly at the earnest impatience on Ianto's face. "You'll go to your rooms for now, until further notice from me. You can visit your grandfather, if you wish."

"No."

"I really think you should," Johnson's voice was cold and

insistent; Ianto knew it wasn't a suggestion.

She noticed him running his fingers up and down his thumb, as if sliding an invisible pencil.

"Is something bothering you, Ianto?" she asked in a sweet voice. "I like my young new officers to be quite straight with me."

"I'm fine," said Ianto quickly and he slipped past her.

As he walked away he had the disconcerting feeling of being watched and saw Ginny staring into the rotunda, watching him. She looked puzzled, then somebody called out to her and she disappeared. She didn't seem to know what had been done yet, but eventually he knew she and Owen would find out. He walked faster until he was running down the marble corridors, past rows of hanging red and white flags, pushing his way through crowds of bewildered Defense officers. He ran through a doorway and found himself in an empty, dark space. He turned, tried to find his way out of it, but he couldn't, and then suddenly a bright, harsh white light switched on. He stepped back, but it didn't fade.

"Hello?" Ianto called out, but there was no response.

He stepped forward and was swallowed by the light which began to pixilate. It reminded him of the 'Box', but he knew he couldn't be inside of the box as the pixilated squares formed the hulking ruins of Pomander's Lid. Smoke rose around him and streams of blood ran at his feet, over rocks and twisted metal. He stood on a jutting cliff above it all and below him were miles and miles of dead bodies—men, women and children. In the center of it all was Ira, sprawled across the ground. Ianto ran, scrambling over the rock until he dropped down on his knees beside Ira. He was ice cold, eyes glassy and devoid of life.

"He's dead," said Ianto hollowly, scrambling away from the body.

"In this world."

Ianto spun around and saw Jamie standing on the cliff, looking down at him.

"Not yet in yours."

Ianto sat up with a start. He was sprawled on the floor of an empty conference room, his head aching. He rose and quickly left the room.

****

Guards led Ianto to a part of Lossit he had never seen before. It was separate from the main building in a sooty brick structure across a courtyard from Lossit's glass tower. Billows of cloudy gray smoke erupted from funnels on the brick building's tall turrets, releasing the thick smog which blanketed the Capital.

"Go on in," the guards said, stopping and unlocking a round, portal-like metal door which served as the building's entrance.

Ianto stepped inside. The air was thick, hot and steamy, and after a few minutes walking across a narrow ramp above a ten foot drop he felt like he was melting. Down below was the gritty, dirty floor of the workhouse where broken figures shoveled coal into fiery furnaces. The sound of rattling rang in his ears. The figures were secured by long chains to hooks in the wall, unable to move any further than the edge of the workhouse stairs. Ianto saw the glittering eyes of surveillance cameras watching in every corner, but he doubted any specific sound could be recorded over the tumult, and descended a set of narrow and steep stairs. There was an old, gray-haired man among the chaos. He looked like he was on death's doorstep, older than Ianto had ever seen him, but there was a hard expression of determination on his face.

"Grandfather?" Ianto asked when he was standing right beside the man.

Arthur Ambrose turned then, and looked at his grandson as if he was seeing an apparition.

"So they were telling the truth. You aren't dead," the old man grunted.

"You said I couldn't. You said I was special and it wasn't possible," Ianto said.

Arthur Ambrose shook his head, asking in a gravelly voice, "What the hell are you talking about?"

"I dreamed," Ianto said, unable to believe his own words. "You said I never would, but I dreamed."

"They were all dead," Ianto said as he recalled the dream for his grandfather. "Every single one of them. Everything was black and burned and ashy. There were still several fires raging. There was no one left alive to put them out."

"You threw Pomander's Lid to the wolves," said his grandfather. "You abandoned them. So they were destroyed."

"My parents built Pomander's Lid," Ianto said. "I thought I could..." his voice died away.

"Is that what all this has been for? Joining Defense, giving them Pomander's Lid—all out of revenge?" Arthur Ambrose's eyes widened. "You sent people to their deaths to spite Edwin and Lavender?"

"No!" said Ianto quickly. "Jamie was going to die if I didn't—"

"Jamie?" Arthur Ambrose snapped irritably. He moved away from Ianto, his chains rattling noisily. "You never cared for anyone in your life."

"Yes, I—"

"Don't try to pretend you aren't something that you are. You are an Ambrose, boy, and we're bloody selfish stock."

Ianto looked at his grandfather, shaking, "You don't know me! All the time you had me locked up, you hardly bothered with me. You didn't even realize Jamie really mattered to me!"

Arthur Ambrose snorted, "I saw a pet you found to make yourself feel good. To make you feel like a normal human being. He revered you, gods know why. You didn't care about him at all."

"I do care about him! More than I can say for you! But it doesn't matter. I know what's right and what's wrong," Ianto snapped angrily. "I did the only thing I could. I'm not sorry."

Even as he said this, the image flashed in his mind of heavy acrid smoke, of Ira, still, drained, broken on the ground...

"I'm not sorry," Ianto repeated, frantically rubbing his fingers over his thumb, till he was digging his nails into his skin. "I don't care about Pomander's Lid. You can't watch me suffer, because I'm not suffering."

"Why would I want to watch you suffer?" asked Arthur Ambrose, genuinely puzzled.

"You've never liked me," Ianto said looking down. "And now that I'm the Defense officer who revealed the secret location of Pomander's Lid, I know you'll hate me."

Ianto felt his grandfather's hand touch his face. He raised his head. He stared straight into his grandfather's face and was surprised to see the old man's eyes wet, as Arthur Ambrose said, "I'm just glad you didn't get yourself killed."

Alaska found Jakob in the packed main square. He turned around, a conflicted expression passing across his face.

"Alaska, this black slip," he said, before Alaska could speak. "is yours."

Alaska stared down at the black paper Jakob held out to her. She reached for it, then stopped, her arm falling to her side.

"No."

Jakob gaped at her, wide-eyed. "Alaska, you don't know what you're saying."

"That's your only way out," said Alaska.

"Thanks for reminding me. Just take it, head for the ship-hold. They leave at midnight. If you don't take it now, I'm getting on that air-ship and that's it, Alaska. No more chances."

"You're still not completely healed, you don't know—"

"I know Ianto's the traitor, so at the very least I'll know who to strangle in hell," said Jakob. Alaska slapped him across the face.

"Shut up and listen to me. This is not a joke," Alaska yelled at him in a shaky voice as Jakob's eyes widened. "You know your leg is still hurt. You know a fleet of Defense air-ships are coming here, and they won't care, Jakob, they won't care, they'll kill everyone they can. I'm not going to let you die, Jakob Graye."

Jakob took her hand and stuffed the black slip into it.

"I'm not going to die. But you're going to get out of here and save them," Jakob said. "Your parents. Your brother and sister." His tone was desperate and final, as he added, "Don't be stubborn.

You know they need you."

Alaska looked down at the black slip in her hand, her fingers closed around it. She looked back up at Jakob, tears in her eyes. *If loving him makes me mad everyone should be mad,* Alaska thought.

"I don't even know if they're still alive. So please don't die, please. Promise to take care of yourself."

Jakob smiled, a haunted smile that didn't reach his eyes, "I always take care of myself, Alaska." He hesitated as if he was about to say something more, but in the end, he only said, "You better go."

She kissed him then. Time ground to a gentle halt. The screams and desperate crowds evaporated. Jakob kissed her back, wrapping one arm around her.

"I love you," she burst out.

"Don't, don't say that, Alaska," Jakob said, his tone harsh and full of fear. "I'll see you later."

He merged with the crowd and disappeared from view. The tumult of the evacuation came rushing back, hitting her like bitterly cold water. She tried to catch a glimpse of him as she forced her way towards the elevator, but she didn't see anything but hoards of desperate, unfamiliar faces. An alarm blared from the ship-hold, piercing through the shouts of the desperate people, who swallowed her up the moment she got off the elevator, carrying her towards the ship-hold. Lymir was trying to create some sort of order, organizing the movement of giant crates carrying precious cure pills into the cargo holds and assigning each evacuee to a vessel, while guards kept back those without slips trying to break through and make a run for the air-ships. Alaska forced her way through the crowd, holding onto the black slip tightly as many sets of hands grabbed for her, trying to yank it out of her grasp. She tried not to look at the faces. She felt only guilt.

"Alaska Donnel!"

She had reached Lymir, who looked at her, one eyebrow raised. "What are you doing here?"

She held out her black slip. "Permission to board?"

Lymir looked at her in shock for a moment, and then a twisted, wry smile crossed his face.

"You always get what you want, don't you Miss Donnel?" he said, mocking laughter in his voice.

"Just let me through," snapped Alaska, her voice quivering.

Lymir nodded towards the guards, standing on the other side of a red line separating the crowd from the air-ships, "She's..."

Suddenly a woman lunged at her. Alaska clutched the black slip tightly, fighting back with her free arm and kicking out in defense. She looked at Lymir for help, but he watched with an amused expression on his face, putting up his hand for the guards to stop. Blood trickled down Alaska's face as she tried to scramble away and was knocked to the ground by the woman, who grabbed her arm violently, trying to tear the black slip out of Alaska's grasp. Alaska fought back, and the woman fell backwards, winded. Alaska scrambled away quickly before she could recover and crossed the red admittance line. The guards helped her to her feet and she looked back at the woman who had attacked her. A little girl ran over to her and clung anxiously to her arm. Alaska recognized them both. The girl like Leila, the woman who had pleaded with Lymir. Alaska's guilt doubled. She felt sick to her stomach, but she was pushed towards the air-ships and a moment later she was inside one. Every sound in Pomander's Lid was drowned by the whirring of the air-ships taking off, every surface drenched in blood red warning lights. She turned the black slip over in her hand, and noticed for the first time cramped, silver writing on the back: *Thank you, Alaska.*

Out of the window the desperate crowds grew smaller and smaller, the faces blended together in a sea of color, and Alaska knew somewhere beyond them, beyond the crumbling stone walls that held all this life, a fleet of Defense air-ships were coming to silence every voice.

The moment Ianto left the hellish brick building he found himself standing in front of Melissa Johnson.

"Ah, perfect," she said, with a wide smile. "Ianto, you can see Jamie."

Johnson walked back across the courtyard into Lossit's main tower and Ianto followed, though he felt something was wrong, something he couldn't quite put his finger on. They crossed the glass bridge, walked through the rotunda and finally stopped inside of Johnson's office. She shut the door.

"Isn't he in the Crypts?" asked Ianto, suspiciously. Johnson shook her head.

"I promised you I would release him when you finished your task, and you have," said Johnson. "Pomander's Lid is being surrounded as we speak. All thanks to you...through here."

Johnson opened the second door of her office. All Ianto saw through it was a swallowing blackness.

"What's in there?"

"Jamie," Johnson replied.

Ianto shook his head. "I don't think so."

"Then you won't see him," said Johnson tartly. She stepped through and disappeared in the blackness.

He heard the click of her high heels on a floor he couldn't see. He waited, but she didn't return. Curiosity overwhelmed him and he stepped in after her. The corridor leading from the doorway was narrow; he could feel the stone walls on either side of him by reaching out his arms. He stopped as strange blue lights switched on, illuminating the space. They had come to the end; five feet away from him Johnson stood in front of a low concrete wall.

"Where's Jamie?" Ianto asked, and Johnson pointed over the wall.

"He's down there."

Cautiously he approached the wall, staying clear of Johnson. She looked amused.

"I'm not going to push you over, Ianto Ambrose. You have to climb down."

"Right," said Ianto skeptically. "Why would I do that?"

"You don't trust me, Ianto?"

Johnson walked over to the wall. She flipped a switch on a metal control box. The room filled with painful, screeching screams. Ianto clapped his hand over his ears, but it was inside his head, ripping his mind apart. She quickly flipped the switch off. Ianto saw the contorted expression on her face.

"You heard the screams, too, didn't you?" Johnson asked.

Ianto nodded his head. "What are they?"

Johnson smiled. "If you climb down, you'll see."

She climbed over the wall and disappeared down a ladder he couldn't see. He walked over to the edge and looked down. He saw what looked like a bottomless drop, an abyss with only a pinprick of light in the center of the darkness showing that there was anything below. He should turn and run now, he thought, but he wanted to know the cause of the screams, and he wanted to know where Jamie was. He saw the top of Johnson's head disappear into the darkness. He climbed over the side and began to descend the ladder. There was no light and no sound, only the feel of cold steel under his hands. The metal brought flashes of memory, connections to Pomander's Lid. He remembered watching the drones building it, piece by piece.

"You can jump off now," he heard Johnson call up to him from below, but he didn't and continued descending until he felt solid ground beneath his feet.

He stood in a stone cavern with dim lights embedded in the walls. A red path lead straight to the end of it where there was an open tall metal door. Beyond the open door, Ianto saw a corridor bathed in blue light with what looked like jail cells lining the walls.

"What do you think?" Johnson asked.

Ianto looked into Johnson's curious face. An ominous feeling hovered over him as he glanced around the old stone cavern.

"Is Jamie dead?"

Johnson smiled, a twisted, cold smile. "No. You should know by now Defense is not evil. You have helped the Nation immensely, Ianto. And for that we promised to reward you. We keep our word. Follow me and I'll take you to him."

She started down the corridor. Ianto stood still, but finally followed, keeping far behind her, ready to bolt.

"This used to be part of a prison," said Johnson with the enthusiasm of a tour guide. "Everything below-ground, the Crypts, this cavern, already existed before Lossit was built. It is as old as the Nation itself. This is where Magler held the machines that built this world, the drones."

"I've seen drones before," Ianto said and Johnson glanced at him briefly, before turning away.

"They are banned by Defense, but some of the rebels have been known to build and use them," said Johnson distastefully.

"People are being kept here," said Ianto. "The screaming..."

"Not people," said Johnson. "You'll see."

She walked down the red path, past the tall, metal door, and stepped into the corridor bathed in blue light, gesturing for Ianto to follow. Cautiously he stepped forward and peered through the doorway. There were nine doors. All but three were shut, and

Johnson walked towards an open one at the end of the corridor. As they passed by the doors, Ianto read the signs next to them:

#1 *Bhuvan Magler*

#2 *Helen Magler*, (an open door)

#3 *Rose Magler*

#4 *Winter Magler*

#5 *Philip Magler*

#6 *Mir Magler Counta*, (an open door)

#7 *Huizhong Magler*

#8 *Markus Magler Walker*

"What is this place?" Ianto asked, frowning and then he saw door number nine's freshly painted sign:

#9 *Ianto Magler Ambrose*, (an open door)

He looked inside at the small circular room bathed in blue light like the rest of the underground cavern. There was a display case that looked like a glass coffin in the center of the space atop a marble pedestal. On the inside of the case, the base was padded in cream-colored leather, a folded, thin white blanket on top of it. Wires ran from a metal box on it down into the floor.

"Ianto!" Jamie cried out. He was chained behind the glass coffin.

Johnson removed her laser and pointed it at Jamie.

"Don't you say another word," she warned, before turning back to Ianto. "The screams weren't human screams. In fact, they weren't really screams at all, but we interpret them as screams. In reality they are only signals of pain, by half mechanical, half biological monstrosities Magler and his father pitied and saved. Angelorum cadentium, or Magler's Children as they were called by whimsical fools. Defense simply calls them A.C.s. They were used by the outside world as soldiers, but the Maglers used them as guardians of a 'paradise' for refugees. The first colonists were rightfully afraid of them and wanted to kill them, but the Maglers felt the world ought to be contaminated by them."

Johnson walked up to the case and gently touched the glass with her fingertips. "Samson Magler was audacious and cruel. He called them his 'children,' but it was all a ploy to get their loyalty, nothing more. He kept them apart, locked up in chambers only to be taken out when he needed them for something, like slaves. Except his precious Winter, who he paraded about like a trophy. Defense killed Rose, but it was Magler who sacrificed Bhuvan to save his own skin and Philip to have spare parts for his horrible experiments," Johnson's face contorted unwillingly from some strong emotion. "My dear grandfather pretended to treat them like his own children, but he never forgot they weren't human. You know of Markus Walker's plight, of course."

He looked at Johnson in disbelief, remembering videos he had seen of Markus Walker. There was not a man more human, Ianto thought. *How could he be one of these abominations?* Besides, he had carried an alien plague, contaminating the Nation, and only a human could do that, couldn't they?

"I know what you're thinking," Johnson circled the case, her heels clicking noisily against the stone floor. "But much of him was biological, he was a cybernetic organism, not an android, not a drone. He had the same blood and many of the same organs as a human. He could very easily have contracted the disease. He probably felt torturous pain before he died."

"If the things down here are dead, how do they scream?"

"We saved their mechanical brains, that's all," said Johnson simply. "Their black boxes. I can switch them on or off, and when they're on they solve problems for me. They find each other for me. But it's not easy waking up from what you thought was certain death to find yourself locked in a glass coffin and unable to reach the rest of your body, forced to follow orders from your sworn enemies. That's why they scream."

"Why can you hear them? No one around me could hear," Ianto said.

"I have an implant, so I can hear what's going on inside of their heads. Using the Box, I can even see things as if looking through their eyes. I'm their warden," said Johnson, saying the last bit with relish, before she paused. "But Ianto, you haven't asked me the most obvious, most important question yet."

Ianto knew what that question was. He also knew the answer, which was precisely why he hadn't asked the question. He didn't want to hear the answer. He didn't want her to tell him the truth, the explanation of why his parents had never treated him like normal parents did, had never shown the same love for him they showed for others. Why his father had always looked at him like a bug that needed to be squashed, or a monster that would lash out any moment. Why he was so resistant to injury, had never cried, had never before dreamed. No, he didn't want answers.

"I did everything you asked," Ianto said, his voice on edge and frantic. "Now let me and Jamie go."

"Ianto..."

Out of the corner of Ianto's eye, he saw Jamie's face go pale.

"Ianto, you're one..."

Johnson shot him in the leg. Jamie howled and doubled over in pain on the floor. Ianto wanted to go over to him but Johnson redirected the laser at him.

"I know you can feel pain, Ianto."

Ianto stopped. Johnson pushed a button on the case and the glass top lifted.

"Your so-called parents were devout followers of Magler's. They did anything for him, even joined the order he formed just before his death to protect his precious little toys. The Nightghosts. They endured your unnatural presence in their lives out of reverence for a dead dictator. I doubt you remember him. The Maglers and

Ambroses have wiped your memory and reprogrammed you so many times. You think you're fifteen, but you're as old as the Nation itself, and you'd have kept going on like that, if you hadn't met me," Johnson said in a voice barely higher than a whisper, not taking her laser off Ianto. "Lifetimes of pain and suffering. It'll end. All you have to do is solve the problems, and if you do that, nothing bad will ever happen to you again."

"If I get in there, you'll kill Jamie, won't you?"

A small, cruel smile crossed Johnson's face. "Look at him, Ianto, he hates you now he knows who you are. He knows you aren't clever or funny, you're just copying and fulfilling your programming. He knows you thanked your guardians with constant betrayals and tried to run away from your 'grandfather' because your programming is flawed, with a strange bent toward disloyalty and selfishness, perhaps to better mimic humanity, but it is all programming. You're a heartless monster. A beast, a thing to run away and hide from. There's nothing here for you to save."

She nodded her head in Jamie's direction, her smile broadening. "Go on, go and see for yourself."

"Don't come near me!" Jamie shouted as Ianto took a step towards him. He tried to scoot across the floor, away from Ianto, tugging at the chains that bound him to the base of coffin's pedestal. "You're a thing, you're a..."

"Shut up, Jamie," said Ianto. He turned and looked at Johnson with a calm, clear expression. "I hate you."

She just smiled. Ianto looked at the display case for a long moment, then hoisted himself up and climbed into it.

"You're lucky, you'll still have your body," Johnson said, her voice suddenly cold and flat. "Pull the blanket over yourself. It will be painless when the paralysis begins."

She bent down to push the button and replace the glass cover.

Ianto leapt out of the case and knocked her to the ground. She scrambled back onto her feet and pointed her laser at him.

"Get back in the box!"

"I'd rather die than go in your stupid box!"

Johnson pointed her laser away from Ianto to Jamie. Suddenly the blue light in the room turned blood red and sirens blared. There was a groaning and rumbling as the cavern rocked violently. With a crash, half the ceiling caved in. Ianto scrambled across the room to the stablest part and dropped to the ground, throwing his hands over his head as a shower of concrete and dust came down. He gasped for air and then forced his way upwards through the rubble, managing to scrabble on top. Above him, he could see clear blue sky bathing the dark space in daylight.

He didn't see any sign of Melissa Johnson, except a lost red high heel. He clambered over the rubble, until he found Jamie, still chained to the pedestal, under an precarious overhang of ceiling. His breathing was ragged and wheezy, blood drenched his clothes, staining the rocks around him red. Johnson had shot him in the side before the ceiling collapsed. It only took a second for Ianto to know Jamie was dying and there was nothing that could be done. Shaking, Ianto cradled Jamie's limp head in his arms as Jamie's eyes lolled, fixing weakly on Ianto's face.

"I was only pretending," Jamie whispered. "She told me about you. She told me if I pretended, she'd let me live."

"I'm sorry," said Ianto, his hands shaking as a lump grew in his throat. "I'm sorry I got you involved. I didn't want to be on my own. I didn't care, I never thought...I lo—"

"I'm...I'm not sorry," Jamie gasped. His eyes bulged from a surge of pain. "You were the only real friend I ever had." His eyes rolled and then he went perfectly still.

"No! No, no, no!" Ianto screamed as Jamie's body went lifeless and fell against the rubble like a sack of rocks. "I loved you."

His grandfather said he didn't feel, he didn't care, he didn't love, but if that was true, Ianto wondered why he felt like knives were ripping through his insides, twisting and contorting them. Ianto would have cried then, if he could have, but he couldn't. Monsters like him didn't cry, he thought, monsters that got innocent, stupid little boys killed.

anto heard the sound of laser gun fire and explosions. He let go of Jamie's lifeless body and rose to his feet. The corridor was still there and the ladder. He climbed up into the remains of Johnson's office. All around was pandemonium and the shrieking of more sirens. He ran to the rotunda and was immediately jostled by officers frantically scattering in all directions. Then came the roar of more bomb detonations. Ianto looked upwards through the domed glass ceiling. Something dark flew over it, blocking the light. A shot was fired from it. A hand grabbed him, yanking him to safety as the glass shattered and fell to the floor in a shower of deadly rain. He looked around to see his savior and recognized Owen.

"Where's Ira?" Owen yelled above the din of sirens and people.

"Ira's not with me. You tried to kill me before," Ianto said breathlessly.

"Why isn't Ira with you?" Owen removed a laser gun from his weapons belt and Ianto backed away in alarm. "Do you really think I'd save you just to shoot you?" Owen said quickly, glancing around. "This isn't for you. Why did you come back without him? Ginny said she saw you and Melissa Johnson talking."

Owen started running and Ianto followed, the noise of explosions sounding throughout the building all around them.

"What's going on?" Ianto asked.

"Isn't that why you came?" said Owen, looking at Ianto in surprise. "Because of the siege?"

Another shot came at their left, and Owen veered out of the

way as a hole was blown in the ceiling, allowing a breeze to blow and scatter papers everywhere.

"Come on, we need to get the prisoners out!" Owen said. "Faster, faster."

"I'm running fast!" Ianto snapped at him, picking up his pace.

"This way," Owen said quickly, going through a doorway.

"We need to get out of here now!" Ianto said as bits of ceiling fell down all around them.

"Not before we free the prisoners," Owen grinned widely, and he passed Ianto a knowing look before he took off.

Ianto had no idea what that look was supposed to mean, but he suspected nothing good as he followed Owen down the dark passageway to the Crypts, heavily guarded despite the bombardment above. Owen flashed a card at one of them, but the guard didn't move.

"You're not authorized to enter the Crypts."

"Yes I am."

"The card has been revoked. You were ordered to remain at your duty station."

"There's fighting going on, if you haven't noticed. It isn't safe."

The guard just stared at him. "I suggest you return there." He nodded to one of the other guards. "They can escort you back."

A vise-like hand closed around Ianto's arm.

"Let go of me," Ianto said, in a deceptively calm, flat voice.

He felt as if he was overflowing with sadness and anger. Whether they were real emotions or not, they made it very hard for him think clearly. *Focus*, he told himself. *Don't draw attention to yourself, get to Pomander's Lid, save Ira, fix this mess.* But that's not what he did.

"Let go of me now," Ianto repeated impatiently, trying to wrestle his arm free.

"That's it, you've earned yourself a nice, cushy spot in the

Crypts," the guard tugged on his arm, pulling him into the Crypts.

Ianto ferociously yanked his arm free. He heard a horrible ripping sound and a crack as the guard crumpled to the ground, unconscious, his sleeve drenched red with dripping blood. Ianto ran forward, seeing flashes of white all around him, as Owen shot the remaining guards, many of which stood with their mouths hanging open, stunned after seeing what Ianto had done to their colleague.

"What did you do?" Owen gasped, catching up with Ianto, his eyes wide. "Did you...did you yank his arm out?"

"Doesn't matter. Is there a way out through the Crypts?"

"There's an exit," said Owen, still looking shocked. "Ginny has an air-ship waiting. First we have to get the prisoners out."

"This has to be a quick jailbreak, Owen," said Ianto worriedly as an almost maniacal expression of excitement spread across Owen's face. "We need to get out of here quickly and inconspicuously as possible, not start breaking down doors."

"Sadly, I don't have to break down any doors," said Owen, flashing a red card in Ianto's face. "This'll work for most of the cells. I swiped it off one of those guards, when you yanked the guy's arm off. That was incredible, by the way. You have to show me how to do that some time."

Ianto sighed, knowing he was stuck following the directions of a madman with a gun.

"Just take me to the exit, and quickly."

Instead, Owen ran ahead of Ianto, periodically unlocking cell doors. They didn't have time to unlock all of them as Ianto pulled at Owen several times to stop him from taking too long. He felt an invisible clock ticking inside his head the whole time. The skeletal, ragged prisoners stepped tentatively out of their cells, unable to believe their good luck.

"This way," Owen called back at them. "This way, quickly!"

A tall, dark-skinned man with very little hair fell in step beside Ianto. "What is happening? Where are we going?"

Owen answered for him, "There's a safe house, we'll take you there."

"My family is in the workhouse," the man said. "I'm not leaving without them."

"I'll take him to the workhouse and meet you at the air-ship," said Ianto immediately to Owen.

Owen nodded affirmatively. Ianto led the way down the corridor, the man following close beside him. A few others fell in behind them. They came to the unconscious Defense guards and switched into their uniforms. Through the chaos, nobody paid much attention to the group as they made their way across the rotunda full of shattered glass, and then across the bridge, Ianto breathing a sigh of relief when he crossed it for the last time. Doors opened for Ianto, and he tried not to think about the reason why, the reason he had just discovered. There were no guards at the exit leading out into the courtyard, but when they came to the workhouse door, they ran into a blond-haired young officer holding his laser out in front of him with trembling hands.

"Don't come any further, or I'll shoot you all."

"Evers?" said the man standing beside Ianto, and the boy's eyes widened as he recognized the man, "Mr....Mr. Donnel?"

"Evers, I know you don't want to do this, you don't want to hurt anyone," the man, Mr. Donnel replied. "You won't get in trouble if you let them go, I can promise you that."

The boy seemed to get over his initial shock. "I've orders to kill any prisoners trying to escape. I have to do this, or it's my head. You understand, Mr. Donnel?"

"Nobody has to know," said Mr. Donnel. "Nobody here will tell. Nobody will blame you for being overpowered by such a large group."

The laser lowered a bit in the young officer's hands, but he didn't put it down. Instead he aimed it at Ianto.

"I'll kill him first, if you don't turn around."

"Yuri Evers," Mr. Donnel's voice was sad and calm. "You've never been put on execution duty, have you? You've never seen what it's like, when you've killed another human being. It's not like patrolling, or manning a door. It's not something you do on orders and then forget when you lay down at night. It's not something you can sleep away. It's something that haunts you every waking hour of every day. And when you shut your eyes it'll haunt you then too, in your dreams."

"Mr. Donnel..." Yuri Evers's face was pale. "Mr. Donnel, I must ask you to stop or I will shoot!"

"You'll see their face, hear their voice everywhere, in places where you thought you were safe. You think you killed them, but truth is, you've killed yourself. Because you'll never be the same person again, Evers."

Evers' face contorted as he looked Ianto in the face. He tightened his grip on the laser, and then he let it fall to his side and thrust open the door.

"Hurry up. Then get out of here."

The escapees rushed inside like a flood. Through the hazy air Ianto saw the workers below, trying to free themselves from their manacles. Ianto scrambled down the stairs, going from prisoner to prisoner, breaking the chains, and then he found his grandfather, huddled in a corner, perfectly still. A shot of panic ran through Ianto as he dropped down on his knees beside the old man. Arthur Ambrose turned his head, his mouth falling open when he saw his grandson.

"Ianto?"

"You're leaving," Ianto said.

"I'm in chains," Arthur Ambrose rattled the manacles around

his ankles.

"I can get rid of them," Ianto said immediately. "You don't know what I can do."

"Ianto, I've looked after you for two years and I know very well what you can do," Arthur Ambrose's tone became slightly less gruff. "I'm an old man, and I've spent my whole life running. I've cheated death, but you can't cheat death forever. You always used to ask me when I was going to die, Ianto, well that time is now."

"First, I never meant that, and second, no, it's not," said Ianto through gritted teeth as he freed his grandfather. "I'm getting you out of here. Guess I'm not an Ambrose after all."

He wrapped his arm around his grandfather, supporting him on his feet.

"Where are we going to go?" Arthur Ambrose asked, and Ianto whispered into his ear.

"I did the wrong thing when I betrayed Pomander's Lid. I have to go back. I have to save those people. I don't want them to die like I almost did, wondering why nobody came back for them."

They made it back up the stairs and out into the air, which seemed impossibly cool after the heat of the furnaces. Yuri Evers stood by the door staring at the waves of wide-eyed people emerging from inside.

Mr. Donnel stepped forward. "Thank you, Evers," he said and Yuri Evers nodded before he suddenly crashed to the ground, unconscious from a punch to the head by Mr. Donnel as the last prisoners poured out the door.

"He'll understand when he wakes up," Mr. Donnel said, casting one last sad look back at the him, before he left, moving towards four figures standing nearby. Ianto saw an air-ship in the distance, hidden well out of the fray in a tight grouping of trees and guessed it was Owen and Ginny's, as it was clearly too old and battered to be a Defense air-ship. He looked up and saw several Defense darters overhead between them and the air-ship. He didn't know whose control they were under, but there wasn't much time to think about it. He tightened his grip around Arthur Ambrose and ran, hearing the others' footsteps pounding after him. They were instantly under attack, and he kept running, not stopping until he reached the cover of the trees. When he looked back, he saw Owen with ten others, the only survivors. Mr. Donnel was among them, holding a little girl who had been hit and was bleeding from her leg.

"Okay, quick, into the air-ship," Ianto said.

Ginny jumped down from the hatch. "In, in!" she said, and seeing Owen she added, "The Mariner's down."

Inside, the injured were ushered away, his grandfather among them. The air-ship shuddered and creaked as it lifted off. Several protestor air-ships came to their defense as Defense darters tried to shoot the old air-ship down.

"Medical supplies are in the first cabin on the right," Ginny instructed them, before she noticed Ianto for the first time.

Her mouth fell open, "What are you doing here?"

"I need to get to the cockpit," Ianto said impatiently, pushing past her. He overheard Owen and Ginny conversing behind him as he made his way to the cockpit.

"Yeah, he got me in," Owen went on to describe the jailbreak in enthusiastic, gory detail.

"But what about Ira?" Ginny called to Ianto. "Did you make it to Pomander's Lid? Is he alright?"

Ianto entered the large cockpit and rushed to the controls.

"It's on autopilot, it'll take us to a safe location," Ginny said, joining Ianto.

"No, we've got to get to Pomander's Lid," said Ianto firmly. "I'll give you the location."

"But we have injured on board! We can't go to Pomander's

Lid right now. We have to get these people to a safe house and doctors."

He ignored her protestations and entered the approximate coordinates of Pomander's Lid. Immediately the air-ship changed course, following the black water of the river.

"Why are we going to Pomander's Lid?" Ginny asked, growing annoyed when Ianto continued to ignore her questions. She laid a hand on Ianto's arm. "Answer my question, or I'll stun you and eject you off this ship."

He glared at her, his voice cold. "We're going to Pomander's Lid because if we don't, Defense will destroy it and kill everyone inside."

Ginny froze, startled, and then she said, in a horrified voice, "Are you saying it's been betrayed?"

"Yes," said Ianto, looking down at the computer's estimate of how long a trip to Pomander's Lid would take.

It would take too long; they had to reach it in the next few hours, and even then he knew it might be too late. Could he get more power? Was there a faster route?

"Who?" It was Owen who spoke in a short, angry outburst.

"I don't know," Ianto said, turning back to the controls as he tried to figure out how to make the air-ship go faster.

"You must know. What's their name? What's their name?" Owen spat. "I'll find them and rip them apart."

"Shut your mouth, Owen," Ginny said. "Ianto, how did this happen? You must know something."

"Listen," Ianto looked from Ginny to Owen. "If I can't concentrate, Ira is going to die. I know both of you don't want him to die, so let me figure this out."

Owen immediately opened his mouth to rebuke him, but Ginny said in a low voice, "Be quiet, Owen."

Ianto turned back to the controls, staring at them for some time as the air-ship went as fast as it could along the river. *Too slow, too slow,* was all he could think. Ginny seemed unable to remain silent any longer and finally burst out, "How are we going to get there in time?"

He needed more power. *Power...* An idea popped into his head, a nonsensical, crazy, painful sort of idea. Yet it was his only idea. He laughed, causing Ginny and Owen to stare at him. He instinctively started banging on a section of the console, trying to break it open. Ginny tried to stop him.

"What the hell are you doing?"

"I need to connect myself to the computer."

"You can't do that."

"Weren't these old ships originally piloted by drones? Where is the drone pilot access panel?" Ianto asked, frantically touching every control on the console. Ginny looked at him like he had lost his mind.

"You're going to crash the ship!"

"No, I'm not. Trust me. I know what I'm doing. Now, where is the drone access?"

Ginny hesitantly put her hand over a section of the console area. It lit up red, than slid aside, revealing a small compartment containing what looked like a headset. "There you go."

Ianto picked it up and started to put it on his head. Owen tried pulling it away from him.

"You're crazy! Come on buddy, I think you've blown a fuse. Happens to the best of us. Let's you and me go back and get—" Owen said as he wrestled with Ianto. Ianto quickly got him into a chokehold.

"I'm going to power this ship," Ianto replied coldly, but without malice. Owen vigorously struggled against him but to no avail. Ginny repeatedly hit Ianto to try to break his grip, but he held onto Owen until he began to grow limp and passed out. Then he casually dropped Owen on the floor. Ginny fell down beside Owen and checked his pulse. He was still alive, just unconscious. She was out of breath from her fruitless repeated attacks against Ianto who seemed unperturbed as he put the headset on.

"Stop, Ianto! This is ridiculous, humans can't power machines with their minds. That doesn't make any sense. It'll electrocute you! The ship will go down and we'll all die!" Ginny screamed at him.

You don't know me, Ianto thought. "Sometimes you have to do things that don't make sense!" he yelled back at her.

Ginny's mouth fell open. "You really are crazy!"

"Great," he said, ignoring Ginny while running a diagnostic program in his head. He immediately knew it worked. Now what to do next?

"Stop now." Ginny aimed a laser gun at him. "Stop now, or I swear I will kill you."

No time. His mind melded with the computer. He was the air-ship, every circuit and every electrical pulse. He was the engines and he roared into overdrive. And then he was just pure energy, a brilliant, buoyant light. He opened his eyes. He felt weak and confused. He took the headset off and dropped it on the floor. He collapsed on the ground beside it. Ginny's face swam in front of his eyes.

"What's happening?" Owen asked groggily as he got up and joined Ginny who was stooped over Ianto's unconscious body lying on the floor.

She shook her head. "I don't understand it."

"Did he get electrocuted?"

"No, no, but there was a power surge to the engines. I don't know how in the hell he did it, but we're going at twice the speed as before, and I don't know how that's possible. How did he connect that way?"

"Is he dead?" Owen mumbled.

The world was vanishing, turning into black and white static. Ianto could barely distinguish their faces anymore...

Silence.

71

Alaska walked towards the air-ship cabin assigned to her, her mind distracted by thoughts about what would happen now at Pomander's Lid. She bumped into an elderly hunchbacked woman leaning heavily on an old, gnarled cane, a heavy steel pendant of a bird hanging around her neck.

"I'm sorry," said Alaska hastily. She noticed an emptiness in the woman's gaze, fixed so steadily on Alaska's face as if she was looking at Alaska, but not seeing her. "Oh, you're a Still."

The woman touched Alaska's face gently. "Winter."

"What?" said Alaska, staring at the Still incredulously, but the old woman hobbled away around the corner of the corridor.

Alaska entered her cabin, a small metal cubicle with a barred window. Alaska guessed this had once been a Defense prison air-ship. She passed by a bunkbed, dresser and sink as she went to the window and peered out. They'd just left Pomander's Lid and were out in the desert. She couldn't see anything except the shadowy outlines of rolling, sandy hills and darkening sky as the night stretched on.

"Alaska?" she turned her head and saw Tarana standing in the doorway. She had been so distracted by her encounter with the old woman Still, she had left her door wide open.

Tarana's eyes were red and she clutched a raggedy shawl draped around her head. She looked startled to see Alaska.

"Hello, Tarana," Alaska said, forcing a smile.

"You're not supposed to be here," Tarana said. "You weren't picked, love."

"Jakob...Jakob gave me his black slip," Alaska said quietly, turning back to the window.

There were bright lights on the horizon, growing brighter and brighter. She and Tarana stared in horror as the lights gave way to massive, white ships, moving far faster than their air-ship.

"Defense!" Tarana cried.

Their air-ship and the other evacuating air-ships changed course back towards Pomander's Lid, fleeing the approaching army. Pomander's Lid loomed back into sight. They were moving as fast as they could, the entire air-ship rattling dangerously as they hurtled through the air. Then there was a terrible boom of an explosion and the pilot yelled over the com, "Emergency landing! Brace for emergency landing!"

It landed roughly, slamming into the ground, sending Alaska and Tarana flying to the floor. Alaska's head hit the windowsill as she went crashing downwards and she groaned, blinking her eyes. The lights switched off, plunging the air-ship into darkness. She felt along the floor, and found Tarana, unconscious.

"Tarana, wake up, wake up!" Alaska said desperately, but she remained unconscious.

Alaska reluctantly left her and went out into the corridor. Lights flickered on and off eerily. Everything was quiet, far too quiet, Alaska thought. She took a deep breath and felt her way along the corridor in the dark. Then she heard screams coming from somewhere beyond, horrible, gut-wrenching screams and sharply barked orders. She ran in the opposite direction as the sound of running footsteps came towards her. She turned a corner, and saw a partially open door. Lymir lay on the blood-slicked floor, his eyes unseeing. She froze, horrified, then heard voices approaching from up ahead, too close to run away from. She scrambled inside his room and looked around for a hiding place. She decided on the space under the bunkbed. As she ran over to it, she saw the sky outside of the room's window, lit up by what looked like hundreds of bright lights—Defense air-ships!

"Clear the ship, every inch. Johnson wants every last head, understood?"

Alaska dropped to the floor and slid under the bed, for once glad of her small size. The voices closed in and the door to the room creaked open a little further.

"Room's been checked, sir."

Why was that voice familiar?

"Check again."

"Yes, sir."

Alaska's heart beat fast as she saw the dark polished shoes of the officer approach Lymir's body. He bent down and inspected it, then turned to leave. She held her breath, then gasped as she saw the trailing hems of Nightghosts' robes as they surrounded the bed. She banged her head against the bed, and a moment later she saw a face looking right at her with watery blue eyes behind spectacles.

"Hugh?"

Hugh Maisel froze, his hand halfway reaching for the laser clipped to the belt of his Defense uniform. Alaska couldn't believe it, her best friend from the Capital standing in front of her. She felt instant relief, and wanted to rush out and hug him, then realized he was wearing their uniform—he had somehow become a Defense officer. The relief ended, leaving only a nauseating sickness.

"What are you doing here?" Hugh whispered, looking as horrified as her. "Why are you with this people? They're evil. They used my father. He's dead because of them!"

"Defense took my parents. They killed your father!" Alaska argued. "It wasn't the protestors who killed your father. Defense is using you, Hugh."

Hugh's voice shook as he stubbornly whispered, "Defense cured the plague, they saved hundreds of lives. They protect us from the provincials. They showed me the things the protestors do. Protestors lie and steal and kill. Protestors take children, Alaska, and do experiments on them."

"The people in Pomander's Lid don't take children. They don't lie and if they steal or kill, it's because Defense has left them no other choice."

"They have no choice but to steal from clinics? To take medicine?"

"They're trying to find a cure, Hugh. Defense has tried to keep control over all of us with their partial cure. They don't want a real cure to be found because it would make them a lot less powerful. I saw Defense kill a scientist to stop a real solution from being found. They've done nothing since they took power but hurt the Nation. The protestors are trying to save it!"

"You're saying these things to try and poison me!" Hugh said. They heard footsteps in the hallway and he quickly said, "I'll distract them. Run, Alaska, as soon as you can. I don't want to ever see you again."

He got to his feet and let her scramble out from under the bed. The footsteps got closer, and Hugh ran to the door and disappeared into the hall. A moment later Alaska heard a horrible thunk sound and realized he had been knocked out by someone. Her grip tightened around Magler's dagger, which she had decided to always carry with her. Then Tarana appeared in the doorway, a stun gun in her hand.

"Come on," Tarana said, grabbing Alaska's hand. "We have to get out of here."

"Thank you," Alaska managed to say, as they ran down the corridor towards an exit door.

"Don't thank me," said Tarana, her voice incredibly sad. "I let the Nightghosts take you."

72

The whole world had gone mad.

"I told them your family was out of the house," Tarana whispered. "I was too weak to protect you, too scared of them. It's my fault the Nightghosts kidnapped you." Tears streamed down Tarana's bloodied face. "Alaska, I know you won't understand, but I'm sorry."

Alaska backed away from Tarana, shocked.

"I'm so sorry," Tarana sobbed as she reached out for Alaska, but Alaska ran away from her. She yanked open the exit door and stumbled out into the frigid night air and desert sand.

Tarana of all people. How could Tarana have done that to her? Above her head she saw the Defense air-ships battering the mountain range where Pomander's Lid lay, but it was the only place to run towards. She doubted they could see her in the darkness, yet she felt dangerously exposed as several shots hit the ground not far from her, like giant lightning bolts. She felt the heat radiating from them, like flames licking at her.

"Alaska!" she heard a scream behind her and turned to see Tarana hurtling towards her. "Watch out!"

She looked up, and leapt sideways, plunging to the sand and rolled away just in time to avoid being hit by a laser bolt. The ground trembled with tremendous force and the heat scorched the air all around her. She threw her hands in front of her eyes to protect them from the intense light. When it was over she lay gasping, covered in grit, painful burns on her hands and legs. She blinked, trying to make out what was going on around her.

Tarana lay on the ground, unmoving. Alaska scrambled over to her, forcing herself to move despite the pain coursing through her body. One side of Tarana's tear-stained, bloodied face was ruined, though her eyes were untouched, and they looked up at Alaska, with an expression of incredible pain and shock. Tarana let out a short gasp and Alaska dropped to her knees beside her.

"I'm sorry," Tarana managed to whisper in a raspy voice.

Alaska nodded her head solemnly, knowing painfully there was nothing that could be said or done.

"I'm sorry too."

Tarana reached for Alaska's hand, closing her hand around Alaska's. "I was sixteen. I was frightened," she whispered, in a shaking voice. "When they took you I should have died then. I should have died instead of letting it happen. I was a coward, Alaska. I let them take you away. I wasn't strong enough. I let them..."

Tarana's eyes closed, her breathing stopped.

"Tarana!" Alaska cried, gently nudging her. "Tarana, please!"

Alaska collapsed onto the sand, tears running down her cheeks. A shot struck nearby and she jumped to her feet. She didn't want to leave Tarana alone, but she knew she had no choice. She ran towards Pomander's Lid, not stopping when she saw a flash of white light in the corner of her eye, or heard a boom. The ground became rocky, and she clambered over the stones and boulders, taking cover in their shadow several times before she heard a voice calling out, "Whose there?"

With relief, she saw it was Ira.

"Alaska!" she shouted over the tumult of the siege. "Alaska Donnel!"

"Alaska!" Ira said in surprise, running towards her. When he reached her, she didn't mind that he embraced her. She never thought she would be happy to see him. He was a liar, murderer, and overall secretive jerk but he was all she had in the midst of the chaos.

"You're trembling. Come on. What happened to the ship? The others? How many of the evacuation fleet made it?"

"I couldn't see what happened to the others," was all Alaska said. "Is Jakob alive?"

"He's fine," Ira responded flatly, a shadow crossing his face, but Alaska didn't notice.

She followed him through a secret tunnel entrance that led them back inside Pomander's Lid. She gawked at the devastation; there had been several cave-ins, buildings lay in ruins all around, a clock hung from a wooden pole, its glass face cracked, its hands unmoving. Alaska looked away and saw Cassandra clambering over debris towards them.

"Ira Graye!" said Cassandra, looking aghast, irate and tired. "Well, since you're here you might as well be our extra pilot."

Alaska noticed that Ira briefly looked pleased, before Cassandra turned to her.

"I want you to check the tunnels, make sure everyone's been rescued from the prison."

"It would be better..." Ira began.

Cassandra continued, ignoring him. "Your friend Holly, I believe, is down there."

Alaska nodded her head, "I'll do that." She started towards the tunnels, and Ira stopped her.

"Here. Take this." He discreetly handed her a laser gun. She took it quickly and hid it in an interior pocket of her tunic. "Alaska, be careful."

Alaska nodded affirmatively, and Ira looked as if he was about to say something more, when Cassandra yelled out, "IRA GRAYE!"

He left, following Cassandra, and Alaska entered the tunnels. The sound of explosions above were muffled by the heavy rock and eventually they disappeared completely, leaving Alaska in utter silence. She felt along the wall, and finally found a lantern. She tried to remember the path to go back, but there were several rock collapses which forced her to take unfamiliar paths until she was sure she was lost. She came to a spot that smelt terrible and saw the tunnel branched off, one way blocked by a partial collapse. Twisted metal bars lay on the ground, and she saw a sign hanging off one screw: *Pomander's Lid Prison.*

"Help me!" a call echoed from inside the partially collasped tunnel.

Alaska scrambled over piles of fallen rocks, and then she saw a figure lying on the ground. Holly looked up in relief at seeing Alaska, though she tried to disguise her pained expression. Alaska held up the lantern and saw Holly's leg was pinned under a heavy rock. Alaska pulled and grunted at the rock until she managed to lift it enough that Holly could move her leg from under it. There was a lot of blood, but Alaska couldn't tell how bad the injury was. She tore fabric from the hem of her tunic and wrapped it tightly around the wound.

"Can you stand?" Alaska asked her.

Holly shook her head. "Not without help."

Alaska wrapped her arm around Holly's waist and helped her up. Holly stood on one foot, hopping along as Alaska supported her. She looked back at the mangled remains of the prison.

"Is anyone else alive?"

Holly shook her head. "They killed everyone, but I hid."

Alaska froze. "They?"

"The Defense officers." Holly looked up at Alaska worriedly. "Aren't they everywhere now?"

Alaska heard voices nearby in the tunnels.

"I heard something! Check for survivors, take no prisoners!"

Alaska scrambled in the tunnel, pulling Holly along with her.

She saw a Defense officer behind her and pulled out the laser gun Ira had given her. She fired it and knocked him to the ground, before finally making it out of the tunnels with Holly.

"Defense officers—"

She stopped, seeing sky above her head. People ran and screamed as huge chunks of rock crashed to the ground below. Pomander's Lid was breached, ripped open, and dark tendrils of rope descended from twenty Defense air-ships above. Officers climbed down them and overwhelmed the fighting crowds below. The only clear place of shelter was the town hall. Alaska darted towards it, dragging Holly along with her.

"Duck!"

Alaska whipped around to see Cassandra's horrified face before something came hurtling towards her and Holly, and they dived out of the way. Something broke on the ground where they'd been a moment before, releasing a cloud of smoky gray vapor. The stone around it turned to black powder, and an acrid smell filled the air. Coughing, Alaska tried to blink away the fog. A hand pulled her away from it, and she saw Holly's pained face.

"Come on, Alaska."

They made it up the steps and inside of the building. Holly tried to drop to the ground, but Alaska pulled her up and struggled on wordlessly. They had to get deep inside of the building, Alaska knew, somewhere hidden and unexposed. The power had been cut, and everything was dark as they climbed the stairs as quickly as possible to the second floor. There was a light shining and through a doorway Alaska could see its source, a candle. Several people had gathered around it on the floor. Most of them were children, one ran to the window to look out and an elderly woman quickly stepped forward to shut it and drew the curtains. Corridor 3. Alaska dragged Holly down it, feeling the walls in the dark with her foot to find her way. Her right foot hit a door frame and after a minute of fumbling she found the handle and stepped inside. It was the control room. There were lights, electric lights, not candle flames, and one of the screens was on, flashing "com" in front of her. A backup generator had survived the barrage. Alaska helped Holly down to the floor and found a few blankets in a storage closet to wrap tightly around Holly's injury. Holly bit her lip and tried not to scream. Alaska wrapped another blanket around herself before she shut the door, putting a chair up against it.

"A chair's not going to stop them," Holly said matter-of-factly, though there was a tremor in her voice.

Alaska replied, "It's the best we've got."

She hurried over to the com panel, picked up a microphone and stared at the controls. There was one for every section of Pomander's Lid and every defense and evacuation air-ship. She tried them one by one and got replies from a quarter of them, feeling a twinge of relief every time a response came and dread every time one did not.

"Pomander's Lid is breached, get as far away as possible," Alaska repeated on every call. "Don't try coming back."

"Hello?" she said on the last one.

Ira responded, "Alaska?" There was relief and confusion in his voice. "What are you doing there? We lost contact with Control ages ago."

"I know, the room was empty when I arrived," Alaska said. "Ira, some of the evacuees made it."

"Just sit tight in town hall, I'm coming to get you."

"No! Ira, you have to go to the evacuees. They need protection. Defense will go after them."

"Wait, I can't—Alaska, stay there. I'm coming for you." The transmission broke up—static.

"Alaska!"

Alaska turned at Holly's frightened exclamation. They heard

screams and noises from outside the room. Then a bright white light spilled around the edges of the closed control room door. *Defense officers are in the building on the second floor!* Alaska thought. There was a high-pitched noise from the control console as the com switched on.

"Alaska?" Ira shouted at her through the com.

"Everything's alright," Alaska said, trying to keep the fear out of her voice. "Just keep going to help the evacuees. Don't worry about me. I'm just going to be cut off for a moment." Alaska looked around and saw a portable communicator. She pinned it to her shirt. "I'm going to have to leave town hall, but I'll keep in contact."

"Alaska?"

She grabbed Holly's arm, "Come on."

Holly shook her head, "I'll slow you down. Just leave me."

"Holly Gizel, I'm not leaving you," said Alaska, determined to save her.

She forced Holly to her feet and hurried out the door. A light was getting closer. She could hear the approaching heavy sound of the Defense officers' boots. They ran down a corridor, trying to find an exit in the dark. They could not get to the first floor which was blocked off by Defense officers. Alaska heard more doors banged open. She could follow their progress, closer and closer, by the sound of screams. Alaska stopped at the end of a corridor as Holly gasped for breath. Three unmarked doors. There was a window to her left, but looking out of it, she knew they were up too high to jump. She could survive it, but she'd injure herself badly, and she couldn't afford that now. Three unmarked doors. She shut her eyes. Helen, in the back room of the cathedral, had shown her maps of all of Pomander's Lid, including the town hall. But now, her mind was whizzing, she couldn't concentrate, she needed to concentrate. *Remember,* she thought furiously, *remember.*

The footsteps sounded as if they were directly behind her so she quickly opened one of the unmarked doors and dragged Holly inside the room. She shut it right before a flash of light. The door was incinerated behind them, but they were already running again. Alaska knew where she was now. The town hall had an emergency exit on the second floor, and it was this way, she was sure of it.

"Alaska, I haven't heard from you, what's happening?"

It was Ira again, his voice coming through clearly from the com badge. The sound startled Alaska.

"We're running for our lives!" Holly cried.

"Holly's with you? What's the situation?"

"Are you protecting the evacuees?" Alaska asked.

"I'm nearly there," Ira said. "What did Holly say...are you alright?"

The exit door was very near. She saw it up ahead and forced herself to run faster when something caught her eye out a window. Defense officers were climbing up the exit stairs, towards the landing. Towards her. Behind her she could hear more of them closing in. Suddenly, Holly collapsed against her, and she slipped, falling to the floor, feeling the cold, polished stone meet her skull with a dull thunk. Her head felt as if it had been split in half.

"Alaska, talk to me!" Ira yelled over the com.

She tried to speak, but she couldn't find her voice. She crawled towards the window, feeling a gut wrenching pain with every movement. Holly lay unconscious on the floor.

"Alaska, what's wrong? Tell me!" There was clear frustration in Ira's voice at her silence.

"I'm trapped," Alaska said, her voice shaking uncontrollably.

"I'm coming for you."

"What about the evacuees?"

"I've dealt with that. They're safe. Where are you?"

"In the town hall, second floor, by the emergency exit."

She pulled herself up to look out a window. Below were broken glass shards on the pavement of the square. She saw a reflection...

"Sit tight," Ira said.

Alaska turned around. They stood in a semicircle around her, nine of them, their dark cloaks trailing on the ground. There was no way the Nightghosts could have suddenly gotten in. *I am hallucinating*, Alaska realized. *They are in my head.* The revelation actually felt like a relief.

"I know you aren't real," Alaska whispered, putting her hand over the com.

"You are so scared," their voices were full of curiosity. "So full of a fear you haven't felt since you were twelve."

"Go away. I don't want you here."

The false Nightghosts looked utterly taken aback by Alaska's command. They glanced at one another in confusion, no longer menacing. Then all nine vanished like smoke. Alaska felt a moment of triumph, then there was a flash of light behind her and she turned her head. There was a loud banging on the exit door. Alaska sank against the wall and shut her eyes. *This is it*, she thought. *The end.* The exit door was bashed open, and she opened her eyes to find herself face-to-face with Ianto Ambrose.

73

She hurled herself with what strength she had left and knocked Ianto to the ground.

"Come back to finish the job!" she snarled, but he was already back on his feet, his hands held in front of himself in surrender.

"I'm here to help. Where's Ira?" Ianto asked immediately.

"How could you come back after what you did?"

He looked drained, covered in dust, his auburn hair clinging to his face. He turned away from her and looked down at Holly's unconscious figure.

"I'm saving your life and you're welcome," said Ianto. "Ginny and Owen have a ship, once we find Ira we can get out of here."

"Ginny and Owen came with you?"

"I have a ship!" said Ianto impatiently.

Alaska didn't move and then she saw Ginny appear in the exit. "Ianto, come on!"

She saw Alaska and her mouth fell open, curling into a smile. "The Donnel girl! Oh, you're bleeding!"

Alaska reached up and felt the wetness on her face. It was hard to see in the relative darkness, but she knew it was blood trickling from a head wound. She felt dizzy and her legs suddenly went wobbly.

"Take Holly," said Alaska immediately. She nodded towards Ianto. "Don't trust him, no matter what he's told you."

Ginny and Ianto picked Holly up and carried her out. Suddenly the building shook and in seconds Alaska saw a flash of metal hurtling towards her. A Defense air-ship crashed into the side of the building and the ceiling collapsed.

****

"She's covered in bruises."

Alaska opened her eyes weakly, blinking. Sterile white lights blinded her.

"She's a very lucky girl."

"Lucky? That is an understatement."

She sat bolt upright and saw she was in a ship infirmary. Out of a far window she could see the sky lit as if with crackles of lightning. Dawn was approaching over the horizon. Then she remembered, and began to scream, "Where am I? What happened? Ira!"

"Hush, hush," a woman in a medical uniform tried to push her back down, but she shoved the woman away.

"Where am I?" Alaska screamed hysterically as the woman, who seemed to be a nurse, restrained her. The nurse was familiar, she'd seen her in the hospital wing. Alaska relaxed a little.

"Is this Ira's ship?" she asked, her voice hoarse from screaming.

"Yes. Just sit still, you've been—"

"How many evacuees made it? Are all the air-ships safe?" Alaska asked.

The nurse looked at her, confused. "How should I know? We didn't leave Pomander's Lid. And none have returned."

Alaska looked at the nurse in shock, then asked, her voice shaking, "Where is he? Ira Graye, where is he?"

"That doesn't matter, dear, you have to sit still here so that I can bandage your arm and—"

"Take me to him NOW."

Alaska scrambled onto her feet. The air-ship jolted and she instinctively stretched out her arms to brace herself, sending a surge of pain through her injured arm.

Alaska collapsed back onto the infirmary bed, biting back tears.

"I'm serious," Alaska said hoarsely.

"I'm serious too, but if you're going to be hardheaded about it..." The nurse took Alaska by the hand, helped her up and through the door then down a corridor until they reached the cockpit.

Alaska could see Ira sitting in front of a large screen, circling the ruins of the destroyed town hall. He seemed to be looking for other survivors.

"Ianto's back," said Alaska. "With Ginny and Owen."

"I wasn't expecting them that quickly," Ira didn't look terribly surprised, briefly glancing over his shoulder as the nurse slipped away. "How are you doing, Alaska?"

"You never even tried to help them," Alaska said angrily. "You told me you had it sorted."

"I didn't have time for the evacuees. If I'd gone, you'd be dead. What was I supposed to say?"

"You lied and let them die," said Alaska coldly.

"I did what I had to," Ira snapped.

"Did you lie about Jakob?"

Suddenly the whole air-ship shook violently as something slammed into it hard. Ira turned back to the screen. Eight of thirteen remaining Defense air-ships had broken off and were coming. Ira quickly maneuvered the air-ship to avoid another attack.

"Did you find anyone in the tunnels?" Ira inquired.

"Holly. She's with Ginny and Owen. What about Jakob?"

"I don't know about every single person, Alaska," Ira snapped. "But yes, I think so."

They were hit hard. Alaska and Ira were thrown against a wall. She scrambled to her feet when the air-ship stopped rocking.

"Come in, cockpit." It was the nurse. "Ira?"

"We're fine!" Ira said, scrambling back onto his feet, blood trickling down from his hair. "Just wait a minute."

Ira took the controls back and started rapidly heading upwards in a sudden and sharp ascent. Alaska couldn't see anything above except dark, midnight blue sky.

"What are you doing?" Alaska asked worriedly. "Where are we going?"

The sky changed as their air-ship went higher and higher with Defense air-ships following in pursuit, closing in around them.

"Ira, they're going to kill us!" Alaska yelled, but he didn't respond. Then she saw what he had been so focused on. It ripped across the sky, a bright, white hole, with a blinding light. Tendrils of lightning radiated out from it, reaching towards their air-ship.

"Ira, stop!" Alaska screamed as their air-ship continued to approach it. "I've seen this before," she whispered, remembering the day with Jakob on the observation deck when she had looked up and seen the crack in the sky. "It'll destroy the ship!" Alaska shrieked, but Ira didn't say a word. "Ira, stop now!"

He seemed hypnotized by it, completely oblivious to her cries. She saw the strange brilliant glow about to strike them. Suddenly, she watched in shock and awe as one of her hands involuntarily raised up, past Ira's face, towards the front window. One finger pointed towards the Defense air-ships. The beam of light changed direction and smashed into the enemy vessels. One exploded, and the others immediately went dead before crashing out of the sky. A piece of wreckage from the exploded Defense air-ship flew towards them and slammed into their air-ship. The ship rocked dangerously and Alaska gripped the back of the pilot's chair, while Ira was thrown to the floor. As another piece of the Defense air-ship flew towards them, she quickly took over the controls, swerving the vessel out of the way. She sank into the pilot's chair, relieved and confused. She stared down at her hand. She didn't know why she had reached out, or why the lightning had changed direction. *I couldn't have redirected it*, she thought quickly, *that's absurd.* The lightning striking where her finger pointed must have only been a freak concidence and the strange movement of her hand itself only an instinctive, panicked gesture. Alaska flew away from the rip, and it closed up again, the sky returning to normal as if nothing had ever been there. She didn't have anymore time to think about the phenomenon she had just witnessed as another Defense air-ship appeared. She fired a few laser shots at it. The Defense air-ship fired back and followed her past the ruined mountainside. On the floor, she heard Ira groan hoarsely, "What's going on, Alaska?"

"Don't move," Alaska said before she rammed the air-ship through the railing of the observation deck Jakob had found.

The air-ship rocked dangerously, but kept going as she neared the lighthouse turret. She looked down at the controls. From her flying lesson with Jakob, she knew which switch dumped the fuel. Alaska passed the turret and flipped the switch, then tore off in the air-ship. When she felt the air-ship was a reasonably safe distance, she fired the rear weapons into the cloud of fuel. The explosion was massive, a ball of fire that ripped apart the pursuing Defense air-ship and all that was left of the Records. She heard Ira groan and turned to see he was standing right behind her, rubbing his head where he'd hit it on the floor.

"That was clever," Ira said breathlessly, looking around in bewilderment. "Alaska!"

She faced forward and saw a Defense air-ship fire at them. She tried diving but the air-ship was hit head-on. The controls immediately went dead. The air-ship began to plummet as the power drained from the systems, leaving it lifeless.

"Massive damage!" she heard somebody scream through the com. "Abandon ship! Evacuate now..."

Alaska grabbed Ira's hand, pulled him out of the cockpit, and ran down the corridor. They were plummeting, faster and faster towards the ground below. Ira ran ahead and guided her down corridors with blinking red warning lights.

"Hatch!" Ira yelled and pointed. They were at the end of a corridor. Other people had already assembled there, some jumping off the air-ship. There was a rock ledge jutting out from the side of a collasped cave, and the air-ship was just above it, hurtling towards it. Ira jumped, nearly falling off the ledge. He thought Alaska would follow but the air-ship sped up its descent and whipped past the ledge before she could jump.

"Ira!" she yelled, and then the dead air-ship slammed into the ground and everything was engulfed in flames.

74

"**M**y name is Oxsana Cathar Hemming." Alaska looked up and saw the face of a young woman swimming in front of her. "I'm here to help you."

Alaska tried to sit up, but she was shackled to a cot. She cried out in alarm, twisting to see the rest of the room and saw a mirror behind the woman. She was twelve years old. She was disoriented as the room swam before her eyes, and she felt a strange soft pressure weighing down her head, like a pillow being pressed firmly into her brow.

"When you return home, you won't remember any of this," said Oxsana. "Don't struggle, please."

Alaska immediately fought her shackles and cried out louder when the metal dug into her wrists.

"See? Resistance is pointless," said Oxsana. "Here, drink some water."

She pressed something to Alaska's dry, cracked lips. Alaska tasted something sweet, with a metallic aftertaste. *The water is drugged*, she thought in panic. She tried to press her lips closed, but she was too desperately thirsty. She let the water flood her mouth and go down her throat, dragging her away from consciousness. Everything was melting away. Suddenly, she heard a scream that violently brought her back to reality, "Where is MIR COUNTA?"

Ira burst into the room, bruises on his face, his hair wild and unkempt.

"Let her go! She's just a child!" he cried out. "You're sick, every single one of you!"

"Somebody restrain the prisoner!" shouted Oxsana.

Ira ran around Oxsana who tried to grab him, but he nimbly avoided her, making it to the cot.

"Help me," Alaska whispered, unsure if she had actually spoken, the words unnaturally loud in her head.

Ira wrestled with the chains holding Alaska down. Oxsana grabbed him from behind and threw him across the room. He fought back, but Oxsana was stronger. She managed to get him out of the room. Alaska vaguely saw two people haul him away. She heard Ira's screams and tried to jump off the cot, but she could do nothing as her body was slowly immobilized and her mind floated away again.

****

Alaska awoke from the memory in twisted, splintered wreckage. She tried to rise to her feet. Her legs wobbled dangerously, agonizing pain coursed through her whole body. She limped forward, planting a hand firmly along the broken hull of the airship to guide herself through the wreckage one step after another, each impossibly excruciating. Her nostrils were full of smoke and her head was swimming. She touched one finger to her forehead gingerly, and it came away slicked with blood. Figures lay on the ground all about her. She dropped down on her knees near a man in his sixties, but she knew there was nothing she could do. There was a stun gun next to him, and she picked it up, then heard a muffled shout.

"Alaska! Alaska, where are you?"

She recognized Ira's voice, panic-stricken like before in her memory. She moved towards the voice, and yelled back, "I'm here!"

She listened hard for a response, and then suddenly came a piercing scream. She knew immediately it was Ira, just like in the memory when he had tried to save her.

"Ira!" she called. "Ira!"

She wasn't letting anything happen to him, not again. She moved as quickly as she could. And then she saw a terrible sight.

Ianto looked around. Since he and Ginny had dragged Holly out of harm's way, the fight had completely changed. Defense only had four air-ships left. He ran through the crowds of fleeing people looking for Ira and found himself face-to-face with someone familiar.

"Hey you! You're that boy who attacked me!" the Defense guard growled. It was the guard that had tried to take his blood sample in Johnson's office that first day at Lossit. Ianto quickly raised the stun gun Ginny had given him and fired.

The guard ducked just in time to avoid it and fired his laser in Ianto's direction. Ianto ran, hearing the sound of the guard in pursuit behind him. The crowds made it nearly impossible to move as he fought and clawed his way through. Then the crowds became almost insurmountable, a stampede hurtling towards him as everyone who'd just run past him was now running back towards him at breakneck speeds. He braced himself as he was nearly knocked off his feet and crushed in a wave of desperation. He tried to see what they were running from, back into the arms of the advancing lines of shocked Defense officers, and saw a dark shadow hurtling out of the sky. An air-ship. People were jumping out of it onto the ledges of the cave walls, desperately abandoning the doomed vessel. It crashed with a deafening noise that drowned out all the screams. Shots were fired into the air from the ground at the Defense air-ships, one of which swerved too far towards the mountainside to shield itself. It lost control of its badly damaged systems and was dashed to pieces against the rock. The last remaining Defense air-ships retreated, and the officers on the ground followed them.

"Ira!" Ianto yelled, blinking away the smoke and clambering around the flames now pluming from the vessel.

Rain started to fall hard, deluging the people below. The defeated enemy Defense guards ran out of the ruin of Pomander's Lid. It was over. But where was Ira? Ianto entered the wreckage and looked around. Looking at the twisted hulk, he didn't see how anyone could have survived. People lay everywhere clearly dead, but none of them was Ira. He stepped over them, making his way till he found what appeared to be a narrow corridor. He heard a scream and ran down it. A young man lay on his back, covered in blood and dust. He had been hit on the head by a blunt object. It was Ira Graye, like in his dream, perfectly still, dead. Ianto fell to the ground beside him on his knees.

"Should I kill you now, Ianto Ambrose?"

He looked up and froze. He saw a woman in red looking down at him. Melissa Johnson's hair was wet and plastered to her face, her clothes were dusty and ragged, but there was no sign of injury on her.

"You were pinned under feet of rocks," said Ianto, breathing heavily. "You're supposed to be dead."

"Maybe I got out before the collapse." She stepped towards him, and Ianto stepped back, shaking his head.

"No way, I would have seen you."

"You're right," there was a twisted smile on Melissa Johnson's face. "A human would be dead. A human, but not a monster, Ianto. Which is why you're still alive. Which is how we are both here."

She pointed her laser at him. He reached for his stun gun, but it was gone, and then he saw it in Melissa Johnson's belt. She had taken it from him in the stampede, and he'd never noticed.

Stupid, he thought, *stupid*. It was too late now.

"I was like them once," Melissa Johnson said as she slowly approached him. "All these human beings. I suppose some part of me still is like them. But I was severely injured, smashed up in a terrible accident, and instead of letting me die like he should have done, my dear grandfather Samson Magler decided to make an experiment out of me."

"You aren't like the other Magler's Children," said Ianto, backing away. Johnson nodded.

"I was beyond saving in that accident." Melissa Johnson's voice was cold as she came closer and closer to him. "So Magler made me the 10th Magler's child. He carved out the body of another Magler's Child and put my mind inside of it. This existence is not living. Did it hurt when you learned what you were?"

Ianto felt the hull of the air-ship wreckage behind him and knew there was nowhere left to run.

"No, I'm sure it didn't hurt. Because you feel nothing when you want to or when you feel like you ought to. There's only emptiness and wires inside of your head. I'm sure it's so much easier for you. You're nothing but piles upon piles of coded commands and duties and commandments. I'm a human mind that's been entombed in steel. I can think for myself. You have no free will of your own."

"Shut up," Ianto said, shaking. "Shut up."

"You've never made a free choice before in your life, Ianto, and you never will," said Melissa Johnson. "You thought you were so clever, so different sneaking away from your grandfather, but that was all programming, nothing more. Everything and anything you do. The idiotic, seemingly irrational act of trusting me for Jamie's sake or going back for Ira, it's really just programming too. You don't care about him, or anyone else in this godforsaken place. You will live forever, an empty, Frankenstein body packed full of wires, nothing more. Not a soul or a mind. I know what it's like to not have a soul. It didn't come with me in the transfer. I found that out when Magler killed everyone important to me and robbed me of my humanity because I didn't care. It doesn't matter to me I'm a monster, or that people die. Only Defense matters to me anymore. My grandfather and your 'parents' tried to save Melissa Magler but they killed her, just like the others. And now Defense and I have killed everyone important to you and robbed you of your delusions of humanity."

Ianto stared at her, unable to speak and she smiled, "We're so similar."

Ianto looked down at Ira's dusty, bloodied figure in front of him. Then he looked back at Melissa Johnson and said through gritted teeth, "I'm not a monster."

Melissa Johnson's face contorted and she angrily fired at Ianto. He threw his hand up in front of his face to block the laser beam and felt the heat engulf him, along with a searing, gut-wrenching pain as he collapsed onto the ground. He looked at his hand and saw the skin had melted, clinging in a fleshy, bloody mess to an artificial bone. He saw wires poking through, intact in metal casings. Ianto screamed. It was the loudest scream he remembered in his life, piercing all of Pomander's Lid. Melissa Johnson clutched her head.

"Stop doing that!"

Melissa Johnson's face leered over him as she smashed the bottom of her red high heel into his hand, mangling a wire. Feeling left his hand, releasing the pain and his screams stopped as he gasped, crumpling to the ground. Melissa Johnson pointed the laser at him again, saying coldly, "I've won. This fight is over."

"This fight *is* over," came a girl's voice from behind Melissa Johnson.

Melissa Johnson turned, startled, then collapsed. She hit the ground hard, the laser knocked out of her hand. Ianto saw Alaska Donnel standing by the fallen woman, clutching a stun gun.

Alaska looked in horror at Ianto's mangled hand. "You aren't human...you're an android."

"Cyborg," said Ianto. "There's a difference. At least I'm a little human."

To his relief she didn't ask more questions. He looked down at the hand and saw it was already beginning to heal, the skin spreading itself over the crushed mess again, slightly stretched and unnatural looking, with scar marks. His fingernails slid back into place, but he still couldn't feel a thing. The wire inside was still crushed.

"Ira," she whispered, her legs buckling beneath her. She knelt down on the ground beside him.

Ianto noticed for the first time how battered she looked.

"I checked, he's still breathing," Ianto said. "He's coming to."

The relief on Ianto's face was strange because it seemed so real and made him look more human than Alaska had ever seen him, even though she knew he wasn't, even though she wanted to hate him more than anything except Defense and the Nightghosts. She looked away and gingerly raised Ira up and held him in her arms. His eyes flew open, wide from shock. Though his breathing was ragged, he was still alive. His gaze fixed on Alaska.

"It was you."

"Ira, you're badly hurt..." Alaska began.

Ira cried out in a raspy, pained voice, "It was you. You caused the lightning."

"No," Alaska said, dumbfounded, her hands shaking. "You're disoriented, Ira. I didn't cause the lightning. How could I?"

"I know what you can do. I know what the Nightghosts did now..." Ira's voice died away as he closed his eyes and slumped against her.

There was the sound of voices as people approached them to help and Ianto ran. Alaska watched him disappear, right before Hawk arrived, a group of people behind him. They helped her onto her feet and carried her and Ira to a makeshift hospital tent set up to take care of the wounded. Outside of the wreckage, smoke rose around the smoldering ruins of Pomander's Lid. The Defense air-ships lay all around, dashed to pieces on the ground. Tattered black flags flew over the rubble. Alaska turned and saw Jakob. There was a burn on the side of his neck, and he looked incredibly tired, but he was alive. She froze as he saw her as well, and then ran over and hugged her, ignoring the disapproving yells of the medical team taking care of her injuries. Neither of them spoke for several minutes as they held each other, and finally Alaska said, with tears running down her face, "I thought you were dead."

"Nah, you should know by now I don't die so easily, Alaska Donnel."

In the distance, Cassandra climbed up the steps of what remained of the town hall and faced the gathering crowd of survivors.

"The battle's over!" Cassandra yelled. "We've won!"

Not yet, Alaska thought, as cheers rang out. The protestors had won this fight, but Defense was still out there, and now they knew where they were.

Alaska opened her eyes and looked out over the wreckage strewn landscape. The battle of Pomander's Lid had ended only a day ago, and yet it all felt like a strange, twisted dream. She turned her head, and saw Cassandra sitting in a chair beside her cot.

"Alaska," Cassandra said, a tight smile crossing her face when she saw the girl awake and watching her. "I underestimated you and for that I am sorry. I thought you were just a child from the Capital, but I heard it was you that piloted our ship, that turned the battle for us. You are invaluable."

"Thank you," Alaska said in a hoarse voice, surprised.

"We've contained ourselves for too long, thinking we could build a new life here away from the Capital, but Defense and Pomander's Lid could never coexist. Pomander's Lid is ruined, but the people survived because of you, Alaska. The people are Pomander's Lid, not the stone and mortar. I think it's time to bring our 'contagion' to Defense's doorstep, to the Capital itself. You could help us bring down Defense. We need your knowledge and skills for the coming battles," Cassandra urged.

"I'm not a soldier," Alaska said, shaking her head.

"Your tactical skills were key to destroying those Defense airships and ending the slaughter."

"I shot down those ships to save my life and everyone else's!" said Alaska, her voice trembling as she pointed a shaking finger at Cassandra. "That doesn't make me a soldier. I'm not a soldier."

Cassandra glared at Alaska. "You have talent, Alaska Donnel, and thousands of innocent people need it in order to survive. The front line is the Capital and there will be no shades of gray, no middle path to stand on, Alaska. There will only be two armies, and one truth, spreading across the country. I know you are not on Defense's side, Alaska."

Alaska sensed someone was standing nearby and turned to see Ira standing just outside the tent.

"I thought you were dead at first when I saw you lying on the ground. You shouldn't be out of bed," Alaska said with a weak smile as he stepped inside with a bandage around his head and sat down on the edge of the cot.

"Well, think about what I said, Alaska. You owe it to your family, at least," Cassandra said as she left them alone.

A shadow passed across Alaska's face at the mention of her family. Were they dead now? In all likelihood, yes. Ira interrupted her dark thoughts.

"I'm not so badly hurt," Ira said. "Besides, I had to return this."

He set a mother of pearl music box on the cot beside Alaska. She recognized it as the one Helen had given her, the one she remembered having as a little girl.

"They found it in the wreckage," he went on. "If you don't want it..."

"I'll keep it," Alaska hesitated. "When I crashed, I remembered something."

Ira's eyes widened. "What?"

"From the time with the Nightghosts. You were there," Alaska said. "They had you prisoner, too. You were trying to help me."

"They captured and held me after Winter's execution," said Ira grimly. "I escaped, but they caught me again right after you arrived. There were other children being held with you, too. I didn't want to tell you about it...I didn't want to give you anything that might make you remember. Being a captive of the Nightghosts is a horrible thing. When they take your memory, it's the kindest thing they do. I just wish they'd taken mine."

"I had a right to know."

"I know."

"When you tried to help me," said Alaska, looking down. "They hurt you, didn't they? I heard you screaming."

Ira went silent and looked away. Finally he abruptly said, "No one can find Melissa Johnson. It turns out she's a Magler's Child. She could be halfway back to the Capital already."

"You're changing the subject, Ira," said Alaska.

"Yes, they hurt me. But don't you want to know why I said you caused the lightning?"

The final question. What had the Nightghosts done? She realized then she didn't want the answer. She was afraid of it, not ready to hear it, or believe it.

The entrance of the tent was open and Alaska saw a procession pass by, led by Cassandra and Hawk. Gloriana Davies was dragged past in chains, struggling to bite the guards who shoved her forward. Temple's body came after her, born on a twisted metal door, a look of sheer determination immortally plastered on his face.

"He must be dead," she heard Hawk say. "He never had such presence in life."

"Alaska, I know you're afraid of the Nightghosts..." Ira started, breaking the silence but Alaska shook her head.

"I'm not afraid of Nightghosts, Ira. They're just a fairy tale. I'm only worried about the people who inspired the story. The people I let scare me into seeing hallucinations and demons everywhere. The people who kidnapped me when I couldn't defend myself. I can't face my real monsters."

Ira hesitated. "Alaska, you fought Defense and won. You can do anything. Let me show you something."

He helped Alaska off the cot, a surge of pain running through her side as she exited the tent with him. They walked across the camp. People waved as they passed, flashing Alaska friendly, but unnervingly reverent looks. By now, they all knew she had been piloting the air-ship that turned the battle. Alaska pointed at a black tent with four guards in front of it.

"Who is in there?"

"Ianto," said Ira. "They caught him. They won't execute him because he's a Magler's Child. They'll want to examine him, use him, like Defense used him."

As much as Alaska hated Ianto Ambrose, she couldn't help imagining the young, cyborg boy sitting alone in the tent in chains, forever someone's captive, no matter what he tried to do. She felt sorry for him. They climbed a hill, and in the distance she could see the ruins of Pomander's Lid, so calm and placid unlike the carnage the day before. Ira stopped at the top of the hill and looked down. She followed his gaze. A battered old Defense air-ship was parked below, exactly like one she'd seen a long time ago, in the basement of an old antiques shop, in another world she'd lost forever, where everything had seemed so right and normal, and she'd had a best friend named Hugh.

A camp had been set up around it, and she saw Hawk shaking hands with people, all dressed in dusty rags and emaciated. Jakob was there too, and he walked past a young girl and man, running around in circles in a game of tag. Alaska knew who they were immediately, and she forgot everything else as tears sprang to her eyes in a wave of grief and joy. They were so different, so changed, and yet they were the same. They were here, they were really here, just down the slope!

"Malcolm," she whispered. "Leila."

"I told you they would be saved," Ira said, smiling. "But they're not what I wanted to show you. Make it rain."

"What?" Alaska asked, bewildered. "I can't make it rain!"

"Yes, you can, but only if you believe you can. Otherwise, you won't even try. Go on, wish for it."

Alaska turned and looked out over the desert. It looked dry and barren, and there was nothing but bright sunlight, not a single cloud in sight. She shut her eyes, imagining a deluge, like the one the previous night at the end of the battle. Alaska quickly opened her eyes as something cold and wet hit the bridge of her nose. It was rain. At first the rain fell as a soft drizzle, then a downpour. It drenched her to the bone. The people downhill ran towards the air-ship for cover. *It is not raining*, Alaska thought desperately. *It's the middle of the desert and everything is supposed to be bone dry. I can't make it rain.* The rain stopped, and it suddenly became bright and sunny again.

She turned to Ira, her voice shaking as she asked, "How?"

"I don't know yet," Ira admitted. "But you can connect to the dome and possibly more of this world in a way no other human can."

"No other human," Alaska said. She saw her reflection distorted in a puddle. "But I have to be human. I know I'm human!"

"You are human, Alaska, don't worry," said Ira quickly.

Alaska's eyes widened as a terrible idea crossed her mind, "Do they want me to be their weapon?"

"Maybe. Some people will go to any length to win, even use a child. Everyone wants their Joan of Arc. I must admit, they're probably perplexed why you didn't kill Melissa Johnson when you had the chance," said Ira.

"I'm not a murderer!" Alaska said adamantly. "I'm not a weapon, I won't do it! Cassandra wants me to do the same thing, she wants me to be a soldier. I don't want to do that, Ira. All I can think about since I shot down those ships are the people who died, the people who are dead...dead because of me." She looked away from Ira and down the slope.

"You said there's a cure," Alaska said. "I'm not going with Cassandra. I'm going to find it. That's the way to end this."

"The key's in your pocket," Ira said.

Alaska reached a hand into her pocket and felt the intricate gold skeleton key attached to its tattered ribbon.

"Are we friends now, Alaska Donnel?"

She hesitated before she said, "Yes."

"I promise I'll help you, Alaska, but you have to trust me. Don't do anything yet. Not till we know more. When the time is right, you'll know and then you'll have to run."

Alaska opened her mouth to ask more questions but Ira nodded in the direction down the slope and said before she could speak, "They're waiting for you."

She looked down and saw Cassandra conversing with Hawk. She felt the cold metal surface of the key in her hand. She remembered the hunger in Cassandra's expression.

"What if Cassandra..." she turned back towards Ira, but he was gone.

"Ira?"

Alaska was alone at the top of the slope, with no Nightghosts, no voices. But she was still sopping wet, a cold reminder of who she was and what she had to do. She slipped the key around her neck, then took a deep breath and descended the slope to join her family.

End of Book One

About the Author

S. K. Gabriel is a 17-year old author who began writing the Immortal Children series in 2009 while being homeschooled. Gabriel lives in a mysterious corner of the world called Western Massachusetts, surrounded by secretly plotting farm animals, Harry Potter books, and family. *The Nightghosts' Child* is her first published novel.

www.ingramcontent.com/pod-product-compliance
Lightning Source LLC
Chambersburg PA
CBHW071636260626
47170CB00001B/118